TO TELL THE TRUTH

Also by Anna Smith

The Dead Won't Sleep

TO TELL
THE TRUTH

Anna Smith

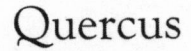

Quercus

First published in Great Britain in 2012 by

Quercus
55 Baker Street
7th Floor,
South Block
London
W1U 8EW

A CIP catalogue record for this book is available
from the British Library

ISBN 978 0 85738 296 2 (TPB)
ISBN 978 1 78087 164 6 (HB)

10 9 8 7 6 5 4 3 2 1

Typeset by Ellipsis Digital Limited, Glasgow

Printed and bound in Great Britain by Clays Ltd, St Ives plc

For my mother, who gave so much,
and climbed a mountain every day.

'I have found the paradox, that if you love until it hurts, there can be no more hurt, only more love.'

Mother Teresa of Calcutta

PROLOGUE

Costa del Sol, July 1998

In the blink of an eye she was gone. It was easy. The kid was just sitting there on the beach, picking up handfuls of sand and letting it run through her fingers. She was like a little fairy, smiling up at him with one eye closed against the harsh glare of the midday sun. She didn't even make a sound when he scooped her up. It was only when he walked swiftly, carrying her to his car on the little sidestreet, that she shouted loud for her mummy, but he was too quick. He bundled her into the boot and sped out of the street. Minutes were all it took. As he cut onto the dual carriageway, he turned up the radio to drown out her muffled cries. He lit a cigarette and wiped the sweat from his forehead. Job done. That's how it all began. As quick as that.

In the bedroom of the beachside villa, Jenny was coming so hard she nearly passed out. But somewhere in her euphoria she heard the cry. Call it a mother's instinct, something primal that needs no explaining that your entire world has come tumbling down.

'Christ! It's Amy!' She heaved Jamie off her and leapt out of the bed, throwing on a robe over her naked body. Heading to the door, she tripped over clothes and flip flops, discarded earlier in the heat of forbidden passion.

'What the fu—?' Jamie rolled over. Then he sat up, asking 'What's the matter?'

But Jenny was gone. All he could hear were her shouts: 'Amy! Amy!'

'Oh, fuck!' He jumped up and pulled on his shorts and T-shirt. 'Oh fuck, no!' he muttered, hurrying into the kitchen, from where he saw through the open patio door Jenny running up and down the beach, calling.

'Amy! Amy! Amy!'

She put her hand to her mouth and almost buckled to her knees as Jamie ran towards her. He held her.

'Oh, Jamie! She's gone. She's gone, Jamie, Amy's gone. She was sleeping. She must have got out. Where is she? Where is she, Jamie? What if she's gone into the sea?'

'Sssh, Jen. She'll be here,' Jamie said, attempting to comfort her. But his stomach dropped as his eyes darted across the stretch of deserted beach. Nothing. A windsurfer was just a speck on the horizon.

'She can't be far, she'll have wandered off. You wait here and I'll run round the back and see if she's walked somewhere.'

He let go of Jenny and ran into the sidestreet, desolate and chilly in the shade. A shiver ran through him. He looked around at the empty street, silent but for the roar of speeding traffic above on the nearby dual carriageway. He shivered again and swallowed to stop himself being sick.

'Jesus,' he murmured.

Right there and then, Jamie knew his life, everyone's lives, had changed forever. This was his best friend's little girl, and he'd just been shagging his best friend's wife. Shit! Maybe he would wake up in a second. He ran back to the house, dizzy with panic. Jenny's face crumpled in sobs when she saw him return alone. They looked at each other.

'Oh, Jamie!' She collapsed in his arms, clinging to him. 'What have we done? Jesus, what have we done! Call the police. We have to. Phone Martin. I need to get Martin . . . Oh, God, Martin!'

Jamie reached into his pocket for his mobile phone. He took a deep breath. Whatever he said, both of them said, in the next ten minutes would come back to haunt them if they didn't get it right. Twelve years as a criminal lawyer defending liars had taught him that. He took Jenny by the shoulders and spoke calmly.

'Jenny. Listen. We'll find her. I promise.' His mouth was tight. 'Go and put some clothes on. I'll call the police. I'll phone Martin. He'll be on his way back by now. We have to get our story right. We have to.'

He shook her shoulders gently. He hoped he was getting through to her. Guilt was for another day.

Two people witnessed this drama as it unfolded, but nobody could see them. They were high up on the balcony of a villa cut out of the craggy coastline, from where they could look down at the shimmering heat and the soothing surf washing onto the shore.

The older man groaned as he spilled himself into the mouth of the teenage boy, who looked up with smiling eyes as he swallowed.

He ruffled the young Moroccan's thick wavy locks. 'Taha. You are the sweetest boy,' he said. Taha stood up, his naked brown body glistening in the sunlight. Then they heard the screaming.

'What the hell's that?' The older man sat forward in his chair, pulling a white bathrobe over his nakedness.

'A woman screaming, sir,' the boy said, pointing down. 'Look. Is from the place we saw the small girl on the beach.'

The man stood up and strained to look, careful not to get so close that anyone passing could spot him. Discretion was everything.

'Hmmn. Certainly seems to be some kind of panic on.' He was always a master of understatement.

Taha continued to watch as the older man went indoors and returned fully dressed, buckling the belt in his khaki linen trousers.

'Maybe is the girl, sir.' The boy turned around and looked him up and down. 'You know? The man? Remember when we were on the balcony at first? He took her?' The boy looked out to the beach. 'Maybe she stolen.'

The older man's eyes narrowed.

'Time to go now, Taha.' He ran his hand across the boy's bony shoulder. 'You have a vivid imagination, dear boy.' He smiled, looked at his watch. 'Come on, get dressed. Time I got back. I have a late lunch engagement.' He handed the boy a one-hundred-euro note. 'You know the drill, Taha. Let yourself out.'

'Thank you, sir. Thank you.' The boy took the money and bowed, almost like a servant. 'I see you again? Maybe next week, sir?'

The older man smiled like a benign headmaster to his favourite pupil, then turned and left.

Taha went back to the edge of the balcony and watched the couple standing on the beach. He could see the woman was crying. Then he heard a police siren. He went back into the villa, pulled on his shorts and vest and shoved the money in his pocket. He would be rich tonight, even after he had given his Russian pimp boss his cut.

As he was about to leave, he saw something on the floor. It looked like a credit card, but when he picked it up he saw it was some kind of pass, with a photograph of the man who had just paid him a hundred euros to rent him for two hours of sex. Taha tried to read the card. He couldn't understand what Rt. Hon. meant, and the name was different, but he recognised the picture of the man he knew as 'Thomas'.

He shrugged, stuffed the card into his pocket, then left.

CHAPTER 1

Rosie stretched out on the lounger, relishing the late afternoon sunshine. It felt luxurious after the coldness of the pool. Fifty straight lengths she was up to. She congratulated herself. By the time she got back to Glasgow in ten days, she would be as fit as a butcher's dog. Get yourself fit physically, she'd told herself as she'd packed for Spain, and the head will follow. But it hadn't really, not yet.

The first week had been the worst, her mind still rushing around the deadlines that ruled her life even though there weren't any here. She created them herself: a time to eat, a deadline to swim, to walk, to read, even to drink. Deadlines made it easier, that was for sure. No time to think of all the crap. Having this much time on her hands had frightened the hell out of Rosie during the first few days, but now she was at least getting there. Opening the boxes inside her head. Tidying them. Putting them away again.

The mobile on the table rang and she picked it up. She could see it was McGuire's private number at the *Post*.

'Gilmour! Howsit going?'

'Try to picture the scene, McGuire.' Rosie smiled, glad of the distraction. 'From where I'm sunning myself on the roof terrace of my villa, I can see little fishing boats in the harbour, where hard-working fishermen with calloused hands have just sailed in with something for my dinner tonight. Need I go on? Still pissing down in Glasgow?'

'And how,' McGuire replied, 'but stop gloating about the weather. Have you seen the news today?'

'No, Mick. I have *not* seen the news today. You told me not to watch the news. Remember?'

'Yeah, I know I did, Rosie.' McGuire's tone changed a little. 'But listen sweetheart. There's a big story going on down in the Costa del Sol, few miles from Marbella. Missing Scots kid. Little girl of three and a half has vanished from the beach.'

'God almighty! Really?' She knew what was coming next. 'What's happened?'

'We know fuck all at the moment. The Spanish cops never tell anybody anything. It only happened yesterday and we didn't get word about it until last night. Late. But this could run and run.'

Rosie wondered why he wasn't sending one of his best news reporters down to Spain. She wasn't a hack any more, after all. Since all the trouble six months ago when she nearly got killed in Glasgow, she'd taken the assistant editor's job in charge of investigations. She didn't have to get her hands dirty these days.

'Why me, Mick? I'm off the road.'

Pause. She could imagine McGuire putting his feet up on the desk and pushing back on his chair.

'Well, Rosie, missing kid? It's too big to send anybody but you. I can't afford to be on the sidelines, leaving some youngster to work with the pack of journos, churning out the same old shite. I want you to do it, Rosie . . . Can you get yourself down there? I'll make it up to you . . . Another time . . .'

Rosie knew it wasn't really a question. 'Yeah. Sure you will.' She stood up and walked across the terrace. 'What's the sketch? Do we know anything at all?'

'Only that it's three couples on holiday with their families. All friends. The kid vanished from the beach in broad daylight. The villa is in quite a secluded area. They're not poor, these people. One of them owns some vineyard in France, and the kid's dad's a property dealer in Glasgow. Mother's some kind of insurance broker.'

'Where were they when the kid went missing?'

'Don't know yet, Rosie.' McGuire sounded like he didn't want to talk all day. 'That's why I want you down there pronto, sweetheart. Think the mum just turned her back for a minute and the kid was on the beach. One minute she was there, then she wasn't.'

'Jesus, that's awful. Is there no intelligence on it? What's the thinking?

Rosie was already running through the possibilities in her mind. She'd covered plenty of missing kids in her time. Some came home. Most didn't.

'Christ, who knows?' McGuire said. 'Plenty of sickos out there. Paedos, serial killers, gypsies stealing kids. All sorts of shit.'

'Right. OK, Mick.' Rosie was already walking towards

her bedroom. 'Get Marion to call me. She'll have to get me a hotel in Marbella. And I'll need money. Who you sending pic-wise?'

'Matt,' McGuire said. 'He's on a plane this afternoon. He'll call you when he arrives. I'll get Marion to phone you shortly.'

'OK.' Rosie felt that little punch of adrenalin that had been missing. 'I'm on it.'

'Great,' McGuire said. 'I'll sleep tonight. Thanks, Rosie, talk tomorrow. Good luck.' The phone clicked.

Rosie shook her head. Good luck? Jesus! At the end of the day, McGuire was hoping for good luck not so much for the kid as the story. Some things never change.

She dragged her suitcase from below the bed, opened the wardrobe, and looked at her watch. From where she was on the Costa de la Luz, it would take three hours minimum to drive to Marbella but she should be there for dinner. She felt really alive for the first time in six months.

On the motorway, Rosie kept to the outside lane for a while until she got used to the speed of the road. She hated driving on the right, and even on a motorway she freaked out a little when cars came thundering past her on the inside. Having a car for her month-long holiday in Spain was not something she would normally have done, but the villa, the whole trip, had been arranged by the *Post*, so she'd decided she might as well give it a go. She'd enjoyed the challenge of driving for the first few days because it had given her something to focus on.

Something to get stressed about. And in truth, once she got the hang of it, she loved the freedom of being able to flit in and out of little villages dotted along the west coast that she would otherwise not have seen.

These last days had been the best Rosie had felt in a long time. After the beating in February by the hoodlums who wanted to stop her story, she had been ordered off work when she got out of hospital. But by the start of the third week, she was going stir crazy in her flat. She'd insisted on coming back to work to get stuck into her new job as assistant editor. It had felt really odd at first, not getting out on the streets for the big investigations, but Rosie had been enjoying the newness of it. She hadn't realised until now that she'd actually missed being on the road so much, and she hadn't even reached the scene yet! She smiled to herself, wondering when she would ever learn.

McGuire had told her to take a month at the company's expense as a thank-you for the work she'd done in bringing down that bastard police chief Gavin Fox and exposing the sex scandal at the children's home. And she'd decided that getting completely off the treadmill for a month would do her a world of good. The truth was that she'd been fighting off panic attacks in the aftermath of the beating, so the holiday had been partly under doctor's orders. Game on.

In three weeks she'd blitzed all the tourist haunts around Jerez, including the obligatory sherry tour which had left her with an almighty hangover she was convinced might actually be terminal. Rosie had read so many paperbacks she was having trouble working out what was real life and what was fiction. With so little to do, it was only a matter of time before she fell into the wrong hands – literally. And so the clichés came rolling in faster than the Atlantic breakers on the beach at Rota – the little gem of a town where she was living in some splendour in a villa overlooking the ocean.

In one local restaurant she'd got a lot of attention from the owner, a handsome Spaniard with a story to tell and a twinkle in his eye. She felt a little embarrassed even now that she'd allowed him to charm his way right into her bed. The single brooding woman all alone, and the handsome Spanish man who was allegedly different from the usual Lothario. Jesus. Such a cliche. He'd be using his B-movie script on some other bird next month.

Brits were few and far between in Rota. But the US Naval base at the edge of the town ensured there was plenty of beef to look at on the beach for a woman with far too much energy. Her next distraction was in the solid shape of a US Marine Major with a crewcut, whom she'd met in a cafe one lazy afternoon. Rosie never could resist a man in uniform, and she knew what was on the cards even before they made a lunch date for the following day. After lunch, he'd taken her to a secluded beach nearby, where they played out the rest of the afternoon not unlike the classic scene in *From Here to Eternity*. The recollection still brought a smile.

These interludes had lifted the ennui and the loneliness which, even in the beautiful surroundings, had sometimes pulled Rosie down. And what the heck, the sex had been particularly good, and she'd resolved to take it up as a proper hobby when she got back home. At least while she was preoccupied with uncomplicated sex, she could put the misery of TJ out of her mind.

She flipped on the stereo and pushed in a CD. The sweeping soundtrack from the movie *Out of Africa* filled the car. Soothing. Perfect for the time of day, with the sun lower in the sky and twinkling on the sea. Sure beat the hell out of the East End of Glasgow on a wet Monday.

As always in her quieter moments, no matter how hard she tried to forget, Rosie's thoughts drifted back to TJ. She couldn't believe he had never once got in touch with her after he left for New York. She'd tormented herself with all sorts of thoughts of what happened that morning when she couldn't keep her date with him because she was in hospital. In truth, she didn't even know if she'd have kept it anyway. The night when the killer came to her house, she'd been planning to take the whole evening to make up her mind. In the end, she didn't get a chance. And from then on she was tortured with 'what if' agony, that TJ may have been standing waiting for her at the airport. But his words that day when he'd told her he was going and had given her the airline ticket, still rang in her ears.

'If you come, fine. If not, don't call me. I hate good-byes.'

Even though she'd waited by her phone for days after he left, she knew deep down he wouldn't call. She'd tried to contact him, believing that once he knew what had happened to her, TJ would be so shocked and caring, he'd get in touch. Maybe he would even come back. But he never answered his phone. He had simply left her behind. That was the hardest thing to take. It was her own fault, she'd told herself, as she threw herself into the new job. She'd let her guard down, and that was her mistake. She'd opened up to TJ more than to anyone else in her whole life, and he walked away. Never again.

That was nearly six months ago, and still the tears welled up in her eyes when she thought of it. It wasn't just the man/woman thing, the romance. It was the whole damn friendship. The baring of her soul, those deeply buried scars from her childhood that he'd brought to the surface. How could he do that then just disappear? She imagined TJ living in New York; wondered if there was another woman, and if he was sharing the same laughs and arguments with her that they used to have. Christ, this was driving her nuts. She was glad when her mobile rang.

'Hey, Rosie.'

She recognised Marion, the editor's secretary.

'Marion. How you doing?'

'Well, it's pissin' down in July, and I forgot to take my washing in before I went to work this morning. It's Friday afternoon and my date for the night just called off. You could say, life is not smiling on me.'

Rosie chuckled. 'Ah, that's men for you, Marion. Play hard to get next time he calls.' She promised herself she would do that if TJ ever phoned. But she knew she wouldn't.

'I'm too old to play hard to get,' Marion said. 'Somebody

asks me out, I'm standing with my hat and coat on in case they change their mind! Anyway, enough of my nonsense. Listen, Rosie. I booked you at the Puente Romano in Marbella. Unfortunately, it's a five-star hotel, but I'm sure you'll cope. And I'm about to wire some dosh into your account. Same number as last time alright?'

'Yeah,' Rosie said. 'That's brilliant. How much money?'

'Five hundred quid. The editor says don't spend it all at once. It'll do for starters. Matt's got his own money.'

'Don't worry, Marion. I'll try to lay off the lobster and champagne. And I'll bring you back a Spanish donkey.'

'Yeah. Do that, Rosie. And make sure it's a two-legged one.'

CHAPTER 2

Besmir had been watching them for days, the whole crowd of them. Eating, drinking, laughing. The men always seemed to be making jokes with each other and guffawing, and the women would shake their heads and smile the way older people did when children were being silly. He didn't like any of them. They were puffed up like peacocks, full of their own importance.

One time, in a cafe at lunchtime, when he was at a table too far and too insignificant for them to notice him, he saw one of the men give the young waiter a dressing down. He couldn't understand what the boy was being berated for, but the others sniggered when he walked away, his head bowed, close to tears. Besmir wanted to go up and grab the waiter and tell him to go back to the table and punch the shit out of the guy. That's what he would have done. Fighting was all Besmir knew. In Albania, you either fought or you were a victim and you got trampled on. The more he watched them, the more he disliked them, and that was good. Because soon they would have a lot more to worry them than whether a waiter served them well.

He had planned to take the girl in the night, when the family were sleeping in their villa on the beach. They were so stupid they slept with the patio door unlocked. He had even been in there while they were fast asleep and he'd looked at the little girl in her bed. She was beautiful. In the end, they'd made it easy for him. She was just out there, on the beach by herself when he walked past for the second time, doing a recce. From a distance earlier, he'd seen the husband of the woman going out wearing shorts and running shoes. He'd run in the opposite direction from where Besmir was, but he'd slipped into the shadows in the sidestreet just in case.

It was only a few minutes later that he saw the other man come by and talk to the woman on the patio. The little girl was nowhere to be seen. Besmir watched as the man and woman disappeared into the house together. He was surprised when he saw the kid come tottering out by herself and sit on the sand. His heart missed a beat. He would do it now. If he was quick, it could be done and over in a minute. He could have her delivered in two hours and get his money. He waited a few minutes in case the mother came out. And when she didn't, he moved.

Now the crying had stopped, and Besmir hoped the girl had fallen asleep. He hated it when children cried like that. It reminded him of the incessant crying in the orphanage, day and night, children constantly crying. The pictures in his head were sometimes blurred these days. He'd made them that way, but he could remember the crying more clearly than anything. He remembered his own crying and saw himself looking through the bars of the cot, the other miserable children rocking back and forth and wailing. But there was no point. Nobody came. Besmir had no recollection of when he stopped crying, but one day he just did. And he had never cried again. Not once.

He pulled the car off the road and up a quiet, twisting lane. He got out, lit a cigarette and checked to make sure there was nobody around. He went to the boot and clicked it open. She lay curled up and asleep, clutching an oily rag among the tools and debris. Her face was deathly pale and her dark brown curls looked even darker against her white skin. For a second he thought she may have suffocated, and he reached out to touch her arm to feel if there was a pulse. But as he did, she stirred. He closed the boot in case the light would wake her up and start her crying again. He got back into the car and drove on. He called Elira from his mobile to tell her he would be in Algeciras in an hour.

The traffic began to back up as he got closer to Algeciras, and Besmir had to slow down until the line of cars was nearly bumper to bumper. He wondered what had caused the hold-up and rolled his window down to stick his head out. Shit. The cops seemed to be stopping people. He looked at his watch. He had been on the road for nearly two hours. The cops would have been alerted by now and would be looking for the missing kid. But maybe they wouldn't be this far down yet. The traffic slowed even more. It could be a roadblock. He began to sweat. He didn't have any papers if he got stopped. Leka had promised him a fake passport and identity card if he did just one more job. Leka always pushed the end game further and further away. He said he would give him three thousand euros for the job. With that kind of money Besmir could be free to go anywhere he wanted. Or he could stay, and become a bigger part of the organisation.

They were everywhere now, the Albanians. From Italy to Spain to London. They were huge and powerful, providing people to order for gangmasters and whorehouses all over Europe. Some people were sold privately as individuals to whoever paid the highest price. There were no restrictions on age or gender. The only rule was that you never crossed the Albanians or the Russians. Ever. Anyone who made that mistake never lived to see the sunset. Especially if they crossed Leka.

Besmir inched closer to the roadblock, and he could see the cop put his hand up to stop the car four in front of him. His heart began to pound. The car was stifling, so the boot would be boiling. All he needed now was for the kid to wake up and start screaming. The fat cop waddled along the line of cars, his pistol in his holster. Besmir made sure he didn't make eye contact when the cop stopped at his car. Besmir looked up with the bored expression of someone caught in a traffic jam. The cop turned around and walked back down the line. He waved the cars on. Besmir gripped the steering wheel hard to stop his hands shaking.

The port of Algeciras was heaving with activity in the late afternoon, a mix of tourist ferries and freight boats going to and from Morocco. Besmir weaved his car in and out of the traffic, past the docks and up through the tight warren of back streets. The air was heavy with smells from the exotic mix of restaurants and street stalls. Fried garlic and Moroccan spices mingled with the searing heat and traffic fumes. Cars honked above the din and drivers cut each other up, swerving to avoid pedestrians shouting abuse.

Besmir wanted to get to the house quickly as the girl must surely be awake by now with this noise. He turned into a one-way cobbled street and raced up, knowing he could cut across the alley half way. It was cooler now as he drove towards the block, where he could see Elira standing on the balcony looking down at him. She lifted her chin a little to acknowledge him, then she disappeared inside. He pulled his car to the side of the road and ran upstairs.

'We must get her out quickly,' Besmir said as Elira opened the door to him. 'We can't wait till it's dark, or leave her there any longer.'

Elira drew on her cigarette and puffed the smoke out of her fat cheeks. A puppy came bounding out of the small kitchen and slipped comically on the stone floor rushing to greet the visitor.

Elira smiled, her face softening. 'Look. The girl will have a little friend. It will help to stop her crying.'

Besmir picked up the puppy and it immediately started licking his face and nuzzling him. He pulled the puppy away and put it back on the floor.

'I'll get the girl.' He headed for the door.

'Leka is on his way,' Elira said.

'Good.' Besmir went out and down the narrow stone staircase to the car.

He looked around the street before he opened the boot. All was quiet, so he clicked it open. The girl's eyes were wide and blinking. A shaft of setting sunlight streaming between the buildings lit up her face, making her eyes the brightest blue he'd ever seen. It looked at odds with the dark hair and pale face. For a second, he thought the girl was going to smile, but she just stared at him, bewildered. He reached in and picked her up. He held her close to him in case she would start to scream. She felt soft and warm. Like the puppy. He went quickly upstairs. Elira opened the door. As soon as the kid saw her, her lip quivered. The sob started somewhere in her chest like a choking, muffled breath, then exploded in an agonising wail. Besmir handed her to Elira who tried to shush her, but the girl was inconsolable.

'Ah, ssssh . . . shhhh baby . . . Sssh.' Elira sat down on the sofa and rocked her against her heavy bosom.

But the girl sobbed, huge tears running down her face. Besmir looked away. Then the puppy clambered up beside them.

'Look. Look,' Besmir said. 'Look at your little friend.' He held the puppy close to the girl and she stopped crying instantly.

She looked at the puppy, then at Elira and Besmir, and she started to bubble again, but it was more of a sniffle. The puppy kept licking her face, and she stopped.

Besmir and Elira glanced at each other when they heard footsteps on the stairs, followed by one loud knock at the door and then the voice they knew. Besmir walked across the room and slid the heavy bolt across and opened the door. Leka stepped in.

'Besmir.' He stood for a second and they looked at each other.

Leka's mouth curled a little, but his eyes were cold. He nodded and looked beyond Besmir to the girl on Elira's lap and back to Besmir. Now he did smile.

'You did good, my friend.'

Besmir said nothing. You didn't make idle chat with Leka. You did what was required and you left. But he knew better than to ask for his money. Leka looked at him, as though reading his thoughts. He touched Besmir's arm.

'All in good time, Besmir.' He walked over to Elira and bent to kiss her on the cheek and run his hand gently over her face.

'You have a pretty baby there, Elira, yes?' He surveyed the little girl who was so preoccupied with the puppy she didn't even look at him. He took hold of her face and gently turned it towards him. Leka made a soft whistling sound with his lips.

'The eyes, Elira. Look at the eyes. Beautiful. I think her price just went up.'

He walked across to the window and opened one of

the shutters a little. The dismal room suddenly looked less glum.

'Besmir?' He didn't turn around. 'There is a change of plan my friend.'

Besmir's stomach tightened. Leka turned to face him.

'I want you to deliver the girl to Morocco. To Tangiers.'

Besmir opened his mouth to speak. Leka put his hand up as though to stop him.

'Don't worry, it will be safe. I have it all planned. I just don't trust anyone else to do it.' He waved his hand in the direction of the girl. 'Look how successful you have been here. You showed that you have good instincts by taking the girl the way you did. How could I trust anyone else to finish the job?'

'But Leka,' Besmir hoped his voice didn't sound desperate. 'You promised. We agreed. My job was only to get her.'

He folded his arms and stood tall. But Leka was taller, and he looked down at him.

Leka nodded. 'I know. I know, Besmir.' His steely eyes fixed him. 'But this is new business. Totally new. We have never done this before. Nobody has. And I want to do it well. The people in Morocco have plans for this one. They never expected us to pull it off, but we have. And I want to prove to them that we can do anything. We are in charge here.' He sighed. 'You must. Then you can have what you need.' He put his hands in his pockets. 'But to be honest, it would be my wish for you to remain working for us. You are strong and fearless. So are lots of my men. But you, Besmir, you are not stupid. You are different.'

He turned back to the window.

'Go now and come back tomorrow at four. Everything will be arranged for you.'

Besmir looked at Elira who looked back blankly. He felt the colour rise in his cheeks. He knew he had no choice.

'OK, Leka,' he said. 'Tomorrow.'

CHAPTER 3

The Rt. Hon. Michael Carter-Smith MP turned back the cuffs of his immaculate white linen shirt and pulled the gold Rolex watch over his suntanned wrist. He walked closer to the mirror to examine his face, smooth and tanned after twelve days in the sun. His bronzed complexion made his eyes an even deeper blue, striking as they already were, fringed with thick black lashes. The newspapers and magazines who were fascinated by him always said he looked a decade younger than his fifty-one years, and he knew it. And, as they often added in veiled reference to his homosexuality, the Home Secretary wasn't just a pretty face.

No. Carter-Smith was the acceptable face of New Labour. The face that had helped get them elected because it was he who was instrumental in them winning over the Middle Englanders whose traditions were steeped in Toryism, but who had become disillusioned after Thatcher's reign. If someone like Carter-Smith, the privileged son of a wealthy banker, with credentials that were true-blue Tory, could put himself at the centre of New Labour, then perhaps they'd give the Party a chance. And they did.

His appointment to the Home Office after they won the General Election was not unexpected: it had been leaked to the newspapers before it was announced. Carter-Smith made sure of that. Nobody did underhand tactics better than he. The campaign trail was littered with the political dead he'd backstabbed as he climbed his way to the top. When he came out of the closet and was outspoken about his homosexuality a year before the General Election, his kudos actually went up. He had made sure the story emerged in such as way that even the buttoned-up old cloth caps in the Labour ranks would admire him.

You could send Carter-Smith anywhere. He could charm the wives at the working men's club in his constituency just as much as the ladies who lunched at the Dorchester. Men loved to hate him, but they accepted him, and everyone admired him. The gay community, of course, had much to thank him for, and they all did – with their votes.

No red-top tabloids had ever turned Michael Carter-Smith over. Even those who hated New Labour wouldn't dare, because he was the very soul of discretion in his private life. He had to be. The Home Secretary's little sexual peccadillo was his penchant for fresh young teenage boys. He loved the danger almost as much as the thrill and responsive enthusiasm of their tight young bodies. He never made mistakes. The word arrogant was invented for him . . .

He looked at the time. In precisely one hour he'd be on board the yacht of his multi-billionaire Russian businessman friend. If the tabloids got a sniff of that, they'd be all over him. He left his bedroom and headed down the marbled hallway to the living-room where his oldest chum, Oliver Woolard, was waiting for him.

'Ah, Michael.' Oliver handed him a drink. 'Shaken, just enough to excite it, but not stirred,' he said. 'Just the way you like it.'

Carter-Smith grinned. He knew Oliver could never resist a dig. They had been at boarding school together and nobody knew more of his secrets than Oliver Woolard did. But Carter-Smith knew plenty of his too, and he watched, amused, at Oliver fawning over his beautiful wife, Connie, as though she was the only woman who had ever lived. But before the night was out, no matter how beguiling his wife was – and she truly was – he would be lapping up the variety of young women served on a plate for him by their Russian host.

Michael knocked back half his martini and put the glass down on the table. He looked at his watch.

'Come on, Oliver. Car will be waiting.'

Oliver gave Connie a lingering kiss on the lips and held her lush dark mane of hair before letting it tumble onto her bare shoulders. He squeezed her bottom, encased in a tight electric-blue satin dress.

'I might be terribly late, darling. Don't wait up.' He kissed her hand.

All dressed up, nowhere to go...? Michael kissed Connie on the cheek as they left, wondering if she felt sufficiently warmed up now for the young fitness instructor who would steal into the villa by the time their car was arriving at the harbour in Estepona.

Michael had only been staying with the Woolards for a few days when he noticed the attention Connie was getting from the young man, her personal trainer from the hotel beach club nearby. In fact, he'd even heard them one afternoon when he returned to the villa while Oliver was out on business. He didn't blame her. He assumed Oliver knew about Connie's little distractions while her husband was empire-building across the world. If he did, he had never spoken about it, but then 'all's fair in love and war' was Oliver's motto.

The days Michael had spent with his friends in their sumptuous villa in the hills high above Marbella had been idyllic, filled with leisurely lunches, and lavish dinners in nearby restaurants where the Woolards were adored. It had become an annual jaunt for the Home Secretary: an opportunity not only to catch up with his old friend, but also to get away from London and do exactly what he wanted – as long as he managed to give his private protection officers the slip. And when he felt the urge, he had only to make a phone call to a contact on the Costa and something would be discreetly arranged, to his particular taste and at an address not too far away . . .

As they got into the car, they both looked up to where Connie was blowing them a kiss from the terrace. In the back seat, Michael glanced up again and thought she looked slightly forlorn. Oliver's mind, though, was already miles away, focusing on his next business.

When the Daimler dropped them on the harbour, close to the yacht, the two men were greeted by an elegantly dressed but stern-faced East European man in his thirties, who raised his eyebrows enquiringly as though waiting for them to introduce themselves.

'Would you be good enough to tell Mr Daletsky that Michael Carter-Smith is here, please?' He smiled engagingly.

The man said nothing, but beckoned them to follow him. As they did so, Michael noticed the bulge of a gun on the back of their escort's finely tailored suit. They walked up the gangplank onto the yacht. Moored discreetly at the far end of the harbour and as big as a cruise liner, it was a splendid, gleaming vision in the setting sun. Here, multi-million-pound floating palaces took pride of place, far enough away from the people who merely *thought* they were rich with their half-a-million-pound yachts. There was so much money here in the port it was mesmerising; and most of it was dirty. But none of that bothered Carter-Smith.

On the open deck, wearing cream flannels and a black shirt, and surrounded by sycophants, stood Viktor Daletsky, oil baron, electronics magnate and exporter. He also had other credentials on his formidable CV, if you believed the tabloids. And a small, deep scar on his cheekbone told of a way of life far removed from the one he was living now. But nobody knew enough, or had enough proof, to write about it.

As Michael and Oliver walked onto the deck, Daletsky excused himself and made his way towards them.

'Michael.' His Russian voice was deep and rich. He stretched out his hand. 'So glad you could come. How are you my friend?' he said, flicking a glance at Oliver.

'I'm very well, Viktor, very well indeed. How are you?' He turned his body towards Oliver. 'This is Oliver Woolard, of Woolard Institutions, who we've spoken about a few times . . . ?'

Daletsky raised his eyebrows and shook Oliver's hand vigorously.

'Oliver. I am very pleased to meet you. Very pleased. I hope we can have some time to talk tonight.'

He ushered them towards a podium where a waiter was opening a bottle of Krug. Three stunning, very young, Eastern European women stood by. Oliver's eyes lit up.

'Some champagne,' Daletsky said, handing Michael a champagne flute so fine he could have shaved with it. Then one to Oliver.

'We must drink to new friends.' He raised his glass. 'To new possibilities.' He made eye contact with Oliver.

'To new possibilities,' Oliver said, as one of the young girls sidled a little closer to him.

Daletsky took a mouthful of his champagne then put down his glass. He looked across the deck and nodded to a tall man in a black suit who had just arrived.

'Excuse me, for the moment, gentlemen.' He crossed to greet the newcomer, who stood silently surveying his surroundings.

Daletsky lowered his voice, but Carter-Smith heard him address the man as Leka.

CHAPTER 4

As usual, the splendour of the five-star hotel was lost on Rosie. By the time she arrived at the Puente Romano in the heart of Marbella, her head was already buzzing, thinking how she could take the story forward so she'd have a good line for Monday's paper.

Since the kid went missing yesterday, a formidable pack of big hitters from UK newspapers and television would be there already. They would be all over this story, pushing for exclusives, while theories and motives on the kidnapping were aired and dissected over hearty dinners by journalists on bloated expense accounts. They were always bloated when they went out of town on a job – especially on a foreign. Most hacks saw expenses as a kind of fine for taking you away from your own bed, your family, and what the rest of the world call a life, and replacing it with the frenetic round-the-clock graft of an assignment abroad.

The bottom line for Rosie was this: if she was abroad on a story, someone was dead – usually, a lot of people were dead. That kind of shit got to you after a while. So what if she ate some decent lobster washed down with a glass or two of vintage wine. It was by way of compensation for making her the dysfunctional human being that all frontline journalists eventually became.

At the hotel reception, she checked in and had a quick shufti round the main bar to see if there were any other hacks around. If there were, she didn't recognise them. Rosie didn't like working with the press pack when there was a big story on the go. There was the one advantage that you never missed anything, but it also meant you had to share, and she didn't like sharing – in case she managed to dig up something by herself. She'd once said she was a lucky reporter when, as a youngster, she'd had a great run of exclusives against the odds. But a wily old news editor told her you made your own luck in this game. Always keep two steps ahead of the pack and you wouldn't miss out, he'd said. It was good advice.

In her beachfront room, she threw open the doors leading to the private terrace and took in the view of the tantalising deep-blue sea. The room was luxurious and massive, with a bed that would take at least five people – all of it perfect if you were here for a few days pampering. Rosie plugged in her laptop and connected to the hotel's internet.

Two emails. One from Marion confirming the cash, and the other from McGuire with forwarded copy from the newsdesk. McGuire's message was curt: 'This is all we have so far. Hope you can do better. x'

The copy was more detailed. There were three couples

on this holiday, each with a villa about a ten-minute walk from the others. The men had all gone to university together and had been friends for fifteen years. The missing kid was called Amy Lennon, only daughter of Jenny and Martin. The dad, a property dealer, was boss of Lennon Properties, a Glasgow family estate agents with interests in Scotland and abroad. He took over from his father, Martin senior, who had died six months ago. That didn't ring any bells with Rosie. The mum was an insurance broker. Amy would be four at the end of August. The story was that the little girl had been sound asleep in her bedroom at the beach-side villa the couple were renting on Mijas Costa. The mother was having a shower while her husband was out on his four-mile morning jog. When she came out of the shower, Amy was gone. As she read those particular words, Rosie winced, imagining the mother's horror when she discovered her child was gone. She read on.

The next name was one she did recognise – Jamie O'Hara. A well-known Glasgow criminal lawyer, he'd made his name getting crooks off the hook for everything from murder to drugs to extortion. O'Hara was a big shot who relished the limelight, and though he was not yet forty he'd already made pots of money defending the kind of arseholes Rosie would gladly have strung up. She knew him, but not well, and she didn't particularly like him. Apart from anything else, he was far too handsome for his own good. His wife, Alison, was a chemist. O'Hara's story was that he was out for a walk and had decided to drop in to say hello to the Lennons, but as he approached the villa he was met with Jenny running out of the house screaming that Amy was gone. He immediately called the police, and Martin.

The other couple were the Reillys, John and Margaret. For the past five years they'd been living in France, where she taught English and he was trying to build up a small vineyard so he could export his own wine. They had been at the market together in Fuengirola when Amy went missing and knew nothing until they received a telephone call from Alison O'Hara.

The email went on to say that the Guarda Civil had launched an immediate full-scale hunt with helicopters and tracker dogs, and had at least a hundred officers scanning the beaches and nearby vacant villas and apartments. They'd said it was early days and they were confident they would find Amy. But at the bottom of the story, as it was describing the exact location, Rosie's heart sank. The villa from where Amy vanished was only a minute's drive from the main dual carriageway that goes from Malaga right along the coast and joins the motorway to Algeciras and Tarifa – the ports to Morocco. Within two hours of her being snatched, the child could be anywhere. She could have been taken to Portugal, or north towards France and the Netherlands. But if her kidnapper had gone to Morocco, that was a different story. She could simply vanish without trace.

Rosie sat down with a glass of ice-cold mineral water. She looked at her watch. The kid had now been missing more than a day and a half. She sighed. Soon they'd probably find a body. She hoped it would be soon, for the sake of the parents. Her mobile rang.

'*Buenos tardes*, Rosie. *Voulez vous coucher avec moi?*' It was Matt, full of the usual shit.

'That's Spanish and French both, you twat.' Rosie was glad to hear from him. 'Where are you?'

'I'm in the bar, darlin', and I'm starvin'. I just got here half an hour ago. Had a quick shower and change.'

'I'm only just here,' Rosie said. 'Tell you what, Matt, I'm going to jump in the shower, then I'll meet you down-stairs for a drink, and we'll have dinner.' She was taking off her clothes as she spoke. 'I'm going to put a quick call in to the cops, see if I can get anyone who speaks English. And find out if there's any press stuff going on tonight or what. We don't need it tonight, but I want to see what's what for tomorrow. See if they're going to put the parents up.'

'Yeah,' Matt said. 'There were a couple of relatives of the other couples back in Scotland talking on the telly. But nothing much getting said. They're all in a mess.'

'Can imagine.' Rosie was naked now. 'See you down-stairs in fifteen, Matt.' She hung up.

Rosie made a call to the Guarda Civil in Marbella, and in her fractured Spanish asked if there was anyone dealing with press inquiries. She was put through to a man whose English was better than her Spanish. No. There would be no press conference with the family. They were still staying at the villa. There would be a press conference early tomorrow afternoon where the Guarda Civil would talk of their search.

CHAPTER 5

By eleven the following morning, there was a posse of press camped on the sidestreet close to the Lennon villa. Mobile TV broadcast units from Spain jostled for position alongside the British TV stations, and the whole place was buzzing with activity. Camera crews and sound men stood around smoking and chatting, waiting for something to happen.

The press pack were dotted all over the street. You spent so much time just waiting, you had to get used to the tedium. It was the reason why there was so much black humour around journalists on frontlines everywhere.

A few locals and some British tourists also stood around in the ghoulish way that people do when there is a big tragedy playing out. Rosie had walked away from the journalists and was talking to McGuire, who was barking at her down the phone from his home.

'I don't really give a fuck what these Spanish coppers say, Rosie. The Guarda Civil are like the Taliban. This couple have got to get the message that if they don't get their faces in the papers, then everyone will lose interest in their kid.'

'I know, I know,' Rosie told him. 'I was going to do it shortly anyway, but there are two cops on the door at the moment. I was going to stick a letter through.'

'Yeah, yeah. Better idea. But tell them, Rosie, that the paper will give away posters in Monday's edition for people to pull out and stick on their windows and cars. Tell them if anyone can get them huge publicity, it's the *Post*. Our marketing people are already talking to people down on the Costa about putting up Find Amy posters done up like a *Post* front page all over the towns. That should look the business. We need to boost sales down there anyway.'

'Yeah,' Rosie said, wishing McGuire didn't think marketing at a time like this.

She knew that television was always in a better position to get publicity than the papers, and that they would also be thinking posters. McGuire was right – you had to move quickly on someone else's misery if you wanted to win points.

'Tell you what, Rosie. Tell them we'll put up a reward. Ten thousand pounds for information leading to getting Amy back.'

'Has the managing director okayed that, Mick?'

'Fuck the managing director. I'll make sure it happens. Just do it, sweetheart. Get me something for Monday, something different.'

'OK, Mick, I'll do the letter now. Talk later.' She hung up.

'What's the sketch?' Matt said as she walked towards their hired car.

'McGuire wants us to offer a reward, put up pull-out posters. The lot. He's offering ten grand, and I bet he hasn't even spoken to the management yet.'

Matt whistled. 'Great. That's brilliant. The bean counters will shit themselves. But they'll go for it.'

Rosie was in the car writing a letter on hotel notepaper she'd brought with her. She knew she wouldn't be the only hack looking for a way in. Despite what McGuire had said, Rosie knew in her gut that their only hope for Monday was a picture of the couple together and – if they were really lucky – a few words. If she wanted an exclusive, she would have to look further than the front door of the Lennon villa.

She was feeling a little rough from last night's lengthy dinner with Matt. It was one of those nights where the banter bounced off the walls and the wine flowed freely, while frontline stories from past foreign sojourns were rolled out. Rosie drank plenty of wine, but she wasn't that drunk. If it had ended there it would have been fine, but Rosie took a call from one of her pals on a London paper, and she and Matt went to join him and a few others in a bar in Marbella's old town until three in the morning. It had been the usual battery of journos, old and young, in various stages of drunkenness. And despite the tragic story they were working on, it turned into a bit of a party, as these things often did. By two in the morning at least two of the hacks were belting out songs on the karaoke along with a few of the ex-pat Brits who hung around drinking with the press pack.

Rosie had bailed out when a knuckle trailer with a thick Glasgow accent, clearly wasted on cocaine, began to noise everyone up, pushing people around and shouting that the press were a bunch of wankers. Given that one of the London reporters was leading the sing-song, he might have had a point. The place was busy with the collection of usual suspects you found in any Costa del Sol British bar. If you took a straw poll round the suntanned faces in the room, you could guarantee that at least three of them were on the Crimestoppers wanted list, and the bulk of the customers had the added glory of having done a stretch in jail. They had stories about the Old Bill that were so far fetched they had to be true. Everyone, it seemed, was ducking and diving, as you do on the Costa where asking too many questions to the wrong person could get you a bullet in the back.

The guy pestering Rosie made her uncomfortable because he was vaguely familiar. Her mind flicked through a filing system of Glasgow hoodlums down the years, and the photofit she came up with was a minder for a coke dealer who'd moved to Marbella five years ago, but was killed in a car crash. When he squared up to Rosie and said he recognised her from somewhere, she did her best to ignore him and grabbed Matt so they could make a sharp exit. The last thing she needed down here was more aggro from Glasgow.

*　　*　　*

Now knackered after such a late night, she took a gulp from a bottle of mineral water and put the letter she'd written in her bag. The reporters she'd been drinking with last night were now gathered yards from the Lennon house. Without even glancing in their direction, Rosie walked up to the front door and knocked. She looked at the patio, at the children's toys scattered around – the remnants of normality before the world caved in. A towel was draped over a chair, and a little red and white stripey bathing suit. A kid's drinking cup. She could almost hear the laughter of a family enjoying an afternoon in the sun. Now the place looked empty and sad.

Rosie gazed out across the beach, where a few people out strolling had stopped to glare at the villa they'd seen plastered all over the TV news and papers. The sea was calm and flat, eerie in this atmosphere. Suddenly the door opened and a female Guarda Civil officer stood there. In Spanish, Rosie asked if she could speak to the parents. The woman answered in English that no she could not. Rosie handed her the letter. The policewoman took it, looked at it and did that little bored shrugging gesture with her shoulders that the Mediterraneans have turned into an art form, before closing the door in Rosie's face. Rosie could sense the rest of the press pack straining to see. She knew a few of them, one or two whom she had turned over in her day, and they knew not to trust her. One grizzled older hack from a London paper came marching towards her.

'What you doing, Rosie? Fucking everyone over?'

He looked rough. The last time Rosie had seen him was

on the dance floor with a rose between his teeth at three that morning.

'Hi, Andy.' She smiled broadly. 'I thought for a minute you were going to ask me to dance.'

He laughed. 'Christ, I'm as rough as a badger's arse this morning.'

'Maybe it was the ice, Andy. That's a killer in this country.'

'Yeah. Nothing to do with the eight Jack Daniels and five tequilas.'

'Well, it certainly brought out your dancing feet,' Rosie laughed. She knew Andy Simpson would not be for shifting in case he missed anything. He was a London-based investigative reporter for the *Post*'s main rival in England and Scotland, and though they were both old hands who respected each other, she knew he would turn her over at the drop of a hat.

She heard the door open, and was surprised to see Jamie O'Hara standing in front of her.

'Rosie,' he said, as if they knew each other better than they did.

'Hello, Jamie.' Rosie took a deep breath. She'd be lucky if she got one sentence out. She spoke fast.

'Listen, Jamie, I'm really sorry. Really very sorry. It's a terrible time, but I just want to try to impress upon the family that we can be of some help. We need to get Amy's picture everywhere. I know it's hard—'

Jamie put his hand up to silence her. Rosie saw it was trembling slightly. So unlike him. She had seen Jamie O'Hara on the steps of the High Court in Glasgow many a time, triumphantly making a speech about a miscarriage of justice as some toe-rag villain who'd just got off stood smirking beside him. Now O'Hara looked pale and drawn, his eyes bloodshot. Amy was his best friend's little girl, and Rosie could imagine that he was trying to keep it together to support the Lennons as another day passed without news of the kid. She almost warmed to him.

'Look, Rosie,' he said. 'I've seen the letter. I see what your paper is trying to do and I understand. We've all had a talk in there.' He jerked his head in the direction of the house. 'I'm sure you'll understand that Jenny and Martin are in a real state. They're completely beside themselves. Honestly.' His lip slightly quivered.

Rosie was a little surprised he seemed to be finding it hard to cope. He took a deep breath.

'So . . . So what we can't do – won't do – is give an exclusive to anyone. Martin and Jenny aren't even in a position to talk today, but they will come out to the door and you can all have a minute to take a picture. The only statement will be delivered by me. We've put together some brief words, but there will be no questions.'

No surprise or disappointment there. She had expected something to come from the family, but despite McGuire's ambitions, she'd known the *Post* wouldn't be allowed to run the show.

Rosie spread her hands in submission. 'That's fine, Jamie. That's perfectly fine. I can understand the family don't want to say anything at the moment. But if they feel up to it another time, I hope you'll bear me in mind.'

Jamie nodded, and turned to go inside.

'And, of course, all of the press would be the same,' Andy called as the door was closed.

'Christ,' he said, as they walked away from the door. 'That Gilmour charm. Works every time. You're a chancing Arab, you know that?'

Rosie smiled. 'Gie's peace. I got you a picture you wouldn't have had, you ungrateful bastard.'

'Yeah, but you were trying to pull a sneaky one on the rest of us.'

'Well.' Rosie took his arm. 'You'd be disappointed if I wasn't, pet.'

Ten minutes later, when the front door opened, the news teams were five deep on the patio.

Jenny Lennon blinked as the flashbulbs went off, and clutched her husband's hand so tightly that Rosie could see her knuckles turn white. Her face was ashen, her eyes swollen from crying. Her auburn hair was swept back, emphasising her high cheekbones and the hollows of her face. Jenny was a beauty, better-looking in the flesh than in the pictures in today's papers. But she looked gaunt already, and it had only been two days since Amy vanished. Martin's dark eyes were watery and distant, and he was clearly blinking back tears. The cameras whirred and the TV crews filmed for a minute before Jamie O'Hara stepped forward and cleared his throat.

'Thank you for your support.' His voice shook. He swallowed. 'As you can imagine, this is the worst nightmare for any parent. Jenny and Martin are understandably too upset to be interviewed, so they have asked me to appeal to anyone who has any information on Amy's disappearance to contact the Guarda Civil.'

He looked up, his eyes intense, then back at the paper.

'We know that by now Amy could be anywhere, so we are asking everyone – wherever you are – to take a look at her picture and please contact the police if you have any information at all that may lead to her being found.' He swallowed again and there was a pause as reporters waited to see if he was finished.

Tears streamed down Jenny's cheeks. Martin put his arm around her shoulder.

'Do you have a message for the person or persons who took Amy?' Rosie chanced it.

Jamie looked at her. Tears spilled out of Martin's eyes.

'All we can say is please, please don't harm Amy. She's just an innocent little girl. And she'll be missing her mum and dad,' Jamie said as he ushered the Lennons back into the house.

A voice from the huddle of reporters shouted, 'Can anyone go through the events of the morning she vanished please, Mr O'Hara?'

Jamie O'Hara looked over his shoulder and glanced briefly before turning away. His face was grey.

Rosie had never ever seen him like that.

CHAPTER 6

As soon as Jenny woke up, the agony came coursing through her like a torrent. Her eyes were tight and stinging from crying herself to sleep.

She could hear Martin moving quietly in the kitchen and she turned over, stretching across to his side of the bed where it was still warm and she could feel and smell where he had lain all night with his eyes open, staring at the ceiling.

In the stillness, the rush of the sea on the shore was rhythmic and constant. She'd slept fitfully, in the crook of Martin's arm, but even as he stroked her hair and whispered words of encouragement, Jenny had wondered if it was her guilt that made her sense that he wasn't the same. Surely he couldn't suspect anything, she'd asked herself over and over again? It wasn't as though she and Jamie had always flirted with each other. There had been nothing. Nothing in the fifteen years they'd known each other would have made her think they – she – could have done what they did.

The night before it happened was the first time Jamie had ever behaved as though he had any desire for her. Even then, it should never in a million years have interested her, but it did. She agonised over it. Maybe it was the predictability of her life every day that made her step out of the mundaneness for one reckless walk on the wild side. Or perhaps, deep down, she hadn't forgiven Martin for that one indiscretion he'd confessed to last year with the girl in his office, and somewhere in her head she wanted to get even. But suddenly, the night before, Jamie had come on to her in the bar and Jenny had responded, and had been stupid enough to allow it to carry on the next morning.

She curled up, wrapping her arms around herself. If only Jamie hadn't come to the house, catching her off guard. If only she had just pushed him away, laughed it off, she and Martin would be lying here waiting for Amy to come bounding into the bedroom, eager for the day to begin.

She dragged herself out of bed, her fit, athletic body now weary and heavy, and padded into the kitchen where Martin stood with his back to her, staring out as the early morning light spread across the beach.

'There's coffee,' he said, without turning around.

Jenny's stomach dropped. He knew something. He suspected.

She crossed the kitchen, poured herself a coffee and sat at the table. Martin came over and sat down without looking at her for a moment. Then when he did, she could see the redness of his eyes, the dark shadows on his pale, lean face. He looked suddenly old. Silence hung in the room.

'I keep thinking,' Martin said, his fingers clasped around the mug. 'I keep thinking, if only I hadn't gone out for a run. If only I'd relaxed, read a book, just sat around the villa. But no. I had to go fucking running. Like I had something to run for. I'm supposed to be on holiday, so why couldn't I sit on my arse and relax instead of this fucking running regime every day. If I'd just been in the house and you were in the shower and Amy got up, I'd have been here. But I wasn't here.' He shook his head. Tears welled up. 'I wasn't here for her Jenny, and she got up. And maybe someone took her. And her daddy wasn't here to stop them.' He started to sob.

Tears rolled down Jenny's face. She ached with guilt. She leaned over and put her arms around him, holding him tight to her chest.

'Sssh . . . Ssssh. Don't. Don't beat yourself up like that. It's not your fault, Martin. It's not, it's not.' Jenny stroked his hair. 'We'll find her, Martin. We'll find Amy.'

If she kept telling herself that, if she kept hoping, maybe just for an instant Jenny would forget that this was all her fault. Maybe she could put the guilt away and hide it so he would never know. Then Martin looked up at her and spoke.

'I keep thinking,' he said. 'Did Jamie not see anything as he was walking down here. I mean he wouldn't be thinking of Amy or anything else, but is there anything at all he might have seen? Might have missed?'

Jenny said nothing. She eased herself away from Martin and went back to her chair.

'Jenny,' Martin said, softly. 'What was Jamie doing anyway, coming down to visit when he didn't even know if we were in? He knows I'm always out running. I mean, you and Amy could have been out walking.'

Jenny looked at him.

'I don't know, Martin. What difference does that make? Jamie just happened to be out for a walk. Who knows? You can't make him feel he should have seen something. He was just out for a walk.'

Jenny got up and went to the sink. She turned on the tap and started to rinse her cup vigorously. She could feel Martin's eyes on her. Her legs felt weak. She heard him get up from the table and then his arms went around her. He turned her to face him and looked into her eyes. Jenny looked back, her eyes filling with tears. Martin studied her face for a moment, his dark eyes suddenly seeming cold. He shook his head.

'We'd best get organised, Jenny. We have to be at the police station this morning to go over everything again.' He left the room.

From the balcony off his bedroom, Jamie watched his two sons playing football on the beach. Daniel dived after the ball with his big brother and collapsed into fits of laughter when Sam jinked away from him and shoved him on his backside.

At not quite five, Daniel was too young to know what was going on. When he asked where Amy was, he was told she was away for the moment but they were looking for her. He had questioned a bit more, but Alison was always on hand to change the subject, giving him something else to focus on. Sam knew though, and he had looked dark and confused these past two days. He was six, and had enjoyed being the little man of the three kids, ordering them around and showing them who was boss. Amy had followed him everywhere like a shadow, and Jamie could see he missed her and was confused by all the activity.

He pulled on a pair of light trousers and a fresh shirt and looked at himself in the mirror. His suntanned face was paler now and his eyes were tired. He could hear Alison working in the kitchen, preparing lunch for the the Reillys who were coming round to hear more about the police investigation while Jenny and Martin were at the police station.

He bit his lip, thinking of how meticulous the police had been when they interviewed him about what happened the morning Amy disappeared. He had his story down to a tee, so much so that he was beginning to believe it himself.

He knew that was the only way. To be totally convincing, he had to convince himself that all he was doing was walking on the beach and decided to visit Jenny and Martin. If he really concentrated, he could put out of his mind that stupid moment where he brushed against Jenny in the kitchen and suddenly they were all over each other. What in the name of Christ possessed him, he kept asking himself. The night before when he made a pass at her, it was because he was quite drunk, but for some reason he couldn't get it out of his mind. He woke up horny the following morning at the thought of her, and that's what drove him to go down there.

He knew Martin would be out for a run. But what the hell was he thinking about? He rubbed his face with his hands as he thought of Amy. Someone must have taken her. They must have. But when the cops were asking him details of his every move that morning, they kept quizzing him, asking did he not see anyone at all on the beach?

Jamie told them that all he saw was the windsurfer getting his board sorted. They asked again and again, their eyes searching his face, but he knew he could keep his expression deadpan even though he thought they suspected something. He managed to keep it up, although the little police sergeant never took his eyes off him all the time the other cops were asking questions. And he was the same with Martin and the Reillys when they were all together in the house, all of them catatonic with shock and panic. They had sat all night talking, crying, going over and over it again. Jamie had stuck to his story, and so had Jenny. But he felt that John Reilly had a look on his face that said he knew Jamie and Jenny weren't telling the truth. And poor Martin. He just kept blaming himself for being out of the house. That was the hardest part. How could he tell his best friend that it wasn't his fault?

But Alison knew. Jamie was sure of it. Even while she was comforting Jenny, Jamie could sense that she knew. Because of his womanising all their married life, Alison had stopped believing him years ago. She knew by instinct that he was with Jenny when Amy disappeared. It was written in her face. But he also knew that for the sake of Daniel and Sam she would go to her grave before she would ever do anything about it.

CHAPTER 7

Rosie sat sipping iced tea in the shade of a pristine white canvas umbrella on the sprawling terrace of the Puente Romano. Through the palm trees and rose-bush-lined paths to the beach, she could see wealthy hotel guests basking in the afternoon sun on blue-and-white striped loungers. There was so much Botox and so many silicon tits, it was hard to know who was middle aged. You could never tell down in Marbella, as Rosie had found during previous assignments on the Costa. The whole place was a blizzard of cocaine, where the rich partied so hard it was easy to look middle-aged by the time you were twenty-seven. But one thing was certain, nobody roughed it around here: 'If you've got it flaunt it' was stamped all over them, from their Louis Vuitton beach bags and gleaming Rolex watches to the fake breasts as hard as Tupperware -pudding bowls. The idle rich . . . That crap about the meek inheriting the earth was obviously just something God threw in to help you cope when you were on the bare bones of your arse.

Rosie had ordered smoked salmon salad while she waited for Matt to come back from uploading the morning's pictures onto his laptop in his bedroom. She pondered on the doorstep scene earlier with Amy's parents and Jamie O'Hara. The tension and the sense of tragedy had been palpable. Jenny and Martin Lennon were completely broken. The chances of their little girl being found alive were getting slimmer by the hour.

'Hello. Excuse me, Miss?'

A voice from behind. Rosie glanced over her shoulder and was surprised to see a young boy approaching. He looked hesitant and apologetic.

'Me?' Rosie said, lifting her sunglasses above her eyes. She looked up at the boy. She wondered if he worked in the hotel, but he wasn't wearing a uniform.

'Yes. Sorry, Miss.' The boy was at her side, shifting nervously from one foot to the other. 'May I speak with you?'

Rosie swung round so she was facing him. She looked him up and down. Dark and skinny, but strikingly beautiful. He looked like a rent boy, and she half smiled to herself. Surely she didn't look old enough to be in the market for a gigolo? She waited for him to say something.

'Excuse me,' the boy cleared his throat, 'but I saw you this morning. Earlier. At the beach. You are newspaper woman? Yes? I can tell you something.' He spoke carefully, as though trying to remember the English words.

A little switch flicked inside her head. This boy had followed her here.

'Yes,' she said. 'That's right.' She motioned him to sit. 'But how did you know I was here?'

The boy sat down. He looked at her with large liquid brown eyes that dominated his face and gave him an innocent look. But the dark smudges under those eyes told another story.

'I heard you say to someone you are going back to the Puente Romano, so I think maybe you living here.' He shifted in his seat. 'I wanted . . . I want to talk to you because you are in the newspapers. And I think I have some information for you.'

Rosie's heart did a little dance and her instincts told her to brace herself. From where she was sitting on a Saturday afternoon, she didn't have a story for Monday's newspaper that wouldn't have been all over the weekend papers and television. Anything, however off the wall, even if it came in broken English from a skinny rent boy, had to be listened to.

'Sure,' she said. 'I'd be glad to have a talk with you. Would you like a drink? Something to eat? Are you hungry?'

Her eyes flicked up and down the boy. He looked vulnerable, like a little vagrant who had scrubbed his face and combed his hair so he could get past the reception in a place that would happily kick people like him into the gutter. But Rosie wasn't daft. He would be on the make alright. He wouldn't have followed her here otherwise. Any minute now he'd name a price, but she knew she would have to listen. The white-waistcoated waiter appeared with her salmon salad and a basket of bread. The boy looked at it and swallowed.

'Can you bring some of the special chicken, please,' Rosie said to the waiter. She looked at the boy.

'You okay with some chicken? A drink?'

'Yes, thank-you.' His eyes brightened. 'I'm hungry. Can I also have Coca-Cola please?'

Rosie told the waiter, then pushed her salad to the middle of the table.

'Here,' Rosie said. 'Help yourself. We'll share. They'll bring more food in a minute.' She stuck her fork into a piece of salmon, inviting him to do the same.

'Thank you,' the boy said gratefully, lifting a piece of salmon with the knife. 'I did not have food since last night.' He stuffed the salmon into his mouth and tore off a piece of bread.

Rosie watched him for a moment as he ate, his lean face smooth and brown under a mop of black curly hair. His pale blue shirt was ragged at the cuffs, and his flimsy beach-boy trousers were frayed and turned up at the bottom, revealing broken leather sandals. He looked out of place amid the elegance of the white wicker chairs and stiff linen table-cloths. Rosie was surprised he had got this far into the hotel without someone turfing him out. Top marks for endeavour, whoever he was.

'So, who are you?' Rosie said, looking straight into his eyes. He may have followed her, but from now on, she was in charge.

'My name is Taha.' The boy wiped his hand on his trousers and stretched it across to Rosie. She shook it. It was soft, like the hand of a child.

He glanced back at the food as if he was afraid it would disappear. Rosie nodded to him to eat.

'I am from Morocco. But I am here now in Spain for one year and two months. Working,' he told her between mouthfuls.

Rosie decided not to ask. If he said he was anything other than a rent boy, she wouldn't have believed him anyway. The boy looked at her as though he knew what she was thinking. His eyes looked sad. He'd probably practised that look in the mirror. When he swallowed Rosie could see his Adam's apple move in his slender neck. He looked over his shoulder fleetingly, then pulled his chair a little closer to the table, seeming nervous.

'I saw something,' he said. 'That girl. The missing girl. But I cannot tell the police because I am illegal here. They would send me back, and I cannot go back now. I am making some money for my parents in our village. I don't want to talk to police, but I know things.'

Rosie looked at his face, watching for some flaw, some sign that he was a chancer. A sudden image of Mags Gillick, the murdered prostitute who had confided in her over Gavin Fox's corrupt exploits, flashed across her mind and she banished it. That same look – fear and loneliness – had haunted her since Mags' murder. Don't even go there, she told herself. She decided to let him talk, make him feel at ease. If he had something interesting then fine. If not, it had brightened up a dull afternoon.

'Listen, Taha.' Rosie stretched her hand across so it brushed his wrist. 'Before we start talking here, you have to know you can trust me. I won't betray you. But if you know something about the little girl, about Amy, then we have to find a way to let the police know. But whatever you tell me, be assured, you can trust me to look after you.'

Taha took a sip of his coke. He wiped his mouth with the back of his hand.

'OK. I understand. But I am worry . . . Because of what I do and the people I work for. They are not good people. Dangerous.' Taha looked edgy.

'I understand,' Rosie said. 'But you have to trust me. My name is Rosie Gilmour, and I work for a newspaper in Scotland called the *Post*. OK? I am over here to look at the story of the little girl. She might have been stolen. Maybe kidnapped . . . ?'

The boy looked down, twisted his glass on the table cloth for a few moments, then looked up at Rosie.

'Yes,' he said. 'I think she was stolen. I saw. I saw someone.'

She took a deep breath. She read his face for lies, for any sign of a set-up. If he was lying he was good, very good.

'Tell me, Taha. What did you see? Were you on the beach?'

He looked down again. 'No. I was in a villa. But close. I could see—' He bit the inside of his jaw. 'I was with someone on the balcony. We saw the girl on the beach. Someone took her.'

Rosie sat back. She let the silence take over for a moment. She knew Taha was waiting for her to ask.

'You were with a client?'

'Yes.' Taha looked a little sheepish, but Rosie probed.

'A man?'

'Yes. A British man. A big important man, I think.'

Rosie took a sip of her iced tea.

'Taha.' She spoke quietly, almost in a whisper. 'Can you tell me what you saw. Just what you saw from the balcony.'

'Okay,' he said. 'I was on the balcony. With the man. It was before we . . . Before . . . You know?'

Rosie nodded her understanding, waved him to go on.

'We were talking a bit and looking at the sea. A small girl was on the beach. No people with her. Then a man came and lifted her up and took her away.'

'Maybe it was her father,' Rosie said. 'What made you think it wasn't her father?'

Taha shrugged. 'It was nothing to us then. Nothing, when it happened. But after . . . After some time, we saw the woman come out of the house nearby, and another man also came out of the house a bit later. They were running and the woman cried a lot. She called a name, like she was looking for somebody. That was when I think maybe she is stolen. Then the papers and television say a small girl is taken.'

Rosie listened. It had Monday's splash and spread stamped all over it. If what he'd seen was Jenny Lennon and O'Hara coming outside, then this was not the version they'd told the world. O'Hara had said he was walking down the beach when he heard Jenny coming out of the house screaming. This was a different account entirely.

But based on what, she could hear McGuire saying. The word of a rent boy? She'd been here before.

'Did you see anything before that, Taha?' Rosie wanted to be clear. 'Did you see a man coming down the beach towards the woman who was screaming?'

'No,' he said, looking bewildered. 'I only saw the girl, then a man take her, then after some time the man and woman come from the house. That's all.'

Rosie nodded.

'So what did you do after that? Did you see anything else. Would you recognise the man?'

'I don't know,' the boy said. 'I don't think so. After that my friend – the man – he left. Then I left. It is the normal thing when I go to that house with a client.'

'So the man was a client?' Rosie asked. 'The British man?'

'Yes,' Taha nodded. 'I been there with him before. Once last week, and twice last year, when first I come to Spain. He's a good man. And he pays well.'

Rosie didn't really want the details. They were written all over the face of this beautiful young boy. He was sixteen or seventeen, if that, and already ruined.

'Taha,' she said. 'You said the man was an important man. Do you know his name?'

Taha nodded. He reached into his pocket and took out something. 'I knew him as Thomas,' he said. 'But the name is different. On this.'

He opened his hand, and in his palm was what Rosie recognised as a House of Commons security pass. He handed it to her. She didn't need to look at the name, because the photo on the pass was enough to make her head swim. The Home Secretary, the Rt. Hon. Michael Carter-Smith, was looking back at her with that arrogant expression which dared anyone to take him on.

CHAPTER 8

She was like the puppy, snuggling against him, and it was an odd feeling. He wasn't used to having someone close to him like that.

In the back of the car, Besmir moved the sleeping child's arm away from him. He looked at her pale face as she slept, exhausted, her eyelids puffy from crying. The car was stifling, and a tiny strip of sweat gathered under her hairline. His fingers reached out and almost stroked her forehead, but he pulled back. She was nothing to him. Just a package to be delivered. He rolled down the window, but the air coming in was dry and sweltering, so he closed it again. He put his head back and closed his eyes. He would be glad when this was over.

The worst moment had been the journey from Elira's apartment in Algeciras. They had to leave at first light and the girl had started to scream as Besmir put her into the boot of the car. They had to be vigilant in case police were looking in every car for the missing girl. A private boat would take him to the Tangiers coast, but he would return by the ferry, using a fake German passport Leka had given him.

Elira had insisted he take the puppy with them, despite Besmir's protests that he'd have enough with the girl. But she'd said it would help once they were on the journey as it might keep the girl calm. Elira had named the girl Kaltrina, Albanian for 'the blue girl', because of her striking blue eyes.

Besmir didn't like the way Elira was fawning over the kid as if it was her own. Just get on with the job. Get to Tangiers and deliver the girl, then get back to Spain and his money. He promised himself that as soon as Leka paid him he'd get on the road and none of them would ever see him again. But for now, he was stuck with this little girl and a puppy in the back of the car.

The motor boat had dropped them off at the small isolated cove on the Moroccan coast. It hadn't been able to come right up to the shore because of the rocks in the shallow waters. It had put out a small rubber dingy to take them to the shore, but it still left them some way out from the beach. Besmir cursed as he carried the sobbing girl and the puppy, wading knee-deep in the sea towards the young Moroccan man waiting for him on the beach.

He'd been tempted to give the girl the drink Elira had given him to put her to sleep, but he was scared in case it would kill her. Knowing Leka, the last thing he wanted to do was deliver the package dead.

The young driver said nothing when Besmir emerged from the sea. He simply nodded and walked away, Besmir following him towards a battered car parked on the dirt-track road. As they approached he noticed there was someone in the passenger seat. A small, fat Moroccan smoked furiously and spat out of the window as Besmir got into the car with the girl clinging round his neck.

'Can you shut her up?' the fat man said, tossing his cigarette out of the window.

'Just take us to where we have to go,' Besmir snapped at him, prodding his back firmly with his finger, as he got into the back seat.

Whoever this fat old Moroccan was, he was not in charge here, and Besmir wanted to make sure he was in no doubt about that.

'How far?' Besmir asked the driver. 'How long to drive?'

'Maybe two hours,' he said. 'Roads no good. We don't go the coast road as there is more traffic and people. But the small roads to Tangiers are not good.'

'Then let's go.' Besmir poked his shoulder for effect.

The girl had sobbed for a little longer, but she stopped when Besmir gave her some water and a soft sugar sweet Elira had put in the bag for the journey. The puppy licked her fingers as Besmir settled her down so she was lying across the seat. But she kept twisting herself around so she could lie with her arm wrapped across him. He automatically put his arm over hers. He looked out of the window.

The car clanked and jerked its way along the road, which became little more than tyre tracks in the desolate scrubland. The young driver repeated it was better to keep away from the main roads, and kept turning his head round to Besmir to reassure him that everything was alright. Besmir guessed he was about the same age as himself, but he could see that he was a little afraid of him, and he resolved to keep it that way.

He didn't like the little fat man and immediately sensed he couldn't trust him. He was a bully. Besmir knew he'd made an instant enemy from the moment he had talked down to him at the start of the journey, but that didn't worry him. He had met enough bullying little men on his way through life, and he feared none of them. You had to get the better of them straight away or they would crush you into the ground like a beetle.

He looked out at the heat rising in waves across the barren landscape. They'd hardly gone past any villages, just miles and miles of empty track and a few straggling herds of goats, some – to his amazement – perched precariously in the trees nibbling on the leaves. He smiled to himself when he saw them teetering on the branches. The goats weren't afraid to take a risk. He liked that.

The driver pointed to a small stream in the distance and asked if they could stop for a few minutes to eat some food. He had been working since daybreak he said, and was hungry. Besmir agreed, and thought he should give the girl something to eat if she woke up. They got out of the car and the fat man lit a cigarette, walking towards the stream and opening his trousers to have a pee as he went. Besmir opened the back door and could see that the girl was waking up. He crouched down and looked at her face, smiling at her.

'Hello, little Kaltrina.' He lifted the bag out to look for

some food, then produced a piece of bread. 'Look, Kaltrina. Hungry? You want some food?'

The puppy jumped out and leapt up at him. He gave it a piece of bread which it devoured in one gulp. The girl giggled, and put her hands out for some food. Besmir broke off a piece of bread and handed it to her. She immediately stretched her hand towards the dog who leapt up and snatched it from her fingers. Besmir watched her face as she looked up at him, her blue eyes piercing in the sunlight.

'Kaltrina. Look. Eat.' He put some bread in his mouth and she put her arms up for him to lift her. He took her out of the car and sat her on the ground, kneeling beside her. Besmir broke more bread and some hard cheese from the bag and gave a small piece to her. He watched as she munched it, then put her hands out for the water and orange juice mix Elira had given them. She was thirsty, and gulped the lukewarm drink. Then she stood up. She fidgeted from one leg to the other, and clutched between her legs. Besmir looked at her, confused, then at the driver, who smiled a gap-toothed smile.

'She want go to toilet,' he said, pointing at her. Besmir felt awkward. He looked at the driver.

'You want I take her?' he said. 'I have little sisters. Is no problem for me to take them to toilet.'

Besmir said nothing but motioned with his hand to take the girl. He watched as the driver picked her up and went a few yards away. He seemed to be at ease around the child. How different their lives were, though they were similar ages. He wondered what it must be like to be easy with people, to be with a family, eating together in the evenings and sitting by the fire. Of course he'd seen it in pictures and on television, but it was alien to him. There was no point in being close to anything or anybody. You could get by in life without all that. Even for sex. You could just do it and feel the rush inside you when you let all the tension go. But you didn't have to lie around touching the woman, because who knows what that would make you feel. You'd want them to be with you all the time, and maybe they wouldn't come back and you'd be left on your own – like the old days, before the crying stopped.

Besmir could see the skyline of Tangiers in the distance, apartment blocks stacked close close under the shimmering heat of the late afternoon sun. He was glad the girl was asleep again, but it wouldn't be for long; as they came closer to the town, the noise of the horns and traffic began building up. He fidgeted in his seat, feeling hot and tired. The driver turned around as though sensing his discomfort.

'Not long now. Just few minutes.'

The fat man sat up straight in his seat and half turned to Besmir.

'I been told that when we get to the place, you take the girl in and then you go,' he said. 'Your job finish.' He jerked his thumb towards the driver. 'He drive you to the harbour and you can take a boat back to Spain.' He opened, the window, hawked and spat.

Besmir leaned forward. 'When Leka gets the call from

the man I am delivering to, then I will go. When Leka calls me.'

The fat man shrugged. 'Leka? I do not know him. My boss is Moroccan.'

'No.' Besmir talked close to his ear. 'You may not know Leka, but he will know you. He will know who you are and where to find you. He will know everything about everyone involved in this. That is how Leka works.'

'Should I be frightened of this man Leka?' The fat man was sarcastic, more confident now that he was deep in his own turf.

'Yes,' Besmir said. 'You should be afraid. Very afraid.' He sat back in the seat and looked out of the window as they continued the rest of the journey in silence.

The girl woke up as they snaked their way through the tight backstreets. Somewhere amid the crowded apartment blocks and buildings, the Muslim call to prayer rose up into the cloudless sky. Besmir smiled at the girl and lifted her onto his lap, surprising himself at how natural it felt. She started crying again, and he tried to shush her, but she was calling for her mother.

'Look, look,' Besmir said, trying to distract her by pointing to things outside in the busy street. He wiped her tears with the palm of his hand.

'We are here,' the driver said, pulling into a little cobbled street.

They got out of the car and Besmir lifted the girl into his arms. She wrapped her arms so tightly around his neck she almost choked him. The driver lifted the puppy and gestured for them to follow him and the fat man along the cloistered sidestreet and across a maze of narrow alleyways until they finally came to a two-storey white building with a massive metal door. The fat man knocked twice.

Besmir stood, his face like flint, steadying himself for whatever was behind the door. It opened slowly and the fat man went in, followed by the driver who nodded to Besmir to come. Inside the massive hall the mosaic tiles on the floor and the walls were like an explosion of colour. The air was heavy with the smell of spices and cigarette smoke. A middle-aged woman wearing a flowing kaftan, with a pashmina covering her head, emerged from a corridor and looked at the fat man, then at Besmir. She smiled.

'The girl,' she said, her heavily made-up eyes bright. She went towards Besmir with her arms outstretched.

'What a pretty girl. Does she have a name?' Her perfume wafted with her every move.

'We called her Kaltrina. In Albanian, it means the blue girl,' Besmir said flatly. 'Look. Her eyes.'

The girl looked confused as the woman tried to take her out of Besmir's arms. She clung onto him, whimpering.

'She is beautiful. This blue girl.' She looked at Besmir.

He was surprised to find himself holding the girl tightly, and the woman stared at him. He loosened his grip, but still held onto her.

A door opened at the far corner of the room and a big, well-built, older Moroccan man with dyed black hair came walking in. He wore white trousers, and a black shirt open at the neck to reveal a heavy gold chain and medal-lion resting on his very hairy chest. Two thickset henchmen dressed in Moroccan tunics followed him. Besmir pulled himself up to stand tall.

'You must be Besmir,' the man said, striding across the room with his hand outstretched. 'Leka told me.' He looked at the girl. 'And he was not wrong about the girl. A beauty.'

'The blue girl,' the woman piped up. 'They have called her Kaltrina. It means the blue girl because of her blue eyes. Look at them. Look how lovely she is.'

The man nodded and touched the girl's face softly.

'My beautiful blue girl,' he murmured. 'You are like gold.'

He looked at Besmir.

'Thank you,' he said. 'Your work here is finished now. The driver will take you back to the port. I will call Leka to tell him you delivered safely.' He smiled to Besmir, his dark skin like creased brown paper.

The woman came forward and put her arms out for the girl, but she buried her head in Besmir's neck. The woman gently prised the girl off him and held her close, whispering to her. Besmir could still feel the softness of her skin on his. Her eyes filled with tears and she started screaming for her mother. The woman stroked her hair and turned to walk quickly out of the room. Besmir tried not to look as he heard the girl sobbing as she stretched her arms out towards him. He could still see the blue of her eyes as she disappeared behind the door.

'You can go now, Besmir.' The man shook his hand. 'Thank you for your good work.'

Besmir said nothing. He glanced at the fat man whose face was wearing a smirk that he would remember long after this day was over.

CHAPTER 9

'Let me just run that past you, Rosie,' McGuire said. 'In case I've blacked out or I'm dreaming. Are you telling me that our esteemed Home Secretary not only may have witnessed the kidnapping of little Amy, but was rogering some dusky rent boy at the same time? Oh, fuck me, Rosie! I think I'm going to faint. Just saying it makes me lightheaded.'

Rosie could almost hear McGuire's brain rattling as he tried to process the information. Nobody relished the dismantling of a public figure more than he, and she knew even before she phoned him that he'd bite her hand off when she told him what the Taha boy had told her.

'Yep, that's right, Mick. The boy might be lying through his back teeth, I don't know, but as we speak, I have in my hot little palm Michael Carter-Smith's House of Commons pass. His privileged face is looking right at me.'

'Jesus almighty.' Silence. 'Right, Rosie. We need to stand back and work this out.'

McGuire offered a few scenarios. By this time, Carter-

Smith would have noticed that his pass was missing –
though if he was still on holiday, he might not notice
until he got back to London. If he'd noticed it was gone,
he'd be in a flap, trying to retrace his steps.

'He'll be shitting himself.' McGuire said.

'I know,' Rosie said, closing the terrace doors. 'What I
can't understand is why people like him carry these things
around with them when they're out picking up rough
trade of a morning. I mean anything could happen.'

'Do you think this little poofter is making it all up,
Rosie? What if Carter-Smith has innocently dropped the
pass out of his pocket on the street, for example, or in a
restaurant or bar, and this little toe-rag stumbled across
it and decided to invent a story for money. I take it that
has crossed your mind?'

'Of course, but he hasn't asked for money. Well, not
yet. And he didn't even ask for money when he gave me
the pass.'

'Yeah. But he will. You know that.'

'I know. But he hasn't, Mick. And he's given me the
pass.'

'So you think he's telling the truth?'

Rosie sat down on the bed, plumped up the pillows
and lay back.

'It's hard to say, but I don't think he's making it up.
My instincts tell me that. Just something about him, the
way he told the story. I know he looks like a little kid,
and that guys from the street like him could probably
buy and sell most of us. Yet I get the feeling that he's
just found himself in the middle of something and he

wants to get it out there. His information about someone lifting the kid won't make a whole lot of difference to the hunt. I suppose he can describe to the cops what he remembers of the man on the beach, though that's not really going to help track Amy down. It'll be too vague, plus it's a bit late. But for us, the story is not just in what he saw, it's in who he claims he was with. It's going to take a bit of digging, but it will be massive if we can do it. Massive.'

McGuire went quiet for a moment.

'Tell you what, Rosie. I need to make a couple of discreet inquiries with my political allies, and see what Carter-Smith does in Spain at this time of year ... if he has a place, or visits friends or whatever. We might find out what he's doing there, and if he has police protection and stuff. And what about this boy? Where is he now? Are you going to see him again?'

'Yes, I've arranged to meet him tonight. He called me a little while ago. He says he has some more information but I don't know what it is. I need to keep him totally on side so I might drop him some cash. Keep him sweet.'

'Great. Tell Matt to get a picture of him.'

'Already done. I called Matt just after we spoke and got him to bag a snatch pic of Taha as he was leaving the hotel.'

'Excellent. Well, let's see what he says tonight. I'll talk to some friends, then we'll speak again tomorrow. The arse will fall out of the empire if we can run this story.'

Rosie now told him what Taha had said about the man

and the woman coming out of the house, and how it differed from the version given by Jenny and O'Hara.

'This is beginning to stink a bit, Rosie.'

'I know,' she said. 'But there's a missing girl here, Mick. Let's not forget the bigger picture.'

'Yeah, but it's something we have to bear in mind. We'll see how it goes. Talk tomorrow.' He hung up.

Behind the bravado as she talked the story up to McGuire, Rosie was already troubled, again thinking of Mags Gillick. She could see her face, clear as that day when they'd first met in the cafe and Mags spilled the lot about Gavin Fox. Rosie thought she'd dealt with the guilt of Mags being murdered because she'd blabbed to her about the corrupt cops, but this Moroccan kid with his story was bringing it all back. She told herself to get a grip. She had a job to do.

It was already after eight by the time Rosie arrived at the restaurant in Fuengirola. Taha had said he would meet her in the last *chirunguito*, the Spanish name for the beach restaurants strung along promenade. It would be easy for her to find. Matt dropped her off and was waiting nearby. She'd give him a call when the time was right, but Rosie wanted meet Taha on her own and gain his complete confidence.

The restaurant was quiet except for three older Spanish men sitting at a table watching basketball on the wall-mounted television in the corner. Rosie nodded to the waiter and walked past him to sit outside in the warm night air, choosing a table as far away as possible from two British couples who were finishing their meal and talking loudly. They were moaning that the problem in the Costa was that it took the Spanish forever to do anything.

'*Mañana*, always *mañana*,' the leathery-faced English guy with the shaved head and tattooed biceps ranted. His mate chirped in with some anecdote about getting a Spanish plumber to do some work around their house. Their fat women giggled as the guy did a poor impression of the hapless Spanish waiter Manuel in *Fawlty Towers*.

Typical Brits abroad. No wonder everyone hated them. When were they going to get the message that their empire had disappeared up its own arse decades ago.

Rosie grimaced ruefully at the waiter who took her drinks order. He made a bored face. He'd heard it all before. She sipped her red wine and looked at the moon on the water. She took her mobile out of her bag and fiddled around with it, going through the directory of names and stopping at TJ's. She resisted the urge to ring it, to see if the number was still dead. And anyway, she'd moved on, hadn't she? A sudden wave of loneliness swept over her, taking her by surprise. She shook herself immediately out of it. No time for that crap. She sat herself up straight and got her head into work mode. Where was this little bastard?

On cue, Taha arrived from behind her and sat down.

'Hello, Rosie.' He smiled at her with his big brown eyes. 'I am very happy to see you again. You are very nice lady.'

Rosie looked at him. Surely to Christ he wasn't going

to offer himself for rent. She gave him a blank look and waved the waiter over. Taha ordered a coke, and asked if he could have a sandwich.

'Of course.' Rosie handed him the menu.

'Is it okay to have a steak sandwich?' He looked genuinely concerned.

Rosie noticed he was a little fidgety.

'Sure. Of course.' She turned to the waiter. 'With French fries.' She smiled at Taha. 'What the hell. Let's push the boat out.'

'Thank you,' Taha said. 'I am very hungry.' He shifted in his seat. 'Always hungry, because I am always running around and working. Last night I worked on the boat. Very late. So I not get time to eat much. Or sleep.'

He pulled his chair a little closer to the table so when he leaned forward he was nearer Rosie. The dark smudges under his eyes were more pronounced than yesterday. 'That is what I want to talk to you about.'

Rosie watched him, wondering if he was on something. He was a lot more jumpy than he'd been yesterday. She wasn't sure if she wanted to know the gory details of his work, but she'd better listen anyway.

'The boat?' she said. 'You worked on the boat? What boat?'

'Yes,' Taha said. 'It belong to the Russian. The big boss Mr Daletsky. Mr Viktor Daletsky. He is very rich man. He own everything. Everywhere.'

Rosie looked at him. No bells rang. 'Daletsky?'

'You know him?' Taha said.

'No, I don't. What were you doing on his boat?' Rosie

hoped he would spare her the graphic details of bottoms being breached.

Taha took a swig of coke. His steak sandwich arrived and he scooped up a handful of chips as soon as the waiter put the plate on the table. He chewed fast and gulped the food down.

'I work in the kitchens for a little while. They have some kind of big party last night. Lot of people. Then I am there in case anyone asks for me.' He sighed. 'You know, like . . . the clients. If my boss tells me someone wants me for a while, then I will go to one of the rooms on the boat. The cabins.'

Rosie kept looking at him curiously, wondering why he was telling her all this.

'Who is your boss? Is he Russian too?'

'Yes. He is Russian, but also he has a boss and he is the Albanian called Leka. He is a big boss. Very big man. Everybody afraid of Leka. My boss is scared of him. He runs all the business for them.'

Rosie was feeling a bit lost. What had the Russian millionaire and the Albanians got to do with this rent boy – apart from the obvious, that he was just part of their prostitution racket that in turn was part of their empire. She took a deep breath and leaned towards Taha.

'Taha,' she said. 'Why are you telling me about the boat and the Russian? What has this got to do with what you told me earlier? About the little girl and the British man?'

Taha looked at her surprised.

'He was there,' he said. 'The man. The British man in the picture card I gave you. He was on the boat too. With

Mr Daletsky. I saw them drinking champagne, and another man was there too. I think he also English. They were laughing together. I was working in the kitchen and I saw from the doorway the man I was with. But he didn't see me.' He leaned towards Rosie and spoke softly. 'I saw a picture in the English newspaper of the man on the card I give you. He is a big politician.'

Rosie hoped her eyes hadn't popped. Carter-Smith and a Russian millionaire! It was a headline in itself. Most of the Russian tycoons were gangsters who had plundered and murdered their way through the country after the fall of the Soviet Union, then legitimised themselves in business in the new Russia. But scratch a Russian oligarch and you found the same corruption and ruthlessness the world over.

Daletsky. Whoever he was, he was worth looking at. The very fact that Carter-Smith was rubbing shoulders with a guy like him on a yacht on the Costa del Sol was a story in itself. She would run a check on Daletsky on the web when she got back, and then talk to McGuire.

'Can you tell me any more about Viktor Daletsky?' she said.

Taha shrugged. 'Don't know. Just that he has a big company that exports things. But all the people who work for him are bad people. Leka. He is the worst. Drugs. And also they sell people. Girls from Russia and other places. Lithuania and Ukraine. They kidnap them and sell them. That's all I know. And this man, this British man in the picture I give to you, was with them on the boat.'

Rosie looked at him but said nothing. He was brighter

than she'd thought: smart enough to know that a politician on a boat with a bunch of Russian and Albanian gangsters was worth something. She waited for him to ask.

He ate the sandwich and they sat in silence. Then he spoke.

'I want to go away from here, Rosie. Can you help me? I need to go.'

'Why do you want to go away?' Rosie said.

'I think now it is dangerous. I think I should not give you the card with the picture of the man. Now I am frightened because he knows Leka and Daletsky. I didn't know he knew them so much.' He swallowed and looked at his feet.

'But they don't know you had the pass. The man could have dropped it anywhere. He might not even talk to anyone about it. If anybody asks you, just say you have no idea. He won't know where he lost it.'

'I cannot do that,' Taha said. 'I know how they are. They won't just ask me. They will just start to beat me and beat me until I tell them the truth. I have to go away before they ask me, because they won't believe me, and if they keep beating me I will tell them. Then they will kill me.' He looked away. His eyes filled with tears.

Jesus. He was just a kid, and Rosie could sense his fear was genuine. It was a different world these days, with the Russian and Albanian gangsters moving in on all the rackets from drugs to people-smuggling. A boy like this was nothing to them, just someone who could be supplied to a client until they had no further use for him. By the time he was all used up, he'd probably be a hopeless junkie and they would toss him into the gutter. But that would be the least of his worries. For talking to her, and for giving her the security pass of someone who must be one of their top clients, he was already a dead man walking.

'Do you think you can give me some money, Rosie? I want to go somewhere tonight. Just get in a train and keep going. Maybe Barcelona. Maybe France.'

Rosie looked at him.

'Why do you have to go immediately? I know you're scared, but why now? And you have no passport, Taha. You are illegal.'

Taha rubbed his face. His hands were trembling. He took a deep breath.

'Because . . .' His voice was almost a whisper. He looked over his shoulder. 'Because when Leka came onto the boat last night, I had to take drinks through to him and Mr Daletsky in the office. I heard them saying that the girl was in Tangiers. I think they mean the missing girl. They said Besmir had taken her there. I know him. He's Albanian and he works for Leka. I think it was Besmir who stole the girl. I think they kidnap her to sell her.'

Rosie looked into his eyes.

'But if you know this man Besmir, you would have known it was him who took the girl, would you not? You would have recognised him.'

Taha shook his head. 'When the girl was taken, I just saw the man from the back for few seconds. It was nothing to me then. I didn't see the man's face. And I have only met Besmir once. But now, last night on the boat when they said Besmir's name and the girl in Tangiers, I am thinking that it was him I saw. He was big man like Besmir. But I didn't see his face so I am not sure.'

'But it could have been anybody they were talking about on the boat, Taha.'

He nodded. 'I know. But I think I am right. I think I hear too much. And now, because I talk to you and give you the card, I am worry. I need to go away. When I am far away from here I can hide. I won't go through any borders. I know how to hide from police. Can you help me? Please Rosie. I have no friends here. Only the boys like me who work for them. You are the only one I can ask for help.'

CHAPTER 10

It was getting dark by the time Rosie typed the final paragraph of her story. To clear her head, she threw open her bedroom doors and went out into the evening air. The chatter and clinking of glasses on the terrace bar below drifted up as hotel guests gathered for an aperitif before dinner.

She went back in and read the story one more time before sending it to McGuire's private email, then she sat back and waited for his call.

The last two days had been non-stop work with she and Matt digging around to find out where Carter-Smith was staying. Rosie had also spent hours trawling through internet cuttings on the Russian billionaire Daletsky.

He was a piece of work. There were articles on him in one of the broadsheet newspapers in the last couple of years, and a couple in the tabloids. But none was specific enough to pin anything on him. That was the trouble with these Russians once they had amassed this level of wealth. Their fortunes gave them a tag of respectability, and Daletsky wasn't the only Russian with a dodgy background who now had legitimate dealings with established companies across the world. But Rosie's Special Branch pal in Glasgow had talked to his mates in London and given her the lowdown on just who he was.

There was enough dubiousness about Viktor Daletsky to cause a stir if it was revealed that he was entertaining the Home Secretary and one of his ex-public schoolboy pals, the millionaire businessmen Oliver Woolard of Woolard Institutions. That kind of stuff never looked good on paper.

McGuire's political connections had established that Carter-Smith had been staying at Woolard's villa on his annual jaunt, so now the pieces were beginning to fit together. There was no proof that Carter-Smith and Woolard had been on the yacht, other than the word of a rent boy, but he decided to wing it and see if Carter-Smith burst. He'd never thought there was any substance to Carter-Smith, and believed that if put under serious pressure, his bottle would crash. McGuire loved a bit of bluff. His attitude was that Carter-Smith would already be bricking it because he knew he'd lost his House of Commons pass. The longer the pass was missing, the more it became like a ticking time bomb, waiting to end up in the wrong hands.

So Rosie and Matt had found themselves staking out Woolard's villa since early morning, without any real plan. It brought a whole new meaning to the phrase flying by the seat of your pants.

'Here he comes,' Matt said. 'Come on you big smug fucker.'

Matt was already firing off several pictures, as they came out of the villa towards the chauffeur-driven Daimler.

'Who's that with him, Rosie? That Woolard? He's got that public schoolboy face. Why is it these guys, no matter how old they are, always have that youthful, fucking pampered tosser expression on their faces?'

'Something to do with self-belief,' Rosie said, shrinking down into her seat out of view. 'They don't teach self-belief in the kind of schools we went to, Matt. The first thing public school kids learn is that they are being prepared and groomed to go out and run the world. It's their destiny. They expect.'

'Well, fuck them.' Matt, put the camera down on Rosie's lap, and started the engine as Carter-Smith and Woolard got into the back of the Daimler. 'They'll not be expecting this.'

They waited until the car had gone down to the bottom of the steep hill and turned onto the street before they went after it.

'Let's see where they go. Nothing to lose.'

The Daimler whispered its way out of the *pueblo* and onto the main drag towards Marbella. They kept a discreet distance as the car continued beyond Marbella and turned into the harbour at the town of Estepona.

'Maybe they're going to Daletsky's yacht. Now, that *would* be the equivalent of a decent pools win.'

'Well, it looks like they're going to *someone*'s yacht.'

Matt pulled the car over when they got into the harbour. The Daimler headed for the biggest yacht in the harbour, moored at the far end.

'Don't get any closer. Just do what you can from here, then we go away and discreetly find out who owns that big bastard.'

Matt did as Rosie said, firing off a few shots of Carter-Smith and Woolard getting out of their car and walking up the gangplank behind what looked like a bodyguard.

'I like the look of this, Matt.' She slapped his thigh. 'I like the look of this very much. Come on, I'll buy you lunch.'

In a little tapas restaurant from where they could keep their eye on yacht, they ordered lunch and sat in the shade watching how the other half lived.

'I was made for this kind of life, Rosie,' Matt said, wolfing down tapas as though he was in the office canteen.

'Yeah, I can see that, Matt. The Spaniards spend generations honing the subtle flavours of their delightful tapas and you're horsing it into your mouth as though it was a fried egg roll with brown sauce.' She stabbed at a little dish of potatoes before they disappeared.

'Hmmm,' Matt mumbled with his mouth full. 'But you know what I mean, Rosie. This life. This pavement café lifestyle. Yachts in the background, sunshine and long lunches. I could settle into this quite well. And you know what? I'd always make sure I was kind to the hired help. That's important if you've got class.' He drank his coke and stifled a belch.

Rosie smiled at Matt's attempt to converse with the waiter.

'Si, senor. We are touristas. Beautiful. Bueno. Beautiful harbour. Magnifique boats.'

The waiter nodded at him and looked at Rosie.

'It is a beautiful place. Fantastic yachts,' Rosie said. She pointed her finger. 'The one at the end. The big one. Is it English people who own it? Arabs? Spanish?'

'No, no.' The waiter shook his head. 'The big boat is Russian. Is owned by Russian. Mr Daletsky. He come here some time to this restaurant for lunch. Very nice man. Very rich.' He rubbed his fingers together. 'Very nice man.'

'You fucking beauty,' Matt whispered, picking up a prawn. 'You fucking beauty.'

'Who says I'm not a lucky reporter,' Rosie clinked her coffee cup with Matt's glass.

Over the long lunch they'd talked tactics and decided not to approach Carter-Smith here. If Daletsky was anything like his heavy reputation, he'd dispose of a couple of tabloid hacks – and not in a good way.

Just before five came the first sign of movement. Matt was positioned so he could get into the back seat of the car with the yacht in his sights. Carter-Smith was first to appear on the deck, and at his side a tall foreign-looking figure, chatting and slapping Woolard on the back.

'Jesus, it's him! Fuck me, Matt!' Rosie recognised him as Daletsky from the pictures she'd seen on the web.

'No problem, darlin'. Just let me hose these bastards down first.' He kept snapping all the way until they walked to the edge of the gangplank. Carter-Smith turned and shook hands with Daletsky, then Woolard did the same. The big Russian was smiling broadly and puffing on a cigar.

'Just sit tight,' Rosie said, as the pair got into the back of the Daimler.

It couldn't have been any easier if Carter-Smith had organised a photo-shoot. What was it with the arrogance of these people? They thought they were untouchable. Rosie and Matt waited until the Daimler was well out of the harbour before they set off, following discreetly until the car pulled up at Woolard's hilltop villa. Matt took more pictures as they got out of the car.

'Let's get the hell out of here,' Rosie said when the two men disappeared into the house.

They headed back to the hotel. McGuire would be ecstatic.

Rosie had just stripped off and was about to go into the shower when her mobile rang. It was McGuire.

'By this time tomorrow, Rosie, if you listen closely you'll be able to hear the sound of arses clanging shut in Number Ten.'

'You like it?' Rosie laughed.

All they had to do was put a late afternoon call in to the Home Secretary's office, and by the time the *Post* was coming off the presses, the whole Cabinet would be in a flap. They didn't even have to suggest anything inappropriate. Having the Home Secretary and his pal photographed on a yacht with this dodgy Russian was enough.

'This is brilliant, Rosie,' McGuire said. 'It weakens Carter-Smith so much, and he'll be wondering just how much we know. We've got him by the balls, so to speak.'

He told her the copy was already with the lawyers, and he had no doubt the story would be cleared in time for tomorrow.

'So, I tell you what we want to do now, Rosie,' he said. 'Let's get a hold of that little Toha, or whatever his name is, and go over this with him again. See if he knows any more. I'm going to talk to the lawyers tomorrow about the possibility of running the story of the rent boy and the Home Secretary.'

'You serious?' Rosie knew this was the word of a rent boy who could prove nothing. He did have the security pass, but it could have been found anywhere.

'Yeah,' McGuire said. 'What I'm thinking is, once we've stitched Carter-Smith up with the Russian story, then we let it be known to him that we have more. We drop it on his lap that we know he was with a rent boy nearby when this kid went missing. If he tells us to fuck off, then we'll tell him we have his security pass, left behind when he was podgering the boy. Carter-Smith might look arrogant, but he won't be able to handle that. He'll be coming out with some kind of damage limitation.'

'Mick, there's something else you need to know. A development. The boy Taha told me last night. If it's true then it's dynamite.'

'I'm on the edge of my desk, Gilmour. Come on.'

'Taha,' Rosie said. 'The boy told me last night that when he was on the boat – remember that first night Carter-Smith was on it with Woolard? Well, Taha was in the office of this Daletsky character and he overheard him and one of the other bosses talking to him about a girl and that she was in Tangiers.'

'What do you mean, Gilmour? You mean Amy? The kid?'

'Well, that's what Taha thinks, but he doesn't know. He just told me this last night. He said they mentioned some guy called Besmir – some Albanian – and taking the girl to Tangiers. Taha knows this Besmir, and now he's thinking that's who took her, so they could sell her for money. How explosive is that?'

'Holy fuck, Gilmour! So, if this boy's right, then Carter-Smith was not only a few hundred yards away from the spot where this kid vanished, he was later with the people behind the kidnapping? Are you serious?'

'Yep. I'm serious. But Taha doesn't know for sure. He didn't get a look at the man's face, and he wasn't paying much attention at the time because he didn't know until later that a kid had been stolen.'

McGuire made a soft whistling sound. 'We've got to get this story, Rosie.' He paused. 'But tell me this, why would Daletsky or any of this mob want to steal a little girl? And why this little girl?'

'I don't know the answer to that, Mick.'

'Okay. Well, we have to just work on the information we have, and maybe we'll find out soon enough. But there has to be a reason.'

Rosie agreed. She looked at her watch. Taha would be calling her soon. 'Okay. I'll speak to the boy tonight, then I need to throw him some money. He wants to go away.'

'Not yet, Rosie,' McGuire said. 'He can't go away yet.

Just get him into hiding somewhere. Make sure you know where you can get him for the next couple of days.'

'Okay,' Rosie said.

McGuire hung up.

CHAPTER 11

Rosie had been waiting for over an hour. Taha hadn't turned up for their arranged meeting last night at the *chiringuito* in Fuengirola, nor had he phoned her mobile. She was worried, but when she got back to the hotel later there was a message in the reception saying simply, 'Sorry. See you in Cafe del Rey, seven tomorrow night.' She ordered more tea as her mobile rang. It was McGuire.

'Paper is just about ready for bed, Rosie. All going swimmingly.' McGuire was buoyant.

'Brilliant.' Rosie's mood lifted. 'Have you put the call in to his office?'

'Just been done. Vincent did it from Westminster. We thought that would be better.'

'Yeah. How did it go?'

'Well, Vincent says there was a stony silence. The kind that deafens you. Then he was told snootily that Mr Carter-Smith was on a private holiday and what he did was his business. They tried to strong-arm it a bit, but Vincent is too smart for that crap. He said all they were after was a reaction. The story and pictures were going in the news-paper, and it was perhaps a good idea to say something. So. We're still waiting. But I'd say Carter-Smith's just about lost his appetite if he was going out for dinner tonight.'

Rosie laughed. It was a good start, but she was pre-occupied with Taha. She looked at her watch.

'Great. Can't wait to see what they say.' She paused. 'Mick. I'm still waiting for Taha, the boy. He didn't turn up last night and left a message to say he would meet me tonight, but he hasn't shown up. I'm getting a bit worried.'

'Rent boys don't keep office hours, Rosie. He's probably out getting shagged by some rich ponce.'

'Maybe. I'm just worried he's been got at.'

'Nah. Nobody knows anything yet. Look, I need to go, Rosie . . . Give you a buzz later once we get word from London.' McGuire hung up.

Across the crowded cafe, Rosie saw the skinny figure coming through the door and furtively looking around. He had a black baseball cap pulled down over his eyes, but Rosie knew it was Taha. He spotted her, came across quickly and sat down. Rosie felt sick when she saw his face. His left eye was puffed up like a balloon with fresh bruising, black and red. The eye was almost closed, and when he tried to look at her, she could see it was raw and bloodshot. Taha touched his face with trembling fingers. Then he started to cry. He looked like a little boy.

'Shit, Taha.' Rosie automatically reached out and touched his arm. 'What happened?'

The weeping made his injured eye look even more painful. His lip quivered.

'They beat me. I knew they would. I told you, Rosie. Look.' He quickly lifted his tee shirt, and Rosie flinched as she saw his skinny ribs swollen and streaked with angry red welts. 'Is pain to breathe. They hit me with the bat.'

'I'm sorry, Taha. Who did this to you? Tell me what happened.' She looked at him and her mind flipped again to Mags Gillick in the Glasgow cafe, describing how the cop had beaten her. Suddenly she felt hot and sick. Panic rose from her stomach and surged through her and she felt her face burn and her head swim. Taha looked at her a little confused. She managed a deep breath.

'Sorry, Taha.' She tried to compose herself. 'It's just . . . I'm shocked. Upset for you.'

She couldn't tell him that for months after they'd tried to kill her back in Glasgow, every now and again something triggered the flashbacks, and the panic would come flooding through her without warning. She hadn't told anyone about it except her GP. Anxiety attacks, post traumatic stress, he'd told her. It would just take time. Fortunately it had only happened once at work and she was able to pass it off. But she'd never been put to the test like this, because the safety of the job as assistant editor never pushed her that hard. In the office, she never had to speak to people like Mags or Taha, or the other battered, damaged individuals she'd spent a lifetime with back in Glasgow.

Rosie lifted the cup to her lips only when she was sure her hands had stopped trembling. She wanted to walk away there and then. To phone McGuire and say, sorry, she was out. But where would that leave her? She could never live with herself. She would get through this. What if there was even a slim chance she could find Amy? She cleared her throat and took a deep breath.

The waiter came, but Taha said he wasn't hungry and wanted nothing. Rosie ordered a coke and a sandwich anyway. She moved her chair so she was closer to the boy.

'I'm sorry,' she said, squeezing his arm. 'Taha, I'm going to organise for you to go away somewhere safe. I promise. I'll get some money from the bank and take you to the train. You can go wherever you want.'

Rosie looked over her shoulder. She didn't feel safe. She took out her mobile and phoned Matt to come with the car and meet them at the cafe. Right now, she had to keep going and do the job. This was not her fault, she told herself. She didn't seek this boy out, he had tracked her down. Same as Mags had done. Now she had a job to do. She knew she had to get a picture of Taha like this. She was about to phone McGuire to clear giving Taha some money, but changed her mind. Just do it. Worry about McGuire later. She went into her bag and took out a tape recorder and sat it on the table.

'Taha,' she said, 'I want to ask you to go over everything you said the other day about when you and the man you were with saw the little girl on the beach. I want to have that on tape as it's important for me, if I am going to do the story. For the newspaper. Do you understand?'

He looked at her and then the tape. There was no way

this kid would understand the full implications of being taped. Rosie told him it was for the lawyers, that they would probably never use it. Same as she had told Mags that day. She told herself to get on with it. Either she did it properly, or she walked away now. He nodded. Rosie felt sick. But she still switched the tape on.

'Go from the beginning, Taha. Just tell me everything.'

He told his story. He'd come to Spain from Morocco where he lived in the country with his parents, four other brothers and two sisters. He got a job in a hotel kitchen at first, but another boy told him he went with men for money and urged him to do it too. He introduced Taha to the Russian guy who would be his pimp. He could make a lot more money by doing this than working ten or twelve hours every day in a kitchen. He didn't care what the work was. He just wanted the money. He said he wanted to know what it was like not to be poor. He described the British man and the sex they had. Then he described seeing the girl and the man who took her, and afterwards the woman screaming on the beach. He had found the pass on the floor and wanted to give it back, but by that time the client was gone and he had no way of getting in touch with him. If he'd told his boss, then he would have accused him of stealing the pass and would have beaten him. That's why he'd got the beating now. The client must have gone back to the contact and told him he had lost something and maybe it was when he was with him. They didn't even stop to ask first. They just beat you, Taha said. They beat you and maybe you will tell. They know no other way. Now he had nowhere to go except to run. He told about the night on the boat and how Daletsky and Leka had mentioned Besmir and the girl he had taken to Tangiers. He said he thought the man he saw taking the kid was Besmir. He had met him only once and remembered his name, though on the beach that day he only saw the back of the man who took the girl.

When he finished talking, Rosie took his hand and held it. It was soft and damp.

'Thank you, Taha.'

'Will you help me, Rosie?'

'Yes, Taha. I will help you. I promise.'

She told him to eat the sandwich as she got up and crossed the room to speak to Matt who had just arrived. She explained that they had to go somewhere to take photos of Taha and his injuries. Then she was going to put him on a train.

McGuire would go crazy that she let him go, but she didn't care. She remembered Mags, the last phone call she'd made to her before she was murdered. She wouldn't take a chance with this boy. She hoped he trusted her enough that he would keep in touch. But if he didn't, she'd live with it.

Taha sat silent in the back seat of the car when Rosie got out at the bank cashline. She took enough to get Taha out of the Costa del Sol and somewhere a good distance away. She'd suggested Barcelona. He was to call her and she would meet him there and give him more money. She would meet him no matter where it was, and give him more money. He agreed. Matt drove them to Malaga.

At the train station, Rosie told him to stay in the car and she went in and bought the ticket herself. One way to Barcelona. There was a train leaving in twenty minutes. She went back to the car and told Taha the plan, and he would be in Barcelona by early in the morning. He was to speak to nobody. Once in Barcelona, he should go and get himself some clothes and find a small hostal to stay for a few days. He'd be safe there, Rosie told him. And she even believed it. She gave him the ticket and a wedge of money, which he stuffed in his pocket. They both got out of the car and Rosie walked with him through the train station until they got to the platform. Taha looked around him nervously.

'You'll be okay, Taha.' Rosie smiled at him.

'I am afraid, Rosie.' He swallowed. 'Thank you for the money. I will phone you.'

He suddenly threw his arms around Rosie and she could feel his bones as he held her tight.

'Take care, Taha. Take care. Call me and I will come. I promise.' She eased herself away from him, and touched his face, soft as a child's. She turned away and kept her head down as she walked briskly out of the station.

Rosie didn't see the two men who had been watching them from the shadows. One of them followed her and got into a car. The other stood a little away from where Taha sat on the platform, staring at the ground.

CHAPTER 12

Rosie cursed the mobile for ringing again and again when she was in the shower.

The story of Michael Carter-Smith and the Russian mafia yacht had been plastered all over the *Post*'s front page, and she'd been expecting a few bristly calls from other hacks. She came out of the shower with her hair wrapped in a towel and picked up the phone. Two missed calls from reporters back in Glasgow and one from the *Post*'s man in Westminster. The latest, from Andy Simpson. She sat on the bed listening, and smiled at his snarling message. The press pack on the Amy story would be well pissed off at missing a massive story on their own doorstep. Rosie was tickled. For badness, she phoned Andy back.

'Hey, Andy. Howsit goin?'

'Fuck you, Gilmour.'

'If I didn't know you better, Andy, I'd think you were angry.' Nothing like rubbing it in.

'We wondered where you went to yesterday. The lads

were saying you were probably shafting us on the missing kid, and there you were, working it right up our arses with the Home Secretary – if you'll pardon the pun.'

Rosie allowed herself a giggle. 'Well, somebody's got to do it, Andy. Come on, you wouldn't have expected me to share any of that stuff, would you?'

'Course not. But it doesn't make me hate you any less, you bitch.'

'I love you too, pet.'

'Just tell me this, Rosie. Well, maybe you can't, but where in the name of fuck did that one come from? Was it London? Was it Westminster? That's what I told my desk. I told them it must have come from London. The guys have all told their newsdesks that, otherwise we look like prize pricks.'

Rosie hesitated. What the hell. Let them think it was London. The last thing she needed right now was for them to think there was any other story here involving the Home Secretary.

'Yeah, that's right, Andy. Westminster. Me and Matt were just told to get ourselves around to the yacht and see if he appeared. And to be honest, nobody was more surprised than us when he did.'

'Oh, well. Good luck to you, Rosie. Nice one.' He paused. 'Rosie, listen . . . Do you fancy a bit of dinner tonight? Catch up and all that?'

Rosie paused. She had a bit of history with Andy Simpson in the shape of a drunken snog a very long time ago. There had always been a certain chemistry between them on the rare occasions they'd found themselves working together. The guilty snog had happened after a long, hard four days on a story in the Highlands. The hacks were all letting their hair down on the last night, polishing off the hotel's wine cellar and gantry of liqueurs. She was glad she hadn't slept with him. If she had, it would probably have been round the press pack like wildfire. But, luckily for Rosie, there was always some invisible safety net that stopped her making a fool of herself when it came to men. Well, there used to be a safety net before TJ. She wouldn't make that same mistake again, and certainly not with a journalist, even an attractive old Lothario like Andy Simpson. But what the heck. It was only dinner.

'Yeah. That sounds good, Andy, as long as you don't try to stab me with your steak knife.' Rosie was looking forward to it already. 'Oh, and Matt's here. You know, the photographer? I'm working with him, and we always eat together. You okay with that?'

'Sure.' Andy said. 'My monkey is going out with a few of the other guys tonight. But yeah, I like Matt. It'll be a laugh to listen to the crap he talks.'

Rosie sensed he was covering his disappointment. She knew he was attracted to her and he knew she was off limits. But he wouldn't be Andy if he didn't at least try.

She got up off the bed and rubbed her hair furiously with the towel. The mobile rang again. It was Vincent, the *Post*'s man in Westminster.

'Well, well, Miss Gilmour. So you're trying to bring down the Home Secretary. What next? The government?'

Rosie sat down on the bed. She could picture Vincent's

florid face, pipe in his hand, feigning indignation but loving every minute of her story. He was one of the old school of solid journalists – respected and feared in equal measure. During working visits to the House of Commons, Rosie had enjoyed many a session with him in the bars and restaurants, and she marvelled at how he was on first-name terms with everyone from doormen to Cabinet ministers.

'The government's next week, Vincent. I'm getting some sun on my back first. Howsit going?'

'Great, Rosie. You should have seen their faces here when I hit them with Carter-Smith and the Russian mafia. They were scurrying around like rats up a tight drain-pipe.'

'Great. I love it when that happens. Thanks for getting the reaction for us. Lesser men than you would have been fobbed off by some spin doctor. So thanks, pal.'

'No sweat, darlin'. Any time. Plus I'm sure there will be more to come. That Woolard fucker, he's got business dealings stretching right into Eastern Europe according to my sources. I talked to McGuire on it and we're going to have a serious look at him. If we've got the Home Secretary introducing his rich British pal to this Daletsky character, then we'll make a meal of that.'

'Yeah,' Rosie said. 'But we don't really know what went on in the yacht, Vincent. All we know is they went on, and they came off with Daletsky like a couple of old mates. Long way to go. But I'll leave that down to you. I'm chasing the missing kid here, as you know.'

'Aye. Nightmare. What the fuck happened there, Rosie?

How does a wee thing just get stolen from her house or the beach or wherever it was? It's not right.'

'I know, it's awful,' Rosie said. Vincent obviously didn't know about Carter-Smith and the rent boy, so she would keep it that way. 'It's a terrible story, and it doesn't look good for the kid, the longer she's missing.' Rosie changed the subject. 'Where's Carter-Smith now?'

'I'm told he's on his way home this afternoon. The pack will all be at the airport, so we'll see what he has to say.'

'Great. I'll watch the news to see his face.'

She thought of his House of Commons ID card tucked into the lining of her suitcase.

'You know him. He'll brass his case big time. Just wait till you see him. Keep it up, and give us a shout if you need any help. Have to go, pet. See you.'

'Okay. Bye Vincent.'

Later, in the roof-terrace restaurant of Andy's hotel, Rosie listened, intrigued, though a little crestfallen, as Andy told them what exclusive line he had for his paper in the morning. Deadlines were well past, so he was relaxed enough to reveal his story. She looked at her watch as Matt filled up her glass. They exchanged glances and he shrugged.

'There's shag-all we can do, Rosie. You win some you lose some.' Matt took a mouthful of his beer, then lifted the glass of wine to his lips. He was a never-mind-the-quality-feel-the-width man when it came to booze.

Rosie considered the impact his story would have. She wouldn't get a hard time from McGuire for not having the line, because he knew they were onto the massive world exclusive if they could manage to nail it down. But Andy's information would change things, that's for sure, and he was relishing being the reporter who set the agenda.

He'd always been the same, ever since Rosie'd known him. Something to do with being a Scottish hack in London. There was that chip on their shoulder, outsiders in a city full of English smartarses. It might have been insecurity that made the Scottish hacks feel they had to be better than the rest of the Fleet Street big hitters, but the truth is, most of them were. Rosie had never felt the need to move down to the Big Smoke to prove herself. She was top hand anywhere in the world in the best and biggest of company, and her name had the same respect as any of the big shots – including Andy. So when he was able to get one over on her and the rest of the pack, Andy was really going to enjoy the moment.

His line had been picked up from his Spanish translator, who had contacts in the Guarda Civil. Tomorrow, everyone would be chasing it.

A windsurfer, a Spaniard, had gone to the police with the story of what he saw the morning Amy disappeared. He'd parked his car on the quiet side street next to the beach and taken his surfing board and gear out of the boot. It was a beautiful sunny morning and the beach was deserted. As he was setting up his board with the sail and bits and pieces on the sand in front of him, he happened to look up and saw a guy walking down the beach. He was quite far away from him, but he could see the figure was definitely male. He'd told police the guy was around thirty something or maybe forty.

The windsurfer didn't pay much attention to him, but he could remember that the man was fair haired and was wearing bright yellow shorts. The windsurfer had been having a drink of juice before taking the board into the water. He saw the guy in the yellow shorts go onto the patio of the house and a woman appear at the door and pull it open to let him in. He didn't see the woman clearly and couldn't say what she looked like. That was all he saw. He didn't think anything of it at the time.

He took his board into the water and the wind took him out to sea. His back was to the shore. The surfer said he had been out for a few minutes, not too far out to sea, then back fast along the shallow waters where the surf broke.

He could see, as he was heading back to the area of the beach where he'd started, that a woman was running up and down, shouting. Then the guy in the yellow shorts came out of the house and put his arms around her. He was able to tell police that the woman had short, dark hair and was slim. And he was able to pinpoint the house she'd come out of. He said he still didn't pay much attention to what was going on, and assumed it was a couple having a row. After he dismantled his surfboard and collected his gear, he headed back to his car to drive to his girlfriend's house for lunch.

It was only later when he saw something on the Spanish television news about a missing kid, that he realised it was the same spot as he'd seen the couple. He didn't go to the police until the next day, and only then because his girlfriend had insisted it was important.

'You did well, Andy,' Rosie said. 'It's a right good line. And it could be significant. It could open up a whole new story.'

'Exactly,' Andy lowered his voice. 'So who was the fair-haired guy in the yellow shorts? Martin Lennon's got black hair. And we've already been told the story of that morning, that Martin was out for a jog, and O'Hara only arrived at the house as Jenny was running up and down the beach frantically looking for Amy. So, someone's telling porkies.'

'Looks like it,' Rosie said. 'Is the windsurfer straight? Did you pay him a lot of dosh?'

Andy nodded. 'We paid him. But what he told us is basically what he told the Guarda Civil. He's Spanish. He knows it wouldn't be wise to concoct a story like that in the middle of a missing kid investigation. And we also have his mate saying he left the house on that morning to go windsurfing.'

Rosie drank some water. It was going to be a busy day tomorrow, chasing this windsurfer. But by now the cops will have kicked his arse big time for talking to the press.

Taha's story was right, if the windsurfer's story was true. Someone had been in the house with Jenny Lennon. If the windsurfer wasn't lying, then O'Hara was lying – that's if he was the guy in the yellow shorts. And it meant that Jenny Lennon was also lying. Maybe that's why O'Hara was so grey-faced, and why Jenny was so broken.

Andy smiled. 'Hmmm. You're thinking the same as the rest of us, Rosie? O'Hara's been shagging Jenny Lennon while hubby's out for a jog. And the kid gets stolen from under their noses. There's no way in the world they're going to let that get out. It's dynamite.'

'Have the cops told the Lennons about the windsurfer?' Rosie asked.

Andy looked at his watch. 'About three hours ago, after I phoned them for a reaction to the information, they went to the Lennon house. Then they went to O'Hara's house. I'd love to have been a fly on the wall at those interviews.' He sipped his wine.

Rosie imagined the scene at the Lennon's house when they were confronted by the cops.

'Jesus, Andy. Can you imagine the guilt bouncing off the walls in those houses right now?'

'Oh, yes,' Andy said. He was relishing the turn of events, whereas Rosie was trying to imagine the horror. She never did have that killer punch. Her mobile rang. It was McGuire.

'Rosie. Have you seen the *Mail*?'

'No, but I know the story. The reporter's just told me. Puts an entirely different light on things.'

'That's a fucking understatement, Rosie. All bets are off with these people now. No more Mr Fucking Nice Guy. From what I'm reading between the lines, these people have got something to hide. Maybe O'Hara's been getting his leg over Amy's mum. If that's the story, our readers will crucify them. And so they fucking should.'

'I know,' Rosie said, but she couldn't help the little

pang of sorrow for them. Jenny Lennon's world had fallen apart when her daughter disappeared, and the only thing that could be worse than that would be having to live with the fact that it was her fault. And now, she may be about to be exposed.

'She'll get torn apart. They both will.'

'You bet,' McGuire said. 'And we'll be leading the charge. Listen, Rosie. I'm not at all bothered that we didn't get that story. Though a part of me wishes we could have broken the Taha story about what he saw. But it's not solid enough, coming from a rent boy. Anyway, we're hunting bigger fish. But we need to be on this too. Do you need a runner down there? I can send Joe Dawson to give you a hand, you know, the day-to-day press briefings and stuff? You can concentrate on the bigger picture. Carter-Smith, and that wee rent boy Toha, or whatever he's called. Have a think, and talk to me in the morning.' He hung up.

Rosie's paranoia kicked in. Was McGuire losing faith because she had missed the windsurfer story? Did he think that maybe she wasn't focused enough? Self doubt forever hovered over her shoulder.

CHAPTER 13

Besmir watched as the ferry that should have been taking him back to Algeciras disappeared into the setting sun. He drew on the last of his cigarette and flicked it into the harbour.

He bit the inside of his jaw. What the hell was he playing at? But even though he cursed himself, he felt a surge of adrenaline at the snap decision he'd made. Six months ago, no, six days ago, he would never have done anything like this. But something had changed in him, as though he'd lost the iron self control that had been the very centre of his life. He felt beads of nervous sweat under his arms at what he was about to do. He dialled the number.

'I am here,' he said. 'I didn't take the boat. Come. Meet me at the little bar on the harbour.' He lit another ciga-rette and ordered a coffee and a cognac.

Besmir dialled another number and spoke to Elira. He told her he would not be taking the boat to Spain tonight as planned, and that he'd met a young lady. He was going to relax for the night. He smiled to himself when Elira made a dirty remark. He was a good liar. She said that Leka had been phoned from Morocco and that he was pleased Besmir had made the delivery. She'd let him know he would return tomorrow. He put the fake passport in his pocket, and watched the ferry vanish on the horizon.

The driver had seen something in Besmir that he himself hadn't known he was capable of. He had done other jobs that involved transporting kidnapped women, even girls as young as fourteen or fifteen. It was a job, nothing more. He had never kidnapped anyone before, but he delivered them to wherever Leka told him, he got paid, then he moved on. Besmir didn't analyse what made him the man he was. To do that would be to revisit the orphanage that turned out dehumanised individuals like him as soon as they were able to fend for themselves. Sentimentality was for other people. There just *was* no sentiment for Besmir. He didn't know what it felt like. Until now. Until this little kid kept snuggling into him. Until he'd opened the boot of his car in Algeciras and her pale, confused face stared hopefully up at him. The memory kept returning of her bright blue tearful eyes as the woman carried her out of the room. Something had changed.

Besmir hadn't noticed the driver watching him during the journey to the port. It was only when they'd left the house after delivering the girl that the driver spoke to him.

'Why you do this?'

They were in the car. The driver kept his eyes on the road as he spoke. Besmir looked at him, then straight ahead. But the words hung in the air.

'Just drive.' He rolled down the window.

They stopped in a line of traffic and the driver took a packet of cigarettes from the dashboard and handed it to Besmir. He took two out, lit them and handed him one. They drove on in silence, Besmir staring out of the windscreen. Eventually, the driver spoke.

'They will get lot of money for the blue girl. For sex. They will sell her for sex. A lot of money.'

Besmir watched the smoke circle up from the cigarette between his fingers. He swallowed but his mouth was dry. Leka and Elira had told him the girl was for a rich childless Arab couple who wanted a British girl so they could have British blood in their family line. When you were that rich you could buy whatever genetic make-up you wanted for your future generations, Leka had told him when he gave him the kidnapping job.

'What do you mean, for sex?' He turned his head to look at the driver.

'That is the way.' He shrugged his shoulders. 'Everyone is for sex. It's what they do. Girls. Boys. Women. Doesn't matter. You did not know that?' His expression was quizzical, mocking.

'She is a baby,' Besmir said, surprised at the indignation in his voice.

'Doesn't matter. Some men will fuck a baby. Plenty men will fuck a baby.' He shook his head and puffed through his lips. 'Plenty.'

'Fuck,' Besmir whispered under his breath as the girl's face flashed into his mind. How stupid could he have been not to know, not even to suspect. All he'd cared about was the money.

'Tell me what you know.'

'How do I know you won't kill me?' The driver glanced nervously out of the corner of his eye.

'If you thought I would kill you, you would have kept your mouth shut. Tell me.'

The car stopped again in the queue of traffic. The air was stifling inside and outside of the car. The driver turned to Besmir.

'I saw you with the blue girl. You don't look right. You tough guy, for sure, but you care about the blue girl. I can see it. Why? Is no good to do your job like that if you care. You see her every day now in your head. You see her on the day you will die. Always she will be there. You are prisoner now.'

Anger at his own naivety rushed through him. And guilt. He grabbed the driver's arm and squeezed it, watching him wince.

'What are you? My conscience? Are you the priest? Fuck you.'

'Please,' the driver said, softly. 'I want to tell you.'

Besmir loosened his grip. He listened as the driver told his story.

The blue girl would be taken, perhaps already had been taken, to the place where they keep the young ones before they move them on. The children were mostly from Morocco and some further into Africa. Some from

Romania. Street children, abandoned, most of them. Orphans. Ones like that could disappear and nobody cared.

The kidnapped women were kept in a few houses across Tangiers and Marrakesh, and one or two outside the cities. Most of the women were eventually sold to work as prostitutes in the whorehouses in cities all across Europe. The best-looking ones were sometimes kept to be sold to the Arabs. The Arabs liked the girls from Eastern Europe and Bosnia, but especially the very light ones from Ukraine. Young teenage girls were valuable because of the men who liked children.

But the very young children were special. They were for the sex rings, and for filming. They could end up anywhere. Europe, Bangkok, anywhere. Men who liked children would pay big money for a baby. The blue girl, he said, would be moved to the broken-down farm further away while they waited until things quietened down before they moved her on. They would already have a buyer for her because she is so beautiful. There were other children there, some as young as her, some a little older. They kept them in cages. Like animals.

'Cages?' Besmir felt hot.

'Yes. Cages. Is dark most of the time. They never get outside. At night you can hear them crying.' He shook his head. 'Is a bad sound to hear children crying in the night. Very bad. Like souls from the dead.'

'You have seen this? You have heard this?' Besmir watched his face for lies.

The driver nodded vigorously. 'I am afraid. I am sad. I never tell anybody before. I have little sisters. Young twins, and one older. I cry in case someone takes them. I am like in prison because I have seen this. I drive the car for Khalid, the fat man. That's all I do. But I saw too much and I am trapped. One time I saw the fat man take a girl of maybe only fourteen and he fuck her.' He shook his head. 'He would kill me if he knew I told you this.'

'Fuck the fat man,' Besmir spat.

They'd been getting close to the harbour and the sound of a ship's foghorn rose above the din of the traffic. He'd never cared before about what happened to the people he had dealt with for Leka. It didn't matter if a drug pusher who was slow to pay needed his legs broken, or a few women had to be driven hundreds of miles to be passed onto someone else. He'd made his mind up never to ask questions or care about what happened to any of them. He had dulled himself to anyone's stories many, many years ago. He'd got rid of corpses for Leka and he had killed people. He couldn't have recalled any of their faces if his life depended on it. But this was different. He knew this was the beginning of the end. But he couldn't stop himself.

They were at the harbour.

'You can show me this? You can show me these cages?'

'I can show you,' the driver said. 'But your boat is here.'

Besmir got out of the car, and walked around to the driver's side. He leaned in the window.

'Give me your phone number. If I don't get the boat I will call you. You come back for me and you take me there tonight.' It wasn't a request.

The driver looked worried. 'But tonight? I don't know.'

Besmir grabbed his wrist and looked him in the eye.

'If I call you, you will take me there tonight. You understand?'

The driver nodded. 'I understand.' His hands trembled as he scribbled down his telephone number on a grubby piece of paper and pushed it into Besmir's hand.

Now Besmir sat and waited, watching the tourists drinking in the crowded bar, armed with trinkets and happy memories to take home from Morocco. They lived in a different world. At the table next to him, a middle-aged British couple got up and walked away, leaving behind an English newspaper folded on the seat. The picture caught Besmir's eye, and he reached over and lifted the paper.

It was Daletsky's yacht, and a picture of Daletsky along with two other men, one of whom he recognised. He read the headline slowly:

Home Secretary's Russian Roulette

And underneath, in smaller letters:

Government rocked by revelations of Carter-Smith's Costa del Crime junket with Russian oligarch

The report described how the government minister was pictured going on board the yacht with his old school friend, the businessman Oliver Woolard, where they spent nearly three hours. And there was a picture of them emerging with Daletsky, who had his arm around the minister. A second story, with a picture of Daletsky looking younger, gave an account of his life story with the word 'gangster' in nearly every paragraph.

Besmir glanced around at the British tourists, and allowed himself a wry smile. He had never met Carter-Smith, but he knew he was one of the VIPs who used the rent boys. He favoured the skinny little Moroccan faggot Taha, who Besmir felt sorry for because he'd once witnessed a pimp beating the kid up for turning up late for his appointment with a VIP. Taha had only been in Spain for a few weeks at the time and didn't know his way around the various apartments his pimp used for what he called his special clients. Besmir had to give the boy some wet towels to clean up the blood from his face. He'd told him sharply to stop crying, and that if he didn't toughen up he might as well take the ferry back to his mother in Morocco.

He imagined the crap that would be flying around right at this minute with Daletsky and Leka. He was glad he'd decided not to go back. At least for now.

He saw the car pull in. He got up, stuffing the newspaper under his arm, and walked towards it.

'Come,' the driver said. 'We have a way to drive and is not easy to find in the dark.'

CHAPTER 14

'I know. I hear what you're saying, Mick.' Rosie paced the floor of her hotel bedroom, the mobile phone pressed to her ear. 'But we can't *make* them admit it. Going in there like attack dogs and suggesting anything untoward at a time like this won't get us anywhere.'

She walked out onto the terrace and listened to McGuire ranting on. No matter how she protested, she'd have to doorstep either Jenny Lennon or Jamie O'Hara. Someone was telling porkies, McGuire fumed, and he hated people trying to pull the wool over his eyes.

The day's front pages had been full of the follow-up to Andy's story about the windsurfer spotting a man with yellow shorts going into the Lennon house on the morning Amy disappeared. The press pack had descended on the windsurfer's home first thing to get their own version of what had left them bare-arsed because of Andy's exclusive.

The windsurfer had stuck steadfastly to his story and Rosie saw no reason to doubt him, even if he did admit to smoking cannabis the night before he'd gone to the beach. That admission alone had given O'Hara and Jenny Lennon a lifeline. They blatantly denied his story. They'd rubbished it in a statement they released after the Guarda Civil had interviewed them separately at the police station when the story broke.

Rosie had been with the rest of the press and the growing crowd when Jenny was driven to the police station by one of their friends. There was no sign of her husband. Regardless of whether she was lying or not, it was uncomfortable to watch her as she ran the gauntlet of rage from the righteous locals who had turned up to judge her. The Spanish news had been buzzing all day about the story that police were quizzing the mother and the friend about their statements, following the windsurfer's revelations. Even though there was no evidence that anything had been going on between O'Hara and Jenny, it was looking like they'd lied – and that was enough to damn them. The locals had already made up their minds, and they shouted abuse at Jenny as she walked the narrow, cobbled street into the police station. Rosie cringed when someone shouted, 'Whore!'

Even if the windsurfer had been lying, it suited the Spanish agenda. They were pissed off that their family holiday resort was now known worldwide as the place where a toddler could be snatched from the beach in broad daylight. It wasn't good for tourism. Any sympathy they had for Jenny Lennon was evaporating fast, replaced by anger and distrust.

Jenny's face was grey and there were dark shadows

under her puffy eyes. She looked as though the flesh had dropped off her in just a few days. The loud haranguing had continued when she emerged two hours later, and it was just as bad when O'Hara arrived, his face set hard against the abuse being hurled at him. 'Sonofabitch', someone shouted in Spanish as O'Hara strode down the cobbled street defiantly square shouldered, looking straight ahead. But he was ashen-faced.

When he emerged after a couple of hours, he ignored the questions that were shouted by the journalists, got into his car and drove off. Rosie wondered who would crack first – Jamie or Jenny. If either, or both, of them did, and changed their statement, the Spanish press would crucify them. And the British pack wouldn't be far behind.

'I just don't believe them,' McGuire was saying. 'And it'll be a lot worse for them now they've been given the chance to clarify their statements and are still refusing to do it. They're lying, Rosie. They're fucked.'

'But—' Rosie tried to get a word in.

'I know, Gilmour,' he interrupted, and she could see him pacing his office. 'There's a bigger picture here. A missing kid. Listen. My eye's still firmly on the ball there. But these bastards are lying. They know it, and they're ripping the pish out of us. It's not on.'

'But I can't make them admit it, for Christ's sake.'

'I want you to put it to them that they're lying. Go to O'Hara. He knows you and he knows us. He's a fucking lawyer and he knows about damage limitation. Tell him in no uncertain terms that if he loses our support, he's fucked. His time is running out.'

Rosie sighed. 'Okay. I think he'll already know that. They both will, but I'll try and give it to him right between the eyes. I can't do much more than that. I'll give it my best shot, but they've already rubbished the statement.'

'See what you can get, Gilmour.'

It wasn't until the last media car had gone from outside O'Hara's villa that Rosie and Matt decided to go back. There had been no answer at the door, either there or at the Lennon house when the press pack knocked. Whatever was happening to Jenny and her husband, they were keeping it under wraps. Rosie could only imagine what kind of mess Martin Lennon was in. He'd not only lost his only child, he had probably lost his wife. How could they ever come back from what had happened?

There was no sign of life at the O'Hara apartment, just a few scattered toys in the garden and a football. Rosie guessed they might all be holed up at the Reillys' house for the afternoon, probably trying to get some normality for the sake of the kids.

'Let's take a walk on the beach, Matt,' Rosie said, getting out of the car. 'Pass some time while we're arsing around here. There's a little beach bar along past the rocks. You can buy me a beer.'

'Okay,' Matt said. 'I'll not bring all my toys. Only one camera.' He shoved the smallest of his cameras into his safari waistcoat pocket.

It was Matt who saw him first.

'Fuck me, Rosie. There's O'Hara. Look. On the rocks.' He grabbed Rosie's arm.

Rosie strained her eyes. 'I see him. He's on his own.' She scanned the beach towards the bar which had a few lunchtime punters.

'Let's just take it slowly,' Rosie said, looking at O'Hara who was gazing out to sea.

She watched as he drank from a bottle of beer. There was no sign of the rest of the family. Rosie and Matt walked away from him and out of his eyeshot, so they could eventually come up from behind.

'Looks like he's deep in thought,' Matt said.

'Wouldn't you be? Right now, he must be sitting there looking at his life disintegrate before his eyes. And for what? An illicit shag. What is it with men?'

'I know. Brains and dicks. Maybe they're too far apart to function together.'

He was already taking pictures after putting on the slightly bigger lens.

'I'm getting good shots here, Rosie. Even if nothing else, the picture tells a story.'

'You're good, Matt, I'll give you that. That's why I like going on holiday with you.'

'I can't wait to see where we're going next.' Matt fired off several more shots.

'You wait here,' Rosie said. 'I'm going to slide up and try to tackle him myself.'

Rosie moved up behind O'Hara, and coughed before she reached him so as not to startle him too much. It didn't work. He jerked his head around as though someone had shoved a cattle prod into his back, and she heard his sharp intake of breath. She put her hands up apologetically when she saw the expression on his face. It was somewhere between rage and tears.

'I'm sorry, Jamie, I'm honestly not following you. I just happened to be out walking here. Please, can I have a minute? I know this is difficult, but please. I have something important to say to you.' She rattled out her pitch.

She expected him to get to his feet, ready for attack. But he didn't. He turned his head away from her and looked out to sea. Rosie counted four empty beer bottles strewn around the sand where he sat. He sniffed and shook his head. He wasn't drunk, not on four bottles of beer. But he wasn't sober either. Rosie knew that O'Hara drank a lot anyway. In another world, another life, the one that he used to live before he screwed it all up here on the Costa del Sol on a family holiday, O'Hara could be found holding court in O'Brien's of a Friday early evening along with all the other movers and shakers. A few beers in the afternoon wasn't going to waste him.

'Rosie,' he said, not looking at her. 'I know you've got a job to do, but Christ almighty. Can you not see there are people's lives falling apart here?' He shook his head.

She'd caught him at the right time. He was weak. He'd come out of that police station knowing that his world was being dismantled piece by piece, and even a smart-arse brief like him knew there was nothing he could do to stop it. It was written all over his face, the knowledge that he would never again have a night of normal sleep. His face had aged ten years in the last week. Rosie sensed she could win this.

'I can see all of that,' she said.

She toyed with the idea of sitting down beside him. No. Standing would give her the edge.

'I can see that lives are falling apart, Jamie. I see it in Jenny Lennon's face. I saw it in yours on that first day when you opened the door to me.' She took a breath. 'Don't think I get any enjoyment out of doing this job when it comes down to something like this. I don't. I can promise you that.'

He said nothing. He looked down and lifted a handful of sand, watching as it ran through his fingers.

Just do it, Rosie told herself.

'Jamie,' Rosie said. 'This windsurfer's story is true, isn't it?'

She felt a little explosion in her stomach. He would either get up and start ranting or he would say nothing.

She pressed on. 'It's true, isn't it?'

He said nothing.

'The thing is, if it *is* true, then you and Jenny both know that this isn't going to go away. And three months from now, even if it can never be categorically proved – if it's true now it will be true then. And Amy might still be missing. But by that time . . .'

She bent down a little towards him. 'Trust me on this Jamie. By that time, everyone will have turned against you, because if you lie to people about what happened that morning they will think you have something to hide.

There's no escaping from that. And if you are hiding something, then people will just get angry. The Lennons will have lost the public's support and sympathy, and the media will tear you to pieces both here and back home.'

Still he didn't speak.

Rosie kept going, while she was getting away with it.

'Listen. Seriously. I'll be honest with you, Jamie. It might already be lost, probably is. But if it's true, you have to find a way to limit this damage. I don't know why the two of you would lie, only you do. But I'm giving you a platform here. You and Jenny. Everyone. Find a way to limit the damage, then everyone can go back to making Amy the story.'

She stopped. She took a deep breath. She couldn't believe she was getting away with this.

'Because Amy is all that matters now,' she continued. 'Everything else is finished. You know that. Jenny knows that. It can't be undone.'

O'Hara stood up slowly, as though he had a ton of lead on his shoulders. He turned to Rosie and fixed her with his steel-blue eyes. He didn't speak. He didn't have to. Rosie knew she had him. She held his stare.

'The lies will just get worse. The hole will get bigger. Time to stop digging.'

Rosie felt the rush of adrenalin that made her hands tremble by her sides.

O'Hara sighed and swallowed hard. Rosie thought he was going to burst into tears.

'I need to speak to my wife.'

'It doesn't need to be done with a big press pack interview. I'll do it. Just me. And I'll cover it for everybody. Limit the damage, Jamie, before it's too late.'

O'Hara shot her a glance. 'I have to talk to my wife,' he said again. He walked away, his shoulders slumped.

CHAPTER 15

'Christ,' Matt said as he pulled the car into the middle lane. 'These bastard Spanish. Way they drive. This guy's been up my arse since we left the beach.' He glanced in his rear-view mirror.

Rosie automatically pulled down her visor, and saw a car swerve immediately behind them into the same lane.

'Shit. He's still there,' Matt said. 'Road rage nutters are even worse here.'

'You didn't do anything,' Rosie said, twisting around to clock the silver car almost touching their bumper.

She couldn't make out the driver, other than to notice he didn't look Spanish – more like a Brit.

'He looks too old to be a boy racer. Did you cut out in front of him or something?'

'No. Not that I can remember. He just came from nowhere as I was getting onto the motorway, and he's been there ever since. I thought he wanted me to let him past, but he's still on my tail. Nut job.' Matt hit his brakes and made a hand gesture that would be universally recognised as dickhead.

'Christ, Matt, don't get into any punch-ups. There's a lot of headcases on the Costa, and plenty of them are Brits. It might be some coked-up psycho with a bloody gun.'

'Fuck him.' Matt slowed down and went into the outside lane, then sped up and crossed two lanes until he was on the fast lane.

Rosie looked over her shoulder. 'Shit, Matt. He's following us. Just come off at the next turn-off. I don't like this.'

'But we're not near the hotel turn-off yet. This is into some kind of housing development.'

'Just do it, Matt. I'm not playing games on the motorway with a headcase.'

As Matt was about to hit the turn-off, the car sped up at his side.

'Fuck! He's trying to make us crash.' He tried to steady the car. It swerved, but he just managed to gain control and made it to the turn-off before he hit the barrier. He sped down the slip road and into another quiet road.

'Just go along for a bit, then follow a sign for Marbella and get back on the motorway. The bastard will be menacing someone else now.'

Rosie saw the colour drain from Matt's face.

'No he won't, Rosie. He's behind us. He's following us.'

Rosie's stomach lurched. They'd come off at an urbanization, where there are never any people, just rows and rows of concrete blocks of flats. Rosie looked around anxiously for a sign of a bar or restaurant. Why were there never any fucking people in these places? She glanced behind her. He was still there, almost touching the bumper.

'Just watch for the road back onto the motorway, Matt. It can't be too far away. Just stay calm.'

Then he bumped them. She jolted forward, her knees banging against the glove compartment.

'Fuck.' Matt stepped on the accelerator.

Then everything seemed to blur. Rosie looked out of her window and the car was at her side. The window was coming down in his car and the driver had something in his hand. Gunshot. Their car swerved and the tyres screeched. She screamed.

'Oh fuck, Rosie! The bastard's shooting at us. Oh Christ!' The car shuddered to a stop, mounting the pavement.

'He shot at the tyres.'

Rosie covered her face with her hands.

'Oh fuck, Matt.' She braced herself for the next shot.

'He's gone,' Matt said. 'Look.'

Rosie took her hands away and could see the car speed off with a screech of its tyres.

'He's gone. Fucker.' Matt got out of the car.

'What if he comes back?' Rosie took out her mobile phone and searched recent calls she'd made, looking for the Guarda Civil number. She was ringing the number as she got out of the car.

'I don't think he'll come back.' Matt crouched to look at the tyres. 'Shot your front one and the back on your side. Fuck me. What the fuck was that all about?'

To Rosie's utter surprise she burst into tears. Matt was even more dismayed. He was immediately at her side and took her in his arms. 'It's okay, Rosie.' He let her go and looked at her face.'What the fuck is this? Tears? Gilmour doesn't do tears.'

He smiled, holding her close and stroking her hair.

Christ. She would never live this down. Matt was one of the young team, and if he wanted to, he could dine out on a story about how he gave Rosie Gilmour a shoulder to weep on. She tried to compose herself.

'Sorry, Matt,' she sniffed.

She shook her head, and wiped her eyes with the back of her hand. She tried to speak. How could she tell him that she wasn't as tough as people thought. That ever since the shit back in Glasgow the night she nearly died, she had never been the same woman, never would be. Especially without TJ. She wanted to tell him that the last thought she'd had in her mind when she heard the gunshot was her mother. The same as it had been the last thought in her mind that night on the Clydeside when the shot rang out. She looked at Matt, her eyes filled with tears.

Matt put his finger to her lips.

'Sssh, Rosie. Don't say anything. I know, I know. It's all that shit from a few months ago. You're alright. You're okay.'

He took her face in his hands.

'Listen, Rosie. You never want to mention this again, we won't. It's forgotten about. End of. You want to talk, I'm all ears. I'm not just some daft young boy. I admire you, Rosie. I respect you. You're a legend. But shit happens and it fucks up your head. You're no different from anyone else.'

He took her hand that was still clutching the mobile.

'Look,' he grinned. 'Still ringing out. Where can you get a fucking copper when you need one. Same as home.'

Rosie managed a smile and put the mobile to her ear. Eventually someone answered and she managed to tell them in her fractured Spanish that they'd been attacked in their car by a man with a gun. She gave them the location, miraculously remembering what the slip road sign had said. From what she could grasp from the rapid fire reply, they had to stay where they were. They were on their way.

Matt handed her one of her cigarettes while they watched nervously in case the gunman returned.

'Matt,' Rosie said, drawing on the cigarette. 'That wasn't a road rage nut. I think it's something to do with Taha. They're all connected. All this gangster shit. Russians, Albanians. Missing kid. Christ. Maybe even something to do with that guy in the bar the other night – the Glasgow cokehead who thought he recognised me. Maybe it's something to do with Jake Cox. He's down here somewhere. What if he knows we're here?'

Matt shrugged. 'Don't get your knickers in a twist, Rosie. I can't disagree with you on all counts, but we can't get all paranoid every time someone makes faces at us.'

'He tried to shoot us, Matt. He wasn't making faces.'

'Stop worrying. It's bad for your heart.' He put on his brave Matt grin.

Rosie bit her lip. She hadn't heard from Taha since she'd put him on the train two days ago. He must have been in Barcelona by now and there was nothing to have stopped him getting to a phone and calling her, even if he hadn't gone there.

'My gut instinct is that they're warning us,' she said. 'Maybe they saw us with Taha somewhere. Maybe they were following him.'

'Look. The cavalry.' Matt pointed beyond her.

'Okay, listen,' Rosie said. 'Let's not say anything to them about what we've just talked about. Don't bring the cops anywhere near that. Just say it must have been an angry Spaniard who didn't like the Brit driving. That's what they'll be expecting to hear anyway. I don't want them anywhere near our story.'

Later, back at the hotel, once they'd dispensed with the lengthy bureaucracy of making out reports at the Guarda Civil office, Rosie luxuriated in a steaming hot bath, sipping a glass of red wine. The bathroom light was dimmed so low it was almost dark. She leaned her head back on the cushion and closed her eyes. There was a tightness in her throat, and it had taken all her strength not to blub again in front of Matt when they finally got back to the hotel.

Now she could let it go, and she sank into the water. She felt so alone. It was something she'd learned to live with during those early years with her mother, having to keep the secret from everyone of how drunk she'd be when Rosie got home from school every afternoon. The only person who had ever been able to see her clearly was TJ. It was TJ who'd tried to put the broken bits back together again, and he nearly succeeded. She shook her head and sniffed. Look where that had got her . . . Enough, she told herself. He was out of her life now, gone like he said he would be, and that was it. Finished. She was back to where she started, to where in reality, she was probably more comfortable. Alone.

She wiped her eyes and told herself to get a grip. Enough tears had been shed over TJ. If he'd changed his mind or really wanted her he would have got back in touch. He knew where she worked, where she lived. He could have written. Now it was time to move on. If she said it often enough, maybe she would start believing it.

She put the glass down. No more wine. She was hot and sleepy enough. The two-hour ordeal with the Guarda Civil, giving statements while the translator took them through the story slowly, had left her completely drained. When they'd got back to the hotel, Matt dealt with the car hire people and they both had a quick coffee in the bar. Matt downed two swift gin and tonics, but Rosie knew getting pissed would only make her feel worse. She thought about telling McGuire what had happened, but she and Matt made a pact not to. He would bring her home immediately, and she was damned if she was giving up. She had too much at stake here to walk away and go home. This is what she did. This is who she was. And right now, it was all she had.

She stepped out of the bath and wrapped herself in the fluffy white bath robe. As she splashed her face with cold water, she heard a knock at her bedroom door. Her stomach jolted. She came out of the bathroom and looked at the phone, half thinking of phoning reception or trying Matt on the mobile.

'Rosie. Howsit going?' It was Matt.

'Christ,' she whispered in relief. 'Matt. Hold on.' She pulled the robe tight and opened the door.

Matt grinned. 'Hi, Rosie.' He winked. 'This is my game face. You're looking beautiful.'

He'd clearly been too long in the bar, shaking off the motorway terror. Rosie shook her head.

'I've seen your game face, Matty boy. I'm sure it works every time, but not tonight sweetheart.'

'No?' Matt looked surprised but was still smiling. 'Porque?'

Rosie laughed. 'Okay, try these for starters. You're too young, you're too beautiful, and, you're too pissed. That should do it.'

They stood looking at each other for a minute. Matt seemed to sober up a little and looked into Rosie's eyes.

'You know what, Rosie? I love you. You're the best woman I've ever known. I just want to tell you that.' He stretched his arms out. 'Can I just get a hug, then?' He stepped closer to her.

They hugged and Rosie held him just as tight as he held her. 'Thanks, Matt.' She stopped herself from filling up. 'And thanks for today. I'm so glad it was you with me.'

He let her go. 'I'm here for you, Rosie. Anytime darlin'.' He turned to go, then he grinned back. 'And I'm not too young. No way.'

'Goodnight, Matt.' Rosie blew him a kiss and closed the door.

She looked at her bed. The reckless part of her wished she'd brought him in for the next few hours. A couple of years ago she might have. She shook her head and went back to the bathroom to brush her teeth. She hoped she'd be tired enough to sleep when her head hit the pillow. Then, suddenly, there was another knock at the door. Bloody hell. Enough Matt. She wouldn't open the door this time, just tell him to go to bed.

'Matt, listen. I'm tired, man. We both had a long hard day. Now go to bed. We've got work to do, and I'm knackered.'

'Rosie?' The deep, dark voice from the other side of the door shot through her. It had been seven months since she'd heard it, but she knew.

'Adrian?' Rosie said, utterly confused. 'Adrian?'

'Open the door please, Rosie. Yes. It is me. I must talk with you.'

Rosie opened the door. Adrian, stood there, his deathly pallor a little less pronounced than she remembered, but with the same dark shadows beneath his eyes. His lips moved to something resembling a smile, then his eyes looked down at Rosie and his face softened. Right there and then Rosie knew she was never, ever truly alone.

'My friend. Is good to see you.' Now he did smile.

Rosie opened the door wider and threw her arms around him.

CHAPTER 16

Rosie couldn't stop looking at Adrian as though he were a ghost that would vanish at any moment. She resisted the urge to reach out and touch him.

When he had first come into the room, everything that had happened in the past few months came rushing back. She'd sobbed in his arms and couldn't even get to the point of asking him how the hell he got to be here. She thought she'd buried a lot of the fears from that night when he'd saved her life, but she hadn't. Just the sight of him brought it all back. She could barely remember how Adrian had picked her up and bundled her into the car to rush her to hospital, but it was always Adrian's voice that she would hear when she woke up in the middle of the night in a cold sweat.

She'd come to know the strong, square tones of the Yugoslav in his fractured English long before that night when he'd held her, telling her she would be okay, that she was safe now. Jesus! Here he was again, walking into her life from nowhere, like that first day they'd met in

Glasgow and she had come to his rescue when, as a hungry Bosnian immigrant, he was caught stealing bread in the cafe where she sat. A chance meeting, a gesture of kindness from one human being to another, as she'd stepped in and said he was her friend.

Rosie hadn't seen Adrian since that night when he'd left her in the hospital bed in Glasgow and told her he had to go quickly before the police came and started asking questions. After he'd gone, she had cried so much that her battered ribs and face ached. She wondered if she would ever see him again, longed to see him to thank him for her life. And she'd often wondered why he hadn't ever called to know how she was. The number she had from him had been dead every time she'd tried it. He had disappeared without trace like the shadowy figure he was, and Rosie had accepted it. He had been there when she needed him. Now she sat and listened intently as he told her where he had been for the past few months.

Adrian spoke slowly and deliberately, drawing on a cigarette and staring into the darkness of the Spanish night. He'd been coming to her flat in Glasgow that night to tell her what had happened, and that he was going away for a while, but when he arrived, he heard voices behind her door and realised something was wrong.

What he'd come to tell her was that earlier in the day he had been called by his mother in Sarajevo to tell him that his sister Fiorina had been kidnapped by a gang of people-traffickers after being lured to Spain with the promise of a job. She was just seventeen years old. With a friend, Katya, from their village outside the city, they'd made their way to Sarajevo to answer a newspaper advert looking for girls for office work, promising jobs in the UK, Spain and Italy. Fiorina had learned secretarial work in school, and both she and Katya spoke good English. The girls saw it as a way to get to Western Europe legally and get a job.

Fiorina and her friend had waved goodbye to their families the following day. They flew to Malaga where, as the man who'd interviewed them in Sarajevo had promised, they were met at the airport by two men who took them to a hotel. They were told to wait in a room and the company boss in Spain would come to have coffee with them. But when they left the room, they heard a key turning on the outside. They were locked in. They banged on the door and shouted, but nobody came. They were held there all night, frightened, cold and hungry.

The next day three men came in and the girls were tied up and blindfolded, and were beaten when they cried. Later, they were taken from the hotel in a car. After several hours they stopped in some cafe with a car park. A van came and they were dragged from the car and driven for more hours. There were other girls in the van, shouting and crying, but everyone was blindfolded. Eventually, the van stopped and the blindfolds were taken off. The girls – about twelve of them in all – could see they were outside a house in the country somewhere.

Suddenly Fiorina and her friend Katya broke free and made a dash for it to escape. All the girls then started running. In the confusion that followed, the men tried to run after them, but they couldn't catch Fiorina and Katya, who ran into the woods. But after only a few hundred yards, Fiorina fell and twisted her ankle so badly that she couldn't move. Katya wanted desperately to stay with her, but Fiorina made her go on. She told her she must go on, save herself and get help. Katya, she said, was their only hope.

Adrian rubbed his face with his hands and shook his head.

'My sister is very brave, Rosie. She knew she couldn't make it, but she didn't want her friend to be kidnapped when she had a chance to be free.'

Rosie touched his arm. 'So the girl? Katya? She escaped and made it home?'

He nodded, and told her how Katya had stayed in the woods for two days before making it to the road, where she was picked up by a farmer and taken to the Spanish police. By the time the Guarda Civil came to the place they could find nothing. No girls. No cars. Nothing.

The Guarda contacted the girl's family and she was put on a plane home. It was only when she came back to Sarajevo a few days later that she was able to go to Adrian's mother and tell her what had happened.

'My mother wants to die now. If she never sees her Fiorina again, she told me she cannot live.' He shook his head. 'That day, when she called me, I promised her I would find her, Rosie. I promised.' He swallowed. 'And I will.'

'Did Katya have any details, Adrian? Any details of the other men? Accents? Nationality?'

Adrian nodded. There was some detail, but not much. She said she heard the name Leka and that he was Albanian. She heard the men talking about Spain. They mentioned a place called Marbella. But just one name. Leka. The boss.

'The name was burned into my heart, Rosie. To my soul. After the phone call, I decided I was going to Spain and find this man Leka. I have a friend who works in a hotel in Marbella and he said I could stay with him and he would help me. He is also Bosnian, and the immigrants always hear things. It is like a network. After some time, I found who Leka was. He was some big boss man of these organised gangsters from Albania and Russia, working together, kidnapping people. They take women and very young girls and sell them to the whorehouses. They even take children. Mostly immigrant children. Romanians, Africans. And they sell them.'

Rosie watched as he shook his head.

'My little sister . . . in a whorehouse. I cannot even think about it. I can only think of how I am going to find her. So I find some other people from Eastern Europe who work for this man and I got a job driving for them, working for the organisation.'

'And does Leka know you? Have you met him?'

'He knows me, but only because I saved his neck one night. I was the driver because his normal driver wasn't able to come. So I drove him to meet these people for some deal he is doing. It was in the harbour. I don't know what it was about, but I thought as soon as I see them it is strange. It felt bad. Something in my gut. You know my instincts are good, Rosie. They were going to kill him, and I saved him.'

Since then, Leka paid him well and gave him good jobs to do because he trusted him with his life.

A couple of days ago, he'd come from the latest job.

He looked into Rosie's eyes. 'The boy Taha,' he said. 'The Moroccan boy. I saw you with him at the train station. We had been following you.'

'Jesus, Adrian,' Rosie said, astonished. She dreaded what he was going to tell her.

He put his hand up. 'Don't worry, my friend. He is not dead.'

Rosie bit her lip. 'Were you sent to kill him?'

He shrugged. 'I was told to deal with him. They don't want to see Taha any more.' He sighed. 'He is a little boy. Stupid, but he's only a boy. I let him take the train. I told them I dealt with him.'

He was to get rid of Taha because he had a big mouth and they suspected he was talking to some newspaper woman. He raised his eyebrows and pointed his finger at her. Also, they'd been told that one of the VIP clients had lost his identity card and that the last time he'd had it he was with Taha in one of the apartments. They beat Taha because they thought he stole it, and that he had it, and was maybe selling it to this newspaper woman.

'But also,' Adrian's face grew dark, 'they didn't tell me this, but I heard from someone that Leka is thinking maybe Taha has seen something on the day this little girl was stolen. Because the fact is, he was close by in an

apartment with the VIP client. He is an important politician from Britain.'

'So are you saying they stole the girl? They stole Amy?
This Leka and the Russians stole Amy?' Rosie asked.

Adrian nodded. 'An Albanian called Besmir took her
for Leka. I know who he is.'

'But why?'

'I do not know that. But there is nothing they will not
do. They are Albanians and Russians. They only care about
money. It doesn't matter if it is a little British girl, or a
seventeen-year-old Bosnian girl. They can sell anything.'

He looked away.

'Although, I think you know, Rosie, that a little British
girl is more important, because nobody writes about a
seventeen-year-old Bosnian girl who is kidnapped because
she wants to find herself a better life. Nobody writes about
that, Rosie.'

Rosie looked at him. In all the time she had known
Adrian, it was the first time she'd ever seen any signs of
vulnerability in him.

'I will,' she said. 'I will write about it, Adrian. We must
help each other.'

Adrian sighed. 'I have to find my sister, Rosie. That is
why I came here. That is why I work for these pieces of
shit. Because I have to find my sister.'

'But if everything is connected, then maybe we can
help each other, Adrian. We can find your sister and maybe
we can find the little girl. I want to help you. And I need
your help, Adrian.'

'I know you do, Rosie.'

CHAPTER 17

Jenny sat on the basket chair in the bedroom, clutching Amy's pillow. She kept burying her face in it hoping to feel close to Amy. She could still smell the shampoo and aftersun she'd lovingly rubbed on her daughter's shoulders each evening – but the smell of everything that was innocent and perfect about her beautiful little girl was fading with each day that passed.

She crossed the room and opened the drawer, pulled out a couple of tee shirts and sniffed them. Nothing. Her heart physically ached. In the bed she could still see Amy's sleepy head and her tumbling dark curls, her bright blue eyes smiling when she woke up and saw her mummy. Jenny felt a stab in her stomach at the thought that somewhere Amy might be waking up each day, afraid, wondering where Mummy and Daddy were, crying for them. She closed her eyes to hold back the tears.

From the window she saw Martin coming in from the beach. He'd gone for a walk after they'd come back from the Reilly house, saying he wanted to clear his head. It had been a tense, stifling afternoon with the six of them together. How different everything had been ten days ago when they'd arrived for the holiday; the house full of laughter, kids playing, drinks on the terrace and everyone alive with the excitement of escaping the treadmill for two lazy weeks in the sun.

Today they'd been pent up, the small-talk coming in laboured bursts, the atmosphere crackling with suspicion. They'd talked about the Guarda Civil, and Jamie had ranted about their attitude when they interviewed him at the station the day before. He said they'd put him through the wringer, bullying him over the windsurfer's story.

Jenny avoided eye contact with Jamie throughout the afternoon. She'd been conscious that Martin was watching her, studying both of them. She knew he was suspicious – more than that. And from the way John and Margaret were, she sensed that they too were beginning to doubt. In the pit of her stomach, Jenny knew it was all beginning to unravel. Everything had changed with the windsurfer's account of the morning Amy disappeared from the beach. The yellow shorts had given it away: everyone knew it was Jamie. They'd all been laughing at Jamie's bright yellow shorts from the moment he appeared in them at the start of the holiday.

Now they looked at him and knew he had been lying. Nobody brought it up, but the lie was there, the elephant in the room. The atmosphere was oppressive and Jenny was glad when lunch was over and Martin suggested they go back home in case there was any news. They'd all hugged each other briefly at the door, but she was acutely aware of the coldness of Alison O'Hara's embrace, and the awkwardness of the Reillys. Jamie had squeezed her shoulder as he hugged her, but still they never looked at each other.

Jenny knew she had to tell Martin – and that it would have to be today. There was no way out. She had phoned Jamie on his mobile as soon as Martin went out for a walk. The conversation was brief, distant. There had been silence when she told him that she was going to tell Martin what had happened between them. Then Jamie said quietly, 'I know. I'm going to tell Alison.' Jenny pushed the button to end the call, just as she heard Jamie's voice say, 'I'm sorry, Jenny.'

Sorry. The word seemed so weak, so inappropriate for what they'd done and for its consequences. Sorry would never be enough.

She was in the kitchen when Martin came through the patio doors. His face was pale and his eyes dead. He walked past the kitchen table where she sat, went to the sink and filled the kettle.

'D'you want tea?'

He didn't look round, but Jenny could read his thoughts. His shoulders were slumped. He already knew.

'Martin,' Jenny began, not knowing what she was going to say next. He turned around.

'Martin. I have something to tell you. Can you sit down please.'

Martin's face was grey. He shook his head and looked at Jenny, folding his arms.

'I don't want to sit down, Jenny. I don't need to sit down. So. Tell me.'

She could hear her heart pounding. Her mouth was so dry she could hardly move her tongue. There was no beginning to this squalid episode that had cost everything. It wasn't meant to happen, but it had. How could she explain that?

'Martin. I was with Jamie when Amy went missing.'

The words hung in the air like the fallout from an explosion. Martin was like a ghost. His eyes never left her. Jenny's mouth quivered as she spoke.

'I was with Jamie. We. We were . . . Oh, Martin, I'm so sorry. I'm so, so sorry.'

She broke down and buried her head in her hands.

'You were what?' Martin's voice was calm. 'You were what, Jenny? You and Jamie were what?'

He went across to her and pulled her to her feet.

'Tell me, Jenny. Tell me.' He began to break. His eyes filled with tears.

'I need to hear it from you. Tell me.' He pulled Jenny's hands away from her eyes.

Jenny stood, tears streaming down her face, looking into the eyes of the man she loved, whom she'd destroyed in one momentary lapse.

'We had sex, Martin.' She shook her head. 'Oh Christ, I wish I could turn the clock back. You have no idea how I wish I could turn the clock back. I'm so sorry.'

Martin held her hands to stop her reaching up to her face. She felt his grip strong around her wrists.

'Tell me. Tell me about it. Tell me, Jenny. Tell me how

you were . . . how you were fucking my best friend when our daughter got out of the house. Tell me, you fucking bitch.'

He grabbed her hair, and forced her to look at him. 'Tell me, you bitch.'

'Please, Martin, you're hurting me. Please, let go. Please.'

Jenny wept. Martin released his grip. He took a step back and seemed to buckle at the knees.

'Tell me, Jenny.'

She couldn't speak.

'Was it good sex? Did Jamie make you come really hard? Did he, Jenny? Were you coming when our little girl was looking for you? When she went outside? Is that what happened? *Was* it good sex, Jenny? Was it worth it? Worth losing your fucking daughter for? Worth losing the only thing that is good and decent in this fucking world? Tell me.'

He slumped over the sink, and began to retch. Jenny reached out to him, but he pushed her away.

'Fucking leave me, you bitch. Fuck off.'

'Please, Martin,' Jenny said through her sobs. 'Please. I'm so sorry. I don't know how it happened. There was nothing before. Not ever. Never had I even thought about Jamie like that. It just happened. So suddenly . . . So quickly . . .'

Jenny sat down again before her legs gave way. She buried her face in her hands. She could hear Martin retching and weeping into the sink. When he finally composed himself and stood up, his face was flushed and streaked with tears. He looked at her and shook his head, sniffing.

'How could you, Jenny? How could you! Our baby, our little Amy – *my* baby? Oh, Jenny, how *could* you?'

He didn't wait for her answer, but fled out of the patio doors and onto the beach.

CHAPTER 18

Besmir assumed the driver knew what he was doing, as he negotiated the tight hairpin bends in the dark. After they'd left what passed for a main road he resigned himself to having no control over whether the car stayed on the road or went down the sheer drop into the ravine. Death held no fear or mystery for Besmir. It never had. It was living that had been frightening for him. But that had been a long time ago.

When he'd got into the car at the port in Tangiers, the driver shook his hand and introduced himself as Hassan. As they drove out of the city and into the countryside, he told him that he was twenty-six and lived with his family on a smallholding where they'd farmed for generations. Now he worked in the city, doing labouring jobs in one of the hotels, and also driving for the fat man whenever he needed him. He hated the fat man, but the pay was good, and every five or six weeks he would go home and give some money to his mother and father to help look after them and his three sisters.

Besmir wasn't interested in Hassan's life story. His mind was on other things. He couldn't get the image of the little girl out of his head, and wondered how she was, whether she was crying . . .

'She was on television,' Hassan said. 'The blue girl. I saw her. A picture.'

'You saw her? Tell me.'

'Nothing for you to worry. Nobody sees nothing on the beach.' He handed Besmir the cigarette packet.

Besmir lit his and then gave one to Hassan.

'Tell me. Tell me everything that was said on television.'

'I saw in the afternoon in the bar, after I drop you at the port. First, it was the picture on the television of the blue girl. Not like when she is with us. But very clean and pretty dress on. She was waving her hand and smiling. The hair it was shorter.'

Besmir pictured the girl. He remembered her hair, her soft skin. 'What else? What else did it say?'

'They show helicopters and police searching. Then two people with lot of newspaper people and cameras around them. I think they are the parents. The mother was crying. They were with Spanish police, but not speaking. Then a man read something from piece of paper. But I could not understand what he said. But the mother was crying.'

'What else?'

'That was all. Just the TV reporter say that the girl is maybe kidnapped from the beach. That the mother came outside and she was gone. Nobody say they saw anything.'

Besmir looked straight ahead, but he was conscious of

Hassan glancing at him. They drove on in silence. He knew Hassan was judging him. He knew he wanted to question why he took the girl, how he could do such a thing. But he also knew he would be too afraid to ask. In the middle of nowhere in the dark, the driver was smart enough to know not to say anything that would upset him. Anyone who can steal a child is capable of anything.

'Is it far now?' Besmir eventually broke the silence.

'No. Not far. But we have to be careful when we go off the next road, because then we must drive with the lights off in case anyone see us. And after some time, we have to walk a little. I know the way. We cannot have a torch to light us. We just have to go slow and careful.'

In the stillness, Besmir was surprised to hear voices and laughter as he and Hassan picked their way out of the undergrowth towards the dim light of the building. He looked at Hassan, his eyes questioning.

'Is the television,' Hassan whispered. 'The woman who stay the night here watches a small television and always it is very loud.' He touched Besmir's shoulder. 'Look. See where the light is coming from? That is the room she sits in. She sit and drink all night, then she sleep. She is supposed to listen for the children in case they cry. But she doesn't.' He shook his head and spat. 'She is a fat, ugly drunk.'

'Where are the children?' Besmir whispered as they climbed the fence.

'You see the light where the room I showed you is?'

Besmir nodded.

'Well, we go left there, and quietly around the back. The place made of tin. Is a stable, but no animals are there any more, only children. But they keep them there like animals. You will see. Come.'

Besmir followed him, crouching as they went towards the building. The sound of the television grew louder.

'Any other people? Any men? Guards?'

'Nothing. Nobody. In the daytime, people come and go with food and things. Maybe take a child and bring one, or return one who was taken for a few days. But at night, nobody but the fat bitch.' He grabbed Besmir's arm, and pointed to the building. 'Look. You see her?' He put his fingers to his lips.

Besmir crawled forward ahead of Hassan. He stayed close to the ground until he was almost at the window, then he stuck his head up. In the grim light of the bare bulb, he could see a fat woman, her face bloated like some of the alcoholic women he used to see sleeping rough in the streets of Tirana. She smoked a cigarette and swigged from a tumbler. There was a half empty bottle of vodka next to her. She giggled, watching some game show on television, and stubbed out her cigarette, lighting another immediately. She reminded him of one of the nurses in charge of the orphanage, who used to dish out beatings to any of the children who disobeyed her or who answered back. He blinked the image away and crawled back to Hassan.

'I see her.'

'Come,' Hassan said. 'Follow me. Say nothing. Just follow me.'

As his eyes adjusted to the darkness, Besmir could make out rusting bits of cars and tyres on the ground and was careful not to stumble over anything. He stood back as Hassan went towards the door, heavily padlocked and chained. Hassan turned to him and put his fingers to his lips. Then he crawled a few yards to the left of the house and quietly removed a heavy stone urn. He took a single key from beneath it and held it up to Besmir as though he was hoping to impress him with his insider knowledge. Hassan opened the lock and silently removed the padlock and chain.

'When we go in,' Hassan murmured, 'we must be careful in case any of the children are awake. If they see us they will cry out and everyone will wake up. We cannot stay long. Maybe a minute or two, but no more. Just so you can see.'

'Will the girl Kaltrina be there?' Besmir surprised himself with the question.

Hassan shook his head. 'No. Not yet. Maybe not ever. I don't know.'

Hassan pushed open the door. It was the smell that hit Besmir first. Urine and shit. His head swimming, he was instantly thrust back to the orphanage, to the rows of metal cots where he and other children sat rocking in their own urine and caked shit and scabs for days. He tensed his stomach muscles to keep control. He saw Hassan looking at him.

'You okay?'

He nodded, his face set. His eyes scanned the room; the tiny shaft of light coming in from a broken window showed the little bodies huddled together in cages like puppies. Three, four at a time, sleeping entwined, some who could not be more than three years old, lay sound asleep. They slept on dirty blankets, and even in the dark Besmir could see the children were filthy. A rat scurried across the wooden beams.

He felt vomit rising in his throat and swallowed hard to keep it down. He felt his legs buckle, and to stop himself from fainting, he squatted down and tried to compose himself, determined not to show weakness in front of Hassan.

Until this moment, only in his nightmares had he remembered how it used to be. He'd hardened himself to the memory of childhood behind the grim, damp walls of the orphanage. But the nightmares still haunted him. These days they – and the images – were fading with each passing year. But now this? He was back in hell, among the iron cots like cages where he'd spent the first years of his life.

'You okay, Besmir?' Hassan crouched beside him.

Besmir nodded and stood up.

'We go.' He went outside and was across the yard in seconds. He dropped to his knees and vomited onto the ground.

'What? What's the matter? You are shocked, my friend. I know. It is bad. I told you. Children like animals. But you are very tough man. What's the matter?'

Besmir sat on the ground and wiped his eyes. He shook his head, then got to his feet.

'Come. Take us back to the car. I have seen enough.'

CHAPTER 19

Rosie flinched under the cold shower, keeping her face under the spray to wake herself up from the restless night after Adrian's visit.

They'd talked until almost two in the morning, and he told her everything he knew about Leka and Daletsky, and the whole organisation behind the kidnap of his sister and of Amy. Rosie was not surprised at how meticulous Adrian was, and how calm. It was how he did business. He was always in the background, but he never missed a trick. Having him back after all this time made her feel safer.

He gave her the name of the recruitment organisation that lured his sister and her friend to Spain on the pretext of work, and he watched as Rosie wrote everything down. The company operated out of a small office in the centre of Marbella, but it was really just a room with two desks and a couple of telephones.

The recruitment firm was all part of the bigger company owned by Viktor Daletsky. Driving Leka and Daletsky in the car, he'd overheard Leka giving Daletsky figures for a number of women who were expected in the next few weeks and where they were from.

Brilliant. But Rosie needed proof. To write any kind of story linking Carter-Smith's presence on a yacht with the head of an organisation behind people-smuggling would give the *Post*'s lawyers heart failure, but it could be done. She didn't need to prove anything over Carter-Smith's involvement. He could be completely unaware of the extent of Daletsky's business dealings, and very probably was. Just telling the story would be enough. Let people make up their own minds.

When Adrian finally left, Rosie promised him she'd tell his sister's story. But she'd need the Guarda Civil to confirm that they'd picked up the Bosnian girl, Katya, who had escaped. They would never say it on the record, because it revealed that they'd failed to find the culprits. But if they admitted that it had happened – even off the record – that would be enough.

She'd ask Adrian to get the girl Katya's account to give the story flesh. Once it appeared in the *Post*, it would be picked up by the Spanish press, and the publicity would put pressure on the police to look seriously at the gang-sters behind the people-smuggling – Daletsky included.

But they had to consider Adrian's sister. Once the story broke, it was anybody's guess how Leka and his mob would react to her. Adrian hoped he'd be able to have an inside track. It was a gamble, but they had to try.

Rosie hadn't slept much after Adrian left and was glad when the morning light woke her. She wanted to be showered and fresh, with at least two jags of strong coffee in her before she phoned McGuire with her latest development.

'Rosie. What's happening? Have you got these bastards to talk yet?' McGuire sounded even more caffeined-up than her.

'Not yet. I spoke to O'Hara yesterday, and gave him my best pitch. He was nearly crying. He said he would talk to his wife.'

'Well, Rosie. They're not going to get away with this much longer. That windsurfer's story stitched the pair of them up big time. It's all about damage limitation now.'

'I know. I told O'Hara all that. I explained that if there are lies being told then they will come back to haunt everyone and the public will turn against them. I told him that in the end the only person who mattered was Amy.'

'And did he admit it?'

'No.' Rosie almost laughed. 'Of course not. Jesus, Mick. He's hardly going to admit it just like that. But they know they've been rumbled. I'm hoping when they talk it will be with me. I think I got the better of O'Hara yesterday.'

'He's an asshole, and I don't even know him,' McGuire said. 'But he's got to live with it. And I'll tell you this. For the rest of his life he'll wish he'd have kept it in his trousers – or, to be more accurate, in his yellow shorts.' He gave a little snort at his own wit.

'Oh, you're all heart, McGuire. Listen. I want to talk to you about another development – on the Carter-Smith side. You're going to love this.'

'Okay, let's hear it.'

'You know this Daletsky character? The Russian mobster? Well, I have good information that one of the many tentacles of his organisation is involved in people-trafficking.'

'Fuck! Can it be proved?'

Rosie told him she hoped that at the very worst, once she got her digging done, there would be a way to write a story in some form of words that would have a link – however tenuous it might be – to Daletksy's organisation and the smuggling of girls from Eastern Europe.

'If they can link him to that, and already have Carter-Smith's snout in the trough at his yacht then that has to be worth a resignation. Yes?'

'You fucking bet it would be. But can you prove it? Tell me how you can prove it.'

She told him about the girls who'd been brought to Spain and kidnapped, and that she could get an interview and signed affadavit from one of the girls. The other one was still missing. She didn't mention Adrian. Some things were best kept to herself for now.

'I think I can have a real go at this,' Rosie said.

'We'll have to be very careful, Rosie,' McGuire replied. 'I mean, we know these Russians are all gangsters no matter whether they're businessmen or at the heart of fucking government. But they're also very powerful. And throwing a few million roubles at a lawyer to sue a newspaper would be a drop in the ocean for these bastards. Even one as guilty as Daletsky. So we'll need something really solid to get it past our lawyers.'

'I know that. Hey, Mick, you don't have to tell me how difficult it is to get a story about someone powerful in our bloody paper.' Rosie couldn't resist the dig about her exclusive, exposing a High Court judge and a paedophile ring that the lawyers had been forced to bury six months before.

McGuire let it hang. They both knew he had no defence of that. He moved on. 'They are also dangerous bastards. These guys that had you dangling over the Clyde last year look like pussies next to the Russian mafia. To be honest, Rosie, even as I talk to you, I'm beginning to get a funny feeling in the pit of my stomach.'

'Maybe you shouldn't have had the kippers for breakfast.'

'Don't be a smartarse, Gilmour. You know what I mean. I'm worried about you.'

There was a small, genuinely poignant silence between the two of them. Then McGuire recovered his sarcasm.

'Well, I don't want my best hackette being shot by the mafia to be a footnote in my illustrious career. It might impact on my judgement.'

'Took the words right out of my mouth,' Rosie said. 'Look, Mick, I'll be alright.' She knew what was coming next.

'I'm thinking of sending someone else out to work with you. A bit of support. One of the heavy guys.'

'No,' Rosie said too quickly. 'I mean, it's okay, Mick. I honestly don't need any help. I really work better on my own with something like this. I'm also going to get this Spanish private eye involved. I've worked with him before, and if there's anything to be found, he'll dig it out. I'm meeting him today.'

She couldn't tell him Adrian would also be watching her back.

'But all you've really got is bloody Matt,' McGuire said. 'And he's half daft. He'll be chasing women all the time when he's not taking pictures.'

'No,' Rosie said. 'You're wrong. He's great to work with. We'll be fine. Honest. Look, I have to go. I want to get to my Spanish contact and get him working for me straight away.'

'Okay, Gilmour,' he said. 'Up to you. But be bloody careful, won't you?'

'Course. Talk later. Soon as I have anything to tell you.' Rosie clicked off.

CHAPTER 20

'Hello, Javier.' Rosie came up behind him. She'd been watching him discreetly from the doorway onto the terrace, where he'd arrived at precisely midday as he said he would. Javier was never late. And, knowing him, he probably sensed she'd been watching him. He turned around and stood up, all six-foot-two of him. A big, perfect smile spread across his face.

'Rosie.' Javier opened his arms and wrapped them around her, holding her tightly. Then he let go, kissed her on the lips, and bear-hugged her again. She caught the fresh smell of his skin, mingled with the whiff of cigarette smoke.

'I'm sorry, Javier' – Rosie surprised herself at how choked she felt – 'I did miss you.' How trite that sounded, since they'd only spoken once in almost three years.

'Sure you did.'

He released her, examining her for a moment, and smiled. Then he ruffled her hair, like she was a twelve-year-old kid. She was forgiven. They were friends again.

Nearly three years ago it had ended in a bitter power struggle between two highly charged individuals who fate should have kept apart. Javier wasn't used to women who answered back. Rosie concluded it was a Spanish thing. But despite the explosive interludes, they had worked well together on an investigation in the Costa del Sol that Rosie had been sent to unravel. Javier was impressive, if a little volatile.

He was somewhere around fifty, though he was vague about his age. A former detective with the Guarda Civil, he'd quit the force after he became frustrated, he had told Rosie when they first met. It was only when he got to know her better that he confessed his 'frustration' showed itself when he pushed a murdering thug who was resisting arrest off the roof of a building. It cuts down on the paperwork, he'd said with a shrug. Rosie was the last woman who'd argue with that. His pushing of the drug-dealing thug had never been proved, because there had only been the two of them present at the time, but he'd left under a cloud of investigation. Now, as a private eye, Javier still had all the contacts and respect and could dig things up that nobody else got a sniff of – as long as you didn't challenge or question the fascist in him.

After he and Rosie had spent a successful if sometimes turbulent month working together, things had blown up. Javier thought his integrity was being questioned when she asked for more information than he was providing, and announced you didn't do that to a guy like him. Rosie had replied that she'd question anything she damn well wanted to, because that was how she did business.

An explosion followed and she left Spain without saying goodbye. She could do stubborn better than the best of them. But she needed him now.

'Sit down, Rosie.' He motioned her to the table, and then barked '*Caballero!*' to attract a waiter.

From anyone else, hailing a waiter by shouting '*Caballero*' may have been considered condescending, but Javier got away with it. Like he was born to rule.

Rosie smiled to herself as she sat down obediently. She'd forgotten how the Javier machismo could reduce you to a mere woman.

He ordered coffee for both of them and handed Rosie a cigarette. She held his hand as he lit it for her, knowing he would like that. He sat back and drew on his cigarette, his chocolate eyes fixing her the way they always had, daring her to take him on.

'It took you long enough, Rosie.' He would have his fun. 'I saw your name every day in the newspaper since the kid went missing, and I half expected a call from you in case you needed my help.' He shrugged. 'Of course, a big shot like you probably has several translators and fixers working for you these days – not to mention private investigators.'

Rosie shook her head. When it came to repartee she would struggle to beat him, and right now she didn't want to fight.

'No, Javier. I have nobody working for me. I'm with a photographer.' She paused as the coffees arrived, then continued. 'I thought of calling you earlier, Javier,' she said, and she meant it. Life was too short to stay angry.

'To be honest, the story was all fairly straightforward in the beginning, and because the missing kid is British, the cops have someone translating the statements. And the Guarda Civil, as usual, are saying bugger-all anyway.'

He watched her silently. She wished he wouldn't do that.

'As I said I did want to call you, but I thought you'd still be angry.'

'What's past is past, Rosie. Forgotten about.'

He sipped his coffee, and ran his hand across his face and through his thick hair, greyer now than she remembered. The face was older too, but just as perfect. Olive skin, lightly tanned but no more, like a movie star growing old gracefully. Javier never sunbathed – he was too conceited to allow the sun to age him.

'So, how are you, Rosie? You looking for my help, or did you just call to say hello?'

Rosie was on the backfoot. She cleared her throat.

'Well.' She sat up straight. 'Both, I suppose. I wouldn't have left without trying to meet up, Javier. And, as you said, because you were probably waiting for my call!' She stubbed out her cigarette and forced herself to look away from him.

'But apart from that, yes, I am looking for some help. I have a line on the story but I need an inside track.' She held out her hand with a flourish, as though introducing him on a stage. 'And who better than you, Javier? The man in the know.' She leaned closer. 'Are you working for anyone on the story? Any newspaper? You're not working for the *Mail* are you?'

'Nope.' He shook his head. 'I don't give a shit about the newspapers. They're all crap. And they're all full of crap. Reporters, TV, newspapers. They are all the same.'

Rosie looked away. She could disappear for five minutes and return to find him still delivering the same diatribe about journalists. He had no respect for them. He'd made that clear from the first time they worked together. He called them hyenas. He applauded their cunning, but they were all full of shit.

'Javier.' She squeezed his wrist. 'I've heard it all before. Listen. I want to see if you can find some information for me from your Guarda Civil contacts. Do you want to hear?'

Javier smiled, and lit another cigarette. Still the same chain smoker. He cocked his head to one side and pulled his chair closer to Rosie so their knees were touching.

'So tell me about it.' He wagged a finger. 'And don't even *think* about saying this is just between ourselves, or I walk away now.'

Rosie shook her head. She wondered if they would be tearing each other apart in two days.

'You never bloody change. You'd think the passing years might mellow you a bit.'

'I can be mellow when I die. Tell me what you got and what you need.'

Rosie began. Javier listened, smoking, stubbing his fag out, lighting up again. You could almost see the wheels turning in his head. She told him everything she knew, about Daletsky, about the people-trafficking, of Adrian's sister lured from Sarajevo to Spain with her friend with the promise of a job. He whistled, shook his head, incredulous, when she told him about the boy Taha and Carter-Smith.

The first thing she'd need, Rosie told him, would be an inside track with the Guarda Civil to see if there was anything, even off the record, about the girl who was found after she escaped the kidnappers. That was the first strand of the story she wanted to tackle. When she stopped talking, Javier looked at her and raised an eyebrow.

'You finished?'

He sat back, stretching out his long legs, then crossed them, his khaki trousers riding up his leg a little, exposing a slim, brown ankle. Sign of breeding, he'd once told her. Rosie stole a glance at his tanned feet in the soft, buff loafers he always wore.

He took a deep breath and blew out a sigh.

'To be brutally honest, Rosie, when you mention Albanians and Russians, one thing I know for sure is that it's time for me to get up and walk away. You mess with these people, they kill you just for fun. It doesn't matter who you are or what you are, they don't care. They are a different breed of gangster. You really don't want to get involved in this. You should walk away now while you still can.'

She knew he was right. Her mind flashed back to the night in Glasgow when she nearly got killed. Javier genuinely had her best interests at heart, but she also knew that he knew she would never walk away.

'Javier, you know me well enough to know that I cannot

do that.' She paused. 'But I understand totally if *you* want to walk away.'

He handed her a cigarette and sparked the lighter as she placed the Marlboro Light between her lips.

'What?' He smiled. 'And leave you to get shot by some Russian gangster?'

He slammed the lighter on the table.

'No chance, Rosita. I'm in.'

CHAPTER 21

They drove in silence, the windows rolled down, the stifling night air starting to cool a little once they picked up speed. They didn't speak for some time, and Besmir was aware that Hassan was stealing little glances at him. He knew the driver was afraid to speak.

Besmir had realised quite young that he had a quiet power over people. Instinctively they could sense a danger behind his flat expression. He'd used it to protect himself, but tonight his silence was not about power. He couldn't blink away the images of what he'd seen: children caged like animals, caked in filth. He remembered that desolation, that fear, from a childhood he'd tried all his adult life to blot out.

A red mist clouded his head. Everything had changed. Everything he had done since he was in Spain, working for these people, gaining their respect, didn't matter a damn. It didn't matter that they were much more powerful and dangerous than he. He couldn't stop himself now. He was out. He would deal with the consequences.

'Besmir,' Hassan ventured. 'Is very late to drive all the way back to the city. You come to my house tonight? Please? Eat with my family, stay with us the night. I will drive you to the port in the morning.'

Besmir didn't speak. He stared straight ahead. He knew he wasn't going to the port. Not tomorrow anyway.

'I will come,' he said, without looking at Hassan.

They drove the rest of the journey in silence, through tiny villages that were no more than a scattering of tin or wooden shacks, an occasional oil lamp throwing light on the shadowy figures hunkered down around fires flickering on diesel drums. This was the Morocco the tourists didn't see, where people scratched a living from the land. The smell of spices and cooking meat mingled with the smoke. Ragged children giggled and kicked a burst football in the dark. They drove on along winding roads that led deeper into the countryside. In the blackness, the headlights from the car shone on the stray goats scampering away when the car sped past.

'Is here,' Hassan said, pointing ahead. 'My house. My father's house.'

Besmir could see smoke circling from somewhere, and a dim light coming from what looked like a house built of corrugated tin sheets and brick. The door opened as the car drew up and a man appeared at the door with a woman behind him. She came out from behind her husband into the yard, and the headlamps lit up the big smile on her face. Hassan got out of the car and went towards her and kissed her on both cheeks. His father came outside and Hassan embraced him, too. They spoke in Arabic and Hassan's father looked towards Besmir, his thin face expressionless.

Hassan came back to the car.

'Come, Besmir. Meet my mother and father. We will have dinner soon. Fresh goat.'

Besmir got out of the car and stood up, stretching his legs after the long journey. He walked towards the couple and held out a hand. The woman smiled and took it. The man, who looked much older than his wife, shook his hand, but eyed him suspiciously.

'Please.' Hassan beckoned Besmir to come to the table outside and sit. 'We will have some tea while my mother cooks.'

The men sat in awkward silence while the woman went to the fire and turned meat over on a long blackened grill. She lifted the lid off a huge iron pot and stirred the contents, smiling over to her son and Besmir. He nodded back, not sure what to do or say next.

The door of the house opened and Besmir blinked when he saw the girl, standing like a vision in the half light. She looked straight at him, then her eyes darted away. He swallowed, stunned by her beauty. He glanced at Hassan's father whose eyes burned a hole in him. Hassan looked a little nervous.

'Salima!' Hassan jumped to his feet and went towards his sister, speaking excitedly in Arabic.

She looked at Besmir. Her eyes were a striking green. He stood up when she came towards the table as Hassan moved to introduce him. The girl put down the tray she was carrying and took the glasses of tea and placed them on the table. She smiled awkwardly at Besmir as he stretched out his hand. He could feel her father's eyes on him. He turned and held his stare until the old man looked away.

Later, after they'd eaten, Hassan walked with Besmir around the building, showing him how they worked, proud of his little farm. Besmir feigned interest, unable to get Salima out of his head. He was also unfamiliar with this kind of family warmth, the way they'd sat round the table, laughing, sharing stories and easy in each other's company. Every now and again as they'd all talked over dinner, Hassan would translate the conversation for Besmir. He told them of his twin sisters, asleep in bed, who would be excited to see the stranger in their midst when he awoke in the morning. Besmir smiled politely, though he had no way of relating to this kind of family spirit.

But he did relate to the modest glances of the beautiful Salima who Hassan proudly told him, was working hard at school and hoping to go Tangiers to study medicine. She'd be a doctor and make the family and the whole village proud. The old man continued to eye Besmir as a threat, but he didn't care. He'd made his mind up there and then, before he'd ever had a conversation with her, that she would be his. He was never going back to Spain to work for Leka or anybody else.

But his immediate problem was not Salima, it was the blue girl, and the thought that she could end up in cages like the rest of the captured children. He would not allow that to happen. If there was shame inside him for what he had done, for stealing her, he wouldn't recognise it as shame or remorse. All he knew was that he wanted to put it right.

'Hassan,' Besmir said, as they stood looking out to the pitch darkness. 'Thank you for allowing me to share this night with your family. But I must ask you something now.'

Hassan looked at him.

'Yes, my friend?'

'Can I trust you?'

Besmir asked the question, but he already knew the answer.

'You can trust me. I think you know that.'

'I want to help the children, Hassan,' Besmir said, surprising himself at the choking feeling he had in the back of his throat. 'I want to set them free.' He looked away from Hassan into the dark landscape. 'And I want to find the blue girl and take her back.'

With those words, he knew he was signing his own death warrant. If Hassan was going to betray him then it was already too late. He didn't care.

Silence hung in the air. Crickets rattled in the scrubland. Besmir was conscious of Hassan scrutinising his face.

'You took the girl, Besmir. Now you want to give her back?'

Hassan's tone was measured, but the reprimand was clear in his voice.

'The blue girl. She is under your skin. I could see that.' He smiled a little. 'Like my sister Salima. I can also see that she is under your skin.'

Besmir said nothing.

'But what you are saying, my friend, will get you killed. I think there are some things that when you do them, you cannot go back. They cannot be undone. You may find out that taking the blue girl was one of them. You cannot fight these people, Besmir. Nobody can. Not even a man as angry as you can fight them.' He shook his head and looked away. 'They will kill you.'

They both stood in silence, looking at each other.

'But they will have to kill us both.' He reached out and touched Besmir's arm. 'Come, we will sit at the table and make a plan.'

CHAPTER 22

'You must have hollow legs, the amount of food you shift,' said Rosie, watching as Matt chased the last of the baked beans around his breakfast plate. 'I had so much to eat last night, I can't face a big breakfast.'

Matt looked up from his plate.

'Yeah, yeah, Gilmour. More like you were kept up all night by the big Spaniard, and you're not fit to eat.' Matt winked, biting off a chunk of toast.

Rosie ignored his jibe and poured some more coffee, but she knew he wouldn't let it go. Matt had already been asking what was the story between her and Javier, having watched the chemistry between them at dinner the previous evening.

'Come on, Rosie,' he said, pushing his plate away. 'You can tell me. What's it all about, Rosita?' He chuckled, mocking Javier's accent. 'Bit of an old holiday romance there? That it?'

Rosie shook her head. 'We're friends. Close friends, Matt.

We worked together on a story here a couple of years ago. He's a top drawer operator.'

'And?' Matt raised his eyebrows.

'And nothing. I said friends. I haven't seen him for a while so we had a lot of catching up to do.'

'Hah! I could see that, Rosita. That's why I bailed out after the coffee. I was beginning to get a hot flush.'

'Piss off!' Rosie drank her coffee, then changed the subject. 'Tell you what, though. Javier already had some good info for me by the time he arrived, and I only enlisted his help yesterday afternoon. That's what I call an operator.'

One of his Guarda Civil contacts had confirmed off the record the story about the Bosnian girl, Katya, being found, and that she'd been kidnapped by traffickers.

He hadn't said too much, but after Matt left, Javier took her to a small flamenco bar in the old town and they talked into the night. The Guarda Civil had never released the information about the kidnapped girl, according to his man on the inside, and the case was being handled by a specialist team investigating organised crime on the Costa del Sol. But Javier said the information was solid.

'Yeah. He's one sharp bastardo,' Matt said. 'I liked him.' He laughed. 'I couldn't believe the way he shouted "*caballero*" to the waiters. The last guy I saw doing that was Manolito in the *High Chaparral*.'

Rosie smiled. 'Yeah. It's a Spanish thing. They respect age. They celebrate growing older. Not like in our country, where youth is perceived to be everything, and everyone over fifty is past it.'

'So is Javier past it, Rosita?' Matt lifted Rosie's hand and pretended to kiss it.

'Piss off. It's not like that.'

Rosie's mobile rang. She lifted it off the table, looked at the screen. No name, and she didn't recognise the British number. She looked at Matt and put her finger to her lips for him to keep quiet. It might be Jamie O'Hara offering to give an interview.

'Hello?' Rosie's tone was sharp.

'Rosie Gilmour?' The voice was rough, a little muffled.

'Who's this?'

'You don't know me. Doesn't matter who I am. You Rosie? Don't fuck about.'

Definitely a lisp or some speech impediment. Or he was disguising his voice. Rosie's brain switched to overdrive. She knew voices like this. Thugs, gangsters, and plenty who just talked the talk.

'Hey, listen, pal.' Rosie's voice hardened. 'I don't know who you are, or where you got my number, but don't come on the phone and swear at me. Now, you've got about ten seconds to tell me what this is about or I hang up.'

Silence. Rosie looked at Matt. If the caller was genuine he would start talking. If he was a crank, he'd hang up. Fuck it. She didn't have time to piss around. Whatever this headcase wanted he'd have to be quick.

'Somebody wants to talk to you about that missing kid. That wee lassie that got stole fae the beach.'

Rosie's stomach tightened.

'You in Spain?'

'Naw. Glasgow. It's not me who wants to talk.'

'Then who?'

'He's inside. Just got fifteen years. He's in the Bar-L. For murder. He's a beast. He told me to contact you. He knows things.'

Rosie could feel her heartbeat.

'I'll see him. Of course. I'll come over and see him in jail. Who is he? What's his name?' Rosie's mental filing system tried to remember who had been done for murder recently, but she'd been away for over a month now.

'Frankie Nelson,' the voice said. 'He got done for killing that woman twelve years ago. She was going to the cops about wee boys him and his bum boy Vinny Paterson was shagging. They're paedos. Paterson's on the run so he never got done, but Frankie got caught and he's banged up. It's Frankie who wants to talk to you. Says he knows stuff. Something about films.'

'Films? About kids?'

'Aye. Don't know any more. Films with weans in them. Sick films. For paedos. Look, I don't know. I'm passing the message on, that's all.' The lisp was quite pronounced now.

'I'll come over straight away. Next couple of days. Can you get me a pass for the prison? But I have to go in there as a friend, not as a reporter. It's not allowed. No notebooks, tapes or anything. Make that clear on the pass. That I'm a friend. Just tell him I'll be there, if you get me a pass.'

'I can do that. Will take about two or three days to get. I'll be in touch.'

'By the way, can I ask you something?' Rosie ventured.

'Whit?'

'How do you know him?'

'I'm not a poof, right?' he snapped. 'I'm just out of jail. I was a turnkey before I left and I got talking to Frankie the last wee while. I did ten years. I shot somebody. Frankie's a cold fucker alright, but he wouldn't mess with me or I'd rip his lungs out. He was alright with me. He says to me, he can tell things that might help find that wee lassie. That's all. I said he should tell the papers. If I can get him in touch with you then I've done my bit.'

'You did the right thing, but why is he doing this?'

She already knew the answer – if his information helped to find Amy then maybe he wouldn't be locked up for the rest of his life.

'He's lodged an appeal against his sentence, and he thinks it might do well for him if he helps get this wee girl. I don't give a fuck what happens to him, he's a beast. But if he knows things, then maybe they'll get the wee lassie back.'

'Okay,' Rosie said. 'Call me as soon as you get a pass, and I'll be there the following day.'

The line went dead before she had a chance to say thanks.

Matt looked at her inquisitively. 'Well?'

'I'm going to have to go back to Glasgow. Some beast in jail says he has information about Amy.'

'That him on the phone?'

'No. It was some guy just released from Bar-L. Says a beast called Frankie Nelson wants to talk to me.' Rosie looked for McGuire's number in her mobile.

'Fuck me, Rosie. That could be mega.' Matt stretched out his legs and put his hands behind his head. 'Fucking mega.'

'Yeah. Could also be a complete header, but we can't take a chance. If he wants to talk then he'll talk to someone, and if it's not me it'll be another paper. I need to call McGuire. I want to see if we can nail the people-trafficker story before I go. Don't go anywhere, Matt. We've got addresses to hit this afternoon, offices where the recruitment company is holed up. Javier's coming in a little while.'

Rosie got up and looked at her watch. McGuire would be coming out of the editorial conference around now. She headed to her bedroom.

Once the usual pleasantries were over, with McGuire telling Rosie he was getting impatient waiting for O'Hara or Jenny to buckle and tell all, she was able to get him focused on the people-trafficker story.

She told him her Spanish contact had come up with addresses for the recruitment firm, and he was already running checks on them. Hopefully they'd lead somewhere. But she had to admit that at the moment she only had information that these were connected to Daletsky's widespread empire. She hoped to have something more solid by this afternoon, she told him.

'It has to be buttoned down, Rosie, if we're going to connect this Daletsky to people-trafficking. Nobody has ever had the balls or the evidence to turn him over before, and if we can't prove it one hundred per cent, I'm telling you now it's not going in my paper.'

'I know, Mick. I'm working on it.'

'Same goes for Carter-Smith. He's the fucking Home Secretary. It was fair enough to have him on a yacht with some dubious Russian businessman. But to start talking about people-trafficking . . . well, we're in deep shit if we say that and it can't be proved.'

'Yeah, I know, Mick.'

'Well, Gilmour, let's find the proof, and we can nail them all to the wall.'

'Mick,' Rosie began. 'There's something else. I just took a call on the mobile from some guy who's just out of jail and he says some paedo called Frankie Nelson knows information about Amy. Says he wants to see me in Bar-L.'

'Holy fuck, Rosie. Frankie Nelson? He just got fifteen years, and is appealing against sentence. He is one warped fucker. We had a big background for the trial while you were away. Does the guy who phoned sound genuine?'

'No way of knowing really. But my gut tells me to get to Glasgow if he gets me a pass for Bar-L. He said he would, in a couple of days.'

'Well, only one way to find out, Rosie. Get your arse over to Glasgow. I'll send somebody over to cover press conferences and stuff. Somebody who knows what they're doing. Probably young Declan. He's keen and meticulous, and I'm sure he'll take a telling from you.'

'Great,' Rosie said. 'Declan will be perfect. I'll only be

gone for a few days, and hopefully before I go I can make some headway with the trafficking story. What I'd like to do is get this in the paper soon as, and then get the hell out to Glasgow while the shit hits the fan here.'

'Fine,' McGuire said. 'But we need proof first. Phone me tonight, Rosie. Let me know how you're getting on.'

Rosie was about to hang up when McGuire spoke.

'Hold on. Marion wants a word.'

The line went dead for a second as he transferred her.

'Hey, Rosie. Howsit going on the Costa? I've been watching all the stuff on telly. Christ, it's awful. The longer it goes on, the less chance there is of finding that wee girl.'

'I know, Marion. But I just feel certain she's out there.'

'Would be great if she was. And if she comes back alive. That would be some moment.'

'Sure would.'

'What's up, Marion?

Marion hesitated for a moment.

'Rosie,' she said. 'Can you talk for a second?'

'Course.'

'Listen.' Marion's voice was almost a whisper. 'I didn't really know what to do with this, so I thought I'd just talk to you. I haven't mentioned it to anyone, by the way.'

'Marion, you're making me nervous. What's up?'

'Rosie. Someone came into the front desk the other day and asked for you. A man.'

Rosie's heart jumped. TJ...? Maybe he'd lost her mobile number. Perhaps he'd been phoning her home and getting no answer. Maybe he was back and was going to surprise her.

'An older man. Quite old,' Marion said.

Rosie's heart sank. TJ was older, but you would never call him quite old.

'How old's quite old?'

'Old. Like maybe seventy or something? Hard to say, Rosie. He was rough looking.' She paused. 'Dishevelled. Not well looking. Kind of, well, kind of down and out.'

Rosie was confused. There was a pause.

'Rosie.' Marion cleared her throat. 'He said his name was Martin. Martin Gilmour.'

She hadn't heard the name out loud in thirty-two years. She couldn't speak.

'He . . . He said he was your father, Rosie.'

Silence. Rosie's head swirled. Her father.

'Jesus wept!' Rosie's voice was barely audible.

'I haven't mentioned it to anyone.'

'What . . . What else did he say, Marion?'

Her heart was beating out against her ribs. She shouldn't be like this. Not after all this time.

'He came in asking for you. The front desk called up to me and I went down to see him. He asked if he could see you, and I told him you were out of the country. He looked sad, Rosie. A sad wee man. He wrote down a phone number of some hostel he's staying in. His hands were shaking.'

'Hostel?' Rosie choked the word out.

'That's what he said. Didn't say the name. Just wrote down the phone number. I said I'd pass it on. He was kind of sad when he walked away.'

Rosie recovered her composure. She had to.

'Fine, Marion. Listen. I've got to come to Glasgow in the next couple of days to do something. I'll get the number then. And ... er ... Marion? I know this goes without saying, but can you just keep that between you and me?'

'You don't have to say that.' Marion sounded a little offended.

'I know. I'm sorry, Marion, but ... well, it's ... it's ... well, it's a long story. Look, I'll talk to you when I get to Glasgow. Thanks, Marion.'

'Don't worry, Rosie. Everything will be alright. See you when you get back.'

Rosie hung up. She walked out to the terrace in a daze. He was back.

CHAPTER 23

Rosie stepped out of Glasgow Airport and into a steady drizzle. Welcome home.

She was always amused at the shock and disappointment of people when they arrived back from holidays and were met by the rain. It was never any other way when you got back to Scotland from somewhere warm – especially in July. Always the rain, just to remind you that whoever you thought you were during those carefree two weeks in the sun, this is actually who you were. It's Glasgow. It's pissing down. And you start back at work tomorrow. Deal with it.

She scanned the cars all along the pick-up line, boots open, waiting for returning families, friends, long lost relatives. She wondered what that felt like just for a moment, but not long enough for it to matter.

Somewhere, not far away, was a man waiting for her who said he was her father. But their story was nothing like that of people arriving to be hugged by cherished family and friends. Rosie wished she could conjure up the grainy images of her father that had faded from her mind a long time ago. They haunted her dreams, but right now she couldn't have picked Martin Gilmour out of the crowd if her life depended on it.

She scanned the cars, and sure enough, a car from the taxi firm the *Post* used was there under the 'G' at the big yellow Glasgow Airport sign, as it always was when she returned from her travels. The driver waved when he saw her. She waved back. What the heck. Taxis weren't family, but it was a safe bet that in most cases they were more reliable.

'Hey, Rosie. How you doin?' The driver took her bag and put it in the boot. 'You might have brought the sunshine.'

'Hey, John,' Rosie opened the passenger door and got in. 'It wouldn't be the same with sunshine. We'd have nothing to moan about the whole of July if it wasn't raining.'

The driver eased the car into the exit traffic and onto the motorway towards the city. Rosie looked at her watch. Four-thirty. She had to meet the mystery man with the muffled voice and the prison pass for Frankie Nelson at seven in the Saltmarket. But first she would go into the office and touch base with McGuire before heading to her flat to dump her bag.

Rosie came out of the revolving door into the marbled foyer of the *Post* and climbed the open staircase to the vast expanse of the editorial floor. She lingered just for a second on the top step, drinking in the immediate sense of comfort of being back in the familiar hub where she belonged.

It was five in the afternoon, and editorial was just beginning to bubble with the urgency that could spill over to hysteria as the hours and minutes ticked towards the edition deadline. The news editors had phones glued to their ears, listening to reporters on the ground talking them through their stories and occasionally barking with frustration if the hack wasn't telling them everything they wanted to hear. Let's not spoil a good story with the facts. Go back to the door and tell that fat fucker threatening you with the axe that you are from the *Post* and you are not scared of him or anybody else. That was the kind of encouragement legendary news editors used to dish out in the old days.

The bank of news reporters sat hunched over their computers, or had phones at their ears, faces concentrated, scribbling shorthand notes, in an island of fifteen desks as though they'd been cast adrift to change the world.

It used to be a sight to behold when reporters still used typewriters, and at five in the evening the cacophony of twenty Olivettis rattling like machine-gun fire was deafening as hacks – well, those who were sober enough – battered out their stories.

These days, the reporters may have been driven by the same desire, the same sense of chipping away at the coalface of truth, as the old hacks used to put it, but the scene before Rosie now could easily have been an insurance office. There was little banter because everything was done in front of a computer. No real conversation, just a kind of battery hen operation, with people churning out copy. It was the silence you noticed more than anything.

But the place sparked to life just like in the past when there was a big story on the go. And right now, the story was in the Costa del Sol. Rosie hoped she wouldn't have to be here too long. One or two reporters looked up, surprised to see her, and gave her the thumbs up. She waved back, but didn't stop by her desk, next to Reynolds. The crime reporter had been stewing with resentment ever since the kid went missing and he was told he would not be required to go to Spain on the story. McGuire was emphatic on that. He couldn't prove that Reynolds had been feeding corrupt police chief Gavin Fox inside information from the paper during the last investigation that nearly got Rosie killed, but he was convinced he was guilty. He'd told Rosie that Reynolds would sit out the rest of his time flat on his arse doing crime statistics, until they could find some deal to get rid of him.

Beyond the reporters, at what in newspaper parlance was the backbench where all the decisions were made, McGuire stood listening to some of his sidekicks trying to sell him a page layout. His hands were deep in the pockets of his pinstripe trousers and, in his white shirt with the sleeves rolled up, he looked like something out of an old movie about the newspaper industry. All he needed was a cigar clamped between his teeth. He was pointing to the dummy page – the broad sheet of paper they used to draw out the ideas for the page before it was done on the computer. He turned around, and seeing

Rosie, gave her a wave. She headed to his office, stopping briefly at Marion's desk while she waited for him.

'Hi, Marion,' Rosie said. 'Thanks for all your help over there – and for that stuff about the old guy.'

'No worries, Rosie.'

Marion handed her a piece of paper with the phone number. Rosie put it in her pocket and leaned over Marion's desk.

'Hey. You fancy a quick coffee once I'm finished with your boss? I want to talk to you a bit.'

'Sure. Give me a shout when you're clear and we'll go downstairs and have a cuppa.'

McGuire came breezing up with a smile on his face.

'*Hola*, Rosie,' he greeted her, motioning her into his office ahead of him. 'You've got far too much of a suntan for my liking. I thought you were supposed to be working.'

'Well, I was there for a month before you called me and broke up my holiday, pal.' She'd missed all this banter.

He went behind his desk and sat down, looking at post-it messages Marion had stuck there for him. One by one he read them, crumpled them, and tossed them in the direction of the bin.

Rosie sat on the black leather Chesterfield opposite his desk. McGuire looked at her and she was conscious that he was watching for signs of stress or the effects of what had happened a few months ago. Whatever else he was, however strident at times, he had been genuinely upset at what had happened to her after the Fox investigation. Rosie knew her editor cared about her a lot, but she also knew he wouldn't want to hear about the nightmares or panic attacks that had been part of her life recently. He wanted her strong.

'You alright, Rosie? You look well enough.' He clasped his hands across his stomach and sat back.

'Tell me. Did you have a good rest, get the batteries recharged and all that stuff?' He frowned. 'Whatever you might think, Rosie, I was a bit worried about you before you went. Thought maybe you came back to work a bit too quick. You looked drained. Dunno. Sad or something.'

McGuire seemed genuinely interested. His eyes narrowed.

'So what are you now, Mick? A psychologist? Maybe you should write the Problem Page.' Rosie gave him a sarcastic look.

McGuire was being nice to her, caring, but she was too fragile right now for an arm around the shoulder from him. Combat she could cope with, but sympathy? No thanks.

McGuire rolled up a piece of paper and threw it at her.

'Aye, fine. Full of the usual shit. Good to have you back, Gilmour! Want a coffee?'

'No,' Rosie smiled.

'Okay. So tell me about this wanker who phoned you about Nelson? No ideas who he is?'

'No. Nothing. I'm meeting him at a pub in Saltmarket in a little while.'

'How do you know he's not some psycho who's going to do you in?'

'I don't. What you want me to do? Go home and build a jigsaw?'

McGuire chuckled. 'Okay, we'll deal with him later. So tell me: how far away are you on the people-trafficking story? And by that, Gilmour, I mean a version that I can get past the lawyers and in the paper.'

'Well, here's the lowdown.'

Rosie told him that the day before she left Spain she went with Javier and Matt to the address of the recruitment office. They watched it for a couple of hours, then they left Matt for a while longer by himself, so he could snatch pictures of who was coming in and out. Turned out there wasn't much to see, and no Daletsky. But one guy went in and out a couple of times, and they suspected that he might be Leka, Daletsky's Albanian enforcer and organiser. Rosie told him she had a source who would be able to identify him when she got back, but she didn't tell him it was Adrian.

She also told him that Javier had researched the names behind the recruitment outfit, and there was one small importing company owned by Daletsky whose director was also on the board of the recruitment company. It was a tenuous link, but it placed one of Daletsky's companies at least in the same trough as the recruitment firm who were behind the people-trafficking.

'How do you know it is this recruitment company who are behind the people-trafficking?' McGuire's eyebrows knitted.

'Well,' Rosie said, 'according to my private-eye contact, Javier, the intelligence coming from his connections in the Guarda Civil is that this company is under surveillance for organised crime, and people-trafficking – as you know – is part and parcel of organised crime.'

'Fine. But I want it more solid than that. What actual evidence are we going to get that they are involved in people-trafficking, Rosie? You know what these fucking lawyers are like. I'm not going to them unless I'm fire-proof.'

'I know, and Javier has also come up with a couple of other things from his cop contacts.'

She sat forward in her chair and concentrated. You had to be careful not to tell McGuire too much. Just enough for him to know that it was workable.

'You'll love this, Mick.' Rosie licked her lips. 'You know the girl from Sarajevo who was kidnapped? Well, I have someone who has made contact with her back there and we now have her story. It's brilliant. Puts flesh on the tale, real human interest. But better than that, she remembered the make of the van that took them from the hotel in Malaga to the house where she escaped when they let the girls out of the van. And, amazingly, she even remembered most of the registration number. She said that from the moment they realised they were being taken, her friend – the one who twisted her ankle and got recaptured – told her they must remember everything they could.'

'You're fucking joking,' McGuire said. 'Are you saying that two country bumpkin innocent girls abroad were being kidnapped and they had the savvy to remember a registration number of their kidnappers – when they must have been worried they were going to die? I find that hard to swallow.'

'I did too, Mick, but all we did was get the info from her. She didn't know what we were going to do with it. What I did was give it to Javier and he ran it past his Guarda Civil man. We didn't have the full reg, but Javier's mate said it was near enough. He ran it through the computer and confirmed that it matched a van from a company that subcontracts work for the recruitment firm. That might be as good as it gets, Mick, but tell you what – it's good enough for me.'

McGuire lifted his spectacles from the desk and began polishing the lenses with his tie.

'I like that. I like that a lot, Rosie. A bit of real digging there and proper intrigue, but it will still be hard to get past the lawyers.'

'I know. But when I get back, I might have more, and I'll be ready to write. I've already done up the girl's interview and I'll pop it across to your secret email.'

'How did you trace her?' Mick asked, standing up and looking at his watch, indicating the chat was over.

Rosie got up and put her hands up as though she was under arrest.

'Now, Mick, you don't need to know any of that stuff but it's all true, and her story is verified by police and counselling groups who have dealt with her since she got back to Sarajevo. How we traced her is on a need-to-know basis. And you don't need to know. Not right now anyway.'

He walked past her, and patted her shoulder.

'Well done, Rosie. Go see your mystery man tonight and call me in the morning. And get some sleep as well.'

CHAPTER 24

Rosie stood at the bar, nursing a glass of mineral water that was getting warmer by the minute. She knew better than to ask for ice.

There were bars in parts of Glasgow you only went into if you could guarantee a safe passage out without getting your smile widened. This was one of them. If you happened into one of these bars as a tourist, or just for a walk on the wild side, you wouldn't get the sense straight away of how your night was going to pan out. You might get a cheery word from the barman, or a 'howsit goin' big man?' from a guy propping up the bar. Some bar-room Voltaire might even engage you in friendly conversation. But the secret was to know when it was time to leave. Because what began as genial chat could swiftly become a broken bottle in your neck. That was the Glasgow you wouldn't see in the Good Pub Guide.

The Globe, smack bang in the middle of Saltmarket, ticked all the squalid boxes. It was close enough to the High Court to ensure that most of its patrons were either on their way to jail, or had just been freed because some clever bastard QC managed to outwit the prosecution – so sending another lowlife scumbucket back onto the streets to resume his career. It was in this dingy hole of a place, which stank of piss and stale tobacco, that the 'not guilty' or the 'not proven' came to celebrate alongside their brief – who would later repair to the posh O'Brien's in the city centre and regale the other movers and shakers with tales of his glimpse into the underbelly. And it was at O'Brien's that he would quaff vintage champagne on the strength of the grand a day he was paid in legal aid to defend the indefensible.

The other punters in the Globe, who sat in dark corners, were the old whores and drunks from the street, who'd come in out of the cold for enough cheap wine to blot out the night and the memory of a squandered life.

Rosie was lucky. She was always guaranteed a safe passage out. She'd been in and out of the bar a million times before, during and after a million High Court trials, and down the years she'd become only as close as you would want to be with the bar staff and the owner. She was respected, and nobody bothered her. Sometimes she would come here to gather her thoughts before writing up her copy after a trial, and other times just to soak up the atmosphere, when her mood became melancholy the way it occasionally did.

Anything could happen at any time in the Globe. On one memorable afternoon, Rosie's eyes nearly popped out of her head when she became aware of a blootered old wino in her sixties giving her equally blootered pal a hand-job under a table in the corner. It finished in a punch-up as he jolted his knee upwards when he came, spilling her drink, and she hooked him with her free hand. The romance of the city.

Now, as she stood at the bar, she saw ghostly images of herself down the years as a young reporter learning her craft in and out of places like this. One time, she was here with a prostitute. There were only the two of them in the bar, and a punter came in and beckoned the hooker out. She'd returned, a tenner richer, about six minutes later, laughing that the punter had said it was the other hooker he'd wanted – meaning Rosie.

Now, Rosie was talking to Billy the barman when the swing doors opened and a vision stepped in. She hoped her mouth hadn't dropped open with shock. The guy had no face, in terms of the kind of faces the rest of the world had. His forehead was the size of a biscuit tin, but half his chin was missing, and Rosie could only see one eye. Two holes, as though moulded out of plasticene, were stuck in the middle of this monstrosity. His nose, she assumed. What passed for a mouth was a kind of slanted slit. The entire effect looked as though someone had made a really bad job of hollowing out a Halloween pumpkin. Trick or treat. The whole bar fell silent waiting to see which it was.

Billy leaned over covertly and whispered to Rosie. 'Fuck me. I'm tempted to say "Why the long face?"'

Rosie didn't even flinch. This was her man – which explained the muffled voice. She straightened up, composed herself. She needed a strong stomach for this.

He walked towards the bar and, with the one eye, looked at her squarely and made a sniffing noise.

'Rosie?' The muffled voice. She was right.

Rosie nodded, offered him a drink.

'Aye. Guinness,' he managed to say, then slowly turned his head to the barman. 'Got a straw, mate?'

Billy looked at him, and with all the deadpan delivery of a comedian at the Glasgow Empire in the good old days, he said, 'Happy Hour's just about to start, mate. Straws are compulsory.' He smiled.

If the man was smiling back it was hard to tell.

They moved over to a quiet corner where they could talk in private, and where Rosie hoped people wouldn't keep staring at him. She got up and went to the bar to bring the drinks over.

'Fuckin' hell, Rosie, where did you dig up John Merrick?' Billy whispered, his face straight.

'Shut it, Billy,' Rosie said. 'He's a contact. How much?'

She paid for the drinks as Billy put the straw into the Guinness and gave her a look. She returned to the table and sat down.

'Cheers,' she said, keeping her eyes on his face.

It was the kind of face you saw in fevered nightmares, a face you wanted to look away from, and definitely one you hoped you'd never meet in a dark alley.

'I don't even know your name.' Rosie stuck out her hand.

'Danny.' He took her hand and shook it warmly, and with a firm grip.

If he was able to have an expression, Rosie felt it would

have been one of sadness, resignation. It would be hard to look on the bright side with a face like that.

'You'll be wondering what happened to me,' Danny said, pointing to his face. 'This.' He sniffed through the holes-for-nostrils. 'Some state, eh?'

Rosie didn't know what to say. He lifted the pint of Guinness and pushed the straw into his mouth, sucking in a long drink.

'Shotgun,' he said. 'I shot my girlfriend when I caught her with another guy. Shot him too. Then I tried to do myself in. I didn't make a great job of it.'

'Christ,' Rosie said. 'Did you kill them?'

'Naw.' He sucked on the straw. 'But I made a right fuckin' mess of them. Couldn't finish the job right on myself though.' He put his head back and pointed with his finger. 'I put the gun under my chin, but it slipped when I fired it and all I did was blow half my fuckin' face off.'

Rosie felt she should say something but she didn't have a script for this.

'Look, I don't know you, Danny. But surely nothing is worth killing people for – or killing yourself?'

He put his drink down, took a deep breath and sighed.

'So they tell me. They took ten years in the jail to tell me that – all the different shrinks. But you know what? I knew it wasn't worth it about five fuckin' seconds after I fired the gun at them. I thought I'd killed them. Then, as soon as I did it, I knew it wasn't worth it. I knew I was going down for it. And I just thought, let's get to fuck out of here.'

He turned to Rosie. There was a little dent where his

other eye used to be. The eye that was looking at her filled up.

'Fuck. Why am I even telling you this?'

'Who knows? People tell me things. Must be the reporter in me.'

His swollen forehead was peppered with buckshot scars.

'You paid a big price, Danny. A big price.'

'Aye.' He sighed. 'Anyway, I'm out now, did my time, so I have to get on with it. Try and get some work. I could always haunt houses.'

Rosie kept her face straight. Time to move on.

'So, did you get the pass?'

'Course.' He went into his pocket and handed her the pass for Frankie Nelson, HMP Barlinnie. 'He gets a few visitors, so it'll not be suspicious. Your name's down as Jean Martin.'

'Thanks, Danny. What's he like? I mean to talk to. I know what he is, but what's he like?'

'He's a creepy cunt.' Danny shuddered. 'Makes my flesh crawl. He takes pictures of weans being abused by paedos like him and makes films out of it and sells it to other beasts all over the world.' He shook his head. '*He* needs shooting. Big time.'

'Is he a hardman?'

'He was alright with me. One look at my face and he knew he better not mess. But in the wing with the other beasts he's got a reputation as some fucking sadist. Who knows what these poofy fuckers do, but he likes to hurt people. Sicko.'

'Can you remember anything specific he said about

the missing girl in Spain? Amy? Can you talk me through how the subject came up?'

Danny drank from his pint.

'It was that day it had been all over the telly. There was a longer bit on the news, with people – experts, you know? – talking about what could have happened. Some ex-copper or something said kids got stolen for paedo and sex films. Mostly it happened in foreign countries, like in Thailand and stuff. There was some mention that it had spread to other countries now and people had to be careful with their weans abroad. That kind of stuff.'

Rosie nodded. 'And?'

'Well, I'd got to know him a bit more with being the turnkey, and sometimes he would tell me things. I just listened, because I wanted to see if I could pass any information on. So the day after the news thing, he told me he knew stuff. He didn't say he knew where she was or anything, but he said he'd bet she'd be sold for the paedo films.' He paused. 'Bastards.'

He looked at Rosie.

'And you know what? He even said he knew places where them snuff movies got made. You know, the ones where they film people getting murdered? He said there's some weans get stolen from places in Asia and now and again they get used for snuff movies. So many weans missing in places like that, nobody really gives a fuck. Unbelievable.'

Rosie thought of the picture of Amy the family had put out to the media. Her little white shoes, her curly hair, blue eyes.

'Do you think he was maybe bullshitting, about knowing about the snuff movies?'

Danny shrugged. 'Dunno. He says he doesn't make them movies, but he says there's a market for them. He distributes them films. That's what he and that other fucking poofy paedo pal of his were doing when they were living in Tenerife. I wouldn't put it past him to steal a wean and sell it.'

'But he's been in jail,' Rosie said. 'So he can't have known anything about Amy.'

'Naw, that's right,' Danny said. 'But what he says to me is that he has the connections. He says he can tell people where to look. That kind of thing.'

Rosie was beginning to wonder how much of what Nelson would tell her would be total crap, just a way for him to try to ingratiate himself because he was appealing against the length of his sentence.

She sighed. 'Thing is, you can't really trust that bastard as far as you can throw him. That's the problem. It might just be total rubbish. But I want to see him anyway. You never know.'

Rosie looked at her watch. She'd got as much as she was going to get here. She finished her drink.

Danny pushed his empty glass away and got up. They walked towards the door and Rosie glanced over her shoulder in time to see Billy grinning and giving her the thumbs up, as though she'd pulled.

Outside, the street looked dismal under the squally shower.

'Okay, Danny,' she said, sticking out her hand. 'Thanks

for your help. And I really appreciate you phoning me in Spain and getting this organised. Honestly. Thanks a lot.'

Danny fixed her with his eye as he shook her hand.

'If it helps, then good. Help get that wee lassie back.' He let go her hand. 'I'm not like all them other fuckers in jail. I was alright one time. I had a trade and stuff. Joiner. I just flipped my lid and I don't know why. I'm trying to live with it.'

He stared into the rain.

Rosie didn't know what to say, and found herself giving him a supportive pat on the shoulder.

'I can see that, Danny. It must be tough for you now.'

He nodded. 'I've got a bedsit in Bridgeton, so now it's up to me to get on with it. Anyway, hope it works out for you with Nelson.' He started to walk away.

'Thanks,' Rosie said. 'It was good to talk to you. Take care of yourself.'

He walked towards the traffic lights, and Rosie headed for her car. She was looking forward to getting to her flat and closing the door behind her.

CHAPTER 25

Sleep had been fitful, nightmarish. Rosie was running, terrified, up a cobbled street in the rain, trying to escape. But terror sprang from every corner. Danny's face, blood-stained, the mouth gaping and laughing, his hands grabbing for her. She ran down a dark alley and pushed open the big oak door at the bottom, and was suddenly blinded by the light. When her eyes finally adjusted she looked up, and all she could see were the slippers on the feet of a body, twisting at the end of a rope. Then the phone, ringing and ringing in her dreams, the way it had done that day when her world caved in. And once again she awoke with – as so often all her life – her face wet with tears.

She closed her eyes. She hadn't had the dream in over a month. She'd learned to deal with the nightmares down the years. A shrink friend once told her to imagine her mind like a linen cupboard full of neatly folded sheets and blankets. Sometimes, something happened and got pushed into the cupboard, mixing everything up, disrupting the order, the straight, pristine lines. It stayed messed up until you took out each sheet, folded it, placed it neatly back. That's what she'd taught herself to do. The nightmares always came back. But now they didn't overshadow her whole day. Well, mostly they didn't.

She swung her legs out of bed and stood up, looking at her naked frame in the full-length mirror. She was tanned and pleasantly toned from all the sun and exercise during her month in Spain. She looked at her pale blue eyes in the mirror and they looked back at her sadly. She smiled and they smiled back.

'Come on, Gilmour,' she said aloud. 'Let's get moving.'

She padded, still naked, into the kitchen of her flat and switched on the ring of the stove to brew the jag of Colombian coffee she needed to start her day. Then she went into the living room, pulled open the drapes and opened the doors to the balcony that looked down onto St George's Cross. The sound of the traffic below drifted up in the breeze. It was good to be home.

She noted the screen on her answer machine showed there were twenty-three unanswered messages. She pressed the button, hoping one would be from TJ, even though she knew in her gut it would not. As she listened to all of them, her stomach sinking a little with each one, she made coffee, squeezed two oranges and spooned some Greek yoghurt and muesli into a bowl, then went into the bedroom and pulled on a towelling robe. She put her breakfast on a tray and went out onto the balcony and, amazingly, the sky was bright blue. Al fresco breakfasts were a rarity in Glasgow, so such moments had to be seized.

She sipped her coffee and relished the familiar sounds of the city, but then her mind drifted to the one thought she'd been pushing away from the moment she got home. Her father.

Rosie had lain in her bath last night, trying to find what it was that she felt about him. But there was nothing. He was a figure who had been missing for so much of her life that he was scarcely even a childhood memory now. Those times, when she was just five or six, and he'd come home from wherever he was and take her and her mother to the fairground or to the seaside, were now so distant that she wasn't even sure what she felt. What she did remember clearly was the disappointment on her mother's face every Christmas. She would receive a letter with some far-off postmark, saying he was on his way home, and she'd stay sober during those weeks, as she cleaned and polished and waited. They both waited. Maybe tomorrow, her mother would say each night as she tucked Rosie into bed. But he never came. After a while, they both just stopped waiting and hoping.

Years and years later, Rosie could still call up the depth of that disappointment, and she had never really believed anyone's promises after that. It had taken a very long time for her to find belief in anything again. The only person she could believe in was herself, and she did that without anyone's help. After TJ had gone out of her life, she didn't feel like putting her trust in anyone ever again.

But still, she knew she would have to go and see her father. She finished her coffee and stood up. It was for another day.

First, she must go to Barlinnie Prison and share the same breathing space as a sick bastard called Frankie Nelson, a convicted murderer who raped children. She shook off her ghosts and went inside to get dressed.

Rosie eyed the mountain of mail she'd shoved into a corner when, armed with two bags of supermarket shopping, she'd pushed opened the door of her flat last night. By the look of it, most was junk mail. Saving rainforests was for tree-huggers like Sting with nothing better to do, but if there was a petition to pass a law stopping junk mail, Rosie would sign on the dotted line anytime. She scooped it up with both hands and headed for the bin in the kitchen.

It was only when she tried to stuff it all down to make room, that she did a double take. It was the childlike handwritten scrawl of her name and address on a yellow envelope that caught her attention. She fished out the envelope and examined it, turning it over to open it. Three little kisses were on the back and spidery writing said, 'From Gemma'. Rosie was surprised by the little skip in her stomach. She tore it open carefully as she walked into the living-room.

It was only one page, the writing slanted downwards with words scored out as though she'd taken time to get it right. Rosie's eyes scanned to the last words and she felt a catch in her throat.

I miss you Rosie. Lots and lots of love, Gemma.

Rosie swallowed and read the four lines again.

Hi Rosie. It's Gemma. I'm fine. Are you fine? Can we still get the pizza on your balcony? I like you. I live in a nice house now.

My foster mum says it's okay to see you. Can you come please?
I'd like that. I miss you Rosie. Lots and lots of love, Gemma.

The Glasgow phone number at the end looked as though
it had been written by an adult hand.

Rosie sat back on the sofa and pictured Gemma's face
that day in the cafe with the wreck of a junkie that was
her mum. She wasn't much, but she was all the kid had.
Something in Gemma's eyes had haunted Rosie since then,
and she'd never realised what it was until now. It was
optimism. That belief of a child that anything is possible
as long as your mother is there to hold your hand. Even
a hand as fragile as her mum's, as long as she's telling
you everything will be fine, even though you know she's
lying.

That day when they first met, Gemma didn't know any
better than Rosie had at that same age, that in reality
everything would not be fine, and one day she'd wake
up and her mum wouldn't be there any more. That for
the rest of her life she'd long to hold that hand one more
time, and no matter how many other hands she held,
she would never find one as warm and soft. Yet Gemma
still looked forward. She had tracked her down, written
a letter. And that single act of optimism in itself gave
Rosie hope.

She found herself dialling the number before she'd
thought it through. Then she stopped and put the phone
down. What was she doing? This was the kid of a ruined
young woman who'd walked into her life six months ago
and told her a story. It had cost Mags Gillick her life, and
if Rosie had known at the time that was the price, she'd

have walked away there and then. But she didn't. Mags died with her throat cut in a back alley off the Drag, murdered by someone she thought was a punter but who'd been sent to silence her by the men Rosie was trying to expose. She had never forgotten the expression on Gemma's face later that night when they roused her from sleep in the squalid flat where she lived with her mum. The tired little eyes that had lit up when they saw Rosie in the crowd in the street that night, and her forlorn look as the police car drove her away and Rosie had stood powerless.

But she could not allow herself to get involved in this. Gemma was with foster parents now. She wouldn't grow up in a junkie house where her mother left her alone at night. The reality is she was getting a chance she might never have had if her mother had lived. She didn't need Rosie to walk back into her life and give her hope of other things.

But then she lifted the phone again. What harm could it do to get in touch and just let the kid know she was still thinking about her. She remembered how alone she'd felt when she was taken away after her own mother died. The neighbours, the friends, everything she'd ever known was gone. She was left in a terrifying world where she knew no-one. No. Rosie wouldn't let that happen to Gemma.

'Hello?' The woman on the other end of the phone said.

'Oh. Hello. Er . . . Sorry to disturb you . . . I'm just making sure I've got the right phone number. Actually, can I ask if you are the lady who is fostering Gemma Gillick?'

'Who's this please?'

'Oh. Sorry. My name is Rosie Gilmour. I knew Gemma's mother. I . . . I've got a letter from her. From Gemma.'

The woman's voice changed.

'Aaah, yes, Rosie . . . My name is Alice Martin. I'm sorry about that. It was me who wrote the number on Gemma's letter. She's been driving me mad for weeks now to get in touch. I'm so sorry. Is it a problem for you?'

'No.' Rosie said quickly. 'Of course not. I was delighted to hear from Gemma. I think of her often.'

'Oh, she's the most wonderful little girl. Bright as a button.' She lowered her voice. 'To be honest she was a bit of a mess when she first came, but she's getting on so well now. She's so loving, and such a beautiful little girl.' The woman sounded sad.

'Is everything alright.'

'Yes.' She paused. 'It's just that I'm not too well in myself at the moment.'

'Oh, I'm sorry.'

'Would you like to see Gemma? She keeps asking. I mean, I see your name in the paper and I'm sure you're really busy.'

'Yes,' Rosie said. 'I'd love to see her. Actually I've been away for nearly six weeks – that's why I took so long to get in touch. Maybe we could meet in a cafe or something? Would that be alright? I'll be back in a few weeks.'

'That would be lovely. I have two other kids I foster as well. Do you want to say hello to Gemma? She's in her room watching the telly.'

'I'd love to.'

She heard Gemma's voice babbling away before she came on the phone.

'Hello?' The voice questioning.

'Hi, Gemma, how are you? It's Rosie?'

'Rosie! It's you! I thought you wouldn't phone. I wrote ages ago. Hiya, Rosie. How's you?' There was a little keyed up giggle to her voice and Rosie pictured her beaming at her foster mother and the thrill in her eyes that she had somebody, that she wasn't alone.

'So how are you, Gemma? Do you like your new home? Your foster mum says she'll bring you to see me. We can meet in town or something.'

'Really? Can I really come? Can I come to your house sometime? We never got the pizza. Can we still get the pizza? Or go to the cafe?'

Rosie laughed.

'We'll see, Gemma, we'll see. Put your foster mum back on. I'll see you soon. You be good now.'

'I am, Rosie. You won't forget? I told my pal at school and she said you'd forget, but I knew you'd come.'

'Okay. I will. Bye, Gemma.'

'Bye, Rosie. See you, Rosie. See you.'

CHAPTER 26

In the stuffy waiting room at Barlinnie prison, Rosie waited among the visitors sat in rows of plastic tubular chairs watching for the doors to open.

Angry young men sized up the prison warders, bristling with hate for anything and anyone in authority, especially if they wore the uniform of a cop – even worse if it was a screw. Today they'd be visiting someone who had graduated to the next level, someone doing time who had earned their respect. The only certainty for most of the boys in this room was that tomorrow, or some day soon, it would be their turn. And when that time came they'd stick out their chests and walk the walk in 'C'-Hall. They'd do their time and they'd earn their stripes like everyone else. And so it would continue, as it had done for generations. Like following your father down the pit or into university, depending on how your particular cookie crumbled.

Children ran up and down the aisles, excited. For all the crap that was going on in the lives of the adults around them, there was something resembling a party atmosphere here. Their dad was a hero, and soon he'd be getting marched from his cell to take them onto his knee and fill their head with stories of all the great things that were going to happen when he got home. Young mums, faces made up and dressed sexily, chatted with each other, swapping stories. Then there were the tired faces of mothers visiting sons, disappointment written all over them. Soon they'd be fighting back tears as they sat with their boys, ruined lives unfolding at every table.

Rosie looked around her and wondered how many of them were here to visit a sex offender, and what it must feel like living with the stigma of having a loved one who was a beast. Rapists, child murderers and perverts who made your skin crawl, yet somebody loved them enough to come and see them.

When the doors opened, everyone filed through to the adjacent area where they emptied their pockets and handbags under the scrutiny of a prison warder. Rosie had left her handbag in the boot of her car and now emptied her jacket pockets for the prison officer, who put everything into a locker and gave her a ticket. She had to open her mouth to be examined inside to make sure she wasn't carrying any drugs to pass on to the prisoner via a kiss. Fat chance, Rosie thought, knowing the pond life she was about to encounter.

Along with about twenty other visitors, she was taken to another room, separate from the mainstream visitors. The sex offenders were kept in the segregation wing of Bar-L, away from the hardmen in other halls who would cheerfully rip them open, convinced they were doing society a favour. And the truth is, they probably would be.

Rosie looked at the weary faces of some of the older women – mothers, who could scarcely believe that the baby they'd carried in their womb would turn into the twisted monster of tabloid headlines. Yet still they visited, listened, refused to desert their sons.

In the large, airy hall, the visitors sat at tables, waiting for their prisoner to appear. Rosie had photographs emailed to her in Spain of Frankie Nelson leaving court after his sentence, so she hoped she'd recognise him.

The door at the end of the hall opened and a procession of prisoners came in, some waving as they recognised their visitors. Rosie's eyes scanned the cons in their blue-and-white striped shirts, prison issue for convicted prisoners as opposed to the red and white stripes of those on remand. She'd visited cons several times before, and though some looked fit from working out at the gym, nothing could take away the pasty pallor all prisoners wore from being in jail.

These men looked the same, but they were different. They were the sickos she'd written about when she'd covered trials where the ordeals of their victims were revealed in court, and where jurors sometimes fainted at scene-of-crime photographs of the brutality inflicted on an innocent child or woman who had happened to be in the wrong place at the wrong time.

The last prisoner to come through the door was Frankie Nelson. Rosie's eyes made contact with his, and his lip curled a little, sending a shiver through her. He seemed to pull back his shoulders as he came towards her, with a confident stride bordering on a swagger. He didn't look left or right, but kept his eyes on Rosie.

'Rosie.' Nelson stuck out a hand as he sat down at the table facing her.

'Frankie.' Rosie didn't squeeze his hand. It felt fleshy and damp. She had the creeps already and he hadn't even said anything. She hoped her disgust wasn't written all over her face.

'You don't like this, do you?' he sniffed, 'guys like me. Beasts.'

Nelson held onto her hand for a second too long until she pulled it away. His dead eyes looked at her from beneath thick black eyebrows.

'You meet all kinds of people in my job, Frankie,' she said, looking straight at him.

'Are you scared of me, Rosie?' He sized her up. 'You look edgy.'

'I'm scared of nobody, Frankie.' She leaned closer to him and could smell his sweat. 'Not you, not anybody.'

She raised her eyebrows for added emphasis. Fuck him. A scumbucket like him wasn't going to put the frighteners on her. She clasped her hands on the middle of the table so they were almost touching his.

'So talk to me, Frankie. It was you who asked to see me.'

Silence. Rosie watched him. He looked at her, then down at the table, then back at her.

'How's Spain?' He flicked a glance at her hair then a quick glimpse at her body.

'It's not exactly a holiday,' Rosie said, flatly.

Nelson nodded. 'Aye. That wee lassie. They'll need tae get her soon or they can forget it.'

Rosie waited for him to say more. Tiny beads of sweat appeared above his top lip. It took her by surprise. There was weakness somewhere in his armour.

'I didn't come all the way from Spain for you to tell me that, Frankie.' She spread her hands out. 'What've you got to tell me? If it's useful for the investigation, then every minute is important. You know that.'

He ran his index finger across his top lip, removing the sweat.

'Aye, I know.' He shifted in his seat.

If Rosie didn't know better she'd have thought he was squirming. But this was a monster, who'd just been jailed for fifteen years for his part in the murder of a woman twelve years ago, because she'd threatened to tell police that he and his homosexual partner were abusing boys. People like him didn't squirm. Or did they?

'Do you know anything, Frankie, that you think might help in the hunt for Amy Lennon? Time is running out, if it's not already too late.' Rosie looked at the chewed fingernails on his fat hands.

He took a deep breath.

'There's a big market out there for porn films with kids in them. I used to sell them.' He paused, looking at Rosie for a reaction. 'And I made a few myself. Me and Vinny, before I fucked off. Me and him made films and sold them.'

Silence. His words hung in the air like pollution.

'Did you make the films with the kids you had sex with Frankie?' Rosie couldn't hide her revulsion.

'Fuck you, Rosie.' His eyes grew darker. 'I know you and your kind. You think you can put the world to rights, but you're all fucked up yourself.' His lip curled again, more of a snarl than a smile. 'Hey. I know you nearly got done over in Glasgow, by the way. You rattled a lot of cages. You might rattle one too many one of these days and someone will rip you to bits.' He made a tearing gesture with his hands.

Rosie held his stare.

'It's not about me, Frankie. It's not about you. It's about a frightened wee lassie who doesn't deserve to be taken away from her mammy.'

'Is that what you were, Rosie? A frightened wee lassie who wanted her mammy?'

He smirked. Evil bastard. Rosie wondered if he knew of her past or if he was just pushing any buttons to see if he could rile her.

'Look,' Rosie said, trying to sound less confrontational. She put her hands up. 'Listen. What you are and what you've done is for you to sort out, Frankie. It's not my business. But you want honesty? No. I don't like it, and no, I don't like people like you. But I care about the life of an innocent kid. You want to hate me for that, fine. There's nothing more to say here.' She pushed her chair back. 'I'm sorry to have taken up your time.' She stood up knowing it was a risky move.

'Wait. Sit doon.'

She sat down.

'I'll tell you what I know.'

Rosie listened as Nelson told her how he and his homosexual lover, Vinny Paterson, had moved to Tenerife to escape the heat over the disappearance of the woman neighbour they'd killed twelve years ago in Ayrshire. Vinny was still on the run. They hadn't meant to kill her, it had just got out of hand. They'd only been trying to frighten her because she was going to shop them. He shrugged, and said the boys were all about twelve to fourteen and they were alright with the sex as long as they were getting money. Rosie tried to keep her expression impassive.

'It was Vinny who lost the plot that night,' Nelson said. 'She was drunk when she came in to our house and we had been taking pictures of some boys. She started shouting that she was going to shop us and Vinny slapped her. Then she grabbed the bread knife and lunged at him, and I managed to grab her and get it off her. I shoved her and she hit the floor. I heard her head crack. I didn't know if she was dead but there was blood. Then Vinny just went berserk. He took the knife and stabbed her chest about ten times, so we had to get rid of her. We put her in a wheelie bin and took her to the sea and weighted her down and dumped her.'

He paused.

'So you moved to Tenerife.' Rosie didn't want to hear any more of the murder of his neighbour or his earlier life. She had read about all that in the newspaper cuttings.

'Aye,' Nelson said. 'That's when we really got involved with the porn flicks.'

He told her that he and Vinny made porn films in the basement of an apartment in Las Americas, with kids they had picked up at train stations and on the streets. There was a huge market across Europe where you could buy porn movies with kids in them from almost anywhere in the world – Asia, Africa, India. Take your pick, he said. It had been organised in recent years by Russian and Albanian gangsters who were involved in everything from drugs to people-trafficking. Making porn films with kids was just another strand of their organisation.

'Can you tell me any names, Frankie? Where the main players are?'

'Morocco,' he said. 'People out there who work with the Russians. That's where Vinny is now. Or he was . . .' His voice trailed off.

'What do you mean?' Rosie asked. 'What happened?'

Silence. She waited.

'Okay, I'll tell you something. It's up to you what you do with it, but it's dangerous.'

Rosie nodded.

'Snuff movies.'

She felt an uncomfortable tightness in her chest.

'Vinny wanted us to go into that. Killing weans on film.'

'Jesus,' was all Rosie managed to say.

Nelson shook his head.

'That's not me.' He looked at Rosie. 'You think I'm a monster. I don't care what you think, but I don't kill weans.' He paused. 'But Vinny did.'

'Vinny killed a child? Who did he kill?' Rosie whispered.

'A wee boy in Tenerife. He was always in the papers as reported missing, if you check back. He was never found. But I know what happened to him. Vinny killed him. He filmed it. That's when I left. That night. He filmed it. I haven't seen Vinny since, but I know he's still in this.' He shook his head. 'There was always a streak in Vinny. He wanted to push things further and further. He didn't know when to stop.'

'Do you think Vinny or any of the people he works with could be connected to the missing girl?'

Nelson nodded slowly. 'You find Vinny, and you'll find that wee lassie.'

The bell rang to sound the end of visiting. Nelson stood up and stretched out his hand.

'That's all I can tell you.' He shook Rosie's hand. 'You still think I'm a monster, don't you?'

Rosie looked at him.

'Thanks for your information, Frankie. I hope it helps.'

CHAPTER 27

In the steady drizzle, Rosie drove down London Road in the East End of Glasgow towards St John's Hostel. She'd tried to brace herself for what she might find there when she asked for a man called Martin Gilmour, but how could she really prepare herself for a moment she'd waited for all her life. Now all she had to do was knock on the door.

Part of her wanted to drive past and keep on going. She already had more than enough on her plate. But a much bigger part of her wanted to see what he looked like, to hear his voice, see what childhood memories it would trigger. For so long he'd been like a phantom to her, and when she'd tried to picture him older, the way that Marion had described him when he'd come to the *Post*, she couldn't. The only way to find out was to do it now. By tomorrow night, she'd be back in Spain. Whoever it was she was going to meet now was not a part of her life any more.

She parked her car close to the hostel and hurried through the rain to the front door. She pressed the bell and the door buzzed and unlocked without any voice coming through the intercom. Security obviously wasn't a strong point.

The smell hit her as soon as she stepped into the dingy foyer. Stale cigarette smoke and unwashed clothes mingled with a vague odour of onions and cooking fat. The black and white tiled floor in the hallway looked dirty in the gloomy light, and the reception appeared to be in semi-darkness. If you ended up here, just looking around you would tell you how crap your life had turned out. Rosie shuddered to think what the rooms must look like – though in a place like this there probably weren't rooms, dormitories more likely, with rows of rancid, festering down-and-outs sleeping off the booze.

'Can I help ye?' A skinny girl popped her blonde spiky head up from below the reception desk.

'I'm looking for Martin Gilmour,' Rosie said, stepping towards the desk. 'I believe he's staying here.'

She didn't want to say guest. It wasn't the kind of place that had guests.

'Gilmour?' The girl licked her finger and flicked open a big red book and scanned down the names. She let out a sigh. 'Martin Gilmour. Right. I see him.' She chewed gum with her mouth half open, and looked Rosie up and down. 'Aye. He's staying here.'

Rosie gave her an impatient look. 'Well, do you know if he's in? I'd like to talk to him.'

She would have liked to wipe the bored expression from the teenager's face.

'I'll go and see if he's in the residents' lounge. Everyone's out of their rooms by this time.' She rolled her eyes upwards. 'Pubs are open. Most of them are out of here by now.' She walked from behind the reception. 'Who will I say wants him?'

'I'll come with you,' Rosie said, giving her a look that dared her to try and stop her.

The girl said nothing and her high heels clicked as she walked along the corridor with Rosie at her back. They came to a door with a small glass window. The girl peered through the wire grille into the room.

'He's in there. I think that's him over at the window.'

Rosie glared at her, irritated by the affectation of looking up his name in the book, when she already knew who he was and what he looked like. The girl gave her a dirty look and walked away. Rosie stood in the corridor until she disappeared.

Her mouth felt dry. This was it. For more than thirty years – long after she'd stopped waiting, long after she stopped hoping – she'd wondered what had become of her father. And now a door with a little window was all that stood between them. She put her head to the grille and looked in.

One man sat in an armchair sound asleep, his mouth open. Another was on the couch, reading a newspaper. Then, at the large bay window, a third man with his back to her stood gazing out at the rain.

He was shorter than she remembered, and instead of the shock of wavy black hair that had always been neatly slicked back, she saw a grey unkempt fuzz and a bald patch. The broad shoulders he used to carry her on were slumped. Jesus! Who was this old man? She tried to swallow but there was nothing there. Her stomach churned. She could turn about now, walk away and never look back. An image of her mother, the way she used to be when all three of them sat around the table listening to the animated stories of his travels, flashed behind her eyes.

Rosie felt the cold metal of the door handle on her fingers. She pushed open the door and walked in. The man on the sofa looked up.

'Hello, hen,' he said, and went back to his newspaper.

Rosie didn't look at him. Her eyes were fixed on the man with his back to her, now turning around slowly, as though a sixth sense told him she was there.

Their eyes met. No words were spoken. They just stood there looking at each other. The only remnant of the man she remembered were the pale blue eyes she'd inherited. They'd grown dim with age, but they were his alright. Then, to her dismay, he began to crumple. He opened his mouth to speak, but nothing came out, and she could see tears well up in those blue eyes.

'Rosie,' he said, standing at the window as though frozen to the spot. He shook his head. 'I'm sorry.'

Rosie's tears stung her by surprise and she couldn't stop them. The old man on the couch looked at both of them, then he got up and left the room. Rosie put her hand to her mouth. She tried to speak but her throat was closed.

She took a couple of steps towards him as he stood gazing at her, tears now rolling down his cheeks. This was her father, this sad, weak old man, who used to make the world safe for her, who was now weeping. And she too was crying in this bleak, chilly, damp room, where the stories of thousands of desperate, broken lives must have unfolded down the years.

'Where were you?' Rosie's heard herself saying in a voice that seemed to come from the child inside her. 'Why didn't you come back for me?' She wiped her tears with the back of her hand.

His head dropped to his chest.

'I'm sorry, Rosie. I couldn't. I couldn't face it.' He covered his face with one hand. 'I'm a coward, Rosie. I failed your mammy.' His chest heaved. 'And I couldn't come and get you . . . I knew I couldn't take care of you on my own, Rosie . . . I was a waster.'

Rosie looked at this wreck of a man, remembering his strength, his laughter. She saw the tremor in his hand as he wiped his tears and sniffed. She saw the cuffs of his jumper, ragged at the wrist, and the shapeless trousers that were too long for him, bagging over his scruffy shoes. He wasn't out of place here among the down-and-outs. What had he become?

Rosie shook her head. Even though she knew she owed him nothing, and she could justify it to herself if she turned and walked away right now, she couldn't. Because, in the tired blue eyes that looked back at her, she could picture her mother and the look on her face when she saw her big strong man coming up the path from his travels and waving up to the window where they'd stood bursting with anticipation. Now it was Rosie who found strength.

'Come on,' she said, sniffing. 'Let's get out of here. We'll go for a cup of tea.' She watched as he picked up his jacket. He followed her as she led the way out of the room.

In the cafe around the corner from the hostel, Rosie listened as her father told her his story. While they'd hurried through the rain, Rosie noticed he was out of breath, and his face looked a little grey by the time they got inside. She motioned him to sit down at one of the corner tables, then ordered tea; and he asked for some toast from the waitress, who was looking at them from the counter as though she'd seen it all before.

Rosie waited for him to speak. Eventually he did.

'I didn't know, Rosie,' he said, his voice just above a whisper. 'About your mammy. I . . . I hadn't been home for nearly two years before it happened.'

'I know. We waited every day for you.' She wasn't going to make it easy.

'I'm sorry.' He shook his head and looked at her. 'I know it's too late for that now – sorry's not enough, but . . .' He sighed. 'I don't know what else to say.'

'So how did you find out?' Rosie poured the tea for both of them, and pushed a cup towards him.

She was trying to be detached, as though she was interviewing someone. But inside she was shaking.

'I came back. I'd changed my job. The boat I was working on went out of business and we were stranded in Brazil. I had to find another boat and that took time. Finally, I got a job and started making my way back home.' He

sipped his tea, searching Rosie's face for a flicker of understanding.

'You could have written a letter telling her what
happened.'

'I know,' he nodded, 'but I was that busy trying to
survive and get some kind of job.'

Rosie said nothing. It wasn't that she didn't believe
him, but it wasn't enough just to say he was busy trying
to survive. It wasn't nearly enough, when her mother was
being driven to the point of suicide with every passing
week waiting for word from him.

'So,' he went on, 'I came back in the December.' He
gazed beyond Rosie. 'The boat that was heading to Europe
was taking months, but it was steady work and at least
I knew I was on my way. I left it at Liverpool and made
my way back up the road. I had stuff for you and your
mammy – presents.' He almost smiled. 'I was nearly at
the house when I went into the pub for a drink and who
was standing at the bar but big Joe Campbell from up
the road from us. Remember him?'

Rosie nodded.

'Well. He told me . . . I . . .'

He covered his mouth with his hand and started crying.

'I'm so sorry, Rosie.'

Rosie felt her throat tighten. She wanted to tell him
how, during that December, she was stuck in the children's home in Dundee; how she'd sat at the window
every night looking at the snow falling on the long,
winding driveway, convinced that her daddy would come
for her and take her home. But the words wouldn't come.

And so they sat, both of them imprisoned by memories that had haunted them for so long. Then her father reached across the table and put his trembling hand on hers.

Rosie's mobile rang, crashing in on the moment. She fished it out of her pocket. It was Adrian. She quickly composed herself.

'Hello, Rosie.'

'Adrian. Hi. You okay?'

Adrian would not be calling her unless something was happening.

'When are you coming back? I have very important information for you. Very important.'

'I'm back tomorrow night, Adrian, I'll see you then. But what's happened?' Rosie knew he wouldn't talk much on the phone, but she was curious.

'I know why the girl was taken. Why Amy was kidnapped. Is to do with her grandfather, Martin Lennon's father. Something happened in Russia.'

'What?' Rosie was confused. All she knew about the Lennon family was that Martin's father, who had owned the estate agency, had died of a heart attack while he was in Amsterdam on business a few months ago.

'I can't talk now. I tell you when you come. Call me when you are here.' The phone clicked off.

Rosie looked at her father, conscious that he'd been watching her while she was on the phone.

'What do you want? Why did you come back?' The words were out before she could stop herself, and she could see his face fall.

He looked at the floor and they sat for a moment, both taking in the cruelty of her words.

'I mean, why come back after all this time? Do you have plans to stay here?' She put out her hands almost apologetically. 'I . . . I don't know what to say to you. What do you want to do?'

For what seemed like a long time he said nothing, but just looked at her face, as though he was drinking in every feature. The light seemed to come back in his eyes for a moment as he spoke.

'You're so like her, Rosie. Every move. Except the eyes. They're mine. But you have her spirit.'

'Her spirit was broken, long before she died.' Rosie couldn't help herself.

He nodded, then looked at her with the same sadness as when they'd met just an hour ago.

'I'm dying, Rosie.'

She put her head back and looked at the ceiling, then closed her eyes, shaking her head. She looked at him, but couldn't speak.

'I came home because I want to be buried beside her.'

She didn't need to ask him about the simple wooden cross that had become old and worn with age at the pauper's grave where her mother was buried. But if he'd been there, why hadn't he tried to find her?

He nodded as though reading her mind. 'I'm sorry, Rosie. I put the cross there. It was all I could do.'

They sat in silence as the waitress came up and cleared

the table and Rosie handed her a fiver, waving her away.

Then Rosie gave him his jacket and stood up. He wasn't much, but he was all she had.

'Come on. Let's go home.'

CHAPTER 28

As usual, Leka was late. Besmir was glad to be in the shade, unlike the foreign tourists who sat with their chairs positioned so the sun beat down on them.

Besmir had been waiting at the cafe on Plaza Naranja in the heart of Marbella's old town for thirty minutes. He decided he would give Leka another ten minutes then he would call him. He fidgeted with his lighter, irritated, because he knew that Leka's habitual lateness was all about power. He wouldn't be late if he was meeting Daletsky. He lit a cigarette as he saw Leka coming up the cobbled street towards him, his bodyguard a few steps behind him. He steeled himself.

He and Hassan had made a pact that night at the driver's family home that they would work together to get Amy back and to help the other kidnapped children. They'd talked long into the night making a plan, knowing one wrong move, one sniff of their betrayal and they'd both be history.

It had to begin with Besmir getting out of the

organisation. Leka had promised him that the kidnapping job would be his last, that he'd get his money and be free to do what he wanted. But Besmir knew he would never get out. As an enforcer for Leka, he knew too much – long before he was told to kidnap the little girl.

'Besmir,' Leka, said, stretching out both hands as though greeting a favourite son. 'You did the job well.'

He sat down. The waiter came over and he ordered a beer for himself when Besmir said he was fine with his coffee.

'The Moroccans are very happy with the blue girl. Very happy.' He watched Besmir and lit his cigarette.

Besmir shrugged. 'Is not my business, Leka, but I was wondering, why take the girl to Morocco? What will happen to her?'

Leka looked at him, and Besmir cursed himself for asking such a stupid question. It wasn't a good start.

'I mean, what difference does it make to her, Morocco or here? If she is valuable, she's just as valuable here. No?' He tried to get over his mistake.

Leka said nothing. Then he looked around the cafe and pulled his chair closer to Besmir.

'Why do you ask about the girl, Besmir?' His eyes were cold. 'Did you become attached to the little fëmijë?' He used the Albanian word for baby.

Besmir blew smoke upwards and looked away, aware that Leka was scrutinising him.

'No. I don't care. Is just a job for me. I'm only curious.'

Leka raised a finger and wagged it in mock warning.

'Curiosity, my friend. Not good. It killed the cat, I think the English say.'

Besmir didn't reply and tried to look uninterested.

They sat for a moment in silence, then Leka spoke.

'The girl is no value to us,' he said. 'I sold her to prove a point to the Moroccans. We are making a deal with them. We let them have some of the people we bring into the country for their whorehouses, and in return they give us a share of their drugs trade. They have the drug routes all to themselves. We want some of it – a lot of it. We traded the girl to show these Moroccan bastards that we can do anything. We can even steal a British kid. It shows them how powerful we are. And to make them understand that if they don't do business with us, we will simply take their business away from them.' He examined his manicured fingernails. 'They will sell the girl on. It is nothing to me. Or you.'

Besmir nodded. 'Makes sense.'

Leka went into his pocket and brought out a wad of notes.

'So,' he said. 'Now you get your reward for a job well done.' He kept the money tightly covered in his hand and put it into Besmir's hand.

'Thank you.' Besmir said, stuffing it into his jeans pocket.

'Are you not going to count it?'

'No. I don't need to.'

'But if you count it you will see there is an extra five hundred euros for you – for being so patient when I sent you to Tangiers.'

Besmir raised his eyebrows. 'Thank you. I will need it on my travels.'

Leka looked at him, disappointed.

'You are really going, Besmir?'

'Yes. But only for a little while. I wanted to talk to you about it.'

Leka waited, his expression blank.

'There is a woman,' Besmir lied. 'She is pregnant with my baby, but she is not here just now. She is Spanish, from the north – Galicia. She has gone back there for a while to be with her family, but I want to be there for a couple of months until the baby is born. Then I will come back.' He hoped he was giving a convincing performance.

Leka was quiet for a moment.

'Why not keep the girl here?'

'She want to go back with her family. She want the baby to be born in Galicia. I can bring her here after the baby is born.'

'But you will come back, Besmir? To work? Or have you gone soft now because you are going to be a father? Is that why you asked about the blue girl?'

'No, of course not,' he said quickly. 'I told you. I was just curious. And yes, I am coming back, in a couple of months.'

'You must come back, Besmir. Because for you, this is all there is. You can go and live in the north with a nice Spanish wife, but you will be like all the other peasants from Eastern Europe. Your life will be a struggle wherever you go. Dead-end jobs, everyone hating you because you are foreign, and distrusting you because you are Albanian. People like you and me – Albanians, Russians, Romanians, the people from the Eastern bloc. Nobody wants us. We have to make our own business. Look at Daletsky. I will be the same as him one day. And you could be too. But not in some stupid job like the others.'

Besmir nodded. 'That is what I want, Leka. But for a little while I have to give my woman what she wants – to be with her family in Galicia. Then I will be back.'

'Alright my friend.' Leka stood up. 'You have made your mind up. I wish you well. And I will see you on your return.' He smiled but his eyes were flat. 'With your little baby. I hope it is a boy child. Strong. Like the father.'

Besmir stood up. 'Is okay for me, a boy or girl.'

He watched as Leka turned and walked away. His bodyguard got up from the table next to them and followed behind.

It was getting dark by the time Besmir made his way back to his apartment. He knew Leka didn't believe a word he'd said and he was ready. He hadn't gone straight to the apartment after leaving Leka, but wandered around the town, keeping himself in the sidestreets, getting into taxis and hoping he would lose whoever was following him. He hadn't seen anyone but he was sure Leka would have had him tailed.

When he got to the building he went round the back and up the fire escape onto the roof. He knew he could enter his top floor apartment from a trap door on the roof. He eased it open and silently dropped inside the bedroom.

Besmir moved like a cat, listening, peering in the darkness. He slipped the knife out of his pocket. He saw a door in the living room move a fraction. He pretended he hadn't noticed and walked in, the knife in his hand.

As soon as he put his foot into the room, the man jumped him and stabbed him in the arm. Besmir turned swiftly and plunged his knife into his attacker. It was Sergei, Leka's bodyguard. He dropped like a sack onto the floor.

Blood seeped through Besmir's shirt but he couldn't stop now. He went quickly into the bedroom and threw some things into his small rucksack then climbed down the fire escape and hailed a taxi. He looked at his watch. If he hurried he could get the midnight ferry to Morocco. If he was still in Spain by the morning he would be dead.

CHAPTER 29

'So tell me exactly what they said, Adrian. This is a real turn-up for the books.'

Rosie listened as Adrian gave her the details of the conversation he'd overheard between Daletsky and another of his Russian friends who was visiting. Leka was also in the car. He'd been driving them to Puerto Banus, and Daletsky and his friend were talking in Russian together. What they didn't know was that Adrian had understood most of what they were saying. For nearly two years in Glasgow he'd had a Russian student girl-friend, he told Rosie, and he'd picked up the language.

'You're a revelation every day,' Rosie grinned as she poured him a coffee. He'd been waiting at the hotel for her when she arrived back from Glasgow. He was very excited, which was an eye-opener in itself. Adrian didn't do excited.

As they settled themselves on the terrace of Rosie's bedroom, Adrian had told her that Martin Lennon's father, who died of a heart attack eight months earlier while on business in Amsterdam, had been up to his eyes in scandal. He had been involved in the death of a prostitute in Russia months before. But he had managed to keep it under wraps.

'Daletsky told Leka and the other man that the kid, Amy, was stolen for revenge – payback he said – for an old comrade.'

'Payback?'

'Yes. I heard him say that word, that he had an old friend, a comrade, named Uri, a Ukrainian. This is what he said. They fought together in Afghanistan in the war, and they see many terrible things. It was a long war. But after the war finish, they went different ways – Uri goes home to Ukraine and works in a factory, and Daletsky goes to Russia and made all the money.

'He did not hear again from him until one day this year, when Uri came to Russia, to his business, asking to see him. Daletsky said his friend was like the shadow of the man he knew. It seem his daughter – he had only one daughter – was killed in Moscow. She had left home, and he did not know that she was a prostitute in the hotels, hanging around the bars and picking up Western businessmen. One of them was Martin Lennon. I heard him say the name, and I understood what he was saying, because I know this name. I was very surprised, Rosie.'

'No wonder. Go on.'

In fact, following Adrian's call yesterday, before she'd left Glasgow Rosie had phoned a private eye friend to look into Martin Lennon senior's dealings. So far he hadn't come back to her.

'I am driving, and listening hard,' Adrian continued, 'and I hear Daletsky say that Martin Lennon killed the prostitute in his hotel room in Moscow.' He drew on his cigarette. 'Some sex game goes wrong. She is found the next day in the room with a sheet pushed in her mouth, naked and dead.' He raised his eyebrows at Rosie. 'And she is pregnant. Was.'

They sat quietly for a moment as Rosie processed the information.

'Was anything said about how Martin Lennon could have got out of the country without being arrested, after leaving a dead body in a hotel room? That just doesn't seem possible. In Russia?'

'I don't know, Rosie. It is Russia. It depend on who you know. You can get anything you want in Russia if you know the right people.'

'But Lennon was an estate agent. He bought and sold property, he wasn't a gangster. How would someone like that know anyone in Russia powerful enough to get him out of the country and in those circumstances?'

'Who knows, Rosie? I do not know the answer to that.'

Rosie thought about the Lennons and wondered if they had any inkling that their little girl's grandfather had been involved in the seedy death of a prostitute. Surely they couldn't be hiding something like that from the police investigation.

'It's hard to believe that they would actually kidnap someone's innocent child because of something her grandfather did. Is there anything these people won't do?'

'Nothing, Rosie.' Adrian's jaw tightened. 'I told you. They do anything to protect themselves and their people. They do not care who they kill.'

'So what else did Daletsky say? Was this all some grand plan or something? I mean, how did they know the Lennons were in Spain?'

Adrian blew air out of pursed lips. 'I do not know for sure. Only one thing Daletsky said is that one month ago one of his men made contact with the son of Lennon. With Amy's father.'

'You're kidding.'

'No.'

'And?'

'Well,' Adrian pressed his fingers to his temple, concentrating. 'I did not hear all what he said. But I think he say something about they had spoken about properties in Spain that Lennon would be selling for them. His father had been selling. I think that is what he said. He told them he was coming to Spain for the holiday, and maybe they would have a meeting. They were going to make a deal.'

'So it could be that Daletsky's men were just fishing to find out where he would be, and bingo, he just happens to be coming here? So they start planning their kidnap from then?'

Adrian shrugged. 'Who knows?'

'Christ,' Rosie said. 'This puts a different complexion on things.' She got up and paced the terrace. 'I wonder if Martin Lennon met this man Daletsky or one of his cohorts for talks while he was here. If he did, maybe Martin even told them where he was staying. Maybe he even took his wife and Amy along to the meeting. What if he introduced his kid to the very people who would kidnap her?'

'Is possible, Rosie. Is all possible.'

'So, Adrian,' Rosie said, 'would they really kidnap, maybe even kill, little Amy for sheer badness and revenge? She's innocent. So are the Lennons.'

Adrian sighed. 'Yes, they would, Rosie. They would. I don't know what they did with the girl. All I know is that Daletsky said he got the call from Morocco and that the girl had been delivered. So she is in Morocco. Besmir, the Albanian, took her. Remember, I told you?'

'But why? Delivered to who? What do you think, Adrian?' Rosie felt sick, remembering her conversation with Frankie Nelson and how Vinny was making child porn movies in Morocco.

'Who knows?' Adrian said. 'They would use a little girl to bargain with the Moroccans about anything – drugs, arms trade. That's what they do with people.'

Almost on cue, Rosie's mobile rang. It was Mickey Kavanagh, an ex-cop turned private eye who she'd known for more than a decade. He was more clued up than most working cops.

'Hey, Mickey. Howsit going?'

'Not bad, Rosie. Pissin' down, but I'd rather be here than where you are. At least it's safer.'

'Ha!' Rosie could picture Mickey's cheeky grin. 'What do you mean? Have you found any info on old Martin Lennon?'

'I have. That stuff you said, about something happening in Russia? Well, it's kosher. He was involved with some hooker he picked up.'

'And?' Rosie knew Mickey liked a bit of drama. 'Come on Mickey, I'm on the edge of my seat here.'

Mickey confirmed the story Rosie had heard from Adrian.

'Are you serious, Mickey?'

'As serious as a Moscow lift operator. Have you ever seen the torn faces on these guys? In fact all of the Russians?'

'Come on, Mickey. This is important.'

'Apparently randy old Martin Lennon got off his mark after the kinky legover situation went tits-up, so to speak. He got the first flight out of Moscow, which was to Paris – not his original destination – but he wanted out of Russia smartish. Understandably. Then he's back to the UK as if nothing happened. A few months later he snuffs it of a heart attack in Amsterdam while on business. That was straight up though, nothing dodgy on his death.'

'So how come the cops in Russia didn't follow up on the dead girl? How come they didn't contact Interpol or cops in the UK? He must have at least merited a bit of questioning, a bit of getting his collar felt.'

'That I'm not sure of, Rosie. What I can tell you is that Lennon was over in Moscow on business. He was going to be branching out his estate agent business to Spain, and he was seeing some property developer who was going to show him properties off-plan they were building in Spain.'

'You mean he was meeting with a gangster?'

'They're all gangsters in Russia. There are no businessmen, only hoods.'

'Are you saying Martin Lennon was a gangster? That just doesn't ring true.'

'No. That's the thing, Rosie. He wasn't. He was quite innocent really, in a lot of ways. He'd met this developer in Spain at one of these estate agent conferences they have down on the Costa, and they'd struck up a kind of friendship. They'd kept in touch, but the Russian's property agency was just a money-laundering scam. Lennon appears to have known nothing about that. He'd be getting a using to launder their dirty money. Or if he did know, he was turning a blind eye in order to do the property deal.'

Rosie was still confused. 'But that doesn't explain how he didn't get questioned by Russian police, or even UK police,' she said.

'Well, for starters, Rosie, I don't think anyone in Russia – cops or otherwise – gives a toss about a dead hooker. Plenty more where they came from, so nobody busts a gut to investigate it. The hotel don't want to make a fuss because it's bad for business. Plus, it only takes a few quid greasing some official palms and the whole incident gets buried. That's the end of that.'

Rosie had heard enough. That *was* the end of that, until Lennon's grand-daughter got stolen from a beach in Spain under the nose of her parents. Someone wanted revenge – badly. The conversation Adrian had overheard was now sounding blindingly possible, and Rosie's heart was picking up the pace.

'Okay, Mickey. That's all fascinating stuff. Thanks a lot.'

She didn't need to ask where his info came from. Mickey had contacts everywhere, from the streets to the murky corners of MI6.

'Aye, no worries, Rosie. That's a big dinner you owe me.' He paused. 'But a word in your shell-like darlin': just watch your back. I've an idea why you want this info, but be careful what cages you're rattling over there. These people make big Jake Cox look like the Widow Twanky.'

Rose chuckled, even if it was a nervous chuckle.

'Right. I'll be careful. Big dinner is on when I get back to Glasgow. Thanks, pal.' She had no sooner hung up when her mobile rang again.

'Hola, Javier. I was just about to call you.'

'I'm on my way to your hotel. What room are you in?'

'Give me five minutes and I'll call you back.'

Rosie looked at Adrian. She knew she could trust Javier with her life, but it was only fair to Adrian that no other person saw him with her. She'd told Javier about his sister and that the big Bosnian was crucial to the investigation, but Adrian preferred to be in the background for the moment. He stood up, sensing her unease.

'I will go now, Rosie. You can phone me.' Adrian's mobile rang and he took it out of his pocket. 'It is Leka.' He put the phone to his ear and walked past Rosie. She heard him say 'hello' as he was going out of the bedroom door.

'So has your lover gone?' Javier kissed Rosie fleetingly and walked past her into the room.

'Come in,' Rosie smiled, sarcastic. 'He's having a shower.'

She turned away from him and walked out onto the terrace. 'We can talk out here, Javier – let my lover slip away quietly.'

'Of course.' He gave her a wry smile. 'Discretion is everything.'

He gave her all the information he'd dug up linking one of the offshoots of Daletsky's complex business empire to people-trafficking. It was checked out and solid from his best Guarda Civil contact. Rosie could see that, as ever, Javier had done a meticulous job.

With the interview already done in Sarajevo with Katya, the rescued friend of Adrian's sister, Rosie was ready to write the next big exclusive, linking Carter-Smith to Daletsky's empire. She would have dinner in her room and write it tonight. McGuire would be well pleased.

But Rosie's thoughts were already running to Morocco: Frankie Nelson's 'find Vinny' words were still ringing in her ears.

'Javier, do you have any contacts in Morocco?'

'I don't, but I know a few people who do. What do you need?'

She told him about the interview with Frankie Nelson and what he had said about Vinny and the child porn movie trade in Morocco.

'Sick bastard. I'd kill the *coño* with my bare hands.'

'I'd be in the queue behind you, Javier, believe me, but what do you think the chances are of tracking him down?'

Javier stretched out his long legs.

'I will speak to my people. A Brit paedo in Morocco should be easy to find.' He looked at Rosie as though reading her mind. 'You think the kid is definitely in Morocco?'

'Yep. My friend, Adrian, the Bosnian who's just been here. He told me.'

Javier grinned.

'So that's who was here when I called you, Rosita. Thought you were a bit cagey.'

'Don't be daft, Javier. He's my friend – has been for a while back in Glasgow.' Then the smile went from her face. 'I owe him my life. Quite literally.' She saw Javier's surprise. 'I'll tell you about it some time, when we're drunk. Not now.'

She told him about the conversation Adrian had over-heard about Daletsky's connection to Lennon's late father, and watched his eyes widen at the possibility that this had all been set up for revenge.

'I want to go to Morocco, Javier.'

Javier gave a little laugh and rolled his eyes upwards.

'I knew you were going to say that.'

Rosie wasn't smiling. 'I'm serious, Javier. I want to go there, find that Vinny bastard and get him done. I want to go there and maybe, just maybe, we can track Amy down. We have to try.'

Javier shook his head.

'Don't you think the police should know about this latest information? It changes everything, Rosie. Have you told your editor this?'

She wanted to tell him to stop thinking like a cop but didn't want to risk a punch-up this early.

'I've only just been told about it in the last half hour, Javier. I'm still taking it in.'

'Bullshit, Rosie. I know you too well. You're thinking you can just waltz into Morocco and hunt down Amy's kidnappers. Go for glory.'

'It's not like that, Javier.'

She didn't want to snap, but she was running the show here. She leaned her back on the railing and looked at him.

'If we tell the police, or my paper publishes the story, then the people who have got Amy will feel cornered and could do anything, even kill her to get rid of her.'

'How do you know they've not already done that?'

'I don't. But I want a chance to run at this myself before everyone wades in – police, media, etcetera. If we can track down this Vinny, maybe get Adrian to lean on him, you never know where that might lead us.'

Javier let out a long sigh.

'I worry when you're like this, Rosie. It's dangerous. For all of us.'

'Not for you, Javier. You just have to set us up with the contacts. Get us a minder.' She pushed her hair back and folded her arms.

He laughed.

'Temper, Rosita! You think I would let you go there without me?' He stretched out and touched her arm.

'I hoped you'd say that.'

Javier stood up and leaned on the railing, looking at her. 'Do you want to have dinner, Rosie? We can talk more, make some plans?'

She looked out to sea, knowing he was watching her. She couldn't think of a better way to spend the evening. She sighed.

'Sorry, Javier,' she spread her hands as though she was typing on a keyboard. 'Got to work. I have to write the guts of the story you just told me about Daletsky's sordid little empire. I need to get it written tonight and talk to the editor. Why don't you go ahead and start making some discreet enquiries with your connections and we can gear ourselves up for Morocco. I'll tell Matt to get himself organised. And I'll tell McGuire what I know. He'll agree that I should go and pursue the line a bit on my own to see the strength of it. He won't have a problem with it.'

'Okay, I'll see what I can dig up, but it's dangerous, Rosie. I must be crazy, allowing myself to get involved in this.'

'You won't be saying that if we can find Amy.'

He brushed his lips against her cheek and left.

Rosie felt a mixture of desolation and relief after he'd gone and she was alone on the terrace. Her mind flashed back to the prison visit with Frankie Nelson and the mention of a lowlife called Vinny. She figured that was the moment when this all became much more than just a story.

CHAPTER 30

'Shit, Rosie. This is fraught with all sorts of problems, and only one of them is the possibility you might end up with your throat cut in some back street in Tangiers,' McGuire said. 'And by the way, why are you only telling me now about this Vinny connection of Frankie Nelson's? I don't like being kept in the dark, Rosie.'

Rosie knew she'd pushed her luck by not keeping McGuire briefed about what Nelson had told her.

'I would have told you, Mick, you know I would,' she said. 'But to be honest, I had put it on the back burner. I knew the priority when I got back here was to nail this Daletsky story about people-smuggling, and the Carter-Smith friendship.'

Rosie lied. She would only have told him about Vinny once Javier was closer to finding out where they could track him down in Morocco. If she had that, she knew McGuire wouldn't be able to resist sending her there to have a run at.

'But listen, Mick, there's an even bigger development. You should sit down for this one.'

'I am, Gilmour. Tell me.'

'Martin Lennon may actually have unwittingly met Amy's kidnappers.'

She told him everything Adrian had told her.

'Holy fuck, Rosie! What are we supposed to do with this bombshell?'

'Well,' Rosie said. 'I don't think we should go blasting it on the front page yet, much as I'd like to. I think we should hang fire for a bit.'

'We should be telling the cops about this. That's my gut feeling, Rosie. Convince me why not.'

Rosie sighed. She knew he would react like this, and of course he was right. But she'd seen too many bungled police operations in her time, and who knew what would happen once you got the police forces of Spain and Morocco working together.

'Right, Mick. Think about it this way' – she made sure the terrace doors were closed tight – 'there are a couple of things we could do. We could fire a huge story onto the front page about what we already know: Martin Lennon's dad and the hooker, the Vinny connection, the fact that we've been told Amy's somewhere in Morocco – even that the Lennons may have met the kidnappers. And we could trumpet that we have now passed our explosive dossier to the cops. But what would that achieve? The cops for a start would go nuts, claiming the information being made public would jeopardise their investigation. We'd be in all sorts of trouble. If Amy – who we're hoping is still alive – died as a result of it, they'd blame us. And apart from all that, if we did a story, the rest of the media would invade Morocco and the people who are holding Amy might panic. Those bastards might just kill the kid and dump her somewhere.'

'Yeah, fine, Rosie. I get that,' McGuire said. 'But a part of me feels duty bound to simply pass the information onto the police and play along with them. Maybe get a promise that we'll be in pole position when the big exclusive comes.'

'Christ, Mick, are you serious?!' Rosie paced the floor. 'There's more chance of Carter-Smith going on *Blind Date* to find a woman than Spanish or Moroccan cops keeping us informed in a kidnapping case. If we make a decision to give them the information, then that's all we do, and don't expect us to get anything back from them because we won't. But ask yourself this: why don't they have the same information we have about the Martin Lennon connection? They're the cops, after all. Or do they have the info and they're not telling us? And if the cops are not as well informed as we are, then you have to ask yourself, did they ever have a chance of finding Amy if they haven't discovered that the kid is already in Morocco?'

She took a deep breath. 'My gut feeling, Mick, is that we play this close to our chests. We go to Morocco and very discreetly see what we can dig up. The Lennons will still be here when we get back, so let's try this first.'

Silence. Rosie could picture McGuire, sense his anxiety.

'Right, Rosie. Listen and listen good.' McGuire would be on his feet now.

'I always listen.'

'No, Rosie. You listen, then you do what the fuck you want. But not this time, you understand?'

'Of course, Mick.'

'OK. You go to Morocco. Take that big fucking Bosnian character with you, and Matt, of course.'

'And Javier,' Rosie interrupted. 'He has to go. He's the private eye here, and he's already making some inroads into who's who in Tangiers.'

'Aye, right, then take him as well. But I want *you* to be in the background, doing discreet – and I mean *molto* – discreet digging. I don't want you going anywhere near these fuckers that might be holding this kid, even if they give you a fucking address. You understand what I'm saying?'

'Yes, Mick.'

'If you track down that Vinny bastard, that'll be something in itself, but I don't want any kicking doors in at any level in Morocco. As I've said, you could end up with your throat cut.'

'And, of course, that could get the paper in trouble.'

'Not at all, Gilmour. I'll just say I had no idea what you were doing.'

'You're all heart, Mick.'

'You bet I am. Now keep in touch, no matter where you are. You've got four days – maximum. Then come home and we pass it all to the cops. But before we do that, we'll hit the Lennons and ask them if they knew about grandad's dirty little secret. I love that story.'

'At least Jenny won't feel so responsible that her wee

girl was snatched while she was shagging Martin's best pal. It was all the grandad's fault.'

'Christ, Rosie. I can imagine that front page already. What if they did actually meet the kidnappers . . . You hurry back. And stay safe.'

'Oh, Mick,' Rosie said, remembering. 'You haven't asked about the Daletsky-Carter-Smith piece?'

'What do you mean, Gilmour? Is it not already on my desk? What've you been doing all day? Get your arse away from the swimming pool and start working!'

Rosie had finished her story and sent it to McGuire's private email. The lawyers would pore over every line. It made Carter-Smith look, at the very least, naïve for being anywhere near a Russian oligarch with such a dodgy background as Daletsky. By the time the lawyers started asking questions, Rosie would be in Morocco. She'd written the piece as carefully as possible so that she wouldn't have too much legal comeback while she was on the road.

She'd already eaten dinner in her room and was packed for the trip, buoyed up by the prospect of being off the leash in the hunt for Amy. This is what made Rosie tick – pushing back the barriers, making her own luck, and, more often than not, flying by the seat of her pants. And now, with Adrian and Javier and Matt riding shotgun, she felt unstoppable.

Later, over a gin and tonic in the hotel bar, Rosie gave Matt the lowdown on plans for Morocco while they waited for Adrian. They'd take the late afternoon ferry from Algeciras. Javier had moved swiftly after he left Rosie and he'd already set up a meeting in Tangiers with a friend of a trusted contact who'd look after them. No, he told her, she didn't need to know who he was, just that he had information that would interest them.

When Rosie had called Adrian to say she was going to Morocco and to ask if he would come with them, she was surprised that he was a little vague. It was Adrian who asked to come to the hotel, as he didn't want to talk on the phone.

Rosie saw him coming up the steps from the terrace and to the bar, busy with guests enjoying an after-dinner drink as they listened to an old guy rattling out 'As Time Goes By' on the piano. Eat your heart out, Rick. Rosie smiled to herself at the irony. 'Of all the gin joints in all the towns in all the world ...'

Adrian scanned the room. If he saw Rosie he didn't make eye contact, but she'd put good money on him being able to tell you almost exactly how many people were in the place. He made his way across to their table.

'Rosie.' He looked at her, then at Matt, then back at Rosie.

'Adrian. Good to see you.' Rosie motioned him to sit down. 'This is Matt, the photographer I told you about. We work together a lot. He's the best.'

'Howsit going, big man?' Matt stuck out a hand and Adrian shook it and sat down, his dark eyes fixing Matt long enough to let him know he wasn't about to get involved in blokeish banter. Matt looked a little awkward and took a gulp of his drink.

A waiter came up and Adrian asked for a coffee, while

Rosie ordered another gin and tonic and a Jack Daniels for Matt.

Adrian seemed uneasy, and Rosie hoped he wasn't going to be uncomfortable with the fact that she was introducing him to someone else. He trusted only her, he'd told her, and nobody else must know who he was. But that was back in Glasgow in what seemed a long time ago, and this was a different ball game now. There were four of them, hopefully heading for Morocco. She wondered how Adrian would get on with Javier, and hoped there wouldn't be a clash of machismo.

'You alright, Adrian?'

He nodded and pulled his chair closer to the table.

'We must talk, Rosie,' he said almost whispering. 'I could not say on the phone, but things have changed a bit.'

He looked at Rosie and glanced at Matt as though seeking reassurance.

'It's okay, Adrian. Everything here is between us,' Rosie said.

Adrian lit a cigarette and inhaled deeply.

'I was called by Leka as I was leaving your room,' he said, blowing the smoke out. 'He tells me I must go to Morocco tomorrow, to find Besmir.' His eyes flicked from Matt to Rosie. 'He says Besmir is a traitor and I must deal with him.'

'What do you mean a traitor? What's he done? Did Leka say anything else?'

Adrian nodded.

'You know I told you it was Besmir, the Albanian who

took the girl from the beach? He take her to Tangiers by order of Leka. Some deal they do with the Moroccans is what he told Besmir. But you and me now know different. But Leka says when Besmir came back he is a different man. He says he is going away to Spain in the north with a girlfriend, but Leka knows he is lying and he wants to know why.' Adrian glanced over his shoulder. 'He sent his bodyguard to deal with him two nights ago, because he can't have a traitor in the business. But Besmir killed him.' He made a stabbing motion with his hand. 'The knife in his belly. Then Besmir disappeared.'

'Christ,' Rosie said.

They sat in silence as the waiter put their drinks down.

'So. Now I have to go find Besmir. And deal with him.' Adrian took a long draw on his cigarette and sat back.

The fireworks going off in Rosie's head were louder than the warning bells. That was always her problem. If Adrian took them with him, there was a tantalising possibility he could lead them to Amy. But McGuire was right – she could end up in an alleyway with her throat cut.

'So, Adrian,' Rosie said. 'You're not coming with us then?'

'No. Not travelling together. Is not safe. I take the morning ferry from Tarifa and you go as your plan in the afternoon boat. When you get to Tangiers, you call me and we will speak. I do not know what the plan will be, only that I have to find Besmir. Someone will meet me in Tangiers and tell me more information.'

'Have you been told anything about the girl? About Amy?'

Adrian shook his head. 'Nothing. But Leka thinks Besmir is betraying him some way, I do not know how. I am told only to deal with him.'

Rosie didn't want to ask him any more. The less she knew about 'dealing with' Besmir the better, but she was in no doubt what mission Adrian was on. If Besmir was betraying the boss who sent him to kidnap Amy, his betrayal could involve only one thing – Amy. Maybe he'd decided to sell her himself, ask for a ransom.

'Don't look now, Rosie! Don't,' Matt suddenly interrupted.

'What?' Rosie saw the colour drain from Matt's face. 'What is it, Matt?'

'Big Jake Cox has just walked into the bar.'

'You're fucking joking. Tell me you're joking, Matt.'

'No. I'm not joking. Just keep looking at me and talking. Don't look up. He walked in and he's standing at the bar with two big fucking gorillas.'

'This Jake,' Adrian said softly. 'He is the one whose men tried to kill you in Glasgow, Rosie? Yes?'

Rosie nodded. She took a mouthful of her drink. Sweat stung under her arms.

'I see him,' Adrian said. 'And his friends. He must have found new friends, after the last ones.' He touched Rosie's hand. 'Don't be afraid, Rosie. These are not tough guys. They only think they are tough.'

Rosie bit the inside of her jaw.

'Fucking hell! They're coming over, Rosie,' Matt said under his breath.

'Stay calm,' Adrian said. 'Say nothing.'

'Can I get you a drink, Miss Gilmour?'

Rosie looked up to see the bloated face of Jake Cox, leathery from the Costa sun where he'd been keeping a low profile since the *Post*'s exposé on his links to police corruption. Her mouth was dry as a stick.

'No, you can't, I've got plenty here. But thanks anyway.'

Rosie fixed him with a defiant stare and was surprised and relieved that her voice hadn't come out as a terrified squeak.

Jake smirked. 'That's no very sociable, pal. I thought you'd be wanting to celebrate your survival after that terrible business back in Glasgow.' He did a sharp intake of breath. 'That was a bad old business that, Miss Gilmour.'

Rosie said nothing.

'Did you enjoy your wee holiday after it all? I heard you were up in Jerez. They do a nice sherry up there. I thought about coming up to buy you lunch.'

Rosie could feel the pulse in her neck throbbing. She glanced at Matt who kept his head down, staring at his drink.

'Oh, well,' Jake said. 'Have it your way. I'm off then. Good to see you, Miss Gilmour.' He stepped away then turned back. 'Oh, by the way, Rosie. You were lucky in that wee car crash the other week on the Malaga road. Heard all about it. You'd want to be careful out, hen. Lot of bad people out there.' He sneered. 'I'll be seeing you, Rosie.'

'Bastard,' Rosie said to herself, taking one of Adrian's cigarettes from his packet. But her hand was trembling so much he had to light it for her.

'Don't be afraid, Rosie,' Adrian said, 'he is nobody here.'

Rosie looked at Matt as he knocked back his Jack Daniels in one. 'Fuck me, Rosie,' he laughed nervously. 'I should get danger money working with you.'

Rosie was almost high from the buzz of adrenaline.

'Christ, Matt! I thought I was going to pass out. Just as well we're bailing out of here tomorrow.'

CHAPTER 31

The sound of her own crying woke Rosie. She lay in the darkness and brushed the tears from her face. The dream had been so vivid – they always were.

Now, with the images of the dream fading as she woke, she remembered that her mother and father were hiding from her. They were together at the seaside, but one moment she looked around and they'd gone. She was running down the promenade calling out for them. Then she saw them in the distance at the harbour, heading quickly towards the gangplank of a ferry. They were pushing people out of the way, and every now and then her father looked over his shoulder and Rosie saw the blue of his eyes. He must have seen her. But he didn't stop, and they melted into the crowd . . .

She stretched over to the bedside table and looked at her phone. It was four in the morning. Rosie switched on the light to banish the loneliness of the dark. She wished she could have TJ to hold her the way he did that first time they'd been together, when she'd woken up in his bed and she'd been crying. She let out a long sigh and swung her legs out of the bed.

On the terrace, the light was just beginning to break through. Rosie looked out into the stillness and her thoughts drifted to her father back in Glasgow.

He had wept again when she'd told him in the cafe that she wanted him to come and stay at her flat. He'd said he couldn't possibly impose, but Rosie insisted. She hadn't thought beyond the fact that she was taking home a man to live with her who had been a stranger almost all her life, but it was a basic instinct. Her father was dying. He needed her. But perhaps the truth was that she needed him more.

They'd gone back to the hostel, where Rosie stood watching him pack his things – a whole life shoved into a little black hold-all. In the four-bedded room he shared, two of the other men looked on sadly as he murmured goodbye to them. Rosie sensed their emptiness, the same emptiness she had felt at the children's home when one of the other kids left to go and live with relatives or foster parents.

When she took him home he had looked around in surprise.

'My God, Rosie. You've done well.'

She set him up in the spacious spare room, where she had a sofa and double bed and a television.

'You don't need to feel you have to come out of here and sit with me all the time,' she'd told him. 'I'm not here a lot anyway. You can have your own space, and you can have the guest bathroom. I have one in my bedroom.'

Rosie felt a little awkward, more like a landlady showing round a lodger.

'Thanks, Rosie.' He looked at her. 'If it's alright with you, it would be good to . . . well, I mean . . . I hope maybe we can get to know each other a bit. If you're okay with that?' He looked sad.

'Sure.' Rosie nodded, not sure it was okay at all, but not knowing what to say. 'I'm going to cook us something. You get yourself settled and we'll have a drink before dinner.'

As she was about to leave the room she turned back and saw him still standing there watching her.

'We'll be okay.' She smiled at him.

As she was leaving for Spain she hugged him for the first time. She'd woken up early in the morning, gone shopping to fill the fridge, then gone to her doctor's surgery to register her father and tell her GP that he was dying of cancer. Dr Simon McLeod had known Rosie for a long time and they were on first name terms. He told her he would see him to organise appointments with specialists. The cancer had spread to both lungs in recent weeks, Rosie told Simon, but when she'd asked her father what the prognosis was, he was vague.

Her father had told her over dinner how he had been living mostly in hostels in the last six months, having moved up from Manchester where he'd been living for years. There were huge gaps to be filled in about how and where and with whom he'd shared his life in the past thirty years. But that was for another day. Rosie wasn't even sure she wanted to know. But there was something about having him there with her, surreal as it felt, that brought her closer to her mother.

Now, with her dream still fresh in her mind, she felt the urge to call him. She looked at her watch. It was too early. She watched the sun beginning to emerge behind the palm trees, and thought of TJ. She pictured him strolling somewhere in Manhattan, his sax case slung over his shoulder. She remembered the look in his eye when he'd told her he hated goodbyes, and if she wasn't at the airport he'd take it she didn't want to be with him. For the hundredth time she asked herself how he could do that, just go and never get in touch after everything that had happened between them . . .

Nothing had ever felt as right as those mornings waking up in his bed, the warmth of him next to her, and never once did she have that urge to get up and slip quietly away that she usually had when she'd spent the night with a man. With TJ the mornings were special, lounging around listening to music while he cooked breakfast.

Rosie went into the bathroom and turned on the shower, staring dreamily as steam filled the room. She stood under the water and washed her body, watching the soap run off her breasts and down her thighs. Her hand automatically moved down between her legs and she felt an overwhelming ache for TJ, for his touch, and for the tenderness he'd shown her the night she'd opened up to him about her childhood. She remembered him kissing every part of her until she was breathless and crying out as he held her tightly, and she searched for some release from the crushing loneliness she'd felt since he left.

There was a missed call on her mobile when she got out of the shower, and a message from McGuire to call him.

'Hi, Mick. What's up? It's not even daylight there.'

'Don't tell me you're just getting out of your bed, Gilmour. It's not a holiday, you know.'

McGuire sounded the way he always did when he was running a big story. He lived and breathed it, and Rosie guessed he'd probably been up half the night reading her Carter-Smith copy and planning their next move.

'Listen, Rosie,' he said. 'That's great stuff on that shirtlifter Carter-Smith. I can't wait to see his face turn puce when we put all this to him.'

'You going to use it in the next couple of days?'

'You bet I am, the whole shooting match. That's why I'm calling you. Here's the plan: The lawyers will take a good look at all the copy this morning, and I'm getting Vincent to doorstep Carter-Smith down at Westminster. He'll be told this is not up for discussion. I want to put the rent boy stuff to him as well – that Taha boy. And by the way, I need you to write what the boy told you and I need it on my desk in the next hour, before you hit the trail to Morocco. Oh, and also, get Matt to take a pic of Carter-Smith's ID pass. I want Vincent to shove that under his nose. He'll shit his pants when he sees we've got that.'

'Mick, do you think it's wise to do the Carter-Smith hit when I'm trying to discreetly dig things up in Morocco?' Rosie asked.

'Yes, Rosie. I've already thought about that, but here's my take. The main thrust of the story right now is Carter-Smith's link to Daletsky, and how we can pinpoint Daletsky to people-trafficking via that rescued bird's interview in Sarajevo. But if we can get Vincent to put the rent boy stuff to him, and the fact that they may have seen something the day the kid got snatched, then that will change things. That'll be the splash. Carter-Smith, the rent boy and the kidnapped girl. That should leap off the newsagents' shelves.'

'Don't you think it will have an impact on what's happening in Morocco?' Rosie was not convinced.

'No, Gilmour, I don't think so. There will be no mention anywhere in the story about Morocco. In fact, to put everyone off the scent, I think we'll put a line in saying that we believe the girl has been taken to northern Spain or somewhere like that – maybe even Amsterdam. Let them think that.'

'Okay, Mick,' Rosie said. 'If we do it that way, then it should be safe.'

'Course it will. Plus the fact it will give everyone something to chase while you're away digging in Morocco. It'll be a good distraction tactic. That's part of the reason I'm doing it. That, and the fact that we need to freshen this story up a bit with a right rollicking scandal.'

'Fine.' Rosie looked at her watch. 'I've got the Taha words half written anyway, so I'll put it together and send it within the hour. But don't forget to say that it's believed Amy's been taken somewhere north. Anywhere that's far enough away from Morocco.'

'Don't you worry, Gilmour, just you take care. And phone me tonight.'

An hour later, as promised, Rosie pinged over the interview with Taha to the editor, including the full details of how he and Carter-Smith had sat on the balcony and seen a man pick up a little girl, who now appears to be Amy, off the beach. She told Matt they should be able to hear the sound of Carter-Smith's bottle crashing from Tangiers. Matt had taken a snap of the ID pass and Rosie had hidden it away again.

She stepped out onto her terrace to phone her father. It rang a few times and Rosie was surprised to find herself worried something had happened to him. She pictured him collapsed in the kitchen or lying unconscious in bed. She was thinking of phoning her neighbour to ask her to check on him when to her relief he answered.

'Hello?' He sounded out of breath.

'Hi. Er . . . It's me . . . Rosie.' She couldn't bring herself to say 'dad', and there was an awkward moment. 'Are you okay? You sound breathless. It took you a while to answer the phone.'

'Rosie. Oh, I'm okay,' he said. 'I was lying down. Didn't have a great sleep last night so I was a bit tired.'

'Are you alright?'

Silence. Rosie could hear him breathing.

'My chest's been a bit tight to be honest, so I'm taking things easy. The doctor phoned me and I've to go and see them tomorrow. How are you, Rosie? Are you alright over there? You watching yourself?'

Rosie smiled. 'Yes. I'm fine. Very busy.'

She struggled for things to say to him. But despite that, she found herself missing him.

'When do you think you'll be back? It's quiet here.' He sounded a bit forlorn.

'Might be a couple of weeks at least. I've a lot to do.'

Another silence. Rosie wondered if he was fed up already with being in the one place. He'd spent so much of his life on the move and he'd told her that he was restless by nature. Part of her wondered if he'd still be there when she got back. It was a weird feeling.

'Listen,' she said, trying to sound upbeat. 'When I get back, we'll do some things together. Just go out in the city a bit, maybe take a run down the coast or something. See some things.' She paused. 'Like the old days.'

Rosie saw herself years ago with her mum and dad on the train to Helensburgh, and falling asleep on his shoulder on the way back at night. It could never be like the old days.

'I'd like that, Rosie.'

'Great. So make sure you get to the doctor tomorrow and I'll phone you to see how you're doing. Just try and rest as much as you can. If you've got any problems give me a call and I'll get my neighbour to look in on you.'

'I'm okay. I'll be fine.' He paused. 'And Rosie. Thanks for everything. I mean that.' His voice shook a little.

Rosie swallowed the lump in her throat.

'I'll see you.'

She hung up and shook herself out of the gloom. She had work to do.

CHAPTER 32

Rosie and Matt stepped out of the Rembrandt Hotel into the stifling heat of the Tangiers night.

Adrian would be waiting for them in a cafe close to the Zocco Grande, the square in the bustling heart of the city that was the gateway to the Kasbah. It had been agreed that all three of them were to stay well away from Javier, who'd also be in the cafe but was working on his own.

When they had arrived off the ferry, Javier was picked up by his contact and asked Rosie to take his bag to the hotel. By this evening, he'd told her, he'd know exactly where to find Vinny Paterson. Javier was in bullish mood, the way Rosie had seen him before when he was on a mission, and when he was on this kind of form nothing could stop him. His machismo cards were firmly on the table – in case anyone, including Rosie, thought they were calling the shots. She was prepared to indulge him a little when he was like this – it always got results.

In the back of the taxi Matt and Rosie exchanged glances

as the driver sped through the city like a maniac, cutting up other motorists who honked their horns.

'If ever a man needs to chill with a joint ...' Matt was in the front, fumbling around unsuccessfully trying to clip the seatbelt.

Rosie gripped the back of the passenger seat as the car swerved and bounced along the road. 'There's just too much traffic in this city, but we're not far from the square. Javier said we could have walked, but I'm uncomfortable when I arrive in a place at night. It always seems a bit spooky.'

'Yeah. Something tells me it might get a lot spookier in the next couple of days,' Matt said.

The plan had been worked out during the ferry crossing from Algeciras. Once Javier had located Paterson's whereabouts, he would make the approach by himself. His contact in Tangier was a fixer he'd used before when he was a detective with the Guarda Civil, and he was confident that he could establish very quickly the places where Vinny hung out. Javier would then pose as a dealer who wanted to distribute porno films in Spain. He knew he could carry that off, but he was hoping to strike up enough of a rapport with Vinny to find out if the scumbag had information they could use. No matter how you handled this it was risky, Javier told them. Shadowy bastards like Vinny were always suspicious but they were also greedy, and that made them careless. If a tempting proposition was put to Vinny Paterson, Javier's instincts told him he might go for it. Rosie, Matt and Adrian were to be elsewhere in the cafe looking like ordinary tourists having dinner.

Rosie felt hot and tense. The back of her neck was wet with sweat. She pushed her hair up with one hand and rolled down the car window, hoping for a breeze. Instead she got the thick, hot air and the pungent aromas of the city wafting from bars and restaurants, mingled with the fug of pollution. She leaned her head back. Some food and a couple of drinks would perk her up.

The driver dropped them off at the edge of the Zocco Grande, already heaving with tourists. Matt handed him the money, knowing they were being ripped off. They walked quickly across the square, dismissing the various guides and hustlers who traipsed after them offering everything from tours of the Kasbah to fake Rolex watches.

Beggars looking for easy pickings eyed up tourists who lingered long enough to listen to the buskers sat on the ground in traditional garb, scratching out a mixture of Berber and Arab music on a violin and rattling tambourines and bongo drums. A snake charmer coaxed a cobra out of a basket and his friend invited tourists who were daft enough to pose for snapshots with a snake draped around their neck.

As they left the square towards the labyrinth of the Kasbah, a skinny youth grabbed Rosie by the arm and asked if she wanted a boy for the night.

'I give you good price,' he said. 'I am very good sexy boy.' Just a kid in jeans and a vest, he walked briskly alongside her, and she caught the whiff of days' old sweat.

'I don't think so, pet.' Rosie pushed him away.

'That might be as good as it gets, Rosie,' Matt sniggered.

'I hope it doesn't come to that,' Rosie laughed. 'At least he didn't offer me a shave.'

Once into the Kasbah it became hustling on an industrialised scale, with sellers surrounding them shoving trinkets into their faces. They could barely pick their feet through dimly lit alleys.

'Where the fuck is this place?' Rosie gripped Matt's arm as they tried to squeeze their way through the throng in the tight sloping streets towards the old Jewish quarter. She stifled a wave of panic and claustrophobia. 'We should have got a guide from the hotel to take us. It's not safe here if we get lost.'

'Look. Rue de la Kasbah,' Matt said, pointing up at the street sign. 'We're here.'

'Thank Christ for that.' Rosie breathed a sigh of relief.

Inside the cafe it was dark except for the candlelit tables and some small eyelights over the bar. Ceiling fans rotating slowly did little to disperse the smoke from the hookah pipes bubbling at nearly every table. The beat of an African drum thumped from speakers. Rosie glanced around and saw Adrian sitting at a table close to the bar.

They made their way across the room, and Rosie felt almost relieved that the crowd was mostly tourists. She wasn't in the heart of some dingy Tangiers bar filled with locals where she might disappear and never be heard of again. She wasn't paranoid, but she'd been in some terrifying scrapes working on the frontline. She'd been mugged in a street in Nairobi by a little kid who smiled up at her and called her 'mama' before he ripped the gold chain off her neck as well as some lumps of her skin. In Bokhara Market in Mogadishu, where the guys with the biggest guns ran the show, she was almost lynched by a baying mob as she sat frozen with fear in the back of a pick-up truck. In Bucharest, she was once left stranded in the middle of nowhere by her thieving driver. From then on, whenever she was out of her comfort zone in some distant land, she would look over her shoulder, anticipating trouble on every corner. She was relieved to be with Adrian, and even more so when she spotted Javier in the corner of the bar, deep in conversation with a man she hoped was Vinny. She needed a drink.

'So this man here,' Adrian said, inclining his head a little, as they sat drinking bad wine, 'this man in the corner is the one who makes porn films with children? And kills them in his movies?' The shadows beneath his eyes looked darker under the flickering light. He shook his head and looked at Rosie. 'If is up to me, this man would not make any more movies.'

'Yes, I know,' Rosie said. 'I feel the same, but he might turn out to be useful to us. In his kind of business, maybe the people who have Amy will get in touch with him.' Just saying the words made Rosie feel sick at the thought of it.

From where she was sitting she saw that Javier had evidently struck up some kind of rapport with Vinny. The waiter brought them drinks and both of them appeared to be doing plenty of talking. In the half light she could see the lean face of Vinny, his eyes narrowed in concentration as Javier spoke. Next to the robust figure of Javier, he was very weedy, with wispy hair that was too thin to be worn long.

'He certainly looks like a wee pervert,' Rosie said to Matt. 'I can't wait to hear what he and Javier are talking about.'

'Me too,' Matt said. 'Looks like your Spanish pal has got him eating out of his hand.'

They ordered a platter of local dishes and house specials recommended by the waiter. Adrian told Rosie that he already had some ideas of where to look for Besmir, but he didn't say what he would do if and when he found him. The once or twice he'd met Besmir, he found him distant and quiet, and he always looked unhappy. He couldn't understand what kind of man could steal a small child from its parents. The fact that Besmir could do that meant he was capable of anything. He would tread warily in his hunt for him, he told them.

Later as they sipped coffee, Matt ordered a hookah pipe, joking that it would make them blend in with the tourists. Rosie went along with it, and at one point she caught Javier's eye as she was puffing on it. He gave her a look that said he was getting on well with his new-found pervert amigo.

'When this Vinny leaves, I will follow him,' Adrian said. 'Is useful to know where he goes, where he lives.'

'Good idea. But I don't want any harm to come to him.'

Adrian nodded, his face blank.

After a while Vinny stood up, and Rosie could see just how skinny and creepy he looked. He was wearing baggy combat trousers and his bony chest was exposed by a tight, low cut tee shirt that wouldn't have been out of place on a girl. He looked clammy and pale with hair that had been dyed so many times it wasn't any definable colour.

'He looks like a wee faggot,' Matt said.

They watched as he left the cafe, then Adrian got up.

'I will call you later, Rosie.'

He put his hand into his pocket, but Rosie waved him away.

Rosie's mobile rang. It was Javier, and she looked up to see him in the corner with his phone at his ear.

'*Buenos tardes*,' she said, smiling at him.

'*Hola*, Rosie. I am going to the hotel now. I will eat there, so you can join me. We can talk.'

'How did it go?'

'Very well. He took the bait. I'll tell you later.'

Rosie saw him get up and put the mobile into his pocket. He walked out onto the street.

On the terrace of the hotel rooftop restaurant, Javier poured wine for Rosie and Matt. In between polishing off a steak dinner he related the conversation with Vinny.

'He's a pervy little *coño*,' Javier screwed up his face in disgust. 'I felt like I needed a shower after just talking to him. But I think he's the kind of bastard who will do anything for money, and that's good for us.'

'So he wasn't suspicious of you?' Rosie asked.

'No.' Javier shook his head. 'The little shit can only see pound signs. Once I told him how much money I wanted to move on this deal, he would have listened to anything

I told him. I was purely an investor, and he would assume it was dirty money, from drugs or something. It wouldn't be the first time someone has bought a stash of films from him with dirty money.'

Few people could think on their feet as well as Javier when faced with an ever-changing situation. Rosie was glad she'd got him involved.

'I told him I wanted to buy a collection of films for distribution in Spain. I said I already had a market and clients, and I asked him about the snuff movies. He became a little bit reticent then, but I mentioned the names of one or two films I'd been asked for by clients and he was impressed enough, or stupid enough, to think that I have connections. I got the titles from some contacts I spoke to before I left. I didn't want to see this bastard and not be prepared.'

'I wouldn't have expected anything less, Javier.' Rosie raised her glass in salute.

'So,' Javier continued. 'We were talking about making a deal and he was arranging to meet again tomorrow but not here – in a little town called Salé close to the old city of Rabat. That's where he does the filming. In his place. It's about two hours drive from here.' Javier drained his glass and Rosie waved the waiter over and ordered another bottle of wine.

'Incidentally, I don't know if you could see from where you were sitting but Vinny was drinking large cognacs. He had three while I was with him. I think he has a problem with alcohol because he looks it to me, plus I think he'd already had a few before I got there. Towards the end he was beginning to run off at the mouth.'

'Really? Go on.' Rosie leaned forward.

He looked from Matt to Rosie, lit a cigarette.

'You're going to love this.' He blew the smoke upwards. 'Come closer, because I must talk very quietly.'

Rosie and Matt pulled their chairs up.

'He told me he's making a film the day after tomorrow in Salé with a little kid, and after he sells it, he'll make so much money that he'll be able to retire and go to live in Thailand – no doubt where he can buy as many little boys as he wants. Bastard.'

'Amy? You think he's talking about Amy?'

Javier nodded. 'It's possible. Very possible. Because he did say that when this film came out the whole world would be talking about it.'

'Jesus, Javier.'

She took one of Javier's cigarettes and he lit it for her.

'Obviously I didn't want to make too much of what he said, but I did ask him what would make this one so special. And you know what he said to me?' He looked from one to the other. 'He said because he was going to sell a clip of it to make money. Big money. Was going to sell it to the newspapers, he said.'

'What did he mean?'

'That was the point when I asked him if the kid he was talking about was missing,' Javier said.

'You asked him that?'

Rosie trusted Javier's judgment. He wouldn't have asked that if he thought he'd be rumbled.

'Yes, Rosie. I asked him that. I can see that this little fucker is stupid and drunk enough to say something he shouldn't. And you know what?' Javier smiled. 'He did. He was that stupid.'

'What did he say, Javier?'

Javier drank a mouthful of wine.

'He told me he was doing this film for somebody else, and that he would be paid a lot of money for it. I asked him again why they would pay him so much for a film of this missing kid and what would they do with it if it was just another film. And he said one word.' Javier paused for effect. 'Ransom.' He looked at both of them. 'He didn't elaborate, but my guess is he was going to try to stiff his client by selling the clip himself before they have a chance to do it – maybe sell it to a newspaper or TV channel for big money.'

'Fuck me, Javier!' Matt said.

'Thank you, Matt, but I much prefer your partner.' Javier grinned.

CHAPTER 33

With the click of the trigger being cocked, Besmir's eyes popped wide open. The cold metal of the revolver pressed against his temple. He looked up. In the blackness of the bedroom Adrian's face was lit by the shaft of street light coming through the window. He knew better than to move a muscle. Adrian stared down at him, his face blank. Besmir swallowed, barely breathing.

'You've come to kill me, so kill me, Adrian.' He stared back. 'You would be doing me a favour, my friend.' He could feel sweat stinging his back.

Silence.

'Tell me, Besmir. Why has Leka sent me to kill you?'

Silence. Besmir looked at the hooded eyes of the big Bosnian. He knew Adrian more by reputation than acquaintance, and he was feared by everyone in the organisation except him. Until now. Because now he had a gun at Besmir's head, and he knew that if he didn't tell Adrian what he wanted to know, he had maybe fifteen seconds left. Enough time to consider why Adrian had asked the question in the first place. Because if he asked it, his intention was not to do Leka's dirty work, but to find out why.

'The girl,' Besmir said, feeling his chest tighten with anxiety. 'The girl I took for Leka. He is suspicious.'

'You killed Sergei. Leka sent him to deal with you. So he was right to be suspicious. Why you back in Morocco?'

Besmir felt a trickle of sweat from his hairline run down his forehead. He knew little of Adrian except that he had fought his way out of his besieged Bosnian village after a massacre by Serbian soldiers. And also the legend of how he saved Leka's life from the men who double crossed him in Spain. In the three months Adrian had been working with Leka's mob, they'd spoken only once, and briefly, while they both waited outside Leka's office on business. Besmir had found him quiet, like himself, with a protective wall around him. And like him, he knew Adrian was not to be crossed.

'You don't have much time left, Besmir. Tell me.'

Besmir took as deep a breath as he dared.

'I saw some things. Children. In cages. It changes every-thing.' His voice was almost a whisper.

Adrian's face showed nothing.

'Go on.'

'I was taken by someone to a place where they keep stolen children. Small children, three, four, five years old. They keep them in cages. Like animals. Then they use them for porn films and sometimes to kill them. Or they just keep using them over and over again with perverts.'

Silence.

'Is the kidnap girl there?'

'No, I don't think so. Not yet.'

'So why do you care what happens to the children in cages, or to the British girl? Why all of a sudden you care? You kidnapped her.'

Besmir blinked away the image of his childhood in the iron cots. He thought of Kaltrina and the blue of her eyes.

'I take the girl and bring her to Tangiers as Leka told me, but something happened to me. I don't know what. That is the truth, my friend. You can kill me if you do not believe me. The girl . . . she was frightened. She . . .' He paused. 'She kept leaning, holding on to me. I do not know why. When I gave her to the woman in Tangiers she was crying for me when they took her away. That never happen before to me.' He looked at Adrian. 'I am from the orphanage in Tirana. I remember the cots, like cages, and the crying. All the time we are all crying. And the smell.'

'So?' Adrian kept the gun firmly at his head. 'Why did you come back here?'

'I . . . I want to free the children from that place. And I want to get the girl. Kal—' He stopped before he said the name. 'I want to get the girl and take her back. I did a bad thing.'

'Is very late to know you did a bad thing, Besmir.'

'I know this.' He looked up. 'But why you are asking me this, Adrian? If you come to kill me, why you care?'

Adrian took the gun from his head, but kept it pointed at him.

'I am also looking for the girl, the British one. Amy.'

Relief began to flood through Besmir. Adrian wasn't here to kill him. He too was betraying Leka.

'Can I sit up, Adrian? Please, take the gun away. If you are not going to kill me, do not point the gun. Let me sit up and we talk.'

Adrian took a step back but kept the gun on him.

'When you tell me everything, I will not point the gun. But if you do anything stupid, you will be dead. Be sure of that, Besmir.'

Besmir nodded and sat up on the side of the bed. He took the pack of cigarettes on the bedside table and looked at Adrian for approval before he slowly took one out. He lit up and took a deep draw, letting the smoke fill his lungs and his head.

'I will tell you everything.' He turned his face upwards to where the Bosnian was still standing over him. 'But we must be able to trust each other. If we do, we can maybe do something good. For me, is the first time I do something good in my life.' He put his hand out. Adrian hesitated, then shook it. 'But how can I be sure I can trust you, Adrian?'

'You cannot, but you have run out of choices.' Adrian let go of his hand. 'Only one thing you can be sure of, Besmir. If you betray me, I will kill you. Do you understand? If you betray me, you are already dead.'

Besmir stood up. 'I understand.'

'Talk to me,' Adrian said.

Besmir placed his half-smoked cigarette on the ashtray, went to the washbasin and turned on the cold tap. He splashed water on his face then dabbed it with a small towel. He went back across the room and opened the window. He picked up the cigarette and sat on the narrow window sill with his back to the street. He began to tell Adrian about the journey with the girl, and also about the fat man. He told him about the driver, Hassan, who had mentioned about the children in cages. Leka had told him that the girl he kidnapped would be bought by a family, and that he was selling her to the Moroccans as part of a deal because they would be doing more business together with drugs, and she would be sold to a rich couple. Leka had said nothing about other children. It was only when the driver told him of the other children that he wanted to see for himself. He said he couldn't explain even to himself, but he couldn't stand the thought of the little girl he stole being trapped inside a cage. So he went with the driver and saw the cages for himself.

'So that is all what I can tell you, Adrian, of why I am here,' he said. 'I want to get the girl and save the other children.'

'Save them? Like you are the hero?' Adrian said flatly.

Besmir looked at him, then at the ground.

'Not like the hero,' he said. 'The girl made me think. That is all.' He looked at Adrian. 'But why are you really here, Adrian? You didn't come to kill me, so why?'

Adrian put the gun into his waistband and picked up Besmir's cigarettes. He took one for himself then threw the packet back on the bedside table. He lit his cigarette, then stood staring past Besmir out of the open window at the morning light beginning to break through.

'My sister,' he said. 'My sister has been kidnapped by Leka and his mob.'

'Your sister! She is a child?'

'No.' Adrian shook his head. 'She is seventeen. She come from Sarajevo to Malaga for work. She and her friend were promised jobs, but they are kidnapped. Her friend escape but my sister is not. I cannot find her, but I know she is in Costa del Sol. Marbella maybe.' He sighed. 'You know what happens with the girls. They go to the whore-houses. They are drugged. You know, because sometimes you must drive them.'

Besmir saw that Adrian could barely control his anger. He felt edgy, and stood up, walking past him to the bedside chair, where he picked up his shirt and pulled it on over his vest.

'Not for a long time, Adrian,' he said. 'I haven't driven any girls for a long time.'

'But you know where they go. Don't you?'

'I have taken them only to a house in the country or to some of the clubs. But I am only driving them, I never see them. I don't talk to them or know where they come from. When was your sister taken?'

'Three months ago. That is why I come to Spain. That is why I work with Leka's mob. I come to find her. Find her from the inside.'

Besmir had to admire his guts.

'You came here and hooked in with Leka, just to find your sister? You are a brave man.'

Adrian shrugged. 'I must find my sister. I *will* find her.'

'So why you want to know about the girl? The one I took to Tangiers.'

Silence. Adrian went across and closed the window. He turned to Besmir.

'I am also helping my friend. She is a journalist. British. She has information about what can maybe happen to the girl Amy if we don't find her. And she is helping me find my sister. Come. We go and drink coffee. I will tell you.'

Besmir stuffed his cigarettes into his pocket and followed Adrian out of the door. He had no idea where he was going or what would happen next. But he knew that now Adrian had tracked him down, he had indeed run out of choices.

In the pavement cafe, Besmir listened as Adrian told him what had happened to his sister and how the journalist had promised to help him find her by highlighting the story in her newspaper because of the connection with the British politician. He knew he could get up and walk away now because Adrian wouldn't risk shooting him in the middle of a busy street. But if he did that, Adrian would hunt him down.

He looked at the big man and wondered if he could take him out if it came down to that. The deciding factor would be about who had the most to lose – and it wasn't him. There was nobody waiting for him, nobody depending on him, hoping he would come through for them. An image of Kaltrina flashed through his mind, of the moment when he'd opened the boot of his car in

Tangiers and saw the wide-eyed hopeful look on her face. She wasn't waiting for him. But he knew that with the help of Hassan, they could get her back.

'You see, Adrian,' Besmir said, 'I have a plan. I told you about the driver. He knows from inside what is going on and will find out what the plan is with the girl. I know I can get her back, do the things I told you I want to do – set the children in the cages free. But with someone else involved, it is more difficult.' He sipped his coffee. 'And now you tell me you have this journalist, this newspaper woman, too. Is dangerous with more people in this. You know that?'

'Of course I do. Do not worry about the journalist. I can manage that. She knows danger and she will not do anything stupid.'

Besmir could not dictate terms. It would have to be Adrian's way. His mobile rang and he took it out of his pocket. It was Hassan. He listened, conscious that Adrian was watching him. Then he hung up and put the phone on the table.

'It was my friend, the driver. Hassan. He has news.'

Adrian's expression didn't change.

'Tell me.'

'They are taking the girl tomorrow to another place. Hassan is driving the car, with the fat man I tell you about. They are taking her to some place called Salé. Hassan says it is near Rabat. He said it is where the children are sometimes taken, but he has never driven them there before. He is calling me later and we will plan things.'

Adrian sat forward. 'Listen, Besmir, I think I know what they are doing. I have been working with the journalist and there is a man in Salé, a British paedophile. She is investigating him. This man is called Vinny. I saw him last night. He makes films of adults having sex with children. Also, he makes films where children are killed. I think they are taking the girl there.'

Besmir's stomach turned over. He had made this happen.

'Your face is white, Besmir. You are going to be sick?'

Besmir tried to compose himself. 'I am fine.'

'You should not be shocked, Besmir. What did you think was going to happen to the little girl when you took her? Are you stupid? You have worked for these people for over a year.'

Besmir felt anger rising. Not long ago, he would have kicked the table over and grabbed Adrian by the throat for challenging him like this. Not long ago, it was just another job to him. The fact that he was told by Leka to steal a kid had surprised him, but not enough for him refuse to do it. But whoever he was when he took the little girl from the beach, isn't who he was now.

'Fuck you, Adrian. You are now like the priest who tells people how to live? You think I don't know I was stupid?'

Adrian shook his head. 'That is your problem. But now you know what happens when you kidnap a human being. Their life is over. You should have thought about that. Like my sister. If I don't find my sister, her life is over. And the life of my mother back in Sarajevo.'

Besmir said nothing and looked away. He did not want

to push the Bosnian for fear of what he might unleash.

After a moment, he looked Adrian in the eye, and spoke calmly.

'So. We can do two things, my friend. I can sit here and listen to you telling me I am a bastard. Or we can make a plan. It is up to you.'

'We make the plan.'

CHAPTER 34

'I feel really sick.' Rosie pulled down the sun visor and glanced in the vanity mirror at Matt in the back seat.

'I'm not too clever myself,' Matt said. 'Fucking potholes.'

Adrian kept his eyes on the road as he tried to negotiate the car around the huge craters in the dirt track road.

'Is not really a road,' he said, steering away from another pothole. 'Is just tracks made from other cars. It is very bad.'

'Christ!' Rosie took a sip from her bottle of mineral water, now lukewarm in the midday sun. 'What kind of shithole is this? Bet it doesn't tell you this in the holiday brochure.'

'I don't think you'll find Salé in the holiday brochure, Rosie,' Matt said. 'What a dump.'

Rosie rolled up her window. Sweat broke out on her back and she could feel rising anxiety. The last thing she needed was a panic attack in the middle of this. She tried to take deep breaths without anyone noticing, but she was aware of Adrian stealing a glance at her.

'Is okay, Rosie. We will find the place soon.'

It wasn't the roads and the heat that were troubling Rosie. She felt threatened by the sheer teeming masses in the streets of this ugly ghetto they'd driven into. A few short miles from the charming, ancient city of Rabat, they'd driven into a different world. Salé was a giant slum and looked like someone had emptied half of Morocco into the streets and left them wandering around like refugees. There were few cars, and the streets were littered with piles of rubbish. The occasional rundown cafe was the only sign that there was any life going on. In their hired car they looked like tourists who'd taken a wrong turn. Rosie felt like prey caught in a trap. This really was the kind of place where you could disappear and nobody would ever find you. Looking at Adrian, she told herself to get a grip, and felt a little safer when he waved away the beggars shoving their faces into the car window and holding out their hands.

'No wonder this Vinny bastard makes his sick films in a place like this,' Rosie said, as they turned away from the crowds and up a side street.

'Look.' Matt pointed out a couple of ramshackle buildings that had brand logos of UK High Street stores on their crumbling shopfronts. Security cameras were perched on the high walls and there was razor wire on the huge iron gates.

'This must be where the sweatshops are for the big guns back in the UK. If they had nothing to hide, they wouldn't put them in this sewer of a place. It must be one of these slave labour factories, punters getting paid pennies. Fucking shameful.'

'We are here,' Adrian said. 'This is the street you said, Rosie. I stop here.'

Rosie checked the address in her notebook and looked out of the windscreen along the length of the narrow road.

'I see Javier's hired car. Let's crawl up here until we get closer to the house number, forty-four, Javier said.'

They drove slowly along the street, deserted but for Javier's car.

'Just pull in here, Adrian, would you.'

It had been a hurried plan, concocted between them last night. When Adrian came back to the hotel, he'd told them about his meeting with Besmir and that Amy was being taken down to Salé today. Rosie knew she should be telling the police, but involving them would open up a whole different game. It was too late to do that, even if she'd wanted to.

Javier had already arranged to meet Vinny to see the collection of films he had for distribution. Vinny told him he had to be out of the house by lunchtime as he was was expecting a visitor to his studio.

Matt had rigged Javier up with a hidden camera in the pocket flap of his safari shirt, and he was wired up with a tape recorder strapped to his body. If they got nothing else, Rosie decided, then at least they'd have a spread with this murdering sicko inside his porn den. If all they achieved was to get Vinny arrested and jailed, it was a job worth doing.

It had been Adrian who suggested they go there to see for themselves. He told Rosie to trust him, not to interfere with anything he would do – which was part of the reason she was anxious. Adrian didn't play by anyone's rules, and if something went wrong, nobody knew where they were.

Rosie's mobile rang and she took it out of her bag. Surprised, she showed the screen to Adrian. It was Javier. The arrangement had been that he would send a brief text if all was well. Maybe he changed his mind. She put the phone to her ear.

'Hello, my darling,' Javier breezed.

There had to be a reason for this. They were close, but not this close.

'Hello, darling.' Rosie played along in case someone was listening.

'Listen, darling, I cannot make lunch with you today, as I am in a very important business meeting.'

'Oh,' Rosie said. 'Is it going well for you? When will you be finished, Javier?'

'It's going very well. Everything I'd hoped for, but I can't discuss it. I'll be finished here soon, but I'm a long way from Tangiers. So I will call you when I get back there later this evening.'

'Fine. See you tonight. Glad it's going well.' The line went dead.

'He's talking like in code,' Rosie said. 'Hello, darling, and all that. Looks like it's going well, and he'll be out of there shortly.'

'Good. What now?' Matt said.

'Rosie,' Adrian said. 'I want you to leave the next part to me.' He turned to her. 'You must trust me.'

Rosie glanced at Matt who made an in-for-a-penny kind of face.

'Your shout, Rosie.'

Rosie sighed.

'What's not to trust, Adrian?'

He switched on the engine and moved the car along the road so that it was in front of Javier's. They sat in silence while Adrian rolled down the window and lit a cigarette. Rosie would have liked to smoke, but her bowels were churning as it was. A rush of nicotine was the last thing she needed.

After a few puffs, Adrian flicked the cigarette away and got out of the car. He went to the boot and took out his jacket. Rosie could see in the wing mirror that as he put on the jacket he was feeling something in the inside pocket, and she guessed it wasn't his wallet. She watched as he disappeared down a path and she could no longer see him, or the door of the building.

'I don't know about you, Rosie, but I'm shitting myself,' Matt said.

'Yeah, well that's one way of putting it.'

'What do you think he's up to?'

'Christ knows. But unless there's some heavy duty bouncers in there, I don't think wee Vinny will give Adrian a lot of trouble.'

'Does Javier carry a gun?'

'I don't know, Matt. I don't ask. I don't want to know.'

They sat in tense silence.

'I wonder what they're doing back at the office,' Matt chuckled.

Rosie looked at her watch. 'Lunchtime. There'll be the usual banter around the table in the canteen.'

'Aye. But they'll not be having this much fun.'

Rosie wiped the sweat from the back of her neck.

Silence. She pulled down the visor as a car crawled past them and the Moroccan occupants took a long look at them.

'What do you reckon the big man's going to do, Rosie? I reckon—'

'Ssssh, Matt.' Rosie heard muffled voices. 'I hear something.'

'Oh fuck!' Matt said as, suddenly, Javier emerged, rushing up the path towards them, carrying a holdall.

He opened the driver's door and threw himself in, breathless.

'Fucking hell, Rosie! Fuck me! The Bosnian. He's fucking crazy.' He switched on the engine.

'What's happening, Javier? What happened?'

Javier gave a nervous laugh. 'Oh shit!' He looked at Rosie. 'I'm just about to come out of the house, and this Vinny *coño* is seeing me to the door. And when he opens it, the big fucking Bosnian comes bursting in. Fuck! He pushed passed me and I almost fell on my ass. Then he grabs Vinny by the throat and holds the *coño* till he's turning blue. The guy is nuts.'

That's good coming from you, who pushed a guy off a roof, Rosie thought. But now wasn't the time for sarcastic jokes.

He opened the holdall.

'Christ, Javier. You took his films?'

Javier smiled. 'I just grabbed as much as I could while Adrian was choking him.'

'Fucking hell!' Matt said. 'Do you know what you've got?'

'He showed me a bit of one. A snuff movie. Just the start of it. I've got that. And I grabbed anything else I could. I even took his laptop. Adrian told me to get into your car and drive you. He is coming out in a minute and bringing Vinny with him.'

'Bringing Vinny with him? Fuck! You mean kidnap him?' Rosie heard her voice going up about two octaves.

'Shit! Look, Rosie! Here he comes!' Matt said.

Rosie put her hand to her mouth.

'I don't believe this.'

Then she saw Adrian.

'Jesus wept!'

Rosie turned to Matt whose mouth had dropped open as they saw Adrian appear at the top of the path carrying the struggling, puny figure of Vinny, kicking his legs out like a naughty kid who'd just been picked up by an angry parent. They watched as Adrian opened the boot of Javier's car, then punched Vinny hard once in the face, knocking him out. Then he stuffed him in the boot and slammed it shut.

'Oh fuck!' Javier said.

Adrian walked briskly towards Rosie's window. He didn't even look ruffled.

'I will drive your car, Javier. It's better Vinny is not in the same car as you, Rosie. Let's get out of here, just follow me.'

He turned away and headed to the other car before Rosie could even ask where they were going.

'We do what the man says, Rosita.' Javier took out a packet of cigarettes.

'Can I get one?' Matt said.

'You don't even smoke, Matt,' Rosie said turning around.

'I do now. I just started.'

Rosie felt the rising nausea again as Javier negotiated the craters on the road back out of Salé. They followed Adrian, and she prayed that his punch had been hard enough to keep Vinny unconscious for a while. Her mobile rang. McGuire. Timing was everything.

'Howsit going, Gilmour?'

'Er . . . Not bad, Mick.'

Rosie turned to Matt and mouthed the word McGuire. He grimaced.

'Just working away, Mick. Still doing a bit of digging in Morocco. A couple of things up my sleeve, but it's too early to tell you.'

From the corner of her eye, Rosie could see the smile breaking out on Javier's face.

'Si,' Javier whispered. 'A couple of things up your sleeve – and a body in the boot.'

'How did the story go, Mick? The Daletsky story?' she asked. 'I was away before I could get a chance to phone.'

'Brilliant, Rosie. Vincent fronted him up and he shat himself. We did the whole lot – splash and spread. The people-trafficking we just touched on, but we're going to run that along with the escaped girl's story tomorrow as a follow-up. I decided to go with the rent boy and Carter-Smith witnessing the kidnapping. Vincent put it to him that he was with the boy and that they both saw the girl being taken. He showed him the picture of his Commons security pass.'

'What did he say?'

'He burst right open. Actually to be more accurate he burst into fucking tears.'

'Really?'

'Yeah. Blubbing. Then, once he'd dried his eyes and re-done his make-up he agreed to sit down and tell our man everything. He knew he had no option. It was damage limitation time.' McGuire chortled. 'I love it when that happens.'

'That's amazing. So what did he say?'

'He was a bit vague about seeing the kid. Understandable. They wouldn't have thought anything of it at the time. But it was afterwards he knew that what they'd seen must have been the kid being snatched, and he should have told the cops. But he kept it back, to protect himself, the fucker.'

'Is he going to resign?'

'Oh, yeah. He already had his letter in by the time we hit the presses last night.'

'That's great, Mick.'

'So what are you doing today? I don't mind you plugging away there Rosie, but now that this Carter-Smith revelation is out, it will have repercussions on the Lennon family. We'll need their reaction and stuff. Plus, I'm choking to put that revelation to them about Lennon's old man and the dead Russian tart.'

'Sure, but you can get Declan to pick up on the reaction to Carter-Smith while I'm away. The grandfather line can wait a day or two till I get back. Nobody else has it.'

'Yeah, okay. But I don't want you in Morocco for too long. The story is back in Spain, Rosie.'

'Well, we don't really know that for sure, Mick. We're trying to get leads to find this kid.'

'Right. But what about that Vinny bastard. Have you tracked him down yet?'

'Vinny?' Rosie said. 'Oh, he's not saying much at the moment. But we're working on it.'

She could see Javier looking in his rear view mirror and smiling at Matt.

'Okay, Rosie, keep it going. And be careful. Great job on Carter-Smith. You'll get a big lunch when you come home.'

'Yeah, Mick. Fine.'

'Hey, Rosie. Bet you're enjoying your little sojourn back on the road, eh?'

'Well, Mick, it's definitely more exciting than driving my desk about.'

'You bet. Just be careful, Rosie.'

Rosie slumped back in her seat.

CHAPTER 35

Besmir had already been with Hassan to the place on the back road to Salé, and they'd meticulously planned the exact angle where he would hide his car so that it wouldn't be seen by the oncoming traffic. Not that there was much movement on the deserted road; except for the occasional truck trundling along the dust track carrying oranges or livestock, Besmir had seen nothing in the two hours he'd been here.

He could have waited until later before leaving Tangiers. He was well ahead of the time Hassan said they would be passing the spot, but leaving things to chance was for the lazy. Besmir liked to be organised. So now, with his car hidden out of view behind the derelict goatherd's shelter, he sat in the driver's seat, smoking and staring out at the searing heat rising in waves across the baked scrubland. He took a mouthful from a bottle of water and wiped sweat from his top lip with the back of his hand.

He was nervous. Not because he thought the fat man

would be any serious threat to him, but because he knew that, from the start, he had not thought this whole business through. He'd been driven by only one purpose: get the girl back and take the children from the cages.

Besmir looked at his watch, rested his head back and sighed to himself. Leka's words rang in his ears. He was right. The East Europeans were treated like shit when they came west in search of their fortune. Menial jobs and racist taunts faced them – especially the Albanians and the Romanians – at every turn. The attitude of the Western Europeans he encountered when he left Albania had stunned Besmir when he first arrived in Italy. Like the rest of the Albanians, he had been smuggled in by boat afer paying everything he had to a gangmaster to get him across the short stretch of the Adriatic. It was a different world in Italy. Everyone seemed to have so much, so many possessions. Even in the countryside where it was poorer, people had so much more than he had ever seen in Albania. In the towns he noticed stacks of food in the shops, shiny cars, and people smartly dressed, yet he saw little kindness.

He had been full of hope then. He'd vowed to leave behind his old ways, when he lived on his wits on the streets of Tirana working as an enforcer for the local mafia. He wanted a different life, but with every job he took in Italy, he faced daily insults with bosses treating him and the other Albanians like slaves. He was sacked most weeks for fighting. Finally he left Italy in a hurry, the cops on his tail, after throwing his boss through a plate glass window. He didn't wait around to find out if the man had survived.

In Spain's Costa del Sol, one of Besmir's old friends from Tirana contacted him. He told him there was money to be made for the Albanians, but he wouldn't find it washing dishes or digging ditches. The Albanians, his friend said, were on the rise. They had a reputation across Europe for violence, and they teamed their cunning and ruthlessness with the Russians in establishing a power base. Together they ran their empire, built on money-laundering, fear and murder. The Brits were still the king-pins in the drugs trade and corrupt property markets, but they were constantly looking over their shoulders because the hardmen from the East were on the march.

Until he snatched the kid from the beach, Besmir was on the up. He had the respect of Leka who did the day-to-day running of Daletsky's organisation. Now everything had changed, and he found it hard to make sense of what he was doing. He had kidnapped a little kid without flinching, and now he was risking absolutely everything to get her back. He shook his head at the stupidity of it.

His fingers caressed the keys in the ignition. He could drive away from here right now and just keep on going. He couldn't go back to Spain, that much he knew, because Leka would be looking everywhere for him. But there were plenty of other places he could go, where he could live a low-key life and stay hidden from the cities where the Albanians operated. But he hadn't even thought that far ahead.

And now that the Bosnian was involved it made him even more nervous. He didn't fear Adrian, he liked him – even though he knew he was capable of killing him.

Deep down, maybe they were on the same side, but Adrian had told him he had this journalist woman with him. You didn't take journalists on jobs like this, and certainly not women.

At last, through the heat haze, Besmir saw the roof of the car emerging. He slipped out of the driver's seat and into the concrete shelter, and watched the car pull in at the side of the road fifty yards away. Hassan got out first, and glanced back at the shelter where they'd arranged for Besmir to hide. Hassan stretched his arms above his head and turned towards the fat man who got out of the car and lit a cigarette. Hassan walked away from him to the trees nearby and stood having a pee, with his back to Besmir. So far so good. Besmir crept out of shelter. He'd already worked out that it would take him only a few seconds to sprint to Hassan's car where he'd be shielded from the fat man's view. He waited for the shout.

'Khalid! Khalid! Come!' The urgency in Hassan's voice was just as they'd rehearsed it yesterday.

The fat man turned towards Hassan and looked irritated, but walked towards him. Besmir moved fast, reaching the car in a few strides. He crouched behind it, out of view, and watched as the fat man approached Hassan.

'What? What is the problem, stupid? Have you shit your pants?' the fat man said, as he came closer to Hassan.

'Look,' Hassan said. 'Here, in the bushes. There's a goat. It's dying. It must have been attacked. We should put it out of its misery.' He pointed to the clump of bushes.

When he got alongside Hassan, the fat man peered

into he trees but could see nothing – because there was nothing to see. If he was suspicious, the fat man did not get the chance for his reflexes to react. By the time he realised there was no goat, Besmir had come up behind him and plunged the knife between his shoulder blades. The only thing that registered on his face was surprise, before he dropped to the ground with a gasp.

'Quick. Get the girl.' Besmir knelt down, pulled the fat man's head back by the hair and drew the knife across his throat. He wiped the knife on his victim's back and walked away as the the blood seeped from the dead man's fat neck into the dirt.

Hassan went into the fat man's trouser pocket and took out a wad of notes, then went to his car, carefully picked up the little girl from the back seat, and rushed towards Besmir.

'Here. In the back. Is she alright?'

'Yes. She is drugged a bit to make her sleep. But she is alright.'

They got into Besmir's car and the wheels spun and sprayed up a cloud of dust as Hassan hit the accelerator. Besmir looked back at the corpse then turned around and stared straight ahead in silence as the car sped off.

Eventually, he glanced at Hassan.

'No going back now, my friend.'

Hassan's face broke into a smile, and Besmir took his mobile from his pocket and punched in a number.

'Adrian,' he said. 'We have the girl. Follow the directions I told you. We will be waiting for you.'

CHAPTER 36

'Where the hell is Adrian going?' Rosie said.

'Fucked if I know.' Matt looked out of the windscreen at Adrian's car a couple of hundred yards ahead of them.

'We passed the exit for Tangiers half an hour ago,' Javier said. 'We're going deeper into the countryside this way. What do you think, Rosie? I'm not sure I like this.'

Javier's unease made Rosie even more nervous. She looked at him but said nothing. Adrian had saved her life back in Glasgow, not once but twice. She pushed the niggle away that one of these days Adrian's luck would run out.

Rosie punched numbers in her mobile.

'Rosie.' Adrian answered the phone after two rings. 'You are afraid?' He sounded as relaxed as ever.

'Well, Adrian, we're wondering what's happening.'

'I told you I will look after you. But you must trust me.'

'But Adrian,' Rosie persisted. 'Where exactly are we going? And what do you plan to do with Vinny in the boot of the car? I mean he might be dead by now in this heat.'

'So what if he's dead, Rosie. You think people will miss a piece of shit like that?'

'No. Course not. But if he's dead, Adrian, he's dead in my hired car. And we *are* in Morocco.'

'Just trust me. It's better you don't know. I will look after you and your friends. Do not worry.' He hung up.

Rosie knew Javier was clocking her. If it came to the crunch and their lives were in danger, Javier would simply turn the car around and take them back to Tangiers. He wouldn't put it to a vote.

'What did he say?' Matt tapped Rosie's shoulder.

'He said to trust him. He knows what he's doing.'

'What did he say about Vinny in the boot?' Javier asked.

'He said if he dies people will not miss a piece of shit like that.'

'Terrific.' Matt sat back. 'He dies in our hired car, Rosie. I'm guessing Adrian hasn't seen *Midnight Express*.'

They all laughed nervously.

'That was set in Turkey, Matt,' Rosie said.

'Yeah, I know. Same difference. But I still don't fancy playing hide the sausage in a Moroccan jail.'

Rosie giggled despite the nerves in her stomach.

'Rosie, I think your friend Adrian is a nutter,' Javier said, 'but he can take care of himself – that much I saw. I get the feeling he is taking us to see the guy Besmir. The one he came out here to find.'

'The kidnapper?' Matt said. 'Oh, he sounds like a right nice guy. Fuck me.'

'Listen, Matt, I'm as nervous as you. Imagine having to phone McGuire from the pokey in Tangiers and say "Hey Mick, about that body in the boot . . . You'll laugh when I tell you this . . ."' Rosie snorted. 'Christ, I could get hysterical at the thought of it.'

'He is stopping the car,' Javier said.

He pulled over behind Adrian and they all got out. Everyone looked at Adrian's car as they heard the thuds from the boot and Vinny's muffled shouts.

'I think he said he wants the veal,' Matt said drily.

Everyone sniggered, except for Adrian whose face came close to a smile.

'That is funny,' he said to Matt.

'Adrian.' Rosie spread her arms out in appeal. 'I think you should tell us where we're going. I do trust you, pal. But . . . er . . . we seem to be driving to Algeria or somewhere. This is all getting a bit crazy.'

'Okay, Rosie, I will tell you what I can. We are meeting Besmir. The kidnapper.'

'You serious?'

'Yes. Things have changed with him, Rosie. He took the girl, but now he wants to bring her back.'

A little rocket went up in Rosie's head, blinding her to everything else. Amy being returned by the kidnapper, and she could be at the heart of the story. Christ! She would just about give her right arm for that.

'He wants to bring her back? What? You mean he's still got her?'

'It's complicated, Rosie, but yes. He has the girl now, but he didn't have her until today.'

'What?'

'I cannot explain that. Just trust me. We must go now. We will see Besmir soon, it is arranged. Then we can see what we do. I know he wants to do something else.'

'What else, Adrian? What are you talking about?'

'I cannot tell you now. Please.' He gave her a look and Rosie knew not to ask any more.

'Okay, Adrian.' She turned to Javier and Matt. 'C'mon guys. Let's go. There's only one show in town.'

Rosie's nausea had lifted. All she could see was the reunion picture of Amy with her parents on the front page of the *Post*. Nothing else mattered.

Javier put his arm around Rosie's shoulders as they went to the car.

'You have that look in your eye, Rosie. I've seen it before. It's reckless. You're making me nervous.'

Rosie smiled. 'How can I be reckless, Javier, when you're in charge?'

'If I was in charge, Rosita, we'd be having a siesta and wondering where we are going to have dinner.' He got into the car.

Rosie and Matt exchanged glances as they opened the car doors.

'We might as well strap ourselves in for this,' Rosie said.

As they were about to drive off, Javier's phone rang. He took it out of his pocket and looked at the number.

'*Si. Digame.*' He put the phone to his ear, then turned to Rosie. 'Excuse me. I must take this call.' He opened the door and stepped out.

Rosie wondered why he couldn't have taken the call in the car. She spoke a little Spanish, but not enough to get the gist of a one-sided of conversation between Spaniards. Javier obviously didn't want them to hear, but she trusted him. Whatever he was doing, there was a reason for it.

'Everything okay?' Rosie said, as he got back in the car.

'Yes. It was my friend from the Guarda Civil. They know about the Russian connection, the prostitute and Amy's grandfather. They know about Daletsky.'

'Christ!'

'Doesn't surprise me,' Javier said. 'To be honest, the only surprise is that this has not come out before. But someone somewhere has perhaps been looking at the whole family background and put it together.'

'Or somebody has talked.'

Javier shot her a look.

'No, Javier. Of course I don't mean you. Don't be so paranoid.'

'Fine. I would be very disappointed if you did. But Rosie, listen to me. This changes things. Because if the Guarda Civil know, then you can be assured that Daletsky knows it has come out why the child was taken. And if he knows, they will be moving to close all the doors.'

'What do you mean?'

'I mean Daletsky or Leka, or whoever this Besmir guy was working for. They will want him dead now more than ever before.'

'But why? It's not as if he's going to walk into a police station and confess.'

'No. But if he is caught he might, to save his own skin.'

'I see what you mean. When did your friend find out?'

'This morning. But that is only when *he* found out. I do not know how long the Guarda Civil have known, which means I do not know how long anyone else has known. That makes me worry more.'

Rosie suddenly felt scared again. 'We have to keep going now, Javier. What else can we do? We might turn back and run slap-bang into whoever is chasing Besmir. These guys won't be asking questions. And if we run into cops, well, we've got a guy in the boot of the car.'

'You're right. Let's just hope that there's not a reception party waiting for us when we meet this Besmir.'

CHAPTER 37

No cars had passed them in any direction for miles. The road narrowed to a single dusty track and Javier slowly negotiated the hairpin bends around the hillside. They drove in silence.

Rosie was exhausted. The rush of adrenaline back in Salé had spurred her on, but now the stress and the lack of sleep for the past few nights left her feeling wrecked. She thought of her father back in her flat, imagining him sitting around watching television, bored, wondering where his life had gone now that it was coming to an end. She felt a pang of loneliness for him.

Ahead of them, Adrian was slowing down. Javier took his foot off the accelerator. 'I can see a car is stopped beyond Adrian's,' he said.

Rosie shook herself out of her daydream and rolled down the window to catch some air. The fierce heat was like a hairdryer blowing in her face. Adrian pulled into the side the road and got out. They saw him walking towards the car parked about fifty yards in front. Javier stopped, but kept the engine running.

'That must be him. The Besmir guy. I'd better get my camera ready.' Matt rummaged around in the back.

'You are having a laugh, Matt?'

'No I'm not, Rosie. If the guy who kidnapped Amy Lennon comes out of that car I'm the only guy in the world who's getting a fucking picture of him.'

'Christ sake, Matt. This is a bit dodgy, pal. Even for a kamikaze merchant like you.' Rosie half turned to see Matt fixing a long lens to a camera.

'He'll never see me,' he grinned back at her. 'Not in a million years.'

'Relax, Javier,' Matt said, resting the long lens on Javier's shoulder. 'It'll be over before you know it, and it won't hurt a bit.'

The car door opened and a man got out of the passenger seat and walked towards Adrian. Another got out of the driving seat. Two of them, Rosie thought. If it turned nasty and Besmir decided to take Adrian on, he had help. Her mouth was dry as a stick, and she drank a sip of warm water. She breathed a sigh of relief when the man stretched out his hand to Adrian who shook it.

'You fucking beauty,' Matt whispered. 'Done and dusted. Snap of the year stamped all over it. One more for luck . . . That's it . . . Magic.'

'When this is all over, Matt, let's hope we dine out on that picture.'

Rosie kept her eye on the tall man in conversation with Adrian.

'That must be him. I wonder what they're saying. The guy is looking over here. Shit, he's coming up. Get that camera out of the way, Matt. Quick.'

'It's done, Rosie. Settle petal.'

Rosie tried a deep breath, but it wouldn't come, her chest felt tight. Shit.

'Take it easy, Rosita. Say nothing. Just answer any questions, and don't be smart,' Javier whispered.

'I'm hardly going to be smart,' Rosie snapped back. She was tense enough without Javier rubbing her up the wrong way.

She opened the door and stepped out of the car as Adrian and the man came towards her. The stranger was pale and unshaven with close cropped dark hair, and on the skinny side even for a tall man. His black shirt was open and he was wearing a vest that may even have been white at one time. He gazed straight at Rosie, black eyes under heavy dark eyebrows. He looked haunted, exhausted. Somehow she'd expected a monster, but he looked ordinary. This was the man who had stolen a little child sitting on a beach without a thought for the misery he had caused and the lives he had wrecked. He had no right to look this ordinary.

'This is the man I told you about, Rosie.'

Adrian didn't say his name, and Rosie was grateful that he didn't put his hand out for her to shake, because she couldn't have done it.

'The girl is in the car,' Adrian said, saving Rosie from asking.

Her heartbeat quickened. She was within a few yards of Amy.

'May I see her?' Rosie directed the question to the man. He looked at Adrian.

'Come,' he said and walked away. 'But I don't want to waste time.'

Rosie walked behind them, knowing Matt would be choking to get out of the car and take a picture. In your dreams, Matt. The driver, a sallow, Moroccan boy who looked no more than twenty-five, smiled with his eyes as Rosie approached. He looked gentle, out of place in this kind of company.

Besmir opened the door of the car and there she was. Amy. She was alive! Really alive and lying there right in front of Rosie, fast asleep, like any other kid who'd dropped off to sleep in the back seat of their parents' car. Rosie closed her eyes for a second and blinked to make sure she wasn't dreaming.

'Jesus,' she whispered. 'May I . . . ?'

She leaned in and studied the sleeping child: her pale face dirty and tear-stained, the thatch of unruly curls tumbling onto her thick, dark eyelashes. She looked peaceful, the way all children should look. She shouldn't be here in the middle of nowhere, with nobody to comfort her when she woke up confused and frightened. Rosie felt a lump in her throat, wondering how many tears this little girl had shed in these past weeks. She reached out and brushed her finger against the girl's soft chubby arm, then she stepped back.

'What do you do when she cries for her mother?' The words were out before she could stop herself.

He seemed taken aback. 'I did not hurt her. I want to take her back.' His voice was deep.

Rosie bit her lip to stop herself saying any more. She wasn't afraid of this man.

'Rosie,' Adrian said taking a step between them. 'Listen. There is a place near here, the place I told you about, where children are kept in cages. It is close by. We want to go there now. We will need the others to help to get the children out. We will take the three cars.'

'I do not think the woman should come,' Besmir said. 'Is better she stays close by with the girl.'

'If you think I am staying out here alone while the rest of you go wherever it is, you're very wrong.'

Tense silence.

'Adrian,' Rosie said. 'I need a word. It's important.'

The man turned his back on them and Rosie and Adrian walked to the car. Javier and Matt got out.

'Javier,' Rosie said. 'Tell Adrian what your Guarda Civil man said about the Russian connection.' She turned to Adrian. 'I think this is all about to burst, Adrian. You're probably not the only one sent here to look for Besmir.'

Adrian listened while Javier told him. He blew air out of pursed lips.

'I must tell Besmir.'

'Adrian,' Rosie said. 'Listen to me. I am not staying anywhere by myself. Wherever we're going, we all go together. Make sure he understands that.'

'Rosie.' Adrian looked over his shoulder as the sound

of Vinny's kicking started up again. 'There is another problem. I have already told Besmir. A few minutes ago, I took a call from Leka. He asked me where I was and if I had found Besmir. He sounded suspicious, and I don't think he believed me when I told him I was close to tracking him down. I have no way of knowing for sure, but I think Leka is looking for both of us now.'

'Christ! What do we do?'

'We go ahead with the plan. But first, I am going to deal with this piece of shit.' He jerked his head in the direction of the car.

'Vinny? What you going to do?' Rosie looked around the barren scrubland. 'You just going to leave him here?'

'Is better not to ask. Come.'

He walked off in the direction of Besmir's car.

Rosie, Javier and Matt looked at each other then started walking behind him in silence.

'You wait here with Hassan,' Adrian said. 'Maybe is better you look the other way for a few minutes.'

Rosie felt hot and light-headed. The Moroccan boy gave her a sympathetic look. Besmir and Adrian walked towards Adrian's car, where the noise of Vinny's kicking was growing louder.

When the boot pinged open everything went eerily quiet, then they heard Vinny's muffled scream as Adrian and Besmir dragged him out. Rosie felt Javier's arm around her shoulder as they saw Vinny's bloodied face, twisted in blind panic as he pleaded and tried to scream. Besmir stuffed a rag from the boot into Vinny's mouth, and he struggled and kicked while both of them stood him up, his legs buckling. Vinny had wet his trousers. For a second Rosie made eye contact with him, and the primal part of her that wanted retribution for what he'd done was glad to see the naked terror in his eyes.

'Fuck sake,' Matt said. 'What're they going to do with him? Where are they taking him?' He looked at Hassan.

'Over there.' He pointed to what looked like an old well made out of mud and stones. 'It hasn't been used for a long time. Nobody goes there any more. Is very deep.'

'A well? You mean they're going to throw him in there?' Rosie gripped Javier's arm as they dragged Vinny across the ground.

'Is better you turn away now. If you don't see then you don't know.' Hassan said.

'Turn around, Rosie. Come on,' Javier said.'You too, Matt. It is better that we don't see.'

The four of them turned away and stood in stunned silence. The sound of Vinny's agonised whimpering was barely audible now. Rosie pictured the final moments in her mind, Vinny choking on the rag, knowing his fate was sealed. There was no need for her to turn round, but she did because she couldn't help herself, even though she knew it would be a sight that would haunt her night-mares. She turned just in time to see Adrian bundle Vinny head first over the crumbling lip of the well. The last thing she saw were the soles of Vinny's sandals as he disappeared. The muffled screams stopped.

'*Dios mio*, Rosie,' Javier shook his head. 'I knew you would look. You are one fucking crazy woman.'

Rosie couldn't speak. Besmir shot her a brief look as he walked towards the car and opened the passenger door.

'Come. We must go,' Adrian said.

CHAPTER 38

Jenny Lennon stepped outside onto the patio with a mug of coffee and sat down wearily at the wooden picnic table. She stared out at the deserted stretch of beach and the tears sprung to her eyes. It was the same every morning when she came out here. Amy was everywhere – squealing with delight as she held her hand and they jumped over the waves. She could hear her giggling, see her little legs run across the sand with Martin roaring playfully and chasing her.

Then Jenny saw herself that morning when her world had ended. She shivered as she remembered those frantic moments, running up and down the beach calling Amy's name. The notion that she would never, ever see her daughter's face again was something she hadn't dared consider. She closed her eyes to shut out the image of her and Jamie writhing on the bed. She would never – could never – forgive herself for what she had done. This wasn't her life any more. Her life had gone the moment she came out onto the beach and realised Amy had vanished. Only now was she beginning to understand the possibility that she might never see her again. Whatever life she was living now, she felt that she was merely a spectator in it. This was her fault. She had made it happen.

The only thing Jenny was certain of was that she didn't want to go on living. She didn't know who to tell or what she would do, but she wanted it to end. The hope had died some time during the three weeks since Amy had vanished, but she couldn't remember exactly when. She only knew that inside she was already dead. There was nothing else to live for if Amy was really gone forever. Martin was broken. What they had been to each other had gone, along with their little girl, and there was nothing left.

It had been so still and quiet since everyone left. The Reillys and the others had stayed on an extra few days after they were due to go home because they'd wanted to support their friends. But their lives had to go on, and it was Martin who insisted they go home. In the end, Jenny was glad to see them leave. They all knew the guilty secret of her and Jamie. It was the elephant in the room each time they got together. She knew they judged her, and they were right to judge, but she also felt their sorrow and sympathy for the price she had paid for her mistake. Jenny hadn't even gone to see them the day they left because she didn't want to be anywhere near Jamie. She'd taken to her bed and left it to Martin to say their good-byes.

The pair of them would stay on at the villa, working with the police investigation and praying each day for some scrap of hope. But so far there had been nothing. It was as though Amy had vanished into thin air.

Jenny and Martin were suffocating under a blanket of grief. They rarely spoke to one another unless it was about Amy and the investigation. She could hardly eat and her weight had already dropped by a stone. Pictures of her anguished face, with its hollow cheekbones, had appeared in the newspapers. They'd been snapped walking together on the beach on the advice of the police to help keep their story alive for the press. Jenny had stopped reading the papers. She couldn't cope with all the speculation and theories about what might have happened to Amy. One newspaper suggested she was snatched by gypsies, another that she had been stolen for a childless couple in America. One trashy publication even suggested Martin and Jenny had killed her and disposed of the body. The Spanish police had come down heavily to quash that notion and the newspaper apologised.

But yesterday there had been a bombshell of a story in the *Post* that shook everyone, and made her feel even worse. Their front page said that British Home Secretary Michael Carter-Smith had been in a villa nearby when Amy was taken. He'd been with a rent boy, and they had both witnessed a little girl being taken from the beach by a man. Martin had exploded when he heard the news, smashing plates onto the floor and punching the wall until his fist was bleeding. The bastard Home Secretary had kept quiet about it until the newspaper confronted him. If Carter-Smith had come forward earlier, it might have helped the investigation at the start. But according to the paper, the politican had defended himself, claiming he'd barely noticed the man who took the child. They'd assumed it was an innocent scene of a father with his child. And, in any case, everyone knew that within an hour of being on the motorway the kidnapper could be anywhere. However, Carter-Smith did resign his Cabinet post over the issue. Jenny couldn't even muster any rage about him. He didn't make this happen, she did.

She assumed the reason Martin had been summoned by the Guarda Civil in Marbella was because of the Carter-Smith story. He had left at eight-thirty that morning when they sent a car to pick him up. The police wouldn't discuss the situation when they'd phoned him last night, and would only say that they wanted to talk to him. Martin told Jenny there was no need for her to come. It was the only conversation they'd had all day yesterday.

Now she heard him come in through the back door and steeled herself for another day of silence. She heard him go to the fridge, followed by the rattle of a glass on the worktop. She glanced up when he came out onto the patio and sat opposite her, and gave him an inquiring look. But she could see from his face that whatever the police had wanted to tell him, it was not good news.

'We need to talk, Jenny.'

Jenny couldn't remember when in the last two weeks he had spoken her name. She looked at his grey face and her heart sank at what was left of their lives.

'What is it, Martin?'

'There's something I didn't know about Dad.'

'Your dad?' Jenny was confused.

'Yes.' He took a deep breath. 'Something I didn't know about. I just found out. The Guarda Civil told me.'

'What? Why? I don't understand, Martin. Why are the police talking to you about your dad?'

'They said it's all connected.' He buried his face in his hands. 'Oh, Jenny. Oh Christ, Jenny.'

'Martin. What are you talking about? What's connected? Your dad? Amy?' She stood up and put her hands on his shoulders. 'Martin, talk to me. What the hell are you saying? Tell me. Do you mean Amy?'

He nodded, sniffing. 'Yes. Oh, Jenny . . . Sit down. I need to tell you everything.'

Jenny sat stiffly, various scenarios raging through her mind before Martin spoke.

His father, he had been told, had been involved in the death of some Russian prostitute in a Moscow hotel room. He had left the country in a hurry. Jenny remembered her father-in-law being in Russia last year on a business trip, but he had often done that as he'd tried to build up foreign property contracts in Eastern Europe since the fall of the Berlin wall. They'd already sold property in Poland and the Czech Republic as holiday homes for eager Western investors. The old Eastern bloc, Martin senior had said, was where the next property boom would come. Smart estate agents were the ones who got in on the ground floor.

Jenny sat open mouthed with shock and Martin sounded confused. He said wasn't a hundred percent sure of the detail. He had been so stunned when the police told him that he was barely able to take it in, but apparently the property dealers they'd met with the day after they arrived in Spain were all connected to Amy's disappearance.

'What are you saying, Martin? That . . . That they took Amy?' She stood up. 'Martin, this isn't making any sense. I want to talk to the police. Why didn't you take me with you?'

'Sit down, Jenny. Sit down and listen.' He pulled her by the hand. 'Please, Jenny. This is so fucking important.' His voice was shaking.

Jenny sat down.

'It was all a set-up, that's what the police are working on. They have inside information – don't ask me how because I don't know – I'm only saying what they told me. They said Amy was kidnapped for revenge, because the big boss down here – some Russian mafia billionaire who owns everything corrupt in the Costa – because, they said . . . they said the prostitute who died, who dad had been with, was the daughter of this man's best friend. And they took revenge for her death by kidnapping Amy.'

Jenny felt as though she'd been shot.

'Hold on, Martin. Are they saying your dad killed this prostitute in Moscow?'

'Well, they believe he's responsible because he didn't get help. Christ, I don't *know*.'

Jenny stared at him. Suddenly things seemed clear to her.

'Martin. Don't lie to me, just tell me. Did you know about your father and this . . . this dead Russian prostitute last year?'

Silence. It didn't matter what his answer was. She knew.

'You knew, didn't you, Martin?'

'No. I didn't know.' He avoided her eyes.

'You fucking liar.' Jenny raised her voice.

'Oh, that's good coming from you.'

Jenny stood up.

'You're lying, Martin. It's written all over your face. You can't tell me the truth about the Russian and your dad, because now you know it's all connected you can't afford to tell the truth.'

Martin got up and went inside. Jenny went in after him. She grabbed hold of his arm and tried to turn him round.

'Tell me. You can't tell me, can you?'

'You mean like you couldn't tell me you were fucking my best friend when someone stole Amy? What the fuck would you know about truth?' He spat the words at her.

'Listen, you bastard. You . . . it was *you* who took us to meet some fucking Eastern Europeans. *You* let us take our daughter with us. And all the time you knew that your father had been involved in something dodgy in Moscow.' She slapped his face. 'You are as guilty as I am. What the hell were you thinking about, going anywhere near these people if you knew about your dad? And you've kept this to yourself all along. I can't believe this.'

Martin slumped onto the sofa. He put his head in his hands.

'I didn't want to believe it either, Jenny. I'm sorry. I didn't know the full story about Dad in Russia. He just said to me there was a problem with some girl he picked up when he was drunk one night. I only found out now, this morning, that she had died. He told me that I could do the next trip to Russia because he left in a bit of a hurry. That's when he explained a little about the girl. He said it wasn't important, and I didn't think for a minute the people we were meeting here were connected to that. How could I?'

Silence. Jenny stood looking at him for a few moments before she spoke.

'They took our little girl for revenge because of something your father's supposed to have done? I don't believe this is happening.' She began to cry. 'Oh, Martin . . . Have they killed her? They have, haven't they? They've killed Amy. Is that what they told you? Please, Martin, just tell me everything. Please.'

She sat down beside him while he answered her.

'They've been watching and waiting for some time, the police told me. That's why they phoned me in Glasgow and asked to set up the meeting when I told them we were coming here on holiday. They said if we met here, it would save them coming to Glasgow and it would be easier.'

Jenny wiped her tears.

'So,' Martin went on, 'those phone calls and emails I got from the property dealer here, who wanted us to see the off-plan apartments that Dad had been negotiating to sell . . . It was all a set-up.'

'Didn't you even consider what your dad had been involved in with the prostitute?'

'No, Jenny. He only spoke about it once and said it was

nothing and that he thought she was alive when he left her. He told me she'd just fallen over because they were drunk. And because there were no police or follow-up I just assumed he was telling the truth. The last thing I expected was anything to come of it a year down the line.'

Jenny wiped her face with her hands.

'So, is it possible they're holding Amy somewhere? What do they think? Do they want money, Martin? We'll find the money. We'll sell the house, the business – everything. If it's revenge they want, they . . . they can take me. They can kill me if they want.' Tears spilled out of her eyes.

'The police don't know, Jenny. Nothing has been mentioned about ransom. The police are working on the theory that Amy's in Morocco. They think that's where they took her.'

A light went on somewhere in Jenny's head.

'Martin,' she said, sniffing. 'I think Amy's alive. They could have killed her as soon as they took her so why take her to Morocco?'

Martin took her hand. 'The police think they've sold her. Could be anything. I don't even want to think about what they might have sold her for.'

'No, Martin. Don't. She's alive, Martin. Amy's alive.' Tears streamed down her face. 'We'll find her. I know we will.'

She put her arms around Martin and held him as he sobbed on her shoulder.

CHAPTER 39

'Why the fuck did you look, Rosie? Are you nuts?' Javier flicked the lighter to the cigarette between his lips as he drove.

'I couldn't help it. I just did it from instinct.' Rosie pushed the palms of her hands onto her eyes. 'Christ, I wish I hadn't.'

'Are you alright?' Matt squeezed her shoulder.

'Yeah. Let's just pray we get through this day. We'll be okay. We'll dine out on it when we get home.'

'You bet.'

Rosie stuck her head out of the window to stave off the nausea she was feeling. Javier said there was no time to throw up, they had to keep up with Adrian's car in front as he followed Besmir – all three cars now rattling along faster than was safe on the narrow, twisting roads. They turned off through a concealed entrance and then up a narrow track, bouncing over the potholes. Rosie rubbed her damp palms on her trousers. Javier wiped sweat from his forehead with the back of his hand.

'You okay?' Rosie touched his arm.

'Of course.' He didn't look at her.

In the distance, Rosie saw what looked like farm out-
buildings, made from corrugated metal sheeting like the
kind she'd seen in shanty-town slums in various parts of
the world. They drove behind Besmir into the yard, littered
with rubbish and a couple of burnt-out rusting cars. He
stopped just before the window of one of the dilapidated
buildings and he and Hassan jumped out. Rosie couldn't
hear what he said, but he seemed to be issuing instruc-
tions to Adrian at the window of his car. Then Besmir
and Hassan went towards the door and opened it, disap-
pearing inside. Suddenly they heard a woman screaming
and glass smashing. Then nothing. Rosie, Javier and Matt
looked at each other. Rosie's mobile rang and all three
of them jumped nervously.

It was Adrian. 'When Besmir comes out, just do as he
says. Follow us.'

'What was the screaming? I heard a woman screaming?'

'She is the old bastard who is supposed to look after
the children. She is always drunk. Besmir and Hassan
were just shutting her up.'

Rosie was frightened to ask any more.

'Where are the children?'

'In the place next door. Like a stable or something. You
see it?'

She looked at the ramshackle barn. 'Yes.'

'When Besmir comes, we go in there. We take the children and put them in our cars. Then we go.'

'Where?' Rosie ventured.

'Doesn't matter. Away from here.'

When he hung up, Rosie relayed the information to Javier and Matt.

'This is mental,' Matt said. 'Fucking mental.'

A few seconds later, Besmir, Hassan and Adrian emerged from the building and went to their car. They took Amy from the back seat and carried her to Rosie's car.

'Come,' Besmir said to Rosie.

She got out of the car. He handed her the sleeping child.

'You must take her. Keep hold of her.' He turned. 'Come, we get the other children.'

Hassan and Adrian followed Besmir.

'Let's go.' Rosie looked at Javier and Matt who didn't move. 'Come on, guys. We don't have an option here.'

'Let's go, Matt.' Javier opened his door and got out. 'I can't fucking believe I'm doing this.'

Nothing could have prepared them for what they saw when Besmir kicked in the door. The overpowering stench hit them. Death has a distinctive, unmistakable, rancid smell, and a rotting corpse will knock you off your feet. Even if it's your first encounter with a decaying body, you don't need to ask what it is. You just know.

'Oh, fuck!' Matt's voice was a whisper.

As their eyes adjusted to the dark, they became aware of things moving on the ground. Then scurrying.

'Fuck! Rats! Fuck!' Matt kicked something at his feet.

Then came the sound of a child crying. Rosie peered into the darkness and could see what looked like cages.

Behind the bars, a little figure tried to stand up, but it fell down again.

'Look, Adrian, a little kid ... Over there ... in the corner, in a cage ... Jesus wept!' She held Amy tight to her chest, thankful that she was sound asleep

Besmir picked his way across the floor. He reached up and pulled down the loose planks of wood blocking a high window, suddenly exposing the place to the harsh glare of the sun. Another child started crying, then another, like the sound of cats wailing in a night when sleep won't come. Rosie stood rooted, her eyes flicking across the room. Don't dare pass out, she told herself.

Inside the cages – there were four of them – there were toddlers, and a few a little older, maybe four or five. In the light, Rosie counted at least eight or nine children. Ragged, filthy little things, staggering around barely able to walk, some reaching through the bars, others cowering, sobbing, in the shit-caked straw. Rosie caught a glimpse of the stricken look on Besmir's face, and in that moment, she thought she saw something close to an answer as to why it had come to this, what had brought them here.

'Quick. Get the children. We must move fast. Get them out of here.' Besmir pulled open the cages. He picked up a weeping child, then another.

Matt looked at Rosie, shaking his head slowly in disbelief.

'Come on, Matt, grab these children. Over there.' Javier took him by the shoulder and ushered him to a cage in the corner where two children were lying.

Rosie tried to pick up a tiny girl who was bawling. She couldn't hold both kids in her arms, so put the girl back down and clutched her hand tightly, while trying not to be sick from the smell of excrement. Adrian already had two children in his arms, and Hassan was climbing over a rusty wheel to get to a kid who was hiding in the corner.

'Aw Jesus!' Matt shouted. 'This kid's dead. Aw Christ, Rosie.' He slumped against the wall.

'Ssssh . . . Quiet, Matt. I'll get him,' said Javier. He crouched down where Matt had been trying to lift a small boy who sat with glazed eyes staring, gripping the hand of the little girl lying still next to him.

'It's OK. I've got you, boy . . . Sssh . . . It's OK now. Come on.' Javier gently prised the child's fingers from the stiff, cold hand of the little girl, whispering comfortingly as the boy wrapped his arms around him and buried his face in his shoulder.

'Come. We must go. Let's get them all into the cars and follow me,' Besmir urged.

Suddenly they caught the sound of a single gunshot and something ricocheting off the walls and roof. Everyone stopped in their tracks.

'Where do you think you are going?'

It was Leka. He stood in the doorway with the smoking gun pointing upwards. Something close to a smile cracked his face.

Stunned silence.

'Besmir. Adrian.' He frowned. 'You betrayed me. Big mistake.' He wagged a finger and tutted.

Besmir stared at him, unflinching. Slowly he put the

two children he was carrying down on the floor. Adrian looked beyond Leka.

'Do not think of doing something stupid, Besmir. Or you, Adrian. I am not alone.'

Rosie could feel her knees shaking as Leka looked around the room and his eyes rested on her, then Amy.

'You have my blue girl.' His steely eyes narrowed.

At the window, from the outside, a metal sheet was being stacked up to close the gap, and the room grew darker as it shut out the sunlight. As everyone looked in the direction of the window, Rosie noticed Besmir slide his hand down towards his ankle, and in one seamless movement remove something from under his trouser leg.

In the doorway, behind Leka, three men appeared, two of them carrying petrol cans. They stepped inside and began to pour petrol around the floor and up the walls, the fumes quickly filling the room. A drop of petrol splashed onto Rosie's bare arm, and suddenly in that moment she felt it was over. Here, in this stinking hell-hole, all of them would die, alongside the decomposing body of a small child. There was nobody to save her this time. Adrian was here, and in the semi-darkness she could see by the chalk-white pallor of his face that he too realised his luck had run out.

'Please don't do this,' Rosie heard herself saying. 'Please. I beg you. Please let the children go. They're just children.'

Leka stared at her.

'I know who you are. Your friend Mr Cox told me. You people are parasites, maggots.'

'If you know who I am, then you must know people will come looking for me,' she blurted out, looking at Javier and Matt. 'For all of us.'

He smirked. 'They can look. But there will be nothing left to find.'

'Please. The children. Your blue girl.'

Leka paused, looking at Amy who was beginning to stir in Rosie's arms. He looked around at the rest of them.

'You should not be here, Adrian, Besmir. Why? You should not betray me. You made this happen, you bring me problems. Police are asking questions now in Spain. Mr Daletsky says everything must be destroyed. No trace. You should have done your job and that is all. You are finished.'

'Please,' Rosie pleaded. 'Please let the children go.'

Silence. The men with the petrol cans stepped back out of the doorway. Rosie felt sick. She looked at Matt and Javier, saw the desperation in their eyes.

Then, suddenly, all hell broke loose. Leka buckled over and clutched his stomach. Blood trickled through his fingers as he grabbed at the handle of the knife Besmir had thrown so hard it had pierced straight into him. Besmir and Adrian rushed towards Leka, but the two big minders were faster. They grabbed him and dragged him backwards out of the barn, then pushed the door closed, plunging them all back into the darkness. Adrian and Besmir shoved hard against the door, but they could hear rocks piling up outside, then the noise of a car starting up and being driven towards them. It stopped up against the door barricading it shut.

Then, suddenly, a flaming rag was dropped through a space in the boarded-up window. They heard a whoosh and the blaze caught in seconds. Flames licked the petrol-soaked walls, and began spreading on the ground. Thick black smoke was engulfing the room, making everyone cough and choke.

Rosie tried to find a place, a gap, that wasn't on fire. She could hear the children coughing and crying, and she covered her mouth trying to take short breaths. Still carrying Amy, and holding the hand of the other child, she blinked, the smoke stinging her eyes. As she swallowed more smoke she began to stagger and slip to her knees, and placed Amy on the ground.

'Quick, Besmir. Kick the wall. It's not strong. It will fall if we kick hard.' Adrian began furiously kicking the metal and throwing his shoulder against it.

Besmir and Hassan joined him, all of them kicking and shoving with the full force of their bodies until the wooden beams creaked and metal began to twist and give way, and Hassan pushed himself outside. The sudden surge of air sent the flames higher and the children screamed, but Adrian and Besmir were already picking them up one by one and throwing them outside to Hassan.

Rosie could hear the screams of the children, but she could feel herself losing consciousness.

'Stay with us, Rosie,' Javier urged, coughing and gasping for air himself.

Matt grabbed hold of Rosie and helped her to her feet and they staggered towards the gap in the wall. Matt pushed Rosie outside and went back to grab Amy and the other child and drag them to safety before collapsing on the ground alongside her. She looked up to see Adrian and Besmir emerge from the flames with three more children, and then all of them slumped to the ground. Rosie raised herself up on her elbow and saw at least eight children, some milling around, some unconscious, others crying and coughing. But she couldn't see Javier anywhere.

Suddenly, the roof of the building fell in.

'Javier! He's still in there. Christ, he's trapped.' Rosie screamed.

Adrian stood up unsteadily. Besmir took off his shirt and tied it around his head, covering his mouth. Flames shot up to the sky as another part of the roof fell in. Besmir ran forward and disappeared into the blazing building.

Rosie sobbed as Matt held her in his arms. Then, through the wails of children, they suddenly heard the sound of sirens. In the distance flashing lights could just be seen through the clouds of dust.

'Look, Rosie, cops. Look.' Matt forced himself to get to his feet. 'I need to get pictures,' he gasped, and staggered towards the car to fetch his camera.

The blue lights were getting closer. Rosie looked at the burning building, willing Besmir to appear, and he did, supporting Javier. They staggered out and both collapsed on the ground. Rosie cried with relief when she heard Javier coughing.

Besmir lay on the ground, feeling the breath leave his body. His lungs had felt like a furnace, but now there was no pain. His head felt light. He turned to the side and saw Kaltrina kneeling, her tear-stained face smeared with smoke and dirt. She was looking at him curiously, as though she remembered him. He thought she smiled. The last thing he saw was the sunlight reflected in her blue eyes.

CHAPTER 40

'What the fuck, Gilmour?' It was McGuire.

'Yes, I'm fine, Mick, thanks for asking. I survived.'

'Christ almighty, Rosie, I know you *survived*. I've just fucking seen you on Sky News. What the Christ happened? Are you sure you're alright?'

'Yeah, Mick, I'm fine. I'm just about to leave the hospital. I would have phoned you earlier, but I was suffering from the effects of smoke inhalation, to use the official term.'

'Very funny, Rosie. We were all frantic about you. Can you imagine the flap we were in? I talk to you in the morning and then don't hear from you all day, then suddenly a snap comes on AP wires saying Amy's been found alive in Morocco, and one line that a female newspaper journalist may have been burned to death. That's how it came out here. We've been phoning you for hours, and getting fuck-all information out of the Moroccans.' He paused. 'Christ, Rosie. We thought we'd lost you.'

'Sorry, Mick.' Rosie detected a catch in McGuire's voice. 'I'm sorry. It was . . . Jesus, Mick . . . It was awful, terrible.

Everything happened so fast. We were out in the middle of nowhere and suddenly we were caught up in something and we couldn't turn back. Then we're trapped in this barn with all these poor fucking stolen kids. Christ, Mick, one of them was lying dead in the corner.' Rosie was surprised at how quickly she was losing it. 'Then . . . then these bastards set fire to the barn. Oh, Mick! I thought we were all going to die.'

The bravado was gone. She burst into tears. Shit. That was the last thing she wanted to do.

'Sorry,' she said quickly, sniffing.

'It's alright, Rosie. It's just the relief that's made you a bit overwhelmed.'

'You know you really should be writing self-help books, Mick.'

Get back in the saddle, she told herself. Don't give him your worries. Whatever he says, he really doesn't care if you do it with mirrors, as long as you deliver.

'That's better, Gilmour. But honestly – we were worried sick. Thank Christ we didn't lose you.' The catch in his voice again. He paused. 'Listen. I want you out of there pronto. I'll get you on a plane tonight, You need to be home.'

'No, Mick. No.' Rosie swiftly composed herself.

It had been less than twenty-four hours since the police, ambulance and fire brigade had arrived like the cavalry and scooped everyone up from where they lay on the ground in various stages of consciousness. All of them were rushed to the main hospital in Tangiers where a battery of doctors checked them over. Two of the children nearly didn't make it and were still in intensive care. But Amy was fine, Rosie had been told by a doctor in his fractured English. It only took a few hours before the news spread and a media presence began building up outside the hospital, hoping for a glimpse of the little girl the world was talking about. Adrian, despite coughing his guts up, had got off his mark in the car before the emergency services arrived. He told Rosie he would be back to Spain by evening. Hassan had also vanished.

The Spanish Guarda Civil was sending a special boat to bring Amy back to Tarifa where she'd be reunited with her parents. As soon as Rosie heard that, she got dressed and signed herself out of the hospital. She was shaky and dizzy when she got to her feet, but Matt and Javier helped her out of the ward. If they hurried, they could be on a boat to Spain within the hour. She needed to be there before Amy arrived.

'Mick. They're taking the kid back to her parents tonight and I'm on a boat back to Spain shortly. Me, Matt and Javier. Nothing is going to stop me being there when Amy gets handed over. I didn't come this far and go through all this shit to give the story to someone else. Matt's got amazing pictures of all these kids lying around the ground after the fire. Really dramatic. He's even got a snap of the kidnapper seconds after he died.'

'Listen, I know what you're saying, but I can send someone to help. You're actually part of the story now, Gilmour. Everyone's all over it, trying to find out what happened to you, and how come you were in the middle of it all. We're fighting them off here.'

'Stuff that, Mick. I'll get to that tomorrow. You can put a statement out or something. But I want to tell the story myself in the *Post*. I'm getting on that boat.'

'The Lennons have said they're not doing a press conference, only reunion pics. They just want their daughter back. What a picture that'll be.'

'I know. Imagine how they feel right now. I can understand them saying no to an interview, but that might change. I'm going to make an approach, Mick. I want that interview.'

'Alright, you can try, but the story will be everywhere. And I don't want you busting your gut if you're not ready. I mean, Rosie: you've just been involved in a huge trauma. You could have been killed.'

'Yeah, but I'm still here. I want to see if the Lennons will do a big sit-down with me. If anyone is in the driving seat it's me, Mick. I helped get their daughter back.'

'Of course,' Mick said. 'I'm sure when they take in everything that's happened and your part in it, you'll be in with a shout for an interview. Otherwise they're ungrateful bastards as well as fucking liars. Oh, and by the way, Rosie, Sky News is also saying that the Spanish cops have arrested four men they intercepted on a boat coming from Morocco. Apparently they're behind the kidnapping. One is called Leka or something. Albanian. He had a stab wound. Ring any bells?'

'Yeah, just a few.'

She signalled to Matt who was at the taxi, pointing impatiently to his watch.

'Listen, Mick. We've got other stuff here we need to

talk about when I get to Spain. Lots of big stuff on the porn movies they were making with these kidnapped kids. They stole kids from everywhere – Romania, Morocco, and further into Africa. And that Vinny bastard. We've got a lot of his movies.'

'You've got them?'

'Yeah.'

'Did you talk to him?'

'Er . . . not quite.'

'How did you get them?'

'No trick questions, Mick. I've got them, that's all that matters. Javier had a look at one last night and he thinks the kid in it is the little boy from Tenerife who's been missing for three years. Vinny killed him. He killed him on film. Snuff movies. That's what Frankie Nelson told me in jail.'

'You're fucking joking. That's on film?'

'Yeah, On film. I haven't seen it. Javier and Matt have it.'

'The Spanish cops will want it.'

'They'll get it when we get back to Scotland – not before.'

'Where's this Vinny fucker now?'

'Er . . . hard to say. But I don't think he'll be making any more movies. Forget him.'

'I'm not sure I like the sound of that, Rosie. Is something going to come back to bite us?'

'I wouldn't think so. I need to go now, Mick. Matt and Javier are waiting. We'll talk tonight.'

'You take care, Gilmour. Don't do anything daft. I've had enough excitement for one day.'

'Yeah. I'm sure you have, Mick.' She hung up.

*   *   *

In the office of the Maritime Rescue Agency in Tarifa, Jenny and Martin Lennon sat holding hands and watching the clock. They'd been told they would be reunited with their daughter within the hour. Outside, the press and broadcast media gathered for a glimpse of the boat's arrival.

Jenny was clutching her daughter's favourite soft toy, a furry rabbit with huge floppy ears. Amy never went anywhere without it. She hoped that if her daughter was traumatised, the rabbit would help her to feel secure. What if she'd forgotten about her mum and dad? Jenny had fretted all night after the initial euphoria that Amy was alive. She'd been gone for over three weeks. Nobody knew what she'd been through. Martin told her not to worry. As soon as she saw familiar faces, Amy would be fine.

The news had come in a phone call early yesterday evening. Martin had answered it, and as always happened every time the phone rang, Jenny watched his face for clues when he took the call. As soon as she heard the words, 'Are you sure?', she was at his side. He'd held his hand out to keep her at arm's length while he pressed the phone to his ear, his face set in concentration as he listened.

Then he looked at Jenny. 'She's alive,' he'd said. 'Amy's alive.' He went back to the phone.

Jenny's hands went to her mouth in shock. Then Martin asked whoever he was speaking to if they would hold for a moment and talk to his wife. She heard the words herself. They'd found Amy and she seemed unharmed, but doctors were still checking her over in hospital. The Guarda Civil were on their way to the villa to fill them in with the details.

When they'd come off the phone, Martin and Jenny had clung to each other, weeping with relief. Jenny kept repeating that she was sorry, that she knew she could never expect Martin to forgive her. She pleaded for one last chance. He didn't answer, and just kept saying how he had to see Amy with his own eyes before he would believe it was really true.

Now they could hear a sudden burst of activity around the harbour. Jenny got up and looked out of the window where the journalists and TV cameras were camped at the quayside. A Guarda Civil car was driven to the edge. The office door opened and a policeman came in and smiled broadly at them.

'The boat is arriving in only few minutes. Your daughter is coming.'

'Thank you,' Martin said.

They waited. They paced the floor. They sat down. They stood up, and sat back down again. Then, at last, they heard voices and footsteps in the corridor.

The door opened, and they held their breath as the female police officer came in. They stood up. They could only see the back of her head, a mop of curly dark hair in the policewoman's arms, but Jenny would know it was Amy's anywhere. She had dreamed of touching it, smelling it, every hour of every day.

'Amy . . . ?' Jenny took a tentative step forward, terrified it wasn't her. Amy turned around as she heard her name.

'Amy! Oh Amy!'

For a second, the little girl looked bewildered, then her face lit up.

'Mummy!'

Jenny and Martin went to her with their arms out.

'Daddy!' Amy's eyes widened with delight when she saw Martin.

'There's my beautiful girl! There she is!'

The policewoman handed Amy to Jenny, and Martin wrapped his arms around both of them, a family together again at last. At least for the moment.

Rosie stayed in the car with Javier while Matt joined the scrum of photographers outside the harbour rescue office. They'd been told the Lennons would come outside with Amy for a few minutes to give the photographers their pictures. But no questions, and definitely no interviews. Rosie stayed well out of sight, knowing any press or media who recognised her from the AP story would want to talk to her. She wasn't ready for that yet.

Javier had positioned the car so they'd be able to see the Lennons coming out, but still stay in the background. Rosie would make her pitch for an interview later. Maybe tomorrow. Give them a night to get their breath back.

'So – you okay, Rosita?' Javier's eyes scanned her face.

She wished she could lie to him, but he would know.

'If I'm honest, Javier, I'm wrecked, actually.'

'Me too.' He leaned back on the head rest, his eyes half closed. 'I thought we were finished in that fire. I really did.'

'Yeah. We nearly were.'

He reached across and ruffled her hair affectionately, keeping his hand on the back of her neck and massaging it gently. It felt good. Rosie closed her eyes. Tears weren't far away, but she bit her lip.

'I could sleep for a week,' she said.

'When we get this finished, we should go out and have a big dinner. Let our hair down. Get blind drunk. Go mad.'

Rosie opened one eye and squinted at him, smiling.

'I think we've had enough of mad for one week, Javier.'

'*Olé*! Here they come.' Javier sat up straight. 'Look.'

The Lennons appeared at the doorway.

'Jesus, Javier. That is some sight for sore eyes.'

Now the tears did come. And Javier wiped away his own as well as Rosie's.

The press pack swung into action with shouts of 'Over here, Martin . . . Jenny . . . Over here . . . This way . . . Amy . . . Smile.'

The cameras whirred, the snappers jostled for position among the TV crews. The Lennons stood behind the railing, holding up Amy and telling her to wave to the cameras, as if she'd just won a bonny baby contest at Butlin's. Martin put her on his shoulders and she clapped her hands above her head.

The sorrow, the agony had gone from Martin and Jenny's faces. They smiled, held hands, giggled together as Amy waved both hands and performed for the cameras, even blowing kisses to the delight of the press pack. The Lennons didn't look broken. But they were. Rosie thought she could see it. Somewhere in the eyes of Jenny Lennon there was a look that said, this is what is left of who we were. We will make the best of it.

Even from half a mile away, Hassan could tell there was too much smoke coming from his father's place. He stepped on the accelerator, the car bouncing and scraping on the dirt track as he raced towards the farm. He pulled into the yard and jumped out.

'Mother! Father! Salima . . .'

But he knew by the eerie silence, he was too late. The fire was dead, only the smoke was still swirling up to the sky. He pushed open what was left of the blackened, burnt-out door. Inside was a shell of the house that had been filled with laughter just days ago.

The first of the charred bodies he saw was that of his father, upright in his chair, burned to death where he sat. Hassan stumbled through the debris in a daze. On the kitchen floor, his mother's body was spread out as though she'd been crawling to escape. Nausea rose in his throat and he vomited on the floor. He rushed, dizzy, into the tiny hallway and pushed open his sister's bedroom door. To his surprise, she wasn't burned like the others, and for a moment he thought she was alive. But when he got closer, he could see she was dead, tied to the bed, her face frozen in terror, her green eyes staring at him, asking why. He stumbled to what was left of the blackened, burnt out twins' room, but there was no sign of them. They must have taken them.

Hassan collapsed to his knees, weeping. The sound of

his wailing startled the wild dogs who waited outside in the shadows.

It was getting dark by the time he came around. He teetered to his feet and staggered out of the house. He went to the well and splashed cold water on his face, then stood there, his face dripping, looking out at the blackness. He threw rocks and screamed at the dogs lurking determinedly at the edge of the yard.

Hassan dug in his jeans pocket and pulled out the rolled-up wad of notes he had taken from the fat man. Two hundred American dollars. He shoved the money back into his pocket. He turned and looked back at the house one more time. Then, in the stillness, as he was about to get into the car, he heard his name being called. He stopped and listened, looked around. Again he heard it.

'Hassan, Hassan.'

The twins came running through the darkness and threw themselves into his arms. He scooped them up and hugged as they wrapped themselves around him. Then he ushered them quickly into the car.

The people who came here would be looking for him, so he had to move fast. All they had left was one other.

CHAPTER 41

Rosie sat drinking green tea on the terrace of her room in the Puente Romano. It was a very long time since she'd felt relief on the scale she did right now. After Bosnia, maybe, when she'd sat by herself in the hotel room in the northern Greek town of Thessaloniki after the long drive from the former war zone. She had been glad to be on her way home, but the scenes and eye witness accounts of human suffering she'd witnessed just days before had left her unable to speak to anyone without bursting into tears.

This time was different. This story had a happy ending, unless of course your name was Vinny Paterson. Rosie wondered how she would explain that little nugget to McGuire when she got home. But that was for another day.

Now she had to make up her mind how much of the Lennon interview she was going to tell McGuire. She could, if she wanted, give Martin and Jenny Lennon a break. Just tell the big, heart-rending reunion story of a couple who thought they would never see their little girl again. The headlines wrote themselves. The *Post* would fly off the shelves, what with Matt's reunion pictures, plus all the graphic dramatic snaps of the rescue in Morocco with the blazing building as a backdrop. But it wasn't the whole story. To tell the truth, she would have to break hearts, ruin lives, shatter illusions. She remembered the hurt on Martin and Jenny's faces when she'd put the allegations to them.

The Lennons had agreed to tell their story to Rosie for the *Post*. She'd made the initial approach at the villa when they'd got back after the quayside photo call for the assembled media. The Guarda Civil had appealed to the press to respect the couple's privacy and give them time alone with their daughter, but Rosie went to the door later because she knew nobody else would dare. And anyway, the Lennons would have been told by the Guarda Civil of her role in tracking down their daughter's kidnapper. McGuire told Rosie the Lennons owed her, big time. She was just glad he wasn't negotiating.

Matt and Rosie had arrived at the villa before ten in the morning, and were surprised to be greeted with a hug from a smiling Jenny Lennon. People weren't generally big on doorstep hugs in Glasgow, at least not with tabloid reporters, Matt had joked. Over coffee and biscuits, and with Amy playing on the floor, the interview was going well, with Jenny and Martin saying all the right things – the heartbreak, the terror that they might never see their daughter again, the joy of that moment when they were reunited. In theory, it was enough. It would sell papers. But it wasn't enough for Rosie. She saw Matt watch her anxiously as she began questioning them further.

'Look, Jenny, Martin,' Rosie said. 'I have to ask you some things that you may not be comfortable with, but I need to put them to you, because my job here is to tell all of this story, not just the good bits. I hope you will understand that.' Rosie was confident, controlled. This was her show now.

Jenny looked suddenly pale.

No point in beating about the bush. Rosie moved straight in, addressing her question to Jenny.

'Jenny. It has been suggested that your version of what happened on the morning Amy was snatched is not actually the whole story.' Rosie saw Jenny swallow. 'I understand the Guarda Civil talked to you about the windsurfer's eye-witness account of the person he claims he saw in the yellow shorts?'

Martin looked at the floor. Jenny's lip twitched. The air was thick with tension. Rosie pressed on.

'Jenny. There's no easy way to ask you this. Was there someone in the house with you that morning, after Martin went out for his jog?'

Silence. Martin kept looking at the floor. Jenny did too, then she looked up and straight at Rosie, her eyes pleading.

'Rosie. Is this really necessary?'

'Yes, Jenny, it is. I'm sorry. I'm trying to report the factual account of events as they unfolded that morning.'

'But why? What if there *was* someone else in the house?

Why does anyone need to know that. Do you really think people need to hear some kind of tittle-tattle?'

'Not tittle-tattle, Jenny. The whole country and beyond took the story of Amy's kidnapping to their hearts. The sympathy was overwhelming. Everyone in the country wanted Amy back. This isn't about tittle-tattle. I think people want the truth. I think they deserve it.'

Silence. Then suddenly Martin spoke.

'Jenny, just tell her. Just tell her who was in the house. Get it over with and let's get on with our lives.' He took hold of Jenny's hand.

She swallowed. She shook her head.

'I'm not going to sit here and tell you every single area of my life, Rosie.' She sniffed. 'It's just not anyone's business. But I will say this to you, and nothing more: I made a mistake. The biggest mistake of my life, and if I roast in hell for it, then it will be nothing to what I've been through these past few weeks. I nearly lost my daughter because of that mistake. My family.' She squeezed Martin's hand. 'I will pay for that mistake for the rest of my life. Do you think I'm going to forget what I did?'

'Jenny. Were you with Jamie O'Hara in the house that morning?'

'Yes. I was.'

What the hell, Rosie thought. Just ask.

'Were you and Jamie ... were you together that morning?' The implication of Rosie's question was clear.

Silence. Jenny broke. Her eyes full of tears, she looked at Rosie. She didn't speak. She just nodded.

'You were?'

Jenny nodded. Amy looked up briefly at her mother then went back to her toys.

Silence. Rosie cleared her throat.

'Can I ask both of you a question?'

Martin looked up.

'How have you dealt with this? I mean. Are you able to put this behind you? Are you still together? Do you think you will be able to survive this?'

'Rosie.' Martin spoke softly. His pale grey eyes looked sad. 'We are together. We have our daughter back. That is all that matters. We have a lot to get through, and we can do this.' He put his hands up. 'Can we just put this line of questioning away now, Rosie? We are not on trial here. We are two human beings, capable of making mistakes, we're not monsters. The monsters are the people who kidnapped our daughter. Get this in perspective. Now please – can we move on?'

Rosie lifted her coffee cup, grateful that her hand wasn't trembling. She looked at them and nodded.

'I have one more question, Martin. Just one more thing. We have been told that Amy's kidnapping was connected to your late father. That he was linked to the death of a prostitute in Moscow last year and that Amy was kidnapped as some kind of revenge, with one of the Russian Mafia bosses behind it? Can you talk to me about that?'

Martin shook his head, his eyes closed for a second.

'No. I absolutely won't talk about that. Not on the record, and I hope you will understand that. You have enough meat on your story as it is, Rosie. I won't talk about my father or any talk of revenge. You know why? Because what if this isn't over yet? Off the record, yes, everything you have said there is correct. But if you publish a story like that, you may be placing our lives in danger. Is there no line you won't cross, Rosie?'

'I'll speak to my editor,' Rosie said. 'I understand what you're saying. I will talk to him, Martin. I promise you that.'

'Please don't publish that, Rosie.' Martin stood up.

The interview was over. There were no hugs this time as they walked to the door. Just handshakes and awkwardness. Sometimes the truth was hard to take – for all of them.

'Christ. That was tough,' Rosie said to Matt as they got into the car.

With the press of a key on her laptop, Rosie could lose the Jamie O'Hara line or keep it in. Cut or keep. It was up to her. What good would it actually do to drag the dirty detail out, she asked herself as she read and re-read the interview? Did it make any difference? No, she decided, it didn't. But what was the point of telling a story if you can't tell all of the story? It wouldn't have been the first time Rosie had kept certain facts from McGuire or the newsdesk when she was investigating or writing a story. She operated by her own rules, not those of the bosses who had never knocked on a door in their lives. Part of her wanted to give the Lennons a break, give Jenny a break. She could tell McGuire they wouldn't even discuss the O'Hara connection. No comment. He would believe her. But a bigger part of her wanted to tell the truth. No other bastard had told the truth since the beginning of this sorry tale. Not Jenny. Not O'Hara. Not Carter-Smith. Not Martin. It was supposed to be about truth. Once you buried the truth, you had nothing left.

She read the story one more time and pressed the send key like an assassin squeezing the trigger.

Her mobile rang and she went inside from the balcony and picked it up off the bed.

'Rosie.' It was Adrian.

'You made it.'

'I made it.'

'Are you alright? They arrested Leka.'

'He is out, Rosie. This afternoon. Daletsky has some very top lawyers and he makes things happen.'

'Shit, that's unbelievable. Jesus, Adrian, you have to be careful.'

Silence. Then: 'Listen Rosie. I know where my sister is. I have information. I am going to get her tonight. Will you help me?'

Rosie and Matt were booked on a plane to Glasgow at six-fifteen in the morning. She'd have to be at the airport by four at the latest. But that wasn't the issue. Whatever Adrian was planning, it wasn't going to involve picking up his sister after a shift waiting tables in a tapas bar. He would be rescuing her from some whorehouse. She feared the body count was about to go up. But thinking twice wasn't in Rosie's DNA.

'I'll help, Adrian. Just tell me what you want me to do.'

'Only to be outside with the car. Ready to drive us away when I get her. That is all I need.'

'Fine. I'll be there with Matt. Maybe Javier.' Rosie's stomach knotted.

'Thanks. I pick you up at ten.'

'I'll be ready.'

'And Rosie,' Adrian said. 'Thanks.' The line went dead.

Rosie went to the bedside phone and dialled Matt's room number.

'Matt. Can you come round here. There's a slight change to our dinner plans.'

She phoned Javier. She told him he didn't have to be part of this. He was the guy who had to live here.

'I'm in,' he said immediately. 'Of course I'm coming. You want to go somewhere in a hurry in Spain? I wouldn't leave it to a fucking Brit to drive the car.'

He hung up.

CHAPTER 42

'I've got this feeling of dread in my guts about this,' Matt said from the back seat.

'It's a bit late in the day to start shitting your pants, Matt,' Javier half joked, glancing in his rear view mirror.

Adrian had been gone less than fifteen minutes. He hadn't spoken much on the journey from the Puente Romano to the bar/whorehouse in the outskirts of Fuengirola. He was unnervingly quiet, even for him. Rosie guessed he was more nervous than they were. He had more to lose. If something went wrong inside the whorehouse, both he and his sister could end up dead. He'd admitted that much to them when they'd discussed the plan in Rosie's room before they left the hotel. But once they were in the car, he hardly said a word while Javier negotiated the backstreets and alleys to the bar.

As he got out of the car, Adrian had told them to wait where they were – 'no matter what happens'. It was the 'no matter what happens' bit that worried everyone.

'He's a scary fucker, that Adrian, isn't he?' Matt said.

'He's very different,' Rosie said. 'His story is a million miles away from ours. I think when you've been where he's been, through all that shit in Bosnia, seen the things he saw, you can't expect to engage with other people in the same way the rest of us do. He has a different set of rules.'

'He sure has. I like the way he does business – especially how he dealt with that Vinny bastard. I just hope tonight isn't the night his luck runs out.' Javier drew the smoke from his cigarette deep into his lungs and stared out of the window.

Rosie and Matt had already packed up and checked out of their hotel. The safest place for them to be when this was over would be the busy airport with its police presence – in case it all went tits-up and they were followed.

Once they got Adrian and his sister away from the brothel, the plan was to drop them at a meeting place where his Bosnian friend was waiting with a car. For some reason Adrian didn't explain, his friend could not come into the area they were going to in case he would be recognised.

As Fiorina didn't have a passport, Adrian was going to attempt to drive all the way to Bosnia. It was easier to travel in Europe since the frontiers had been removed, but there were still external checks. He said he would deal with whatever he came up against, but the immediate danger would be over once he was far enough away from the Costa del Sol.

After they'd made the drop, Rosie and Matt would go straight to the airport and sit it out until it was time for their early morning flight. As travel itineraries go, it wasn't ideal.

The bar, a seedy looking place, was up a side street in the part of Fuengirola you didn't go to unless you were searching for this particular den. The fact that it happened to be part owned by Big Jake Cox from Glasgow cranked up the fear factor for Rosie and Matt, when Adrian broke the news to them. In addition to providing rooms with paper sheets and birds you could rent by the hour, there was also a card school in a backroom of the bar every Thursday where a hand-picked few played for big stakes. Tonight Leka would be taking part in a poker game with Jake Cox and one other hoodlum.

Adrian's Bosnian friend had found out yesterday that Fiorina was living in the apartment above the whorehouse with other girls. His friend said she looked just as spaced out as them.

'It's so quiet here,' Rosie said, scanning the darkened empty street. 'Scarily quiet.'

'That's good though. It means we'll be able to get away fast. Christ, Rosie. I can't wait to get back to Glasgow.'

'Yeah. Me too.' Rosie thought again of her father alone in the flat. 'I've been away for ages now. That first month up in Jerez seems like years ago.'

'Sssh . . . Did you hear that?' Javier interrupted.

'Yeah, like a car backfiring,' Matt said.

'No, it's gunfire. Inside the place. Something's kicked off.' He switched on the engine. 'We better get ready.'

'Shit, there it is again.' Rosie glanced at Javier.

'If something doesn't happen soon, someone will call

the cops and they'll be all over the place.' Javier watched the building.

'Look! The side door!' Rosie saw it burst open and a figure emerged from the shadows. 'It's Adrian! He's got a girl with him.'

'Fuck!' Matt said. 'Someone's after him.'

The squat guy chasing Adrian grabbed hold of his arm and pulled him round. Another shot, then another, and the guy fell. Adrian tried to run, holding up the girl, whose legs couldn't keep up with him.

'Open the door,' Javier said.

Adrian was almost carrying the waif-like girl now as he got to the car. He bundled her inside and then dived in himself.

'Quick, let's go. They are coming.'

The car screeched away wheels spinning. Out of her side window Rosie could see two guys running.

'They just got into a jeep, I saw them.' Javier sped up one-way streets towards the edge of town.

'You okay, Adrian?'

He was breathing hard. The girl was crying, her head buried in his chest.

'Mama,' she sobbed. 'Mama.'

Adrian spoke to her in his language and patted the back of her head. He turned to look out of the rear window.

'I don't see anybody behind us. Maybe we lost them already. They are mostly English in there, the henchmen in the bar, so maybe they don't know the roads so well.'

'What happened?' Rosie was almost scared to ask.

'It was bad. Jake Cox was there in the back room. And

Leka, and one other man, English. I don't know who he is. Was. I knew my sister would be in that room with them because they had her working there for the night. My friend told me this. They use the girls for themselves after the poker game. That is why I had to go tonight.'

Rosie turned around to look at him. If his sister had been held by these scumbags for nearly three months, then tonight wasn't her first stint in the whorehouse, that's for sure. By the look on Adrian's face, he knew that too.

'We heard the gunfire,' Rosie said.

Adrian nodded.

'Did you shoot all three of them?'

Adrian looked back at her. He didn't answer. He didn't need to. Rosie wondered if he'd killed Jake Cox. That would be a result in itself. But whoever he killed had help, because now she could see in her wing mirror the jeep was gaining ground.

'Christ, they're behind us now.'

'Come off here, Javier. Quick. This road.'

'I know a back way to get to the place we are going,' Javier said. 'Leave it to me.'

Javier took the next slip road. The tyres screeched as he about-turned and sped through an industrial estate and out the other side.

'There he is. My friend. He is flashing the lights.' Adrian pointed to a deserted piece of wasteland at the edge of the estate.

They pulled up and Adrian got out of the car and carried his sister, helping her to stand upright. Rosie got out.

'We don't have much time, Rosie.' He stepped forward and hugged her. 'Thank you, my friend. I will not forget this.'

'What will you do, Adrian?'

'I have to get away from here. I will go home for a while, take my sister back to our mother. I am safe there. I will come to Glasgow. I am coming back, but I don't know when. When it is safe for me.'

'Goodbye, Adrian. Hurry. You must go.' Rosie swallowed the lump in her throat. She would probably never see him again.

Javier and Matt got out of the car and went forward to shake Adrian's hand. As they did, everyone froze with the sound of screeching brakes.

'Shit!' Javier said. 'Get back in the car, Rosie.'

But it was too late. Bullets smashed the rear window of their car and two, maybe three, pinged off the doors. Adrian pushed his sister to the ground and fired back, bullets ricocheting off the jeep, smashing their windscreen. His friend dragged Fiorina into the car.

'Hurry, Adrian,' he called. 'Hurry.'

Rosie heard more gunfire. Headlights plinked out. The gunfire stopped. She was about to dive onto the ground beside Matt when she felt an arm go round her neck. She heard a shot whizz past her head as she was dragged backwards. Then she saw Javier slumped on the ground groaning.

'Oh Christ, Javier.' She tried to struggle, but she could feel the metal of the gun pressed at the side of her head.

'Shut the fuck up.' The voice screamed in her ear.

The shooting stopped. Rosie saw Adrian standing with his gun pointing.

'Let her go,' he shouted.

'Fuck you,' the voice rasped, dragging Rosie backwards towards his car.

Rosie struggled to breathe as the arm tightened around her neck. From the corner of her eye she could make out Matt lying face down on the ground beside their car, terror in his eyes as he raised his head.

'Let her go or I'll shoot.' Adrian's eyes narrowed, his face ashen.

'On you go, prick. Shoot and she gets it first.'

Rosie's eyes snapped shut with the explosion of the shot, which almost burst her ears. She couldn't feel any pain. The arm around her neck slackened, but it dragged her and she stumbled backwards. He made a gasping sound as she fell on top of him.

'What the fu—?' Rosie was off her attacker in a flash and on her knees, confused. Then she saw Javier, his body raised a little, with the gun in his hand.

'Javier.' Rosie crawled towards him. 'You shot him.'

Javier slumped back, clutching his stomach, a patch of blood spreading quickly across his shirt.

'Javier. Oh, Javier. You saved my life.'

'Fuuuck!' He winced, blood running through his fingers.

'Oh Christ, Javier.' Rosie bent over him, lifting his head.

'Don't worry, you can pay me double. Now get out of here, Rosie. Get in the car and go.'

Adrian came over, the gun still in his hand. He knelt beside Javier.

'Good shot my friend.'

Javier almost smiled.

'Get out of here, Adrian, you have to. I'll be okay. Go.'
He struggled to speak.

Adrian got up and looked at Rosie.

'I *must* go, Rosie.' He looked distressed.

Rosie nodded through tears. Adrian got into the car
and drove off, quickly gathering speed.

'Rosie,' Javier grabbed her hand. 'Listen to me.' His
breathing was laboured. 'Take my mobile out of my pocket
and look for the name Jose. Call the number.'

Rosie rummaged through his trouser pocket. Her hands
trembled as she scrolled down and pressed Jose. It rang
several times.

'Fuck, it's ringing out.' But as she spoke, the voice
answered.

'Jose?' Rosie said.

'Give me the phone.' Javier put his hand out.

He shoved the phone to his ear and spoke in Spanish.
From what Rosie could gather he was giving a location.
The bloodstain on his shirt was spreading across his chest.

'Rosie, listen to me. They're on their way. My friend
Jose, he's a cop. They're coming with an ambulance. You
need to get out of here. Now.'

'I can't leave you like this.'

'Yes you can. You have to. You have all the Vinny tapes.
They'll take them off you and we'll all be in the shit if
they start asking where the bastard is. Get out of here
now, for Christ's sake.'

'Oh, Javier.' Rosie was crying.

'He's right, Rosie.' Matt bent down and touched Rosie's shoulder. 'We need to go. They'll be here for Javier, he'll be fine. Won't you Javier?'

'Yes', he said, his tone hoarse, his breathing becoming laboured. 'Matt. Get her out of here. Go. Please. Go.'

'Come on, Rosie.'

'I'm sorry, Javier.' She leaned down and kissed him on the lips.

'I'll call you, Rosie. Don't worry. I'm okay. It's not as bad as it looks. Just go.' He winced, gripping his stomach.

'Come on, Rosie.' Matt pulled her by the arm.

They got into the car and Matt sped out of the car park and back onto the other carriageway heading for Malaga airport.

'I can't believe we just left him there, Matt. He didn't even have to come with us tonight. What if he dies?'

'He won't die, Rosie. It might not be as bad as it looks. They'll be there in a few minutes and he'll be in hospital by the time we get to the airport. Come on.' Matt reached over and ruffled Rosie's hair.

She tried to compose herself.

'What are we going to do with this car, Matt? It's got fucking bullet holes in it.'

'We'll just dump it at the far side of the car park and hope they won't check it till the morning. Let's hope we're gone by the time they notice it.' Matt chuckled.

Half an hour later they were through check-in and security, and sitting in the departure lounge at Malaga Airport along with all the other holidaymakers in their cut-off trousers and suntans. Matt went to the bar and Rosie sat alone, tears welling up behind her dark glasses.

Her mobile rang and she blinked back the tears trying to see who was calling her. It was her GP back in Glasgow. It could only be bad news.

'Rosie.'

'Simon. Is it my father?'

'I'm afraid so, Rosie. He's in hospital. I had to admit him. Where are you?'

'I'm at the airport in Malaga. I'll be home in the morning. Is it bad, Simon?'

'He's not good, Rosie, he has an infection. Pneumonia. Just get here as soon as you can.'

CHAPTER 43

'Where are you, Gilmour?' McGuire's was the first voice Rosie heard when she switched on her mobile as soon as they arrived at Glasgow.

'We just landed. On my way out of the airport as I speak.' Rosie and Matt walked briskly through the baggage hall.

'Come straight here. I've read your big sit-down with the Lennons. Great stuff. Just come here and we'll have a chat'

'That sounds ominous.'

'No, no. Some things to go through. Some decisions on just how we play it.'

The taxi was waiting in the usual spot and the driver waved at them when they emerged outside and into the rain.

'Rain. Now there's a surprise,' Rosie said as they walked towards the car.

'I don't care if it's blowing a blizzard, Rosie. I'm just

glad we're back. Christ almighty, I honestly thought that was it last night.'

Rosie said nothing. She thought of Javier, and automatically pulled her mobile out and punched in his number. No answer. She had been crying on and off during the entire flight and she could see by the look on Matt's face that he was beginning to think she was falling apart. She told him not to panic. It was a combination of relief, worry about her father and Javier, and sheer exhaustion. She'd be fine when she got back to the office. But she couldn't get Javier out of her mind. The fact that they'd walked away and left him bleeding on the ground . . . If he was dead she would never forgive herself. She rang the mobile again. Still no answer.

'Leave it, Rosie.' Matt seemed to know without even looking who she was phoning. 'He'll be in the hospital. His phone will be switched off.'

'What if he's dead, Matt?'

'He'll be alright. Come on. Stop worrying.'

They got into the car. She should call McGuire, tell him she was going to the hospital first to see her father. He would understand.

'You going to your flat first, Rosie?' the driver asked.

'No,' Rosie replied. She looked out of the side window. 'Straight to the office.'

'You look wrecked,' McGuire said, when she walked into his office.

'Thanks, Mick. It's good to be back.' She gave him a sarcastic look and threw herself wearily on his leather sofa.

'Christ, Mick. I am so knackered. I just want to sleep.'

He watched her for too long.

'What's up?' she said.

'Nothing. You do look exhausted, Rosie. It must have been fucking awful. That fire and the kids and stuff. Are you sure you're alright? I just want to go through a few things with you, then you can go home and sleep.'

'I'm alright.'

'Great.' He rubbed his hands vigorously, and called up her copy on his screen. 'As I said, all great stuff. They must have loved you when you brought up the shagging line. Christ, I wish I'd been a fly on the wall for that. What was it like?'

'Well, you could say it got a little frosty.' Rosie rubbed the tiredness from her eyes.

'I'm sure. Anyway, Rosie, I've made a decision. Fair play to you for having the cheek to ask them about it, but I'm not using any line at all about the shagging.'

'What?' Rosie was surprised, but a little relieved. At least she knew she'd told the full story.

'Well, I talked to the lawyers about it. Number one, Jenny Lennon doesn't go into all the juicy details – unless I can hear her head rattling off the headboard it's not enough for me. And number two, we don't have anything from Jamie O'Hara. He's a lawyer, he's not daft. Never in a million years is he going to admit to shagging her, so I'm going to save you the hassle of asking him. And to be honest, I don't need to complicate their lives by exposing their ill-timed get-together. So I'm just going to leave it out, give them a break. They've been through enough. The interview is great without it. And the pictures are brilliant.'

'If I'm honest with you, Mick, I'm glad. I agonised about putting the line in the story or leaving it out, but thought I'd let you make the decision.' She smiled. 'You're just a big softie, really, you know.'

He looked at her and wagged a finger.

'Aye, sure. But don't you go making decisions on what you'll leave out in a story, madam. That's my job. You're not the editor yet.'

'Yeah. Not yet.'

'But I am using the line about the Russian hooker and his dirty old dad. I know Martin Lennon isn't saying anything much about, or so it seems in your story.' He raised his eyebrows. 'Unless you're holding out on me?'

Rosie shook her head.

'He didn't want to talk about it. He specifically asked not to mention it, Mick, because he's worried that this might not be over yet. I mean if you're talking juice here, the stuff about the Russian mafia involvement is the kind of juice that could get someone killed.'

'The line has already been hinted at in the *Sun*, but no real detail. We've got too much detail not to go with it . . . Fuck it, I'm doing it.'

'Fine. Your decision.'

'Right. That's that then.'

McGuire sat back and put his feet up on the desk. He took his specs off.

'So, tell me about the Vinny tapes and what you've got.'

He buzzed Marion and asked her to bring them in some coffee.

Before Rosie started to talk about Vinny, she told him about last night, about the shoot-out in the whorehouse. He almost fell off his chair when she told him she thought Adrian had shot Jake Cox.

'He also shot Leka, the Albanian mafia guy. I think he may have killed him. And there was some other hoodlum there who got shot too, but I don't know who he is.'

'Jesus, I don't believe this.'

'Oh, believe it, Mick. Strap yourself in. Because this is going to get a lot worse.'

She told him about the car chase and about Javier getting shot. She tried hard not to break down when she described how he saved her life and they'd walked away and left him bleeding on the ground.

'You did the right thing, Rosie.' McGuire could see she was upset. 'If you hadn't, you'd be in a Spanish jail right now, in possession of child porn tapes. It's easier to deal with all of that from here than with you stuck abroad. We'll get him checked out from this end. We'll make sure he gets looked after.'

'Thanks, Mick. He's a good man. He didn't need to be there with us last night, but he wanted to. I feel like shit for leaving him like that. I'll never forgive myself.'

'He'll be alright. Now tell me about the Vinny tapes.'

Rosie told him what Javier had seen in the tape, and that there were several other tapes where children were being sexually abused or posing naked. The tapes would need to be passed on to the police.

'You might want to have a look at them first. I think they'll be pretty grim,' Rosie said.

'Maybe a look. To see the extent of what's there before we hand them over.' He folded his arms. 'So where is this bastard Vinny now?'

The image of the soles of Vinny's sandals flashed up in Rosie's head.

'I don't know.'

McGuire sat forward.

'Yes, you do, Gilmour. It's written all over your face.'

Rosie did a half smile and looked away from him.

'He's in a very large hole in the ground.'

'Fuck! I knew it. But you know what happened to him. Don't you?' McGuire sighed, clasping his hands across his stomach. 'Rosie. Listen. Part of me doesn't want to know, because I have this sense of foreboding that someone bumped this fucker off, and you know about it. That makes me a bit nervous, Rosie. But tell you what. I don't give a fuck if he's dead – shot, trussed up, with his own fist stuffed up his arse. But what does worry me, sweetheart, is that a posse from Interpol is going to come riding in here at any time and drag you out. Hey, and not just you. Me as well.'

Rosie had been here before with McGuire. And when backs were to the wall, she found honesty was almost always the best policy with him. You could tell him stuff that was highly unorthodox and he wouldn't get all hysterical like some editors she'd worked with who played it by the book. But he'd rather know than not know.

She took a deep breath.

'I will deny on a stack of Bibles, Mick, that I ever said this. But, yes. Vinny is dead. The kidnapper – the Albanian guy I told you about, Besmir? He and Adrian threw him into an old well in the middle of nowhere in Morocco.'

'Oh fuck!'

'That's what I thought at the time.'

'Were you there?'

'I was.'

'Did you see it with your own eyes?'

'I was supposed to have my back to it. Me, Matt and Javier. We were all looking the other way. But I turned around. The mad bastard in me couldn't stop myself.'

McGuire burst out laughing.

'Fucking hell, Gilmour! Your nightmares must be brilliant.'

Rosie shook her head.

'Well, you could say they are very varied – and extremely graphic.'

McGuire looked as though he was enjoying it. He'd never actually been a reporter; he'd come up through the newspaper ranks as a sub-editor and then onto the back-bench. But he always relished the inside stories from reporters on the frontline. He valued the reporters at the cutting edge above everyone else at the paper because it was they who were out there, making this happen. That was why Rosie loved him so much.

He drained his coffee cup and ran his fingers through his hair.

'Right. What we need is for you to get yourself home for the rest of the day and have a good kip. The Lennon interview will be the splash and spread tomorrow. But we'll puff the revelations of what may have happened if Amy hadn't been found. Let's have chapter and verse on Vinny and how you tracked him down. Bring in the Frankie Nelson interview in jail. Even though he's a scumbag paedo, his information was crucial. And then just tell the story of your tracking her down. Everything. You coming face to face with the Albanian kidnapper, seeing him die, the fire. The whole shebang, Rosie. Let it run. I'll clear two spreads for Thursday and we'll let rip.' He stood up. 'It's going to be brilliant Rosie.' He raised a finger. 'But I need to get the lawyer in to talk about the Vinny tapes. Obviously we won't repeat what you just told me, but you're going to have to come up with a story about how the tapes came into your possession.'

'We'll just say a contact of our Spanish fixer.'

'Oh, the Javier guy. Yeah. Just say that.' McGuire's phone rang. He answered.

'Really? Fuck me! See what else you can get down there.' He looked at Rosie as he hung up the phone. 'That was Lamont telling me that news coming on the wires is that Jake Cox has been shot in Spain. Last night. In some whore-house.'

'Is he dead?'

'No. But he's not in good shape. Lost a lot of blood. Let's hope the bastard pegs it.'

Rosie's stomach dropped. 'The guys who chased us, who shot Javier. They were Brits. They saw me, Mick. They'll connect it all once they get their thick heads around it.'

McGuire came round from behind his desk.

'We'll get you proper protection, Rosie. This time we won't take any chances. We'll get you a bodyguard.'

'I don't want a bodyguard.'

Rosie stood up and he walked her to the door. He put his hand on her shoulder.

'We'll keep you back in the office for a while, Rosie. Every time you leave the place people get shot. I'm beginning to get nervous around you.'

He laughed and squeezed her shoulder, but Rosie knew he really was nervous.

'Go home. Get some sleep.'

'Sure.' Rosie smiled to Marion as she walked past her and out into the editorial floor.

CHAPTER 44

Rosie was almost flat out with exhaustion by the time she drove into the car park of Glasgow's Western Infirmary. But the mixture of fear and adrenaline of not knowing what she was about to encounter in the next few minutes drove her on.

She hadn't recognised the number that had flashed up on her mobile as she left the *Post*, yet she knew as soon as she heard the voice that this was the end.

'Is that Rosie Gilmour?'

'Yes. It is.'

'This is Sister O'Rourke at Ward 15 of the Western. It's about your father. His condition has deteriorated. The doctor said there may not be much time. I'm sorry.'

'I'm on my way.'

Rosie felt sick. There was a tightness in her chest as she took a deep breath. Her hands trembled as she tried to push her keys into the ignition.

Rosie had witnessed death in various shitholes in the world. Journalists like her would leave their five-star hotels in war-torn troublespots to write loftily that life was cheap, when the truth was that life was never cheap. To anguished mothers who wept over their starving children as they died in some stinking African refugee camp, life was as precious as it was to mothers in the rest of the world. She had sat with mothers in their Glasgow high rises as they wept into tea towels, preparing to bury their junkie kids not yet out of their teens. Life wasn't cheap to them either.

But despite wading through other people's misery, Rosie had never sat with anyone of her own who was dying. By the time she'd found her mother hanging from the banister she was already too late. So much of her life had been defined by that moment, and nothing she had ever seen since would come close to the sense of shock and loss. Life was never cheap. Not for her mother, and not for the sick old man she was about to sit with and try to find a way to say goodbye.

She stood in the lift with the other hospital visitors. Some, grim-faced like her, would be there to hold the hand of a loved one for the final time. Others, more hopeful, carried chocolates, magazines or flowers.

Ward 15 was ghostly quiet and stiflingly hot. A nurse, pushing a medication trolley, looked up as Rosie walked down the corridor.

'Can you tell me where Martin Gilmour is? I got a call to come. He's . . . He's my father.'

'Oh, right. If you'd wait a second, I'll just get Sister.' She turned and walked quickly down the corridor, returning with an older nurse in a dark blue uniform.

'Rosie? I'm Sister O'Rourke. We spoke on the phone.'

'Yes.'

'If you'd come this way, the doctor would like to have a word.'

Rosie followed her into the little airless side room, feeling sweat trickle down her back. The doctor stood waiting for her. He looked all of twenty, but with dark circles under his eyes.

'Hello, Miss Gilmour. I'm Dr Kavanagh.'

They shook hands. He took a deep breath.

'I'm afraid your father is failing fast, Rosie. You know he's a very ill man, and that the lung cancer had spread quite rapidly.'

'I knew he was very ill. He told me.'

The doctor nodded, his face set in concentration. He had a script to deliver, not sympathy.

'He's developed an infection and it has slipped into pneumonia. By the time he was admitted, it was deep into his lungs, which were already very weakened. He doesn't seem to be responding to antibiotics. Your father doesn't have long.' He paused. 'And, I have to ask you, as it's standard procedure, if he goes into cardiac arrest do you want him resuscitated?'

'I don't think there is any point. Do you?' She swallowed.

The doctor made eye contact with her for the first time.

'Your father is not going to get any better, I'm afraid. The best we can do for him now is to make him as comfortable as possible.' He paused. 'I'm sorry.'

Rosie looked at him. She wondered how many times a week he had to deliver that line. And he was just a kid.

'I understand. I think it's best not to resuscitate.'

The nurse produced a form from nowhere like Paul Daniels.

'Would you mind signing here.' Sister O'Rourke gave Rosie a sympathetic look.

Rosie signed, noticing her hands were shaking. The Sister squeezed her arm. Rosie almost burst into tears.

'Can I see him?'

'Of course. Come this way, Rosie.'

Her father had been given the dignity of a private room. It was at the end of the ward, with a tiny window and a plastic blind over it.

For a second she wanted to say this was the wrong room, that they must have made a mistake. She didn't recognise the face with its sunken cheekbones behind the oxygen mask. Her father's chest moved up and down in short, rattling breaths. Rosie couldn't speak. She gasped and swallowed, turned to Sister O'Rourke and burst into tears.

'I don't know what to do,' Rosie shook her head.

'It's alright, Rosie.' The Sister pulled over a chair. 'Just sit with him. Maybe hold his hand.'

'Is he unconscious, or is he sleeping?'

'It's the drugs. He's drifting in and out of consciousness. But he's comfortable, he's not in pain – and I think he'll know you're here.' She patted Rosie's shoulder as she sat down. 'Just be with him. If you need anything, just come out. I'm at the end of the corridor.'

Rosie wiped the tears from her cheeks with the palms of her hands and sniffed, focusing on his face. She noted the grey stubble on his chin and his dry lips. An old defeated man, tired of living. She reached over and took his hand in hers. It was warm and soft. His fingers wrapped around hers and gripped hard. Tears came again.

'Can you hear me? D . . . Dad. I'm here. It's me. Rosie.'

His hand tightened its grip. She looked at his face and his eyes flickered a little. He could hear her.

'I'm going to stay with you now, Daddy. I'm here. Just sleep.'

She watched his face for any reaction. A single tear came out of his eye and rolled down the side of his temple. Rosie swallowed a lump so hard it hurt her chest. His lips moved as though he was trying to speak.

His grip tightened more, and his lips were moving a little.

Rosie stood up and leaned across the bed. She put her face next to his, her ear to his mouth.

'I can hear you, Dad. Are you saying something?'

He breathed the words, not even as loud as a whisper, but Rosie could make them out.

'I'm sorry, Rosie.'

'I know. I know you are, Dad. Sssh.' Rosie held his hand tight. She stroked his papery forehead. 'It's okay now. Just go to sleep. You can sleep away. I'm so glad you came back for me. It's alright to go now. You can be with her.'

Rosie sniffed as tears rolled down her cheeks. She watched as he breathed fast for a few seconds and then nothing. His grip slackened. He was gone.

*   *   *

Rosie sat at the table next to the window in the Grass Cafe. She'd stopped crying, but she knew by the expression on the face of the waitress that her eyes were red and swollen. The girl had given her a sympathetic look when she put her mug of tea on the table.

Rosie always seemed to end up here in the bad times, as though she needed to be here. She could almost see Mags Gillick and Gemma sitting opposite her that first time they met. The inquiring look on Gemma's face, the lost look on Mags'. Something about this place made her feel safe, because no matter what happened outside nothing changed in here.

Rosie closed her eyes, felt them stinging. She tried to blot out the image of her father lying in the hospital bed, his frailty. She thought of his face the previous time they'd seen each other when he'd hugged her hard. She'd looked at him across the table in her flat and had gone to bed that night knowing her father was in the room next door. Strangely she'd slept better than usual. The picture that had always come to her in the past had been from years ago, when he'd looked up and waved as she and her mother watched from the window as he came up the path. But now she had a better picture. She could do this. Her mobile rang.

'Rosie.' The voice hit her like a knock-out punch.

It was TJ.

ACKNOWLEDGEMENTS

So many people make a contribution to my life – whether it's in the love and support of my sister Sadie every day, or the big crowd of family, friends and readers who turn out to book launches, stand in queues and share a drink with me. It's a privilege to have such support and I appreciate it more every time.

I want to thank my brothers, nieces and nephews and all my family – including all my many cousins – for the kindness and strength I get from them.

Without my brilliant techno troops I couldn't function in the modern world, so thanks to my nephew Matthew Costello for designing my website and the computer magician Paul Smith who puts up with my endless, frazzled demands.

Thanks also to my cousin Alice Cowan down in the big smoke, who looks after me, no matter how often I pitch up at the Hatchend Hilton.

My friends Mags, Ann Frances, Mary, Phil, Helen, Louise, Jan, Barbara, Donna and Ross, who are always there for me.

In Ireland, thanks to everyone back West in Ballydavid and Mhuirioch, for making me feel at home.

And in La Cala de Mijas on the Costa del Sol, all the characters who give me a laugh with their stories and their company.

My friend Franco Rey, for the good times, the laughter and the love.

My agent Ali Gunn for just being the brilliant Ali Gunn. The wonderful team at Quercus, in particular my fantastic editor Jane Wood, from whom I've learned a great deal, and, publicity director Lucy Ramsay for getting me out there.